Eldercide

Also by Julie Lomoe
Mood Swing: The Bipolar Murders

"Eldercide," by Julie Lomoe. ISBN 978-1-60264-188-4.

Published 2008 by Virtualbookworm.com Publishing Inc., P.O. Box 9949, College Station, TX 77842, US. ©2008, Julie Lomoe. All rights reserved. No part of this publication may be reproduced, stored in a retrieval system, or transmitted in any form or by any means, electronic, mechanical, recording or otherwise, without the prior written permission of Julie Lomoe.

Manufactured in the United States of America.

July 2008

To Irene —

Eldercide

by

Julie Lomoe

Thanks for including
Eldercide in Oriel!
Best Regards,
Julie Lomoe

For the aides of ElderSource, Inc.,
whose compassionate care
helped inspire this book,
and for my parents,
Wallace and Vi Lomoe,
who bequeathed me their love of writing.

Chapter 1

At first the pinprick sensation in the skin of her neck was so delicate that Harriet Gardener wove it flawlessly into the fabric of her dream. She was lying on a blanket next to Arthur, beneath an enormous maple at the edge of a meadow like the one on the farm where she had grown up, yet much larger, with wheat fields sweeping away to the horizon as far as she could see. As she watched the sun sinking in the west, she realized she had no idea where they were or how to find their way back home.

"Arthur, we'd better leave now," she said. "We must have fallen asleep. It's getting dark, and the mosquitoes are starting to bite."

The pinprick grew sharper, more insistent. As she felt it penetrate her skin, she cried out in pain. A yellow jacket! Why now, so late in the day?

His hand clapped down hard on her mouth, with a brute force so utterly unlike Arthur that her eyes flew open in shock. The brilliance of the light made her blink. She'd been wrong. It was already night, and the meadow was nowhere to be seen. Now she was on a road, caught like a deer, paralyzed in the glare of a single headlight bearing down on her.

The dream had become a nightmare. She jerked frantically, willing herself awake, staring into the glaring light, a shimmering circle surrounded by inky blackness. A full moon, dazzlingly brilliant. No, a flashlight. As her eyes adapted with agonizing slowness, the familiar outlines of the furniture in her darkened bedroom brought her back to the barren reality of her present-day world, her world without Arthur. Now she could make out the black barrel of the flashlight, the ghostly white of the gloved hand gripping it. And in the shadows beyond, the looming contours of a strange man.

Why couldn't she shake free of this nightmare? Why hadn't he gone back into the limbo of bad dreams where he belonged? Now he was hovering above her, pushing her head down and back, deep into the pillow.

And the hornet was still stinging her. Her hands flew to her neck, swatted wildly at the source of the pain, but he blocked them effortlessly with a muscular forearm. Out of the corner of her eye, she caught the flash of something silver.

Her mind raced in frantic circles as she thrashed ineffectually, trying to free herself. Her legs felt leaden, as if she'd been running up a hill so steep, she couldn't take one more step. She willed her arms to move, to fight the numbness creeping over her, but they wouldn't do her bidding. As she gave in to the unaccustomed feeling of no feeling, it occurred to her for the first time that she might be dying. So this is what it's like, she thought. It's not so bad, really.

All at once the breath caught in her throat. Her chest froze, and she couldn't fill her lungs. *I'm not ready! I want to come back!* She stared up at the halo of light, past its shimmering edges at the dark figure beyond, sending him a silent prayer: save me from this horror. But he was motionless. She heard the soft sigh of his breathing. Then, in the distance, the mournful hoot of a barred owl. She used to hoot back to them, she remembered. A little conversation, kind of repetitious, just the same four notes over and over, but it was companionship of a sort. Especially in the stillness of the nights after Arthur was gone.

The halo of light was spilling over now, flooding the darkness, becoming a seamless gray fog. Something soft flitted across her eyelids, stroked them closed with infinite gentleness.

Arthur. You've come for me at last.

——— ——— ———

The trilling of the cell phone was so subtle that the sound carried barely twenty feet from shore, harmonizing with the chirping of the sparrows and the soft cooing of the mourning doves. If not for her dog Freia, Claire Lindstrom would have missed it entirely, but the big blond Labradoodle was dancing on the dock, wagging happily as she bounced around the little black instrument of torture.

"Good girl!" Claire murmured as she steered the kayak in for a landing. She'd taught the dog this silent pantomime in deference to the neighbors, most of whom didn't appreciate being stirred from sleep by a salvo of barks, no matter how magnificent the sunrise.

Setting down the paddle, Claire grabbed the cell phone and peered at the caller ID. The number was Harriet Gardener's.

A shiver swept over her, despite the rising heat of the early September day. As nursing supervisor for a couple of dozen home care clients, Claire was accustomed to getting calls at all hours of the day and night. Call her compulsive, call her a workaholic, but she'd made it clear to everyone on staff that she wanted to be brought up to speed on anything out of the ordinary, no matter what the hour. Most of the clients at Compassionate Care were elderly, and many were gravely ill. The aides knew better than to leave Claire out of the loop when it came to making judgment calls about the people in their charge.

But Harriet Gardener was in excellent health, physically at least. She suffered from mid-stage Alzheimer's and needed supervision to prevent her wandering away or burning down the house with her absent-minded attempts at cooking. But she was strong, and she rarely came down with so much as a sniffle. For the time being, thanks in large part to her live-in aide Dahlia Douglas, her quality of life was excellent. But inevitably that would change. Although they tried not to show it, the fact that she was fated to endure many years of painfully slow decline, culminating in the eventual loss of all her mental and physical functions, distressed her overwrought family no end.

Dahlia wouldn't have phoned at six a.m. without good reason. The possible scenarios played through Claire's mind as she climbed out of the kayak and felt the cool water bathing her bare feet. Most likely Harriet had fallen, maybe broken a hip or hit her head. Or she might have slipped out and wandered away. When the agency first opened her case, Claire had done an exhaustive inventory of the house and supervised the safety proofing of the place, like a conscientious mother safety-proofing the home of a roving toddler. Every door and window that Harriet could possibly reach had been secured with a state-of-the-art locking device.

Still, even with an excellent aide like Dahlia, human error was always a possibility, and Harriet was maddeningly persistent in trying to defeat the locks. Harriet lived in a lovely old farmhouse on acres of rolling land, the kind of land that had once dominated the town of Kooperskill in upstate New York. But urban sprawl was encroaching rapidly, and interlopers from the nearby mini-mansions took the curves of the narrow two-lane highway that bordered her property far faster than they should. Now in her late seventies, Harriet had been born there, and she and her family hung doggedly onto the old homestead, determined to let her die there. Claire just hoped today wasn't the day.

Resisting the impulse to press the call-back button immediately, she shoved the cell phone into her waterproof tote bag, tied the kayak to the dock, and strolled with deliberate slowness back to the house, inhaling deep breaths of calming country air en route. As years of experience had taught her all too well, nursing is a high burnout profession. Claire had stayed in the field this long only by creating her own survival strategies. Keeping an invisible barrier between her personal and professional lives was the key to it all.

By choice, Claire was on call twenty-four seven, but she drew a careful line of demarcation in the physical realm. Inside the cottage, on the deck, even in the garage she had converted to a jewelry studio, she used the laptop and cell phone that tied her to her little community of beleaguered staff and clients. But the chains broke when she descended the stairs to the back yard and immersed herself in the delights of gardening, swimming, kayaking or simply lounging. By and large, she had conditioned herself to banish job-related thoughts when she reached her private sanctuary. Random thoughts of clients or staff broke through occasionally, like a dog lunging through an invisible electronic fence in pursuit of a rabbit or a cat, but usually the boundary held firm.

Not this morning, though. Halfway across the lawn, she had the cell phone out of the bag, her finger poised over the callback button. She jabbed the button as she set foot on the first step, and the phone was ringing by the time she reached the deck.

Dahlia answered on the third ring, her voice weak and shaky. "Harriet's gone," she stammered. "It must have happened sometime in the night."

Claire's heart sank. "But Dahlia, how could she get out without your knowing? Everything's locked up tight. You sleep right across the hall from her, and I know you're a light sleeper."

"Not that kind of gone." Dahlia's careful diction had yielded to the earthy dialect she usually reserved for the other Jamaican aides, and the melodic lilt of her voice was incongruously at odds with her message. "She's gone. I mean she passed. I don't understand. She was fine when I tucked her in bed last night. She had such a strong heart, and you know how the family used to kid around with me. We thought Harriet would outlive us all."

Just like my father. Claire shivered. She took Dahlia's report, somehow got through the formalities, hung up. Then, suddenly wobbly, she sank onto a chaise. Nine years ago, on a flawless September morning much like this one, she'd gotten a call from the nursing home where he'd been admitted the day before, suffering from mild dementia. He had gone to bed ostensibly healthy, died sometime in the night. A previously undiagnosed cardiac problem, they said. Or, as Claire always thought of it, a broken heart. He'd been furious when her mother shunted him off to a nursing home against his wishes, vowed to get out if it was the last thing he did. He had fulfilled his vow, although not the way he planned.

He shouldn't have died that way, abandoned and alone in an institutional bed. His death shocked Claire into abandoning graduate school and entering nursing. She found her way into home care, where she could help keep people away from those warehouses for the dying. All these years spent making amends, and now it had happened again.

————

Across the lake, Gabriel squinted through the telescope. Claire Lindstrom sprawled motionless on the chaise, her head turned toward the morning sun. Her wavy blond hair curtained her face from view. Too bad – he'd have liked to see her expression. When she'd made the call, her back had been turned. He felt a flash of anger. Watching was part of what made his work worthwhile, and she was depriving him of the pleasure.

The scene was deceptively idyllic, like a watercolor on the cover of an L.L. Bean catalog. The slender blonde in a turquoise tee and khaki shorts stretched on the forest green, Adirondack-style chaise, her skin still summer tanned. The big dog, its hair a shade lighter than Claire's, lying nearby on the lawn that swept down to the water. The kayak, a nifty accent in fire engine red, pulled up on the beach, the lake sparkling in the morning sun, encircled by deep green hills.

Maybe he should start painting again. He'd taken a couple of courses in college, and the instructor had told him he had talent worth pursuing. The network kept him fairly busy, but although the number of assignments was increasing, there were still stretches of inactivity. And painting might bleed off some of the nervous energy he felt when he'd successfully completed a mission.

Last night, for example. The old lady's death had progressed perfectly, exactly as planned. He had shone the flashlight full into her face, watched the confusion, the slow dawning of comprehension segueing into terror, the creeping paralysis as the drug took hold. Even after the breathing stopped, the eyes clung desperately to life. It was hard to pinpoint the exact moment she crossed over, but he kept the light focused on her face for a full five minutes as he watched the life glow fade from her eyes. Then, still wearing the latex gloves, he closed her lids.

Death by paralysis had to be ghastly, but at least the suffering was short-lived, infinitely superior to the endlessly prolonged agony and degradation that modern medicine inflicted on the chronically and terminally ill. He'd had his fill of that in the nursing career he'd abandoned.

The new affiliation had come as a godsend, and the money wasn't half bad. But the role they'd cast him in was too limited, too predictable. The powers that be had cautioned him to follow their protocol precisely. No room for creativity or improvisation. He was just a cog in a much larger machine. But that could change with time. If he played by their rules, they promised, the potential for advancement was virtually limitless.

He watched through the scope as Claire climbed off the chaise. She raked her fingers through her hair, daubed at her eyes. He caught a glimpse of her elegant features before she turned and headed for the house. Before long she would probably be at Harriet Gardener's place. He wished he could join her there, savor her reaction. But that was out of the question.

He'd called in his report hours ago, and a day of enforced idleness yawned in front of him. All at once he knew how to spend it: he would drive to New York City, pick up some supplies at that discount art supply store in SoHo. Pearl Paint, on Canal Street, near Chinatown. He'd be down and back before nightfall, and if they had a new assignment for him, they could always reach him on his cell.

He decided to buy oil paints. They had a squishy, sensuous feel that was more satisfying than acrylics. Cadmium red light would be perfect for the kayak, and it was good for mixing flesh tones, too. He wanted to do justice to Claire.

When Claire entered Harriet's bedroom an hour later, she saw at once that Dahlia was right: Harriet Gardener was definitely, unequivocally dead. Her lips were pale, her skin strangely translucent. Lifting the sheet, Claire saw the telltale signs of livor mortis, the purplish puddling on the undersides of the arms and legs. As a formality, she checked the vital signs. There was no pulse, no breath, and Harriet's skin was already cool to the touch. Still smooth and soft, however - Claire flashed back to the way Dahlia used to massage Harriet head to toe with aloe lotion. Harriet loved the sensation, and the massages were one of the ways Dahlia calmed her down when she was feeling agitated, lost and confused.

"That feels so good, Sissie," Claire had heard Harriet say. "I'm so glad you came back to live with me again." She had trouble remembering Dahlia's name, so early on she had taken to calling her Sissie, and a little while after that, she had begun confusing Dahlia with the older sister who had died many years before. Dahlia accepted the new identity with grace and good humor, the way she accepted everything else about Harriet.

Turning away from the bedside to face Dahlia, seeing the unshed tears in the aide's luminous brown eyes, Claire felt her own eyes well with tears. Impulsively, she reached out to Dahlia and they embraced for a long silent moment. Then Claire pulled back in a valiant effort to reclaim a semblance of professionalism. "I'm so sorry, Dahlia. I know how close you were to Harriet."

The aide was weeping openly now. "She was a wonderful woman. She took me into her home and her heart like her own daughter. But the Lord knows best. He has called her to a better place, and now she is at peace."

Claire envied Dahlia her belief and wished her own were as strong. True, Harriet's death was a blessing in its way, cutting short a life that would have grown increasingly painful and pointless as the Alzheimer's ravaged her mind and body. But the woman was blessed with a sunny disposition and a strong constitution, and she still had a robust appetite for life. Her death was puzzling in its suddenness, and it left questions in its wake.

"Was Harriet in any distress last night?" she asked Dahlia. "Did she complain of any unusual pain or discomfort?"

"No, she seemed sleepier than usual, but that was all. I helped her with her bath, then helped her towel dry. I massaged her with the aloe lotion, the same way I did every night. You can see, she's very fresh and clean. She looks so peaceful, don't you think?"

"Yes, she looks beautiful." It was true, Claire thought. Death had stripped years from Harriet's face. The worry lines were gone from her forehead, and her expression was serene.

"I keep thinking there is something I could have done, something I overlooked."

Claire was thinking the same thing, but sharing her misgivings with Dahlia would accomplish nothing other than to intensify the guilt the aide was already feeling. "These things happen sometimes, especially with the elderly," Claire said instead. "There may have been some preexisting condition we didn't know about, an undiagnosed heart problem, perhaps. I'll telephone Dr. D'Attilio, but my guess is that he'll pronounce the death over the phone. Then I'll call the daughter in California, and the funeral home. As I recall, the family's wishes are spelled out in the intake assessment I did when we opened the case."

Calling Harriet "the case" sounded callous, Claire knew, but it injected some much needed professional objectivity into the situation, distancing the two living women from the body that lay beside them.

Dahlia fumbled in her shirt pocket, extricated a crumpled Kleenex, daubed at her eyes, then blew her nose loudly. "Should we do anything to get Harriet ready for the mortician?" she asked.

"You took such good care of her, there's very little to do. First I'll make those phone calls. Then we can just straighten her out a little and pull the covers up to her chin. After that, if you like, you can wait outside for the people from the funeral home. You can probably use a break."

Tears reappeared in Dahlia's eyes. "Thank you, Claire. Do you mind if I go outside right now? I have my period, and it isn't good for me to stay in the same room with a dead person. It may sound silly, but in Jamaica we believe it's very bad for a menstruating woman to stay with a corpse. We believe –"

The last thing Claire needed right now was a discussion of Jamaican folklore. She rested a reassuring hand on the aide's shoulder. "Never mind, Dahlia, no need to explain. Go take a break. I'll tend to the body."

Alone once more, Claire took comfort in the familiar routine of her nursing persona. First she phoned Dr. D'Attilio. His answering service picked up, of course – it wasn't even eight o'clock yet. The operator said she'd page him immediately, and while Claire waited for his call back, she arranged the body. Harriet had been lying on her right side, her limbs bent casually as if still in the comfort of sleep. Claire rolled her gently onto her back, straightened her legs, folded her arms in the formal symmetry of death. Now, before rigor set in. She left her in the nightgown she'd been wearing, pink cotton trimmed with white lace. The body was clean, scented with aloe lotion and baby powder. Too soon for the odor of death.

She was just folding the sheet over the summer-weight blanket at Harriet's chin when Dr. D'Attilio phoned back. As she'd expected, he decided a house call was unnecessary. Based on Claire's description of the physical findings, he estimated the time of death at approximately four a.m., then told her to call the daughter and the funeral home. "You nurses are so much better at that sort of thing," he said lightly.

His flattering tone rubbed her the wrong way, and she fought the urge to tell him exactly what she thought of his weaseling out of the hard part. "Okay, if you think that's best," she said with fake deference.

Next she dialed Joanne Hargreave, the daughter. The answering machine picked up. Not wanting to break the news to a tape, Claire was deliberately vague. "Joanne, please pick up if you're there. I know it's only five o'clock your time, and I'm probably waking you, but it's important. It's about your mother. There's been an incident –"

"What is it?" The voice, foggy with sleep at first, grew clearer by the second. "What kind of incident? What's wrong?"

"I'm sorry to have to tell you this, but your mother passed away early this morning. I'm at her home now, with Dahlia, and I just got off the phone with Dr. D'Attilio. She died peacefully in her bed."

There was total silence, broken at last by Claire. "Joanne, are you there?"

"I'm here. I don't know what to say. I can't believe it."

"Neither can I. She was doing so well. Dahlia didn't notice anything unusual when she went to bed last night. As far as the cause of death is concerned, it's too soon to tell, but –"

"Claire, stop. Please. I can't stand to think about that right now."

"Of course, I understand. Would you like me to call the funeral home? According to the plans we discussed –"

"I remember what we discussed. Go ahead, do what you have to do. Sorry if I sound curt, but I'm still half asleep, and this feels so unreal." There was a brief silence, then what sounded like a muffled sob. "Excuse me, Claire, but I've got to go make some coffee, give this a chance to sink in. I'll make reservations for Frank and me to fly in today. We'll probably land in Albany."

"If there's anything else –" Claire heard a click and stopped mid-phrase. The line had gone dead.

Chapter 2

*P*aula Rhodes took another bite of maple-frosted donut as she watched Claire Lindstrom pause on the footbridge that led to the lobby of their building. The leisurely pace wasn't like Claire, who was usually a whirlwind of purposeful activity. Could Claire be feeling as dejected as Paula? If so, they were in for a hell of a day.

Paula wondered for the umpteenth time what had ever possessed her to think she could run a home health care agency. When she'd launched the business six years ago, she'd been as slim and sylph-like as Claire. She'd worked her butt off ever since, and what did she have to show for it? Not much in the way of money, but she did have fifty new pounds packed onto her five foot, four inch frame, thanks in large part to the mood stabilizers and antidepressants she gulped down daily to keep from freaking out. Not to mention the Dunkin' Donuts just down the block.

She took another bite, savoring the sticky sweetness as she stared down at the turgid brown water that ran below her office window. When she had first rented space in this office complex, the little stream had been one of the features that intrigued her most. Wending its way down from the Taconic foothills to the east, it had been channeled into a cement watercourse that flowed alongside the building, then beneath it and out the other side. A century ago, this rambling brick building south of Troy had been a thriving factory, and the water had powered machines for the dozens of women who sewed shirts for the nation's aspiring businessmen. That industry, like so many others in upstate New York, had languished and died, and the building stood vacant for years, until a savvy real estate developer transformed it into an office complex with just the right mix of nostalgia and modern convenience to appeal to adventurous entrepreneurs like Paula.

This morning she felt anything but adventurous. The caseload at Compassionate Care had grown painfully slowly, in fits and starts. Whenever the bottom line looked reasonably healthy, one of their clients had to up and die. Sometimes she felt like Sisyphus, pushing the same gigantic boulder up the same hill, only to have it roll back down, over and over again.

"Good morning, Paula."

Claire's usually cheery voice had a throaty catch to it. Her back to the door, Paula scarfed down the last bite of donut, wiped the remaining goo onto a paper napkin, then spun her chair around to confront her head nurse. "Morning to you too. But I wouldn't call it good."

Claire looked wilted, wrung out. Her eyes were red, and Paula suspected she'd been crying. "I'm so sorry about Harriet Gardener," the nurse said. "I've just come from the house. Dahlia's still there. Everything's under control."

"Easy for you to say. We can't afford to lose another live-in client!"

"I'm as shocked as you are, Paula." Claire sank into the chair beside Paula's desk. "Aside from the Alzheimer's, Harriet was in excellent health. She was still in the middle stage of the disease, and I expected her to live several more years before it finally killed her."

"So did I. In fact, I was counting on it. Her family paid a month in advance, as regular as clockwork. You have no idea how rare that is, and what it meant for the bottom line. I earmarked that check to cover the Worker's Comp payment every month."

Claire furrowed her brow, and her mouth twitched in distaste. Her priorities were different, Paula knew – nurses didn't have to worry about making payroll. "I'm sorry," Paula said. "I know that sounds crass. That poor family – they must be devastated. The daughter was so sweet. I only met her once, but we talked on the phone a few times."

"I know. She told me how much she enjoyed your conversations. She's flying in from California tonight."

"How's Dahlia taking it?"

"She's awfully shaken." Claire's voice trembled. "She was with Harriet for almost a year; those two were really close. Now that they've taken the body to the funeral home, she wants to stay in the house till Joanne arrives. She's going to do some laundry and cleaning, although God knows the place is already immaculate. But she doesn't think the daughter should come to a house where nobody's home."

Paula forced a smile. "No doubt she'd also rather stay in that beautiful house than go back to her husband in Brooklyn. Seriously, though, that woman's a saint. Sometimes I wish I could just hole up at home and stay in bed for a week so Dahlia could take care of me."

"That's not a bad idea, Paula. As a matter of fact, speaking as your nursing supervisor, I might go so far as to recommend it. No offense, but you seem pretty frazzled."

"I know. Lunesta and Zoloft have been keeping me up nights."

Claire narrowed her eyes appraisingly. "You never told me you were taking those kinds of meds. I can see how Zoloft might give you insomnia, but the Lunesta should counteract that."

"Oh, I guess I didn't tell you. I got two kittens a couple of weeks ago, and I named them Lunesta and Zoloft." Paula paused. To date, by unspoken but mutual consent, she and Claire had kept a certain professional distance. How much should she share? She decided on a half-truth. No need to tell Claire she took Seroquel too. That was a red flag for bipolar disorder or worse. "Actually, I do take Zoloft and Lunesta," she said. "I don't think I could run this agency without them. They're great drugs; that's why I named the kittens after them."

"Oh, that explains –" Claire stopped short.

"My weight gain, I bet you were going to say." Or my mood swings, Paula thought. No doubt Claire had noticed both. "Anyway, you're right about my needing time off. But I don't dare take it right now, and there's no way I could afford a week of Dahlia's services. Once again it looks as if I'll be going into our credit line to make payroll."

"Since you mention it, I see you made another detour to Dunkin' Donuts. All those carbs wreak havoc with your blood sugar, you know. It can't help your mood any."

"Spare me the lecture, okay, Claire? My new diet is –" Paula stopped mid-sentence as Maria Gonzales flounced into the room. "What is it, Maria?" She felt like telling the woman to get lost, but she knew better than to give Maria a hard time about her uninvited entrance. As coordinator, she was responsible for assigning staff to clients, finding the optimum fit in terms of scheduling, skills and temperament. It was a fiendishly difficult job, and Maria had a better knack for it than anyone Paula had ever seen. They had learned to make allowances.

Maria flashed a devilish grin. "Sorry, Paula. I have news so good, it cannot wait. I believe I've found you your very next live-in.

The son, he wants someone to care for his mother immediately, today if possible. Claire, I told him you'd call right back. Dahlia will have a new client to go to. And me, perhaps I'll have that raise I've been asking about. Right, Paula? How about it?"

Paula laughed aloud. Maria could be obnoxious, but her vivacious good humor was so infectious that it was hard to stay annoyed with her for long. Born in Puerto Rico, she had grown up in the South Bronx, and her hard-won street smarts served her admirably in her dealings with the aides. She was equally adept in her telephone contacts with clients, but it was just as well they seldom saw her in person. With her willowy figure and frequently outrageous outfits, Maria projected a visual image that smacked of less reputable business. Today's get-up was typical: clingy black sweater that stopped just short of the navel, burgundy leather miniskirt slung low on the hips, segueing into lacy stockings and black suede stiletto boots.

Paula wheeled herself back to her desk and looked up at Maria expectantly. "Tell me more."

"The lady fell, broke a hip, and she just came out of rehab. The son was trying to take care of her, but he says she's driving him crazy with her demands. The doctor said she shouldn't live alone and recommended they get live-in care from our agency. I told him our rates, and he went into shock at first, but then he said they could handle it for a few weeks."

Paula felt a rush of hope. "Sounds like our kind of people."

"There's just one problem," said Maria. "He started asking about where our aides were from, their backgrounds, that kind of thing. I told him we check them out thoroughly, that they all have good training and references, all the usual stuff, but he wasn't satisfied. Finally he came right out and said the aides would have to be white."

"How did you answer?"

"I said he would have to talk to our nurse about that."

Claire sighed. "Thanks a lot. Just what I need, after dealing with Harriet Gardener's death since six o'clock this morning. This really makes my day."

Why did nurses have to be such prima donnas? Paula gulped down some coffee, felt it begin doing battle with the donut in her stomach. She shot a glare in Claire's direction. "Maria was right to bump it up a level. It's a tricky issue. Don't you agree, Claire?"

"Of course. I'm sorry. It sounds as if you did a great job, Maria. I'll go over there and do some schmoozing, take care of the intake assessment, but I need some down time first, and I have paperwork to catch up on. Why don't you call him back? Set up an appointment for, say, three o'clock."

Paula opened her desk drawer, fished out a Tum. "Thanks, Claire, that sounds like a plan. But Maria, don't tell him our nursing supervisor was dealing with a client who died. He might find it unnerving."

Maria pouted. "Paula, I'd never say anything like that. I'm not stupid!"

"No, on the contrary, you're very bright," said Paula. "But when it comes to sharing information, sometimes less is more."

Claire smiled at Maria. "I know you'll be diplomatic. No need to get into the race and scheduling issues. Just take down the basic information on the face sheet and get directions to the house. I'll deal with the rest when I get there."

Paula let out a sigh of relief so audible that Claire and Maria both grinned. "Go for it, ladies," she said. "Onward and upward with Compassionate Care." *But make it snappy. I want to get back to those donuts.*

Alone in her office at last, Claire pillowed her head in her arms for a few moments of stolen solitude before getting on with the day. On top of worrying about her clients, she was worried about her boss. Paula was sounding frazzled, looking bloated. Coping with the woman's financially driven mood swings could be far more draining than coping with the death of a patient. The news that Paula was on serious medications cast a new light on things, but she resolved to put that out of her mind for now.

For the next few hours, Claire burrowed into her paperwork. But at exactly three minutes to three, she ascended five cement steps and jabbed the bell mounted just to the left of a barn-red door.

She heard a burst of frenetic high-pitched yapping, then a deep male voice. "Shut the fuck up, you crazy bitch!"

Claire recoiled instinctively, then realized the man was addressing the dog. The door opened a crack, a florid red face appeared, and she caught the unmistakable whiff of whiskey. He was holding a blue plastic glass. Around the level of her shins, a small black and white dog scrabbled to get out.

"Don't mind Maizy," the man said. "She won't hurt you." With one beefy leg, he nudged the dog roughly back and out of the way. Then he opened the door another few inches. "I'm Lester Schatz. And you must be the nurse from Compassionate Care. Come on in."

I will if you get your beer belly out of the doorway, Claire wanted to say. Based on what Maria had told her about his racist comments on the phone, she was already prepared to dislike the man, and the way he treated the dog didn't help matters any. But they needed the case, so she extended her hand in a pretense of cordiality. "I'm Claire Lindstrom, the nursing supervisor. I understand you're interested in setting up live-in care for your mother."

He transferred his drink from his right hand to his left, took her hand and held it a beat too long. The cool moisture from the glass coated her palm. Resisting the impulse to wipe it on her skirt, she stood her ground until he stooped, grabbed the dog's collar, and took a step back. "Come on in. Can I offer you something to drink? I'm a Jack Daniel's man myself, but you look more like the gin and tonic type. I've got Beefeater's if you want."

The notion had its appeal, but Claire's professional veneer was firmly in place. "No thanks," she said crisply. "Or on second thought, I could use a glass of tonic without the gin."

"Great. Come on in."

The stench of urine assailed her as soon as she was over the threshold, mingling with stale cigar smoke and the whiskey on his breath.

"Is that a Jack Russell terrier?" she asked. Family pets were great ice breakers, she'd learned over the years.

He grinned, exposing a mouthful of yellowed teeth. "Sure is. She can be a royal pain, but she's the light of my mother's life, aren't you Maizy?" He closed the door and let go of the dog, who retreated to a nearby sofa. "Come on into the kitchen while I get you that tonic."

As Claire trailed him through the living room, she was swamped by an overwhelming miasma of brown. Brown knotty pine walls, brown-flowered upholstery, dark brown wood frames on the family photos that lined the walls. The kitchen, in contrast, was steeped in yellow. The colors of feces and urine, she thought – the colors that all too frequently dominated the lives of her clients. She ought to be grateful, she supposed. After all, it was when they could no longer cope with the most basic of bodily functions that they and their families called on Compassionate Care.

"Lester? Who's there? Why was Maizy barking?"

Turning in the direction of the high reedy voice, Claire found herself facing a dark corridor with light at the far end.

"It's the nurse from the agency, Mom. Remember, I told you?" His ruddy face deepening to an alarming shade of burgundy, the man took a generous gulp of his drink. Hypertension, Claire was willing to bet. Was he on blood pressure medication? If not, he probably should be.

"Damn it, Lester, I already told you, I can do fine on my own. I don't want any nurses in here."

Lester Schatz let out a deep sigh. "Might as well get this over with," he mumbled. "Come on, I'll introduce you." He led Claire through the dusky corridor into a squarish room. Dingy Venetian blinds filtered the light. Against one wall, a frail woman cowered in the corner of a sofa bed.

"Mom, I'd like you to meet Claire Lindstrom. Claire, this is my mother, Minna Schatz."

His manners improved in his mother's presence, Claire noticed. His mother, however, was another story. "You're wasting your time, lady. I don't care what the doctor said, I don't want any strangers in my house. You might as well leave right now."

Just then Maizy wandered through the door and over to Claire. The dog began a thorough inspection of Claire's legs, bristling slightly as she sniffed.

"She must smell my dog." Claire squatted down and submitted herself to Maizy's examination. After a few moments, assured she had passed muster, she began stroking the little dog, scratching behind her ears.

"What kind of dog do you have?" asked Minna.

"A Labradoodle. That's a Labrador-poodle mix."

"Never heard of it," Minna snapped. Her lips curled in the hint of a smile. "But Maizy likes you, and that's a real compliment. She's an excellent judge of character, and she doesn't take to just anybody."

An hour later, Claire was back in the yellow kitchen, sitting across an old Formica table from Lester, going over the contracts for round-the-clock live-in care. "It's amazing how my Mom took to you," he said. "She was dead set against the idea of getting any help, but you had her eating out of your hand in no time."

Claire grinned. "I think Maizy deserves most of the credit. She broke the ice." Better to praise the dog than to brag about her own marketing skills, she thought. Winning over clients to the idea of accepting the care they needed was one of the things she loved most about her job. And the feistier the clients, the better she liked them. Providing care for Minna Schatz was going to be a challenge, but if they could come up with the right aide, this could turn into a long-term case.

"Now there's just one more thing," said Lester. "Like I told the girl on the phone, my mother's what you might call prejudiced. No offense, but we can't have any blacks in here. I'm sure you understand."

Here it was, the deal breaker she'd been anticipating. Taking a deep breath, Claire drew herself erect. "Compassionate Care is an equal opportunity employer. We don't discriminate on the basis of race, color or creed. Legally, we'd be in hot water if we did. Besides, our agency is morally and ethically opposed to any form of discrimination. We have some top-notch aides who happen to be women of color; I'm sure you'll be pleased with them."

"Them? What do you mean them? I thought you'd assign one aide to stay round the clock."

"We do assign a primary aide, but she'll need someone to relieve her every couple of weeks."

"Can I meet her before I decide?"

Aha, thought Claire – the deal's as good as done. Lester's prejudice had given way to minor quibbles that could be easily overcome. "We prefer not to work that way," she said. "The aides are already our employees, and we can vouch for them a hundred percent. Subjecting them to a special interview puts them on the spot and makes things uncomfortable for everyone. Anyway, the woman I have in mind, Dahlia Douglas, is really marvelous. She's not available today, but I think I could talk her into starting tomorrow."

Chapter 3

Claire raised her glass to the setting sun. "To Minna Schatz," she murmured. "May she live a long and happy life with Dahlia Douglas."

She took a lengthy swig of her gin and tonic. She'd already toasted the memory of Harriet Gardener and of her Aunt Alice, who'd bequeathed her this beloved patch of land alongside Kooperskill Lake. The gin was the deep discount variety, and the tonic was diet, but she'd squeezed half a fresh lime into it, and the effect was delicious. Lester Schatz might spring for Beefeater's, but she could barely tell the difference, so why pay extra just for snob appeal? Anyway, there was no one in her life she needed to impress. Not for years now. Not since Mark had died and she'd moved upstate.

She set the glass on the broad wooden arm of her aunt's battered old Adirondack chaise and stretched her arms luxuriously skyward, then reached down to pet Freia, who was sprawled peacefully at her feet. "Just look at those tiny ripples on the lake," she told the dog. "Isn't it gorgeous, the way they reflect the colors of the sunset?" The gin was easing its way warmly through her system, softening the raggedy after-effects of the day she'd just been through.

All at once Freia jumped up, yipping happily, and bounded across the grass toward Angelo and Regina Giordano's yard. Claire turned her head to track Freia's trajectory and saw Angelo making his way along the path that ran through a thicket of overgrown lilacs, linking their two yards.

"Mind if I join you?" he called. "I've got something to discuss."

Claire's heart lurched. Had Regina taken a turn for the worse? Claire had known the couple since earliest childhood, when she and her parents had begun making their annual summer pilgrimages to Alice's lakeside home. She had called them "Uncle Angelo" and "Aunt Regina" back then, although they weren't related by blood, but a few years back, by common consent, they had become just plain Angelo and Regina.

Claire rose, wrapped him in a ritual hug. His body felt frailer than she remembered. She pulled back and looked at him. "So how's Regina doing?"

"Not so good. She's saying she can't face going through another round of chemo."

"It must be terrible for both of you. Please give her my love. Tell her I'm thinking about her."

He forced a smile. "I will. But actually I came over to talk to you about something else. I might have a referral for your agency. My friend George Cropsey is suffering from Parkinson's disease. He's a retired English professor, taught at the State University for umpteen years. He's been staying with his son's family, but they're practically at each other's throats, so he wants to move back home. He's virtually bed bound, so he'd need round-the-clock care. He needs help managing his diabetes, too. Sound like something you can handle?"

"Absolutely. Have you talked with him about our services?"

"A little, and I think he's receptive. I told him you'd give him a call tomorrow."

Claire kissed his cheek. "Angelo, you're a doll. My boss will be thrilled. Our caseload is pretty low. As a matter of fact, one of my favorite clients died this morning."

"I'm sorry. Is that why you're out here all alone, drowning your sorrows?"

"Maybe so. Care to join me?"

"I guess I can spare a few minutes. Then I have to get back to Regina."

"Would you like a gin and tonic? We won't have many more summery nights like this; soon they'll be out of season."

He grimaced. "Ugh, no thanks. Those things are too bitter for my taste."

"Then how about some bourbon? I still have some of that Wild Turkey you brought over when you and Regina were here for dinner last month. On the rocks with a splash of water, right?"

"That would be great."

"So," he said when they were settled down with their drinks. "A lovely young lady like you shouldn't be alone on a gorgeous night like this. It's been three years since Mark died, and you're much too young to remain a widow. You should be out on the town with some handsome young gentleman."

"Actually, I can't think of anyplace I'd rather be than right here by the lake. Or any gentleman I'd rather be with than you."

It was a game they'd played before, this ritual flirtation with its comforting familiarity. It had evolved naturally over the years, and Claire knew it was essentially innocent. Angelo loved his wife with a deep, unwavering devotion. He was in his late seventies now, around the age Claire's father would have been, had he lived. She felt fortunate to have a father figure next door, especially one so gallant and sympathetic, so chock full of old school charm.

Blessed with the kind of craggy Italian looks that age with distinction, Angelo must have been irresistible in his prime.

He nodded in approval as he sipped his bourbon. "You remembered to use the well water, fresh from the tap, right?"

"Of course. You've given me enough lectures on the subject."

"I've trained you well. Our native water is pure ambrosia. It beats the stuff they sell in those fancy bottles." He grinned, and for a moment she glimpsed the carefree man he'd been before his wife's illness. "Want to freshen your drink?" he asked.

"I'd love to, but I don't dare. I have to go back to the house of that client who died today. The daughter's flying in from California, and she should be there in about an hour."

"What's the client's name? Maybe it's someone I know."

"Maybe, but I can't share the name with you. The identities of our clients are strictly confidential."

"Even after they die? What difference can it make? Oh well, never mind, I'll check the obituaries the next couple of days and see who died at home after a long illness."

"Why so curious, Angelo?"

"When you get to be my age, every death hits close to home. There's always a kind of morbid fascination, along with a guilty sense of relief that you beat the odds for one more day. What did this person die of? At least you can tell me that?"

"Actually I can't. She had Alzheimer's, but she was in reasonably good health physically, and we don't know the actual cause of death. We may never know."

"But they'll do an autopsy, right?"

"No, not unless there's something suspicious about the death. Autopsies aren't as common as you might think from watching the TV crime shows. Especially with older people who have a number of physical conditions –"

"But you just said she was physically healthy."

"I thought she was, but there must have been some preexisting condition we hadn't picked up on before."

"Sounds a lot like your father's case. But they did an autopsy then, didn't they?"

Claire felt unexpected tears stinging her eyes. "That was because of the nursing home setting. They wanted to see if there was any negligence or mistreatment involved." There was, she thought. Mine and my mother's. Not the kind that shows up on autopsy.

"Sorry, honey, I shouldn't have brought it up. I can see you're upset."

"It's not your fault. I've been thinking about my father all day. There are definite similarities. The Alzheimer's, the sudden, unexpected death –"

"Then they should do an autopsy, damn it!" He slammed his glass down on the wooden chair arm with such force that the bourbon sloshed over the sides. "When an old person kicks the bucket, the medical establishment should care enough to find out why. People don't just up and die of old age. There's always a reason."

———

Gabriel ripped the page out of the sketchbook, crumpled the sheet and threw it on the floor. God damn that Claire Lindstrom! Why did she have to go into the house just when he was getting the composition down on paper? He'd made a few modifications – eliminated the old man, for one thing. For all he knew, the guy might become a target one of these days, and Gabriel didn't want to jinx the painting he was about to start.

The drawing didn't do justice to Claire, but small wonder. He was frazzled from his whirlwind trip to the city, his figure drawing was rusty, and looking back and forth from the telescope to the paper put yet another barrier in the way. He'd have to figure out a way to study her at closer range.

He splashed some vodka into a tumbler and took a swig as he studied the lake. Half a dozen geese glided low over the water, and its gentle ripples reflected a fractured mirror image of the cloud formations above. Violet, fuschia, rose red, and above it all, a clear, celestial blue darkening to purple. The colors were straight out of the skies in that calendar he had – Maxfield Parrish, the guy who painted nymphs and maidens romping through idyllic landscapes.

A jet arced high overhead, its fuselage fiery orange, its con trail cotton candy pink in the fading light. Heading west into the sunset. Normally he'd have been itching to be aboard, but right now, he was happy to be homebound, especially since Claire was his neighbor.

At first he'd been ticked off when they stuck him up here in the boonies six months ago. They said it was because he knew the area. He ought to: he'd grown up in a little burg less than thirty miles away, out west past the Helderbergs, gone to nursing school in Albany, held a couple of jobs in the region before splitting for New York City. He hadn't expected to return any time soon, but after the filth and chaos of the city, the area looked pretty damn good.

He suspected they were testing him. Blend in naturally without arousing suspicions, acquit himself well, and they'd move him up to more ambitious assignments. He was confident he'd excel. Eldercide: the word they'd used to describe his job had a nice ring to it. The karma was right. Even finding this cottage. Scoping out the Harriet Gardener case, he had trailed Claire Lindstrom home from her office one day, noticed the for-rent sign on the place a third of the way around the little lake. Back at the motel, he'd called the number that same night, paid cash in advance the next morning. One month's rent, one month's security.

The woman's eyes lit up when she took his money. The cottage belonged to her parents, she explained. They had died a few months apart, and the estate was tied up in probate. She and her brothers were still unsure what to do with the property, but in the meantime, it would be a blessing to have someone responsible living there, looking after it. She had no doubt he was trustworthy, and she didn't ask for references. Inspiring confidence, that was one of his many talents.

He felt the vodka easing through his system, damping down the energy that still coursed through his system. You've got to learn to relax, he told himself. You've done enough for today. The Harriet Gardener assignment, the round trip to New York City for art supplies, with side trips to a few SoHo galleries, the preliminary sketches for a painting featuring Claire –

His cell phone trilled. He picked up. "Yes?"

"Gabriel, this is Athena. We've got another assignment for you. Are you ready?"

"Ready as I'll ever be."

The painting could wait.

———————

Once inside, Claire stripped off her clothes and dumped them in the hamper. Standing naked beside the shower stall, she set the water temperature as hot as she could stand it, the pressure to pins-and-needles intensity. Holding the grab bar, stepping cautiously into the cubicle of peach-colored ceramic tiles, she thought of Alice. This bathroom had been a source of pride and joy for her aunt, who had splurged on a state-of-the-art remodeling job a few years back at Claire's insistence.

She remembered their endless arguments. "What do I want with a new bathroom at my age?" Alice had protested. "This one has served me perfectly well for fifty years, and I figure it'll do just fine for the few years I've got left."

"It may very well shorten your life," Claire had replied. "The bathtub's too slippery, and there aren't adequate hand holds for climbing in and out. And with all the hard porcelain and sharp corners, the room is a real menace, an accident waiting to happen. Do me a favor – spring for something better so I won't have to worry so much about you staying here all alone, maybe falling with no way to get up or get help."

In the end, she had worn down Alice's resistance, helped her retrofit the bathroom with the latest in safety-conscious equipment. A big roll-in shower stall with a built-in seat, counters with padded vinyl edges to cushion the impact and lower the risk of injury in the event of falls. But although the low-skid surfaces, the rounded corners, the extra-strong safety bars might have bought some peace of mind, maybe even some borrowed time, they couldn't fend off death forever. Alice had succumbed to a stroke two years ago, leaving the cottage to Claire. Coming so soon after Michael's death, the gift seemed heaven sent. Her life in New York City was inextricably bound up with memories of her husband. Impulsively, she pulled up stakes and moved upstate to Kooperskill, where she'd spent so many idyllic summers as a child, to start anew. The move had been good, on the whole, but memories of Mark still overpowered her at times. Tonight, with early autumn in the air, she ached with the pain of his loss.

As she scrubbed shampoo into her hair, she thought of the nurse in South Pacific, singing about washing a man right out of her hair. She couldn't manage that, nor would she want to. But at least she had her work to turn to. Nursing, she had learned, was the best antidote to missing Mark.

The western sky was a velvety deep purple shading to black as Claire turned into Harriet Gardener's driveway an hour later. Her eyes on the emerging stars, she barely missed ramming the rear end of the agency car parked outside the front door. A black Taurus sedan, the damn thing was practically invisible after dark, not to mention funereal.

And what was the car doing here anyway? Pulling up behind it, turning off the ignition of her Focus hatchback, she took a deep breath to gather her thoughts. Stephen McClellan, their driver and jack of all trades, must be here at the house to pick up Dahlia, but no one had told Claire a thing about it. Why did Maria persist in leaving her out of the loop? She grabbed her cell phone to call Paula and complain, punched the speed-dial number for the agency, then stopped short and snapped it shut. Cool it, she told herself. You're overreacting.

Her breath was coming faster, and it wasn't just anger fueling her upset. Since Stephen McClellan had charmed his way into a job six months ago, he'd made himself indispensable, meeting the aides at the Amtrak station in Rensselaer, ferrying them to the clients' homes, running errands, doing minor carpentry and odd jobs for the clients and their families. The elderly ladies loved him, and why not? He had movie-star looks: tall, well muscled, wavy blond hair, chiseled features, like a young Matthew McConaughey. And a movie star was exactly what he intended to be, he'd told her on more than one occasion. Preferably before he hit thirty. In the meantime, the part-time flexibility of the job at Compassionate Care suited him perfectly, leaving him ample time to bop down to New York City to audition for soaps and off-Broadway productions. Claire suspected Maria of juggling the aide changes to accommodate Stephen's casting calls. But the system worked well enough, so why tamper with it?

Claire sighed. Sitting here musing about Stephen wasn't going to improve the situation one whit. She clambered out of the car, marched to the front door and rapped smartly.

Moments later, the door opened and Stephen stood there in all his splendor, looking deceptively Ivy League in khaki pants and powder blue button-down shirt. "Claire!" he exclaimed. "Come on in, we've been expecting you."

Like a country gentleman welcoming a long lost friend to his manor home, Claire thought. She caught a whiff of cologne, with a musky male undercurrent that sent her pulse rocketing skyward. Damn those pheromones, she thought. She wasn't ready for feelings like this. Not by a long shot.

"I didn't know you were working today," she said.

"I wasn't. I was down in the city auditioning for a new reality show. One of those bachelor things." His sea-green eyes took on a mischievous glint, and he grinned rakishly. "They told me I was too good looking."

Claire tried to look stern. "Stephen, cut to the chase. I gather you're here to pick up Dahlia?"

"Yes, Maria called me on my cell, told me about Harriet and asked me to meet her daughter at the airport, then take Dahlia to the train. I made it in record time. You want to come in?"

"That's the general idea."

He ushered her into the foyer, then the living room, where Joanne Hargreave sat stiffly on the sofa. Harriet Gardener's daughter was a petite woman with cropped black hair. She wore an expensively tailored black suit, as if already set for the funeral.

Claire crossed the space between them and took both Joanne's hands in her own. "I'm so sorry about your mother," she said.

Joanne's hands were cool and dry, and she withdrew them immediately, averting her eyes from Claire's. "Thank you," she murmured. "It happened so suddenly, I still can't believe it."

Being with the bereaved – this was the hardest part of the work. Tuning in to the grieving family, letting them vent. Claire was good at it, but the role was essentially passive, at odds with her need to act. Even worse, it forced her to confront her own feelings of grief and loss, and in this case, her uneasy sense that things should have been different.

She sank down on the sofa next to Joanne and waited for the woman to speak.

"I'm exhausted," Joanne said at last. "It's only five o'clock Pacific Time, but it's already so dark out, it feels like midnight to me. I think I'll turn in for the night."

"Okay, but if you'd like to talk, if you have any questions, maybe I can help."

Joanne stiffened, edged away from Claire. "What kind of questions? It was my mother's time, that's all. In a way, maybe it's for the best. With her Alzheimer's diagnosis, the prognosis was horrible. She was bound to deteriorate until she lost any last semblance of dignity. This way, at least she was spared any suffering."

"Even so, it has to be hard on you, losing your mother so suddenly." As she spoke, Claire flashed on her mother's face. She'd died suddenly too, a few months after Claire's father.

The image evaporated as she grew conscious of Stephen's presence close by, looming over them. "Joanne's exhausted," he said. "All the way from the airport, she was telling me how upset she was about Harriet's death. Maybe she doesn't need to talk any more right now."

The arrogance of the man! Chauffeur, handyman, and now grief counselor to boot? Claire felt a surge of adrenaline, and she held her breath until the wave of anger subsided. "That's really up to Joanne," she said through clenched teeth.

Joanne gave her a sidelong glance. Her long lashes shadowed her dark eyes, and Claire couldn't read her expression. "Stephen's right," Joanne said. "I'm utterly exhausted, so I'm going to turn in. I'll stay in my old room. Mother kept it virtually untouched all these years, so I'll feel right at home."

"Where's Frank? Wasn't he going to come with you?"

"He's so busy with work, I told him there was no need. He'll arrive in time for the funeral Saturday, but to be honest, I wanted the time alone before all the friends and relatives show up. Sorry, but I don't feel exactly cordial right now." She buried her head in her hands. Claire expected the shoulders to shake, the tears to start, but Joanne sat utterly still, shrinking in on herself, silent as stone.

Claire rose, giving Joanne's shoulder a reassuring pat. "If you're sure there's nothing I can do to help, I'll touch base with Dahlia, and then I'll be on my way. But if you want to talk later, don't hesitate to call. Even if it's the middle of the night."

She extracted a business card from her purse, wrote her cell phone number on the back, handed it to Joanne. The woman took it gingerly, cringing as if it were contaminated. Claire knew she wouldn't call.

Claire headed upstairs and was halfway down the hall to Dahlia's room when she heard the soft tread of Stephen's feet behind her. She whirled to face him. "What are you doing up here?"

He stopped short. "I was going to tell Dahlia I'm ready when she is."

"You'll have to wait. I need a few minutes alone with Dahlia to discuss the case she's starting tomorrow."

"Yeah, why she wants to yoyo to Brooklyn and back is beyond me. Why don't you ask Joanne if Dahlia can stay here, or put her up at a motel overnight? It would be cheaper than the round trip on Amtrak"

Now he was playing coordinator. Claire felt another rush of anger. High time to rein him in, she decided. "Look, Stephen, we've got to get some things straight about your job description, but this isn't the time or the place. How about if we meet at Tanya's after you drive Dahlia to the train? Say in about an hour. I'll even buy you a drink."

Stephen grinned. "You're on."

"Good. Now I'd appreciate it if you go wait in the car."

Chapter 4

When Claire pulled up at Tanya's Tavern, the parking lot was jam packed. No doubt the inside would be a zoo. What had possessed her to issue that invitation to Stephen? Sitting in her Focus, staring at the low, rambling roadhouse with its ragged brown siding and neon beer signs, she realized she had no desire to lecture him about his job description. In fact, she had to admit her desires were entirely different where Stephen McClellan was concerned.

Any way you cut it, Stephen was bad news. Easily ten years her junior, totally self-absorbed and enamored of his own considerable charms. A would-be actor, no less. She'd never seen him ply his trade professionally, but he was such a consummate bullshit artist, she imagined he'd be good at it. Even worse, he was involved with Maria Gonzales. Exactly how heavily, Claire wasn't sure, but there was obvious chemistry there. The office was the worst possible place to go trolling for relationships, meaningful or otherwise. Maybe she should warn Maria – she was bound to get hurt, and it would be a shame to lose such a good coordinator.

Speaking of chemistry, the sparks between Claire and Stephen had been palpable since their first meeting. She'd tried to deny it and damp it down, told herself it was ridiculous, but it was only getting worse. Did he have any inkling of the incendiary effect he had on her? Maybe, but she had no intention of admitting it.

She didn't see the Taurus yet, but she could certainly use a drink, and maybe some of Tanya's fabulous baby back ribs. Suddenly ravenous, she clambered out of the Focus, punched the key fob. The car clicked its locks, flashed its lights and gave her a friendly beep as she headed across the parking lot.

Inside, the ambient temperature was pushing ninety degrees. She stood a moment, her senses under assault by the pungent mix of perfume, sweat and beer, then threaded her way toward the bar and ordered a Pinot Grigio.

"Let me get that." Close beside her, a hand slapped a ten-dollar bill onto the dark wood. Startled, she glanced up at its owner, who grinned. "I'm Rick Kozlowski."

"Claire Lindstrom." She eased onto a barstool, angled her knees to carve out some personal space, then studied her new companion. He had an intriguingly angular face framed by curly brown hair tamed only partially with gel. Eyes of a brown so deep, she couldn't see his pupils. Plaid flannel shirt with the sleeves rolled back to reveal sinewy forearms. The tail end of a tattoo, possibly a mermaid, snaked down from the crook of one elbow.

"I've seen you here before," he said. "But never alone."

"No, I usually come with people from my agency. It's only ten minutes from the office, and the food is decent, so it's become our unofficial hangout."

"What kind of agency?"

"Home health care." She was about to leave it at that, but her boss's image flashed across her mind's eye. Claire could almost hear Paula's voice. *Market, market. You never know who you're talking to.* "We're a small, independent agency. Compassionate Care. We specialize in round-the-clock live-ins. I'm the nursing supervisor."

"Talk about instant karma! I'm a RN with Tri-County Home Care." He grinned. "So now you're hobnobbing with the enemy. If your boss only knew."

"I wouldn't exactly call it hobnobbing." He was right about the enemy part, though. The mere mention of Tri-County was enough to throw Paula into a funk. The agency was part of a national chain, with a lock on more contracts than Claire's boss could ever dream of.

He chuckled. "Come to think of it, what exactly is hobnobbing, anyway? It sounds obscene, when you think about it. So what are you doing here? Drowning your sorrows?"

"Actually I was thinking of ordering some ribs. And I'm meeting someone from work."

"Male or female?"

"You ask an awful lot of questions. Did anyone ever tell you that?

"Frequently. Guess I've just got an insatiable curiosity. Seriously, though, it's great to meet a fellow nurse, someone I can talk shop with. How's it going at Compassionate Care? No offense, but you look kind of frazzled. Did you have a rough day?"

Was it that obvious? Claire sipped her wine in silence, wondering how to respond. He'd backed off from the male-female question, and she didn't get the feeling he was coming on to her. It suddenly occurred to her that he might be gay.

"Judging by your silence, that's a big affirmative," he said. "Want to talk about it? I'm a good listener."

Something in the liquid depths of his eyes made her want to plunge ahead. "Actually, one of my favorite clients died early this morning," she said. "It was so completely unexpected, I guess I'm still in shock. I just came from meeting with the daughter at the house."

"That's always tough." He signaled the bartender. "One more round, okay?" He eased his stool closer to Claire's, stared into her eyes. Maybe he wasn't gay after all. She pushed back her stool. The metal feet scraped like chalk on a blackboard, and she winced.

"What was the cause of death?" he asked.

"Sorry, but I don't feel comfortable discussing it."

"Of course. Confidentiality and all that good stuff. We only just met, after all. But if your agency is anything like mine, you deal with a lot of clients who are really pushing the envelope of their allotted life spans. People who wouldn't be here at all if not for the miracles of modern medicine. Sometimes I wonder why we try so hard to keep them alive, when all they've got to look forward to is prolonged pain and suffering."

"I agree quality of life is a major issue. But you sound pretty cynical, especially for a nurse. Do I detect a touch of burn-out?"

"Touché. Brilliant diagnosis, Claire. You're talking to someone in dire need of a career change."

"That's too bad, because –" She stopped short as Stephen McClellan insinuated himself into the space between their barstools. He was wearing jeans and a green microfiber shirt, and he had a freshly showered smell. She wondered fleetingly if he'd just come from a quickie with Maria, reminded herself it was none of her business.

Stephen grinned, a little sheepishly, she thought. "Sorry I'm late."

"No problem. Stephen, I'd like you to meet Rick Kozlowski. He's a nurse at Tri-County."

The two men locked eyes. "We've already met," Stephen said in a tone that suggested the meeting had been less than cordial.

The tension was palpable, and Claire had no desire to referee a testosterone-fueled battle. The day had been dramatic enough already. *I've had it,* she decided. *With Rick, with Stephen, with everybody. I'm drowning in interpersonal relations, and I want to go home.*

She clambered down from the barstool. "No offense, guys, but I suddenly realized how exhausted I am. I'm going to call it a night."

Rick's eyes narrowed. "I thought you were lusting after a rack of ribs."

"I'll swing by KFC for some takeout instead."

Stephen reached out and stroked her shoulder. She quivered, hoped he didn't feel it. "I thought you wanted to talk about my job," he said with a sly smile. "A performance evaluation, so to speak."

"It can wait."

"Yeah, but I don't know if I can. I was looking forward to spending some quality time with you."

Rick was watching their exchange with interest. "You want me to butt out?" he asked.

"Not necessary," Claire said. Suddenly she thought longingly of the lake. A late-night swim with Freia was exactly what she needed. Something to cool her off.

Thirty minutes later, she stood in her bedroom, stripping off her clothes. She pulled on her bathing suit as Freia bounced and whimpered in excitement. "You're so brilliant when it comes to fashion," Claire told the dog. "You know we're going for a swim, don't you."

As Claire pulled on her old sneakers, Freia escalated to whining, then full-fledged barks, all the while crashing into Claire's legs and nibbling at the laces. "Calm down, baby, I'm hurrying as fast as I can. You're not helping any."

No strings attached – that was one of the things she loved about her dog's companionship. Everything was so upfront, so simple and straightforward, whereas with Stephen, if she wasn't careful, things could get awfully complicated in a hurry. He hadn't been happy about her sudden leave taking, but so be it. The idea of discussing his job description over late-night drinks in a roadhouse was ludicrous anyway. It blurred the boundaries, and where Stephen was concerned, she felt blurry enough already.

As she padded across the lawn, she gazed out at the darkness. The lake was ringed with houses, but tonight only a few distant pinpricks of light suggested human habitation. The summer residents were already gone, and the few remaining year-rounders had probably gone to bed. Shivering, she wrapped her beach towel more snugly around her as Freia danced in ecstatic circles, her blond body wraithlike in the faint light of the new moon. Claire knew this might be their last midnight swim of the season. The Labradoodle, with her thick curly coat, could brave the spring-fed lake well into fall, but for Claire, this particular pleasure would soon cease to be.

She stepped from the narrow strip of sand into the lake, shivered as the chilly water lapped her ankles, then her calves. The soles of her well-worn sneakers protected her from the sharp edges of the rocks and pebbles embedded in the muck of the bottom. A few feet from shore, where the seaweed took over, she flung herself forward onto the surface of the water. Floating just below her body, the stuff scraped at her exposed skin like a gigantic loofah sponge. The sensation was peculiar but Claire had long since grown accustomed to it. She couldn't have tolerated the slimy, stringy kind of seaweed, but this curly pondweed wasn't so bad. A small price to pay for having her own private beach.

Twenty feet out, where the water grew colder and the seaweed slacked off, she let her legs sink down until her body was nearly vertical. Treading water, she felt the frigid currents of the lake's hidden springs welling up from the depths, enveloping her. Water this cold could be deadly. How long would it take for hypothermia to set in? Not a bad way to go, if you had the choice. Like drifting off to sleep . . .

All at once something nudged her back. She screamed, flailed wildly, grabbed a handful of matted hair. "Freia! You scared me half to death!" Claire let her legs drift up and floated onto her back. The water was bracingly cool once more, the frigid springs unfelt beneath her. Gazing at the sliver of moon rising over the black silhouettes of the distant hills, she tried to focus on the clear beauty of the night and banish the morbid ruminations from her mind.

——— — ———

Standing in Minna Schatz's sunlit kitchen the next morning, going over the plan of care with Dahlia Douglas, Claire felt utterly exhausted. The events of the day and the late night swim with Freia had jolted her body into a state of wired restlessness that had kept her tossing sleeplessly for much of the night.

Dahlia looked as exhausted as Claire felt. Traveling to Brooklyn and back, she couldn't have gotten much sleep. "Claire, I don't know about this case," the aide muttered. Her fingers dug into Claire's forearm, clinging for dear life, and her brown eyes stared intently into Claire's. "That man Lester Schatz, he hates me. He's evil, I can tell by the way he looks at me with those beady little pig's eyes." Shuddering, she puckered her lips as if biting into a lemon.

Claire's stomach lurched in sympathy. "He doesn't hate you, Dahlia. He hates what's happening to his mother, and the situation they're in."

"No, he hates his mother, and she hates him. They're both nasty. And she doesn't trust me. Remember when she talked about storing all the sterling silver someplace safe? She practically came right out and called me a thief."

"That's just her paranoia kicking in. She'd probably feel the same way about any unfamiliar person in her home."

"Not you. She took to you all right. Because you're white."

Claire pursed her lips. How to field this one? Dahlia was probably right. "I'm sure things will settle down once they get to know you," she said at last. "I warned you this might be a tough situation."

Dahlia sighed deeply. "I know you did, and so did Maria. She told me Mr. Schatz and his mother are racists."

"And you're the perfect person to show them the error of their ways. In no time at all I'll bet Minna and Lester will adore you." Claire patted Dahlia's hand, trying to project a confidence she didn't entirely feel. "How about giving it three or four days? I know it's difficult for you, coming here directly from Harriet's house. We probably should have insisted you take a week off, but I know you're saving to bring your daughters up from Jamaica. If you want, though, I can have Maria schedule someone else to relieve you Friday."

Dahlia's eyes went even wider. "No, Claire, please don't do that. I need the job. I'll stay two weeks, and then we'll see. All right?"

"Okay, but let me know if you change your mind." Claire crossed to the refrigerator, where she'd pinned up the plan of care with a banana-shaped magnet. "I know this situation may be tough psychologically, but the level of care is pretty straightforward. Remember, the most important thing is to stay close by and assist her with transfers from the bed to the chair or the commode and back again. I want you right there supervising when she uses the walker. She needs the exercise, but we don't want her falling. After that hip fracture –"

The sound of Maizy's nails scrabbling on the vinyl tiles broke Claire's train of thought. She wheeled to see the dog bounce into the room, trailed a few seconds later by Minna. As the old woman hobbled out of the dark hallway into the sunny kitchen, the rubber pads of her walker thumped softly on the floor. She paused, blinking against the brightness. "I'll bet you ladies were talking about me."

Claire smiled. "I was just reminding Dahlia to stay close beside you when you're getting from one place to another. But she can't do it unless you tell her when you need help. Remember how we talked about that when we were going over your needs for your plan of care?"

Minna scowled. "Don't use that tone of voice with me. I'm not a child, and my memory is perfectly fine. I remember you talked about all kinds of nonsense. I also remember I didn't agree to it. Anyway, Lester helped me get up. Isn't that right, son?"

Lester shuffled into the room, far too late to have been any help if Minna lost her balance. "That's right, Mother. Now if you ladies are all set, I'm going to be getting back to my own house."

His hands were shaking badly, and Claire guessed he was anxious to get back to his booze. "Go ahead. We'll be fine," she said.

"Speak for yourself," snapped Minna. "Lester, how could you leave me in the hands of strangers? I've told you a million times, I don't need any help. And if I did, you could just as well care for me yourself. It's not as if you had anything more important to do."

Lester's face flushed crimson, and he gulped twice, convulsively. "I'd stay if I could, you know that, Mother," he said in a strangled tone. "But I really think you'll be better off with someone who's trained for this kind of thing." He gave Dahlia a sidelong glance. "I'm sure this girl here will take excellent care of you."

"Either that or she'll kill me. That's what you'd really like, wouldn't you. Then you could get your hands on all my money. Not to mention this house."

"Don't be ridiculous. What would I want with this house? You made it a living hell the whole time I was growing up." He turned abruptly, headed for the dark corridor that led to the front door. "That's it, I'm out of here. Good luck, ladies."

Dahlia shot Claire a long-suffering look. Claire arched her brows, sent back a commiserating smile.

"I caught that." Minna's voice was shrill. "You think you're so high and mighty, think you can put one over on me, but you're wrong. I may not be getting around so good, but there's nothing wrong with my eyes and ears. I'll be watching everything you do."

———————

Two hours later, Minna Schatz patted her stomach contentedly. She hadn't eaten so well in ages. Sautéed chicken breast, fresh green beans and sweet potatoes – this Dahlia sure knew how to cook. A little too much pepper, and the paprika and whatever else she'd scrounged up must have been years old, but all in all it was pretty good. Maizy had liked it too – Minna had slipped her a couple of tastes when Dahlia wasn't looking.

She could get used to this new life style, she realized. Being catered to, waited on hand and foot – it was no more than she deserved, after working so hard all her life. But she wouldn't let on to Dahlia how much she liked it. The girl might get a swelled head, start taking advantage. Snooping around, handling Minna's personal things, stealing her blind. With this class of people, you always had to be on the lookout.

This round-the-clock care had to cost a small fortune. Lester told her not to worry, that they could handle it, but she didn't believe him, and she knew it upset him to shell out money to strangers, money he'd no doubt hoped to inherit some day. Her son was tight-fisted, always had been. She'd taught him well in that respect. She had no idea of her net worth, because Lester had been handling her accounts ever since her husband Harry died ten years ago. That was probably a mistake. Lester told her he'd invested wisely, made a bundle in the market a few years back, but for all she knew, he could have been draining her bank accounts all along. But she didn't trust anyone who wasn't family, and she'd never been good with figures, so she didn't have much choice.

She'd always been careful with money, always saving for that proverbial rainy day. Well, maybe it was finally here, that stormy spell she'd saved for. She might as well enjoy it. She reached for the silver plated bell Lester had dug out of the bottom drawer of the sideboard, a wedding present over fifty years old. She couldn't remember who had given it to her, and she'd hardly ever used it. After all, it was the kind of bell you used for summoning servants, and she'd never had any servants before. Well, she did now.

Wrapping her hand around the cool silver, she gave the bell a vigorous shake. Dahlia appeared a few seconds later, her brown skin almost invisible in the dark doorway. "I need to use the commode," Minna told her. "And when I'm done, Maizy will need her afternoon walk. I wouldn't want her piddling on the floor."

Chapter 5

"We're all at our wits' end," Arlene Cropsey said. "Not to mention at each other's throats." From the quavery sound of her voice on the phone, Claire had the feeling George Cropsey's daughter-in-law was about to burst into tears.

Not another dysfunctional family, Claire thought. This was all she needed after spending the morning with Minna and Lester Schatz. But she had promised Angelo Giordano she'd call, and from the sound of things, his friend George was in dire straits. "It sounds like a tough situation," she said. "If you like, I could drop by later this afternoon. How's three-thirty?"

"Not good. My husband has an important meeting at four, but he said he could get away between one and three if we heard from you. Can you come over right now?"

Claire's stomach growled loudly, protesting the impending loss of yet another lunch. She hoped Arlene didn't hear. "Okay," she said. "Give me directions to your house, and I'll be there in half an hour."

She grabbed her briefcase, her laptop and a low-carb diet bar and headed out of the office. By one o'clock, she was snaking her way along a curvy road through an upscale subdivision of mini-mansions on gargantuan lots. She had an irrational prejudice against these enormous, energy-wasting homes that had gobbled up so much of the area's old farmland, but she didn't actually know anyone who lived in one. She resolved not to succumb to stereotypes and to keep an open mind.

As she slowed to check the addresses on the mailboxes, she glanced in her rearview mirror. A white Lexus loomed close on her tail, and she glimpsed a frowning male face. Why couldn't he swing around her? *Sorry, mister,* she muttered. *You'll just have to cool it.*

Here it was – 136. She swung into the driveway of a brick house with numerous wings and gables, and the Lexus pulled in beside her. Its driver was out of his car before she could shut off her engine. "Paul Cropsey," he said, extending his hand as she scrambled out of her Focus.

"Claire Lindstrom. I'm the nursing supervisor with Compassionate Care."

"Glad you could make it. I'd better fill you in on my father before we go inside."

Claire nodded as she studied the man. The crazed look in his blue eyes reminded her of Lester Schatz, but there the resemblance ended. Paul Cropsey was slim, with a well-tended beard, a navy pinstripe suit, red and blue patterned tie and buttoned-down white shirt. His harried manner suggested he'd rather be anyplace else.

"As Arlene told you, my father's suffering from advanced Parkinson's disease, plus diabetes," Paul said. "And *suffering* is the operative word. Can you imagine the horror he's going through? He's a brilliant man, a retired professor of history at the State University, and he still has all his faculties, but the Parkinson's has affected his speech so much that he's ashamed to talk. He's virtually bed bound now, and he has an indwelling catheter. It takes two people to help him transfer from the bed to the commode when he has to take a crap. On top of that, he needs help with his insulin injections. Needless to say, he's extremely depressed. I ask you – what kind of life is this?"

"It sounds like a tough situation. Is your mother still in the picture?"

"No, they divorced years ago, and they're barely on speaking terms."

"Who's been doing the care giving?"

"My wife, God bless her, along with our three kids. They're all teenagers, two boys and a girl. But it's really not fair to dump this burden on them, let alone on Arlene. She's been running herself ragged, and I told her it has to stop, effective immediately. The kids need a normal home environment, someplace they can bring their friends. They're so stressed out, they can't even study. They're all college bound, assuming we can still afford to send them. Dad was going to help with the tuition, but who knows what will happen now? Paying for your services isn't going to help matters any, but I don't see what choice we have, other than putting him in a nursing home. And he's vehemently opposed to that. He wants to go back to his own home. To die, as he so cheerfully puts it."

He lapsed into silence, took a deep, ragged breath. Even listening to him was exhausting, Claire thought. Imagine living with this level of tension day in, day out. "Perhaps I should see him now," she said. "Your wife said he's expecting my visit."

"Yes, but don't expect him to welcome you with open arms. He's pretty out of it."

"Don't worry about it. If you just introduce us, I can take it from there."

"All right. As a matter of fact, if it's okay with you, I'd like to take off and get back to work."

Claire glanced pointedly at her watch. Couldn't the man stand to take even a couple of hours off for his own father? "I thought your wife said you have until three," she said.

"Yes, but I don't see what good I can do here. I'm a policy analyst with the State Assembly, and things are really frenetic right now. If there's a lot of paperwork involved, you can go over it with Arlene, but don't have her sign anything. Just leave it on the kitchen table and I'll review it tonight."

"Do you have Power of Attorney?"

"Yes, and I'm designated as his Health Care Proxy. He has a DNR order too."

Not everyone spoke so casually about Do Not Resuscitate orders. "Whose idea was that?" Claire asked.

"My father's, but I totally agree. After all, what has he got to look forward to?"

Best to treat the question as rhetorical, Claire decided. She said nothing as Paul Cropsey ushered her through the front door into the foyer, where a slender blond woman stood waiting. "I'm Arlene Cropsey," she said, extending her hand. "Thank you for coming on such short notice."

"Pleased to meet you. I'm Claire Lindstrom." Claire felt the tension coursing through the handshake, noticed the dusky hollows beneath Arlene's carefully shadowed eyes.

"If it's all the same to you ladies, I'm heading back to the office," Paul said.

Arlene's lips parted, but whatever she was about to say, she bit back the words. No question who was the top dog here, or who was the primary caregiver. "If you'll just introduce me to Mr. Cropsey, I can take it from there," Claire said.

As Paul turned tail and disappeared out the front door, Arlene ushered her into the living room. The décor was modern and minimalist, the furnishings in monochromatic tones of beige and desert sand, the carpeting an off-white Berber weave. "He's in the sun room," Arlene said, as she crossed to a pair of doors with curtained glass panes. She rapped, then threw open the door without waiting for a response. "Dad, the nurse from the agency is here."

Stepping over the threshold, Claire found herself in a brilliantly sunlit space. Window walls wrapped around the room on three sides, and green plants were everywhere. Ferns, palm trees, dracaenas, assorted cacti – for a moment Claire felt she had been teleported to a conservatory at the Bronx Botanical Garden.

In the center of it all lay a frail man in a hospital bed. "Welcome to the bird cage," he said.

Claire crossed to the bedside. "Hello, Mr. Cropsey. I'm Claire Lindstrom." As she took his hand, she felt the Parkinsonian tremor. She smiled. "This is a spectacular greenhouse you've got here."

He grimaced. "It's not mine, it's Arlene's. My presence here is ruining the esthetics, I'm afraid."

His voice was faint, but his speech was fairly clear. His gaunt, aristocratic face looked a lot like Paul's, but age and disease had distorted the contours, so that looking at the father was like viewing the son through a funhouse mirror. The resemblance was especially striking around the eyes. But while Paul's were crazed, George's held a look of infinite sorrow.

"So, Mr. Cropsey, I understand you want to go back to your own home. I gather you've talked it over with your family, and everyone is in agreement?"

As he nodded, his blue eyes filled with tears. He raised a hand as if to wipe them away, but the effort appeared to exhaust him, and the hand fell limply back onto the bedclothes. "Yes, I'm tired of being a burden to my family. I think I'll be better off there."

Arlene approached the bed. "Don't talk that way. You're not a burden, Dad."

His face reddened, and he scowled. "Cut the crap, Arlene. It's obvious I'm no good to anyone anymore. I'd be better off dead."

It was all here, Claire thought. The depression, the volatile mood, the physical decline. Classic late-stage Parkinson's, worse in its way than Alzheimer's because the mind was often still intact. She took a deep breath, summoned her most professionally reassuring manner. "Arlene, why don't you take a break? Mr. Cropsey, before we see about moving you back to your own home and setting up care for you, we need to do a thorough assessment. Do you think you're up for that now?"

He summoned a faint smile. "The sooner the better. And please, call me George."

Claire felt a rush of warmth, and she knew at once: this was going to be one of those clients who stole her heart and threatened her objectivity.

"I'll be in the kitchen if you need me," Arlene said. She left the room, closing the double doors behind her.

"Whew." George let out a tremulous sigh. "This death and dying stuff is really the pits. In my humble opinion, society has taken it too far. We should take a lesson from the Eskimos, just put our elders on the nearest hunk of iceberg and float them out to sea. Save everyone a lot of time and aggravation."

———————

The next afternoon, Stephen McClellan caught sight of Claire's Focus before he was close enough to read the mailbox. He stomped on the brake. Cropsey – yes, this was it. He eased the Taurus into the driveway, pulled up behind Claire and killed the engine, then turned to the Jamaican guy in the passenger seat. "Here we are, Errol. Your assignment, should you choose to accept it."

The black man exhaled deeply. His eyes were wide. "I already accepted, and man, I'm glad I did. This place is fabulous!"

"You're lucky Claire decided to give you another chance."

Errol shot Stephen a glare. "What's that supposed to mean?"

"Remember that case a couple of months ago, when you cut short your assignment three days early when we didn't have anyone to relieve you? Maria had a shit fit, and Claire ended up spending the night at the client's house. Tanisha finally ended up filling in, but man, it was a close call. The guy's family was so pissed off, we practically lost the case."

"Yeah, well, it was an emergency. I had a death in the family."

Yeah, right, Stephen thought. The lamest excuse in the books. "Anyway, from what I hear, this case is a tough one," he said. "The man's really in bad shape, can't do anything for himself. He has Parkinson's disease. Diabetes too."

"I know. Claire went over his care with me on the phone. I can handle it."

Arrogant bastard! Stephen didn't like the casual way Errol used Claire's first name, as if they were bosom buddies. What Stephen knew of the case – and it wasn't much – he'd learned from Maria, not Claire. "You're probably not used to places this fancy," he said. "Not in Brooklyn."

Errol turned in his seat and glowered at Stephen. "You'd be surprised what I'm used to. Back in Jamaica –"

"Never mind. Cut the nostalgia crap. I could care less."

Cool it, Stephen. You can't afford a pissing contest, even if the guy's obnoxious. He couldn't see why Claire and Maria were so crazy about these Jamaican aides. Half the time they were probably stoned on weed. They had to be. How else could they stand it, staying in these houses for weeks at a time? The women had a nice way about them, he had to admit – kind of elegant, with a touch of earth mother that made him suspect they'd be great in bed. But this guy, with his tall, rangy build, his black leather jacket, polyester pants and spit-polished shoes, looked like a dope dealer, or maybe a pimp.

As Claire appeared on the front steps, Errol opened the passenger door and eased out of the Taurus. Then he leaned down, tossed Stephen a grin. "I better get inside. You mind bringing in my bag?"

Damn right I mind. I'm not your fucking valet. "Yas, massuh," Stephen muttered under his breath.

"What you say?"

"Nothing." *You'll get yours, asshole. Just you wait.*

Inside the house, Stephen plopped down Errol's bag, then stationed himself in the hallway near the kitchen, where Claire was going over the care plan with the aide. When they finally emerged, Stephen stood his ground, knowing Claire would have to brush past him on her way to George Cropsey's room. "Let's grab a bite after you finish up here," he murmured.

Claire threw him a deer-in-the-headlights glance. "I don't think so, Stephen. This orientation could take awhile. Mr. Cropsey's plan of care is complicated, and I have to make sure Errol remembers how to operate the Hoyer lift."

"I'm in no hurry. I can wait."

Her face flushed. "Sorry, but the answer's no."

As she turned tail and headed down the hall with Errol, Stephen felt his cell phone vibrating in his pocket, low on his hip. He pulled it out, checked the screen. Maria's home number. Damn! When they'd set up this case yesterday afternoon, he had promised to call to let the coordinator know that Errol had caught the right train, that Stephen had met him at the Amtrak station in Rensselaer and they were safely in the house. No problem there, but he knew Maria had more on her mind than the agency's schedule. She had said something about dinner at her place, and he knew the dinner would come with strings attached.

All well and good, sex with Maria was great, but she was too damn clingy. Her desperation was getting to him – all that crap about their relationship and where it was going. Nowhere, that's where. But he couldn't afford to blow her off. As coordinator, Maria had a major impact on his weekly paycheck. She told him who to pick up at the Amtrak station, where to take them and when. Sweet-talked the clients into booking him for grocery shopping or odd jobs around their homes. Scheduled around his time-off requests so he could go down to the city for auditions. Not a bad deal, really. She gave him plenty of assignments, and he gave her plenty of quality time after hours in the sack. Half the time he was fucking her, he was picturing Claire Lindstrom in his mind.

Wonder what Maria would think of that? He felt a familiar stirring. Claire with that Nordic ice princess look. Couldn't be involved for professional reasons, she said. Horse puckey. She wanted him. He could tell by the way her eyes widened when she saw him unexpectedly, like just now in the hall. *Gotcha*, he thought. Maybe not now, but soon. You think you're hot stuff, a RN and all. You're probably saving it for some doctor, but I've got what you really need.

Calling Maria could wait, he decided as he headed down the hall toward the patient's room. Claire was busy orienting Errol, but it couldn't hurt to say hello. He paused in the doorway, then crossed to the bed. "Hey, Mr. Cropsey, how are you doing? I'm Stephen McClellan, the agency's driver and jack of all trades."

The old man in the hospital bed glared at him. "We're busy here, Stephen," Claire said crisply. She reached out a hand, began massaging the patient's bony shoulder. He gave her a twisted smile, more like a grimace, jerked his head up and down spasmodically.

The room smelled of antiseptic and some kind of sickeningly sweet air freshener that made Stephen feel like puking. Or maybe the sweet smell was coming from the enormous pack of adult diapers on top of the dresser. This used to be the library, he supposed; the walls were lined with more books than Stephen would read in a lifetime. Or maybe a family room; there was a

large-screen TV across from the hospital bed, and framed
photographs scattered around the shelves. But now it looked more
like a hospital room, what with the metal-framed bed, the portable
toilet – commode, Claire had told him to call it – and the
enormous hydraulic contraption with chains and netting that
looked like some kind of bondage and discipline machine but was
actually for lifting the patient into and out of bed. Dahlia had
demonstrated it to Stephen one time, on another case.

I'd rather die than live this way, he thought. What was the
point of living when you were trapped in a single room, couldn't
even sit up or get out of bed without help? On the other hand . . .
"Nice work if you can get it, being waited on hand and foot," he
said to Mr. Cropsey.

The man's face reddened. "This is a god damn circus," he
sputtered. "Get the hell out of here."

Claire flew across the room, grabbed Stephen by the arm,
escorted him into the hall. "You're upsetting him. You'd better
go."

———

Claire sighed in relief when Stephen was gone. The day
wasn't over yet, and it already felt endless. Before starting the
orientation with Errol James, she had finished the plan of care,
ordered the pneumatic Hoyer lift from the medical equipment
company and transformed George Cropsey's library into a state-of-
the-art sickroom. Then she and Arlene had helped him make the
transition back to his own home. The last thing she needed was
Stephen coming on to her. What had gotten into him? He'd been
awfully aggressive, even for Stephen. Maybe the presence of Errol
James had him on edge. Over six feet tall, with dark chocolate skin
and the sinuous build of a long-distance runner, Dahlia's cousin
was a magnificent masculine specimen.

She watched as Errol positioned George's sling. The aide steadied the old man with a gentle hand across the shoulders, taking care to double check the alignment and make sure he was centered directly over the hospital bed.

"Ready, Mr. Cropsey?" I'm going to lower you down now," Errol said. George's head jerked in a nod, and Errol cranked the handle of the Hoyer lift. George descended slowly, a fragile cargo. Practically dead weight, Claire thought, then chided herself for even thinking the phrase. He might be immobilized by Parkinson's, his hold on life might be fragile, but the fire of life burned fiercely in his eyes.

Once George was safely on the bed, Errol straightened his limbs, then removed the steel S hooks of the chains from the grommets at the edges of the netting. "Now I'm going to help you roll on your side so I can get this netting out from under you," he said in the lilting Jamaican tone that was so much like Dahlia's.

"This is a weird contraption," George muttered, gazing up at the aide. "I feel like a piece of cargo on the docks, but you're a little skinny for a longshoreman. What are you doing in this line of work, anyway?"

Good question, Claire thought. She'd asked Errol the same thing when she'd first interviewed him, but as she recalled, his answer had been vague.

The aide beamed down at George. "I was the oldest brother in a big family, so I grew up helping people, and I guess it's in my blood. I'm saving up for nursing school."

That was news to Claire. Was it the truth? Errol had the gift of gab, and she wasn't always sure she could take his statements at face value. But he was the best Maria could come up with on such short notice. She just prayed he wouldn't bail on her.

"Well, I guess you'll do," George said with a crooked smile. "You're strong enough, at any rate. I was always afraid Arlene and the boys were going to drop me."

Errol patted the old man on the shoulder. "I've never dropped anybody in my life."

Claire had a good feeling about the chemistry between the men. "I know you two are going to be fine together," she said, hoping her confidence was founded on something more solid than fatigue and delusional thinking.

Chapter 6

*T*he next morning's sky was the same blazing blue it had been three days before, the day Claire had learned of Harriet Gardener's death. Once again Claire was setting off in her kayak, admonishing Freia to sit and stay on the dock, knowing full well the dog would obey her commands for a minute at most before jumping up waggingly to watch Claire's progress around the lake. But today had a decidedly different feel, simultaneously rushed and somber, because Claire had to be at the office by eight. She wanted to phone a few aides and catch up on her charting, then head over to Minna Schatz's house to orient the relief aide, Tanisha Clarkson. Dahlia Douglas would be getting her first time off from her new assignment this morning: she would be riding with Claire to attend Harriet Gardener's funeral.

The maples ringing the lake still wore the lush green of summer, and the weeping willows still had their delicate gray green cast, but the morning air was decidedly cooler now. Soon the life-giving green would drain from the leaves, revealing the reds and golds that betokened the end of the growth cycle. Each season was splendid in its way, and even the bleakness of winter bore the promise of renewal beneath the earth. If only the human life cycle were as comforting. People didn't go out in a blaze of glory, and there was no promise of renewal, at least none that Claire could find it in her heart to believe.

She paddled her usual lap around the lake, but the effort left her more drained than energized. Her mind kept drifting back to Harriet, and the magnificence of the day seemed a mere sham, a fragile façade that failed to mask the decay and chaos beneath. Impatient to get on with the day, she rushed back to the house to shower and dress, and she was at the office well before eight.

Maria beamed up at her as she entered. "Claire, that outfit looks ravishing on you! You should wear black more often – it really sets off your blond hair."

How did Maria do it? She was disgustingly perky for so early in the morning, and her makeup was flawless as usual. She looked ready for happy hour. Still, her grin was infectious, and Claire smiled for the first time that day. "Thank you, Maria, but black's not my thing. I reserve it strictly for funerals."

"Well, you should reconsider. You look really hot."

"Hot wasn't my intention." Claire smoothed her hands over the velvety ultrasuede. She had to admit she'd liked what the dress did for her in the three-way mirror at Macy's last night. A simple sheath that fell almost to the ankles, topped by a long, skinny jacket, it took twenty pounds off her already slender frame. She wondered fleetingly how Stephen would react.

Maria flashed an impish grin. "There's nothing wrong with hot. In that dress, you'll be a magnet for men. Couldn't you stand to spice up your life a little bit?"

Sure, I could, thought Claire. With your boyfriend. That would do wonders for office politics. "I got this dress out of deference to Harriet and her family," she said. "Everything in my closet seemed too colorful, and I didn't want to be disrespectful."

"Whatever. Hey, Claire, you think I could go to the funeral too? There'll probably be a lunch or something afterwards, won't there?"

"Yes, but we need you here to help cover the office. I'm taking Dahlia, and Paula is going, but that'll have to be it. I'm sorry."

Maria shrugged. "Okay, but it's your loss. I might have gotten you some clients."

"Maybe so, but that's not why we're going." *At least not why I'm going. With Paula, the profit motive rules.* "Anyway, Maria, if you want to represent Compassionate Care in the community, we need to talk about your image." She eyed the décolletage of Maria's clinging pink sweater. "You've definitely got your own look, but it might need a little modification."

Maria cocked her head and pouted, then brightened. "Hey, Claire, I've got a great idea! Let's go shopping together at the Huguenot Mall some night after work. We can try things on and give each other some makeover advice. It would have to be after pay day, though – my credit cards are all maxed out."

"Actually that does sound like fun. I'll think about it."

Just then the door opened and Allyson Quigley stomped in. The nurse was wearing her usual long-suffering look. Claire forced a smile. "Good morning, Allyson. How's it going?"

Allyson shot her a glare, then looked away. "About as well as can be expected."

Okay, thought Claire. If that's the way you want to play it, so be it. There was no love lost between the two women – hardly surprising, since Allyson had been demoted from nursing supervisor a month after Claire arrived last year. Claire had made valiant efforts to build a good working relationship with Allyson, but the older woman rebuffed all her overtures.

"Is Paula in? I have to see her." Allyson addressed herself to Maria, ignoring Claire completely.

"She's in, but she's got a lot to do." Maria rolled her eyes. "Paula and Claire are going to Harriet Gardener's funeral. You and I didn't make the grade – we have to stick around and work."

Claire could have strangled Maria. The coordinator was a drama queen, and if things threatened to get too dull, she loved kicking them up a notch. "Believe it or not, Maria, I'm not looking forward to this. If I could send you in my place, I would."

"It's not too late!" Mischief danced in Maria's eyes. "We could even trade clothes if you want. You're a couple inches taller than me, but I bet I could fill out that dress pretty well."

At the sound of her office door slamming, Paula Rhodes practically choked on her coffee. Startled, she glanced up to see Allyson Quigley barreling toward her desk. Grabbing her outsize mug, Paula took a couple of generous swigs to fortify herself, then leaned back in her chair and folded her arms. "What is it, Allyson?"

"Why did you give Claire Lindstrom another case to open? This is really starting to get to me. Bad enough you made her nursing supervisor and made me report to her, but lately you're sending her out to do all the nursing assessments too. I want to know what's up."

What's up is that the clients like her better, Paula wanted to say but didn't. With a dogged persistence that was all too rare among nurses these days, Allyson Quigley had hung in with Compassionate Care for all six years of the agency's existence. She was a smart, competent nurse, but her interpersonal skills left a lot to be desired.

"This particular case has some problematic aspects," Paula said, then paused. As Allyson's boss, she didn't owe the woman any explanation, yet she couldn't afford to alienate her. Loyal nurses were in short supply. "Believe me, from what Claire and Maria have told me, I'm doing you a favor. Minna Schatz and her son aren't easy to deal with."

"You don't think I'm up to dealing with them. That's what you mean, isn't it, Paula? Why not come right out and say it?"

Paula took a deep breath, trying to quell the adrenaline rush that threatened to destroy her diplomatic skills. Oh, the hell with it, she decided. If Allyson wanted answers, she'd give her some. "You're an excellent nurse, Allyson, and I truly value your work. But Claire Lindstrom has a knack for establishing rapport with clients right from the outset, and that's essential with these private-pay people the agency depends on for survival. When we start a new case, they're still deciding whether they want our services or whether they should shop around and go elsewhere."

Allyson puckered her lips as if she'd just gulped a mouthful of sour milk. "So it's all about salesmanship, not quality of care."

"On the contrary, quality of care comes above everything else, and I wouldn't have made Claire Lindstrom nursing supervisor if I didn't have complete confidence in her abilities."

"So she's more than a good-looking figurehead?"

"Obviously. Besides, it makes no difference in your salary or your standing with the agency whether you open cases or not. We're dealing with people, not cars. There's no sales commission involved. As a matter of fact, I've been thinking that with all her other responsibilities, Claire shouldn't be carrying a regular caseload. Once a new client's situation is stabilized, say after a week or two, I'd like to have you take over the ongoing nursing supervision for our live-in clients."

"But that's a lot of extra work. I already supervise half the hourly cases."

Paula felt like screaming. Dealing with Allyson was never a win-win proposition. It was always lose-lose, an exercise in frustration. Leaning forward, she planted both elbows on her desk, tented her fingers and zapped Allyson with her best managerial stare. "I need to leave for the funeral in an hour, and I've got work to do first. Besides, I think we're at cross-purposes. Let's continue this discussion tomorrow, after we've both had time to think things over."

Allyson frowned, opened her mouth to speak, then closed it again with a gulp. Like a bottom-feeding fish, Paula thought. Maybe a catfish, or a wall-eyed pike. The woman was nearing fifty, almost Paula's age, but even in her youth, she couldn't have been attractive. Paula could understand her resentment of Claire, even sympathize. Her own looks didn't exactly stop men in their tracks. But like a general, she had to deploy her troops to maximum advantage. She couldn't let sentiment stand in the way of business.

Paula reached for her day planner. "I'll pencil you in for nine. Unless some other time would be better?"

"Nine is all right, I guess."

"Good. See you then." Paula scribbled a line in her book. A Blackberry would have made a more powerful impact, she realized, but she was mildly technophobic, and the planner had a satisfying heft. She snapped it shut and stood, signaling an end to the discussion. Her mind drifted to Dunkin' Donuts. Would there be time for a pit stop before the funeral? She'd never make it through to the reception without a little sustenance. Today seemed like a Boston cream kind of day.

All in all, she was pleased with the way she'd handled Allyson. Giving her that pitiful little choice of appointment times had been a nice touch, a classic closing maneuver to let the nurse think she had some say in the situation, when actually she had next to none.

———————

An hour later, as Claire stood on the front steps outside Minna Schatz's barn-red door, she heard Lester shouting inside.

Déjà vu all over again, she thought wearily. But this time Lester wasn't shouting at the dog – he was shouting at Minna. "You could have told me last night," he screamed as the door flew open. "This live-in care is just one hassle after another. Maybe the whole thing was a mistake."

Claire gave him a quick once-over. His face was redder than ever, his blood pressure probably off the charts, and his hands were shaking. "Is this private? Should I wait in the car?" she asked.

"No, no, you might as well come in, since it's about the agency. Why didn't anybody tell me you were sending someone to fill in for Dahlia? You said she'd be here for two weeks."

Damn Maria! Claire had instructed her to call both Lester and his mother, but evidently she hadn't. "She will be. I'm taking her to a client's funeral, and I'll have her back by two o'clock at the latest. Then she'll stay with you for the rest of the two weeks."

He cocked his head, scratched it vigorously. "Funeral, huh? Would this be for her last client, by any chance? The case that just ended so conveniently?"

"Yes, as a matter of fact."

"Doesn't say much for your quality of care, does it?" He narrowed his squinty eyes and focused on her hips. "Although I've got to say, I like the way you dressed for the occasion. Whose funeral is it?"

"I'm not at liberty to say, because of client confidentiality."

He grunted. "That doesn't mean much now that the person has croaked. Never mind. I'm sure my mother can pry the information out of Dahlia, if she hasn't already."

Brakes squealed, and Claire wheeled to see the agency's Taurus swerving into the driveway. Stephen climbed out and caught sight of Claire standing on the steps. He puckered his lips and pantomimed a whistle. "Whooey! You're looking mighty fine today, Ms. Lindstrom."

Lester laughed. "You can say that again. I was just telling your nurse how much I liked that dress on her."

Claire felt a blush creep up her neck. Just then Tanisha Clarkson opened the passenger-side door of the sedan and began climbing gracefully out. As Claire descended the steps to greet the relief aide, she sensed the men's eyes following them both. Let them look, she thought, if it distracted Lester from his inquisition. And wait until he got a closer look at Tanisha. With her finely chiseled features and café au lait complexion, the aide looked like a young Halle Berry. If anyone could banish the bigotry from Lester's nasty soul, Tanisha was the one to do it.

Claire grasped Tanisha's hands in both her own. "Am I glad to see you!" she exclaimed. "If things work out today, I can ask Maria to make you the regular relief aide, that is, if you can fit it in with your course work this semester."

"No problem. My classes run Monday afternoons through Thursday mornings, so I can work long weekends whenever you need me."

"Thanks, Tanisha. Now, there are some things you should know about this case. Minna has a definite paranoid streak, and as for Lester –"

"He's a racist pig, right? Maria already warned me, and I had a long phone conversation with Dahlia last night."

"He's prejudiced, yes, but I think he's coming around. I hope they didn't scare you."

Tanisha grinned. "Don't worry, I've dealt with his kind before. I'm sure I can cope."

"I'm sure you can too. Come on, I'll introduce you to Lester and Minna, and then we'll go over the plan of care. Dahlia can show you around before we leave, but we'll have to be pretty speedy. The funeral is at eleven."

As they walked toward the house, Lester ogled Tanisha with undisguised admiration. "My my," he said. "Who's this pretty little lady?"

Tanisha's mouth twitched and she shot Claire a long-suffering look. Then she mustered a grin and extended her hand to Lester. He grasped it with all the ardor of a dog lunging for a particularly juicy bone.

Claire smiled. It never failed to amaze her how quickly prejudice could melt away when the circumstances were right.

From his vantage point in the third pew from the back, Gabriel had an excellent view of Harriet Gardener's funeral. The church was overflowing with mourners, the majority of them elderly. White-haired ladies hobbling painfully up the aisle with walkers, men with canes, murmuring softly to one another.

Claire Lindstrom was nowhere in sight. He felt a flash of anger. He'd been virtually positive she'd come, and he could use another look at Claire if he was going to paint her. Sketching her features from memory just didn't cut it. He'd told Athena he wanted to attend the funeral in order to get more of a feel for the organization's clientele, and that was true too, but it was strictly secondary. Athena hadn't been crazy about the idea when he phoned her yesterday. But she'd been so pleased with the way he'd carried off his latest assignment that she decided to indulge him.

"You might as well make it an on-the-job learning experience. Study the family dynamics," she told him, sounding like the social worker she was. "Keep an eye on the daughter, Joanne Hargreave. She loved her mother; she told me so right up to the moment she handed over the cash for our services. But she didn't love the person her mother was becoming, the confused, childlike creature who sometimes failed to recognize her own daughter. And she definitely didn't love watching her mother's estate evaporate before her eyes, shrinking with every check she wrote to Compassionate Care. Joanne counted on that money for her children's college, and she couldn't stand to see it dribble away."

"I can sympathize," Gabriel said. "Why wipe out the family's resources to sustain a life that was turning into a travesty of its former self? In her right mind, Harriet would never have wanted that."

"Well said," Athena replied. "I'm glad you see it our way. Keep a low profile, blend in with the crowd, and report back to me after the funeral. Maybe we'll be expanding the scope of your assignments before long."

Just so they involve Compassionate Care, he thought. The latest assignment felt like a diversion from his true purpose. Working with clients from other agencies was all well and good, but it didn't bring him closer to Claire.

As Athena had directed, he turned his attention to Joanne Hargreave. She sat in the front pew, her face cradled in both hands, sobbing quietly beneath her sheer black veil. Her grief seemed genuine enough. It was probably compounded by guilt; he could see it in the tense set of her shoulders. But she would get over it, as the others had. In time, she would be grateful for the service he had provided.

A sixth sense told him someone was behind him. He swiveled just in time to catch Claire coming up the aisle, arm in arm with Dahlia Douglas. The aide was weeping quietly, and Claire was murmuring softly, trying to comfort her. As they passed his pew, he caught a whiff of musky cologne. Probably Dahlia's – Claire was too classy for such a cheap scent. The nurse looked terrific. She was wearing a black dress in a soft, velvety material that set off the slim lines of her figure. Resisting the urge to reach out and touch her, he clasped his hands together till his knuckles turned white and she was safely out of reach.

The Gardener job had gone smoothly, according to plan. He hadn't heard a peep out of the aide all the time he was in the house. She'd either been sleeping soundly or scared and pretending to. She probably felt guilty as hell. It couldn't have been pleasant, waking to find the woman in her care already cool, stiffening with death. But she'd get over it, as the daughter would.

On the other hand, for all he knew Dahlia Douglas could be part of his own outfit. The organization was deliberately low profile, and they doled out information on a need-to-know basis. To date, Athena was his only contact, and they had met face to face only once, on the day she put him through that exhaustive interview and battery of tests, then offered him the contract. Athena was merely her code name, she'd told him, just as Gabriel would become his.

Whether Dahlia was involved or not, she looked like a kindly woman. According to Athena, Compassionate Care had already assigned her another case, and he was glad for her. He had nothing against the nurses and aides of any of the agencies. They were dedicated souls, caring for the same clientele he did. It was just that their treatment goals and objectives were somewhat at odds with his.

As the minister walked to the pulpit, the crowd hushed in expectation. Gabriel donned an expression of mournful piety. Kooperskill was a small town, but there were lots of others nearby. And in all of them, so many elders, so many good, upstanding citizens who had saved so diligently for their twilight years.

A warm wave of benevolence swept over him. He was glad he would be sticking around awhile.

Chapter 7

Claire raised her glass to Paula's. "Let's drink to Harriet Gardener. It's exactly one month since her death."

"Really?" Paula clinked her glass against Claire's, a little too forcefully. "I'd rather accentuate the positive, and drink to our burgeoning caseload. Five new live-ins in under a month. I don't know if it's the change of seasons or just our growing reputation, but I'm not going to question our good fortune. And I want to propose a toast to John Lennon."

"I'm sorry?"

"You know, the Beatle. It's his birthday. October 9th. I always celebrate it."

"I didn't know you were a Beatles fan."

"There's a lot you don't know about me." Paula gulped more Pinot Grigio. "I was just a kid when they hit it big, but I was a rabid fan. John was my first major crush." Her luminous eyes grew moist. "And you were just a kid when he was murdered."

"Yes, it's one of my earliest memories. I'd never seen my mother cry like that." Claire felt her own eyes fill with tears, turned her gaze to the window. Paula was treating her to dinner at the Café Hudson, the most elegant and expensive restaurant in the venerable industrial city of Troy. Beyond the expanse of plate glass, across the broad expanse of the Hudson, the lights of Albany glimmered in the distance, but in the water directly below them, she could see only blackness. She shivered, aware of a vague sense of foreboding as she fought back the tears. Her boss was unusually animated, almost manic. She'd just ordered them a second bottle of wine, over Claire's protests. And it wasn't like her to treat Claire to anything, much less spring for an expensive dinner. She wondered if Paula's Zoloft dosage was too high.

Paula reached for the breadbasket, grabbed a second hunk of bread and slathered it with butter. "The hell with my diet. Anyway, back to business. Claire, you've been knocking yourself out getting these cases up and running. You deserve a night on the town."

"Thanks, Paula. If you're in the mood to treat people, maybe you should send a fruit basket over to Mike D'Attilio's medical group. He referred three of the new live-ins."

"Including Minna Schatz, right?"

"Yes, and Rose Dobson, too."

Paula gave her a blank stare, and Claire realized she'd better elaborate. "The lady with advanced Alzheimer's, remember? We opened the case last week with that new aide, Sharon Westerly."

"Oh, right. And to think you were so worried D'Attilio wouldn't refer any more clients after what happened with Harriet Gardener."

"I guess I was being unnecessarily paranoid. Anyway, in terms of getting the new live-ins going, Allyson deserves a lot of the credit. She's jumped in with both feet, taking over the case management, visiting the homes to orient the aides, leaving me free to concentrate mostly on the newest clients, just the way we discussed."

Paula grinned. "I warned her she needed a major attitude adjustment, and I guess she took it to heart. I know there's no love lost between you two, but I gather things are better now?"

"Yes, definitely. She's a good nurse, and I've been telling her I trust her judgment, giving her more autonomy. It seems to have helped."

"I'm glad. This way you're freer to concentrate on expanding our case load."

Claire's stomach lurched. She glanced longingly at the breadbasket, managed to restrain herself. She had to set a good example for her boss. "Strange, I never thought of myself as strong on sales. But I love selling these people on our services, signing the contracts, then collaborating with Maria to match the clients with the best possible aides. In a way it's like running a matchmaking service. We have to balance the aides' skills and experience with the needs of each client, but personalities are equally important. Errol James and George Cropsey are getting along famously. And Tanisha Clarkson is perfect with Minna Schatz, because she loves the challenge of dealing with all Minna's complaints and suspicions, but Tanisha would probably be bouncing off the walls if we put her with one of our advanced Alzheimer's cases like Rose Dobson. Tanisha's bright, a little on the hyper side, and she needs a client she can match wits with. She wouldn't be happy with someone who asks the same question every five minutes."

Paula gazed around, her eyes glazed. "I'm starving. When do you suppose they're bringing our entrees? Anyway, Claire, thank God you're into those kinds of subtleties, because they bore me stiff."

"That's why you're the administrator. You're more into the big picture, the panoramic view, while I prefer the human element and the tight-focus details."

Paula beamed. "Put us together, and we make an unbeatable team. There's a synergy that makes us more powerful than the sum of the parts."

Claire sipped her wine, relieved the discussion had turned back to business. Her emotions were back under control, and so, evidently, were Paula's. Things had verged on the maudlin there for a bit, but it was better this way – purely professional. Better stop drinking, though, or she might lose it again.

Paula poured herself another. "Your idea of bringing aides up from New York City on Amtrak was a stroke of genius, Claire. Being able to staff all these private-pay live-in cases has really given us an edge over the other agencies. Before you came along, we were like everyone else, hustling for those measly Medicare and Medicaid contracts, two hours here, three hours there. And we were always competing for the same sorry pool of employees. Most of them are much too busy coping with their own dysfunctional families and their ne'er-do-well boyfriends to even consider doing round-the-clock live-in care. And their cars are forever breaking down."

"The same thing was true in New York City," Claire said. "Except there they couldn't use their cars as an excuse for not showing up, because they all took the subway."

Paula patted her lips with her napkin, gazed around again for the waiter. "Up here, the aides from the city are virtually stuck. Once Stephen delivers them to these houses in the boonies, they're at our mercy, because they haven't the foggiest idea where they are or how to get away."

Claire laughed. "Some of them are really spooked by the solitude in the country, but most of them love it. Living in these one-family homes has to be better than their apartments in Brooklyn or Queens. I'll never forget the day I first took Dahlia to Harriet's house. She took one look at that big meadow with the

Holstein cows grazing by the stream, and she said, 'God has answered my prayers – this is just like Jamaica!'"

"Maybe I should follow her example and pray for more cases."

"Then you'd better pray for more aides to go with them." The lurching sensation in Claire's stomach intensified. It was anxiety, not hunger, she realized. "Actually, Paula, I've been thinking. Maybe we should hold off on opening new cases until after we bring on more staff. And I'd like more time to check out their skill levels and get to know them before we assign them."

Paula's face reddened. "Our standard hiring practices already cover that. We give them assessment tests, check their references, all that good stuff. We even do criminal background checks."

"Because the law says we have to. But I just have the feeling we should be doing more."

"Well, we can't afford to turn down perfectly good referrals. We'd be shooting ourselves in the foot."

Just then the waiter appeared with their orders – Cajun grilled salmon steak for Claire, a gigantic Porterhouse steak and sweet potato fries for Paula. Perfect timing, Claire thought. Their discussion was escalating into the danger zone.

"Don't give me that look," said Paula as she grabbed for the steak knife. "I know I shouldn't, but what the hell. Fish just doesn't do it for me."

"Now don't go getting paranoid, Paula. If I gave you any kind of look, it was just out of jealousy. I wish I'd ordered the steak."

———————

A few miles away, Sharon Westerly was about to sit down to dinner with Rose Dobson, the lady with Alzheimer's she'd been living with for the past week. The days had dragged endlessly, and Sharon didn't know if she could stand it much longer. The woman was driving her crazy with her never-ending needs, her repetitive questions. But tonight they had company. Allyson Quigley, the nurse who was managing the case, had stopped by unannounced, no doubt to see if she could catch Sharon goofing off on the job. No such luck – fortunately Sharon had bathed and dressed Rose just an hour before, and the nurse would never realize that their client had spent most of the day in a soiled nightgown and dirty Depends.

Sharon had been looking forward to microwaving a couple of Lean Cuisine meals, then sitting down with Rose to watch Entertainment Tonight while they ate. Now instead she had to make nice with Allyson. But anything was better than spending another night alone with Rose, and the nurse had even brought dinner.

"I'm glad I could join you," Allyson told Sharon. "I'm on call anyway, and I really don't have anywhere else to go. So I decided to bring you and Rose some of my special meat loaf. I want to make sure Rose is eating enough. She's at that stage of Alzheimer's where patients are so confused and distracted that they can't focus on food. You also have to monitor them for choking, because their gag reflexes start getting impaired. I made sure to puree everything extra fine, so she shouldn't have any trouble."

Sharon suppressed a sigh as she gazed at the meatloaf. It actually looked pretty good. "I know all that stuff already," she said, giving the nurse a bit of attitude. "You went over it with me the other day. So did Claire Lindstrom when we opened the case. It's all in the plan of care."

"I know, but a little repetition never hurts."

Not unless it's Rose repeating the same questions over and over, thought Sharon. "Can I go home now?" And "Where's my mother?" Rose was a sweet old lady, and Sharon felt sorry for her, but sometimes the woman drove her absolutely crazy.

Speak of the devil, here she came now, shuffling toward the table in those filthy pink slippers. Allyson and Sharon had tried to get Rose into some decent shoes two days ago to keep her from slipping and sliding on the polished wood floors, but Rose had thrown a fit at the idea of parting with them. Allyson had said to let her keep the slippers for now.

Rose glared at Allyson. "I don't know you. What are you doing in my kitchen? I didn't invite anyone over for dinner."

"I'm the nurse from the agency, dear. My name is Allyson Quigley. We already met two days ago. Now, why don't you sit down with us and have some yummy meatloaf? I made it myself."

"Mmm, it smells good." Rose padded to the table and lowered herself cautiously onto a chair. "I might try a little, but we have to save enough for the pot luck at the church later."

"Of course we will. Don't worry about it, dear," said Allyson.

The nurse had a nice way about her. A little too goody-goody for Sharon's taste, but at least Allyson knew better than to correct Rose or argue about whether they had met before. With an Alzheimer's patient, it wouldn't do any good, because five minutes from now they would forget everything you'd told them anyway. Better to just go with the flow, be calm and reassuring, like Claire had said.

This was Sharon's first job with Compassionate Care, and she wanted to make a good impression. "This meat loaf looks delicious," she said, sliding her chair closer to Rose's. "Let's all have some together."

"I'll do the honors and serve if you'll bring me a spatula," Allyson told Sharon. "Meanwhile maybe you can find some vegetables and nuke them in the microwave. This recipe has lots of breadcrumbs in it, so that'll do for the carbohydrate. I even added some bran for regularity."

Jeez, thought Sharon. Next she's probably going to launch into a lecture about the food pyramid. She forced a smile as she pushed back her chair. "I noticed some frozen baby peas in the freezer. I'll put those in the microwave, and then I'll set the table while they're cooking."

"That's a dear," said Allyson.

Sharon tried not to cringe. Allyson reminded her of Mrs. Higgins, the fifth grade teacher who'd always acted sweet as could be, but ended up flunking her and making her repeat a grade. "Isn't this wonderful, Rose," Sharon said as she patted the old lady's shoulder. "We're going to have a dinner party, just the three of us. I don't know about you, but I'm absolutely starving."

———————

Hours later Rose Dobson awoke from a deep sleep. Something had disturbed her – maybe the sound of the door opening, but she wasn't sure. It was a crisp autumn night, with a bit of chill in the air. Clouds scudded across the sky in front of a nearly full moon. Climbing from her bed, she shoved her feet into her fuzzy bunny slippers, then found her pink chenille bathrobe at the foot of the bed where she always left it. She wrapped it tightly around her body and tied the sash. Mother wouldn't like her catching a chill.

She crossed to the window and peered out through the sheer curtains. It was a lovely night. She began singing softly to herself. "Shine on, shine on harvest moon, up in the sky. I ain't had no loving since January, February, June or July." She couldn't remember the rest, so she started at the beginning again. "Shine on, shine on harvest moon –"

"You have a beautiful voice, Rose," someone whispered. A man's voice, so close she could feel his warm breath tickling her ear. She gasped, startled, but before she could scream, she felt a hand clamp down hard on her mouth. "Don't worry," he murmured. "I won't hurt you. I'm going to take good care of you."

She tried to struggle, but he was too strong. He held her from behind, one arm encircling her waist, the other around her neck with the hand on her mouth. She couldn't see him, but the feel of his body against hers was familiar, and the sound of his voice. "Raymond, it's you," she said, but the words were muffled against his hand.

It was her husband, she was positive of that. But why was he being so rough? Maybe he didn't realize who she was, and she couldn't very well tell him, not with her mouth covered like this. She felt suddenly faint. Her knees buckled and she sagged limply toward the floor. He let go her mouth, caught and encircled her in two strong arms.

"Raymond," she whispered. She had to be quiet; there would be hell to pay if her mother found them together in the bedroom. That was why he had covered her mouth – he didn't want her screaming and waking her parents. "Don't worry, I won't scream," she whispered.

"That's a good girl," he said. "But just to be on the safe side, I'm going to cover your mouth again. We wouldn't want anyone disturbing us, now, would we?"

"Mmmph," she said through his fingers.

He had let go of her waist now, and he was rummaging around with his free hand. She couldn't see what he was doing, but she guessed he was unzipping his pants. He was going to take her by force. This wasn't Raymond; he would never treat her so roughly.

Something was terribly wrong. She was starting to struggle when she caught a whiff of scent. Something strange and sickly sweet. There was a flash of white, a handkerchief maybe, coming closer, covering her nose.

"Breathe deeply, my dear," he said softly. "Close your eyes. You're going to feel very peaceful soon. Everything will be all right, you'll see."

She gasped as everything went black and night descended for the last time.

Chapter 8

*T*he next morning was one of those blazingly brilliant October days that seem all the more magnificent for the hint of frost to come. For the first Saturday in ages, Claire wasn't on call. Luxuriating in her unaccustomed freedom, she decided to spend a few hours in her long neglected jewelry studio. But first, in hopes of shaking off the aftereffects of last night's wine, she opted for a brisk jog with Freia. Pulling on her fleece jacket, she caught sight of her cell phone lying on the table in the hall. Forget it, she told herself. Allyson's on call this weekend. But something – compulsiveness, force of habit, a weird sense of foreboding – made her stash the phone in her pocket.

As she headed onto the lakeshore road with Freia, the sun was just climbing over the trees on the eastern shoreline. The foliage hadn't yet peaked, but every so often a crisp breeze wafted through, stealing a few more leaves and carrying them gently to the water.

At first, the musty dimness of her studio nearly drove her back into the sunshine. The gray cinderblock walls and the small, dingy windows close to the ceiling gave the space a claustrophobic feeling. But what did she expect from a converted garage? Armed with a thermos of coffee, she headed for her workbench. Early this morning she had awakened with the amorphous image of a silver filigree necklace swirling through her mind's eye. Her jewelry making skills were rudimentary, and she knew the reality wouldn't measure up to the vision. But her dreams had been full of crises – bungled, incompetent care, missed diagnoses, dying clients. The message was loud and clear: she was in desperate need of diversion.

The first strands of sterling silver wire were coiled in a serpentine pattern, ready for soldering, and she was adjusting the flame on the acetylene torch when the cell phone's tinny snatch of Vivaldi cut through the hiss of the gas. Damn! She turned the control knob, watched the blue flame fade away and set the torch on the fireproof pad, then fished in her jacket pocket for the cell, but by then the tune had stopped. She checked the screen. The number was vaguely familiar – Rose Dobson's, maybe? She called back, let it ring, but no one answered.

So much for jewelry making – she'd better see what was going on. She raced into the house, Freia at her heels, and checked the answering machine. Sure enough, the green message light was blinking. She pushed the "Play" button.

"Claire, it's Allyson. Please pick up if you're there – it's urgent." The nurse's tone was uncharacteristically harried. There were a few seconds of semi-silence, punctuated only by Allyson's breathing. "I'm at Rose Dobson's house. Rose is missing; she must have wandered off some time during the night."

Claire's heart plummeted, began an ominous pounding. Her fingers trembled as she dialed the number again. No one picked up. Why the hell didn't they have an answering machine? They were probably out looking for Rose; she'd better get over there and join them. She glanced down at her jeans and sneakers –

unprofessional, but perfect for searching the woods if it came to that.

The images racing through her mind kept pace with her rapid heartbeat as she drove to Rose Dobson's house, curbing the impulse to speed. Her Focus hatchback took the curving country roads with ease, but every turn, every cresting hill held potential hazards. Children, dogs, deer, raccoons, even the occasional chicken – she'd seen them all on these peaceful back roads, and the last thing she wanted was to create some unintentional road kill.

The half-hour drive seemed endless, but at last she was on the gravelly lane that dead-ended at Rose's driveway. Scrubby forest lined both sides of the road – maples, pines, pin oaks reclaiming what had once been open farmland. She slowed to a crawl, gazed from side to side in hopes of catching a glimpse of Rose. If she had truly wandered away, she could be anywhere.

Why on earth did her family let Rose Dobson keep living out here in the middle of nowhere? She would have been better off in a nursing home, with people to watch her around the clock and activities to stimulate what was left of her deteriorating mind. *No, wait! What are you thinking?* An image of Claire's father flashed into her mind's eye. He had died from the shock of being railroaded into a nursing home – she wouldn't wish that on Rose. *The home environment beats institutionalization, doesn't it, Claire? Isn't that why you went into home health care?*

As she drove into the clearing, Claire caught sight of Allyson and Sharon standing in the front yard, holding coffee mugs and chatting for all the world like two neighbors enjoying the autumn sunshine and passing the time of day. How dare they act so casual when a client's life was at stake? Claire peeled up beside them, stomped on the brake and killed the engine.

Sharon came running to the car, and Claire realized her first impression was deceptive. The aide's deep brown eyes were wide with panic. "I swear I don't know what happened!" she exclaimed. "When I went to Rose's room to get her ready for breakfast, she wasn't there. I looked all over the house, I called her name, but she didn't answer. So I ran outside and looked some more. I kept yelling her name, but she still didn't answer. So I went back inside and called the agency. The service paged Allyson, and she got here as fast as she could. Didn't you, Allyson?"

"That's right," said Allyson, catching up with Sharon. The nurse was short of breath, chest heaving, face deathly pale. "I helped Sharon look around for a few minutes. When we didn't find Rose, I called you right away."

"Did you look in the woods?" Claire asked.

Sharon shuddered. "No, the woods give me the creeps."

"There could be ticks, and Lyme disease –" Allyson gulped. "I mean, I thought it was better to call for help first."

Both women were in a state of panic bordering on hysteria, and the first order of business was to calm them down. "Let's all go inside and catch our breaths," Claire said, trying for a tone of confidence. "It's a beautiful October morning. Rose probably just went for a walk, and I suspect she'll come back any time now. She's lived here all of her adult life, so she knows these woods well."

"But she's so confused, she could still get lost," said Sharon. "Or maybe she fell and broke her hip or something. She could be lying somewhere in agony. But why wouldn't she answer when I called?"

"It's no use speculating," said Claire. "What we need is a plan of action. Who else have you notified?"

"No one," said Allyson. "We were thinking along the same lines as you, hoping she'd come back."

Claire glanced at her watch. "It's nine thirty now. When did you first notice she was missing?"

"About eight," said Sharon. She averted her eyes, studied the ground. "Maybe seven thirty. I don't know."

"We'd better notify the police," said Claire.

Allyson's face turned a shade paler. "Don't you think it's too soon? She's probably out for a walk, like you said."

"I hope so. But they could help with the search. It's cool, probably still in the fifties, and we don't want her suffering from exposure. I'll go in and call them, along with Rose's daughter. She might have some ideas as to where Rose would be likely to go. I'll notify Paula Rhodes as well."

"Oh, God," said Sharon. She began to cry. "This is all my fault. I should have checked on her during the night. But I was sleeping so soundly, I didn't hear a thing."

Claire placed a reassuring hand on Sharon's shoulder. "Don't blame yourself. I made it clear to the family that the level of care we're providing doesn't involve constant round-the-clock supervision. For that, they would need aides on rotating shifts, and they didn't want to pay that much. On live-in cases, the aide is expected to get a decent night's sleep. It's all spelled out in the contract. So rest assured, you didn't do anything wrong."

Sharon took a deep, gasping breath. "Thank God. That's what I thought."

"Absolutely. But Sharon, I do need to ask: was Rose acting agitated last night? Did she talk about wanting to go anywhere?"

"She talked about wanting to go home and see her husband, but she's been saying that all week. I didn't think she meant anything by it." The aide began sobbing again. "See, you do think it's my fault."

It's the agency's fault, Claire thought grimly, for trying to manage care for a severely confused, highly mobile Alzheimer's patient in her own home. Maybe they needed to rethink their priorities, put less emphasis on the bottom line and more emphasis on safety.

"You both keep looking for Rose," she said. "I'm going in to make those calls."

An hour later, the sunlit clearing was crowded with cars. Claire's green Focus was keeping company with a black-and-white police patrol car, Allyson's silver Saturn, Paula's slate blue Prius, and the burgundy Honda SUV that belonged to Barbara Whitman, Rose's daughter. Barbara had arrived just minutes ago and made a beeline for the house, followed by the two police officers, who were presumably interviewing her now. The five cars sparkled in the sunlight, creating an incongruously cheerful riot of color in front of the old house.

With the police on the scene, Claire's role seemed less critical for the moment, and she was able to step back, away from center stage. Gazing toward the trees beyond the clearing, she had a sudden impulse to take to the woods. The sun was climbing higher and illuminating the blazing fall colors of the forest. Perhaps Rose was out there, watching from a distance, confused and frightened by all the strangers swarming around her home. Claire was comfortable in the woods, and she decided she could do the most good right now by searching on her own.

But first she needed to touch base with the others. She strode toward the house. Entering the living room, she found Rose's daughter Barbara with Paula beside her on the sofa. Two officers, one male, one female, occupied the wing chairs on either side.

Catching sight of Claire, Barbara burst up from her seat. "What in God's name were you thinking, calling the police!" Her eyes were wild. "Look at all the aggravation you've caused!"

"I'm truly sorry," Claire began.

Paula shot her a warning glance and cut her short. "We're sorry you're upset, Barbara, but we're doing everything possible to find your mother."

"But why did you have to cause such a ruckus?" asked Barbara. "My mother loves these woods, and she's familiar with every nook and cranny for miles around. I think you jumped the gun. I'm sure she'll be back any time now."

"I certainly hope so," Claire replied. "But in the meantime, I thought the police could help with the search."

"Well, you should have consulted me first. I'm my mother's legal guardian, and I should have been the one to decide what measures to take and when."

"But as nursing supervisor, my obligation –"

"Ladies, please!" The woman officer held up a palm as if to stop traffic. *Officer Frances Milgrim,* her tag read, and her warm hazel eyes had a no-nonsense look that commanded respect. "Ms. Lindstrom did the right thing. As a matter of fact, I'm going to call the office and ask the patrol sergeant if he thinks they should send over more personnel to assist with the search."

Barbara paled. "I'm sure it's not really that serious," she stammered.

Claire took a deep breath. "I hope you're right. Actually, I think I can help matters most by going out to look for Rose. I'm familiar with woods like these; I do a lot of hiking. With all the fallen leaves, maybe I can even pick up some traces of which way she went."

"That's a great idea, Claire!" Paula exclaimed with an enthusiasm so patently phony that Claire could tell her boss just wanted her out of the way.

As she crossed the yard, it occurred to Claire that she should have brought Freia. She flashed on an image of the two of them traipsing through the woods in the dappled sunlight, successfully tracking Rose and returning triumphant with the old lady safely in hand. Too late now – it would take an hour to drive home and get the dog, an hour they couldn't afford.

Standing at the start of an overgrown path at the edge of the woods, she paused to get her bearings. She felt put down, dismissed, like a naughty child whose mother had told her to get out from underfoot, go outside and play. Still, it was just as well. That living room had been crackling with tension, and it was obvious Paula was worried Claire would say the wrong thing and infuriate Rose's daughter even more.

Stretching both arms skyward, flexing her fingers, Claire breathed in the crisp autumn air, trying to center and calm herself. Breathe in the sunlight, she told herself. Breathe out the stale, troubled air of Rose's living room. Breathe in the positive energy of the forest, the old woman's spirit, her love of these woods. Follow in her footsteps. Where would she go? The answer might lie on this path. Claire followed it deeper into the woods.

The trail was carpeted with fallen leaves – the brilliant orange of sugar maples, the gold of beeches, the russet brown of oaks. As she walked, still more leaves twirled lazily down, floating on the soft currents of a playful breeze. They drifted onto the path, creating a constantly changing mosaic. How could she have hoped to track Rose's movements in these woods? Even if Rose had come this way, the leaves would have obscured the traces of her passing.

A few hundred feet from the house, the path dead-ended at a narrow stream. Water trickled thinly among the rocks and stones that lined the bed. Half a dozen rotted boards lay askew across the shallow depression, remnants of what must once have been a narrow footbridge spanning the brook. Years of seasonal flooding had scoured the bank away on the far side, freeing the planks from their moorings.

A few feet downstream from the boards, a flash of dirty pink caught her eye, incongruous amidst the autumn colors. The color of a dead possum, or – no, it couldn't be – a fuzzy slipper. Her breath caught in her throat as she crept closer to be sure. Yes, it was unmistakable. Rose had come this way, perhaps tried to cross the stream. Cautiously, Claire crept down the rocky embankment, parting the brambles with her bare hands, oblivious to the thorns of the wild roses and raspberries raking her arms. With a sucking sound, her sneakers sank into the dark muck at the water's edge as she gazed downstream.

A few feet away she caught another flash of pink, a bigger one this time. Sprawled beneath the near curve of the streambed, almost hidden from view, lay a swathe of pink chenille, a body face down on the rocks, gray hair streaming like seaweed in the brown water.

Running to Rose's side, she squatted in the water, pressed two fingers to the carotid artery in search of a pulse, knowing already that it was too late. The skin was blue-gray, cool to the touch. And on the sharp rock beneath the fragile skull, among the mossy green lichen, a deep crimson stain spread its tentacles like a malevolent flower.

Chapter 9

*C*laire trembled uncontrollably as she gazed down at Rose Dobson's body. A handful of scarlet maple leaves lay atop the pink chenille, and three more floated down, alighting gently on the frail figure. A faint rustle broke the silence. Startled, she glanced up to see a squirrel perched in the forked branches of an enormous maple, twitching its tail and peering curiously down. Somewhere nearby a crow cawed raucously.

Left alone, undiscovered in these woods, how long would Rose's body have remained undisturbed? Probably not long. Within a day, maybe less, it would have been festooned in leaves, besieged by insects, discovered and worried apart by the creatures of the woods. Then the natural process of decay would take over, transform her into humus for the forest floor. She would become an integral part of the woodlands she had loved, an offering of nourishment for the never-ending cycle of death and rebirth.

But modern society had more civilized means of confronting death, and Claire was duty bound to honor the prevailing customs. She began to kneel, then realized the police might construe this as a crime scene. Bending cautiously so as not to disturb the forest tableau more than she already had, she reached down, stroked Rose's stringy silver hair, paused a moment in respect. Then she rose and headed for the house.

The two police officers were walking slowly together on the far side of the yard, their heads bowed as they scrutinized the ground. She considered telling them of her discovery, decided to wait. As next of kin, Barbara had first claim on this grisly knowledge. Softly, Claire crossed the lawn and entered the house unobserved.

In the living room, Paula and Barbara sat silent on the sofa. They glanced up as she entered. Something in her face must have telegraphed the message she hadn't yet translated into words, because Barbara jumped up, her eyes wide with alarm.

Claire held out both hands to her. "I found her," she began.

Barbara drew back, away from her. "She's dead, isn't she?"

"I'm afraid so."

"What was she doing outside the house?"

Claire wondered at Barbara's immediate leap to the worst-case scenario, her matter-of-fact question. Where was the shock, the sorrow? "She must have wandered outside at some point during the night."

Barbara scowled. "That wasn't supposed to happen."

"I'm so sorry."

The woman closed her eyes, shuddered, began to sob in deep, wrenching gasps that seemed wrested from the depths of her being. Then as suddenly as she'd begun, she stopped, opened her eyes and blinked with the bewildered look of someone awakening from a nightmare. She swabbed at her eyes with the sleeve of her blue silk shirt. "Where did you find her?"

"She was in the woods, down near the stream. It looks as if she fell and hit her head on the rocks. I can't say for sure, but I'd guess she was knocked unconscious immediately, so she probably didn't suffer. I know that's scarcely any comfort, but –"

"Oh, but it is." Barbara's blue eyes took on a far-away look. "More than anything, I was afraid of her suffering. Alzheimer's disease is so hideous. I've known people who had it." The tension drained from her face, replaced by an uncanny look of serenity.

"Would you like to go out and see her? I need to escort the police officers out there, but perhaps you should come too."

Barbara shuddered. "I don't think I could stand it. Is there a lot of blood?"

"There's some. Not a lot."

"I feel kind of faint; I'd better stay here. Somehow I always thought she'd die peacefully in bed."

Like Harriet Gardener, Claire thought. "I know this is a shock," she said. "Why don't you just wait here in the living room? Paula can stay with you while I take care of some details."

Still ensconced on the sofa, Paula shot Claire a glare. In return, Claire sent her a slight but encouraging smile. Her boss wasn't big in the TLC department, but a woman who'd just lost her mother shouldn't be left alone.

As Claire was heading back outside, she caught sight of another black-and-white police cruiser pulling into the driveway. The man who emerged moments later was middle-aged and much too thick in the middle. Probably the sergeant that Officer Milgrim had spoken of calling, Claire thought as she watched him stride over to the other two cops. She gave them a few moments together, then headed toward the group. After cursory introductions, she told them of her discovery and offered to lead them to the body.

"It looks to me as though Rose tripped and fell," she said as they made their way along the overgrown path deeper into the woods. Aware of their eyes at her back, she curbed the impulse to fill the silence with nervous chatter. Better to let them look and decide for themselves. In all probability, they would arrive at the same conclusion she had: this was an unfortunate accident, nothing more. On the other hand, if they found anything to raise their suspicions – but why would they? The possibility was ridiculous, wasn't it? She couldn't imagine why the notion had even entered her brain.

The day had grown warmer, and half a dozen flies had discovered the bloody blotch around Rose's head. They buzzed frenetically as the filtered sun struck their wings, adding highlights of iridescent green and purple to the crimson stain. Claire resisted the impulse to step forward and shoo them away.

The three officers stood motionless, studying the scene in silence as time dragged by with tortuous slowness. At last Milgrim fished in her pocket and retrieved a pair of latex gloves. Yanking them over both hands, she squatted down next to the body and laid two fingers on Rose's neck.

"No pulse," she said finally. "You were right. This lady is definitely dead."

Claire sighed. "Do you need me here for anything else?"

The Sergeant cleared his throat. Patrol Sergeant Neil Portman, his name tag read. "Not at the moment, but stick around," he said. "We'll want to talk to you later. Officer Milgrim, have you got your camera on you?"

"Right here, Sir." Milgrim unsnapped a black leather pouch hanging from her belt and extracted a compact digital camera.

He harumphed again. "I want close-ups, long shots, the works. You know the drill."

Milgrim threw him the hint of a glare, then hunkered down and zeroed in on Rose's head. *Like a nurse doing all the work while the doctor calls the shots,* Claire thought. *Hierarchical bullshit.*

Reaching into his pocket, the Sergeant extracted a cell phone. "I'll place a call to the coroner, and we'll wait out here till he arrives. I'll let him decide whether to call in the crime scene technicians."

Claire's heart lurched as she envisioned a cadre of dashing young investigators swarming over the scene. Get a grip, she told herself. This isn't CSI. Not Las Vegas or Miami, much less New York City. "Why?" she asked. "Do you see evidence of anything criminal involved?"

"Not at first glance. But whenever there's an unattended death, it's best to err on the side of caution. This is the optimum time to collect evidence. Now, while it's still fresh, in case we need anything for future reference."

"I see your point," Claire said. "Now, if you'll excuse me, I'm going back inside to call Rose's doctor. He's familiar with her illness, and once I give him the details, he should be able to advise me as to the legal time of death."

Milgrim lowered her camera and stood. Her hazel eyes narrowed, then widened again as she fixed Claire with a silent but sympathetic stare. I know the drill, thought Claire. She's waiting for me to open up to her, maybe say something significant. She's good, but I can play that game too. Widening her own eyes ingenuously, she mirrored the officer's gaze.

"Go ahead and call," the Sergeant said at last. "But since this wasn't a natural death, it's standard procedure for us to notify the coroner. He'll have to look over the scene and sign off on it before we can move the body. You might as well go back inside."

"All right." With deliberate cool, Claire took her leave and retraced her steps to the house. Retreating to the privacy of the kitchen, she perched on one of the battered wooden chairs in the breakfast nook, extracted her cell from her purse and called Dr. D'Attilio's office. He had Saturday morning hours, and with any luck, he might actually be in. His secretary put her on hold, forcing her to endure an endless two minutes of saxophone jazz lite until the doctor picked up.

His side of the dialogue was curt and to the point. "So you took the vital signs and found no pulse? When would you estimate the time of death to be?"

"I'd say she's been dead several hours. I expect the coroner will be able to give the time of death more exactly."

There was silence on the other end. "You already called the coroner?" he said at last.

"No, but the police probably have by now. I left them out by the stream with the body."

She heard a sharp intake of breath. "The police?" he said then. "You didn't say anything about the police being involved."

"I called them as soon as I learned Rose was missing. There are three of them here."

He sighed audibly. "It sounds as if you did everything right. I'm sorry there are all these irrelevant third parties involved, but from what you've told me, this is a straightforward case of a confused woman with fairly advanced Alzheimer's disease wandering out of her home and falling in the woods. I'm sure the police and the coroner will see it that way as well. Don't you think so?"

Why did he sound so worried? If anyone was to blame for Rose Dobson's death, it wasn't the doctor, it was Compassionate Care. Claire had a sudden urge to get off the phone. "Excuse me, Doctor D'Attilio, but I'd better get back out there and see what the police are up to."

"You do that." He clicked off, evidently as eager to end the conversation as she was.

She glanced up to see Paula standing in the stucco archway that marked the entrance to the kitchen, glaring in Claire's direction. "God, this is a disaster," Paula said. "I hope Barbara Whitman isn't one of those litigious types. All I need is a malpractice suit."

Claire felt a rush of anger. "Is that all you care about? For Christ's sake, Paula, a woman has just died. But since you mention it, I'm not happy about the fact that it happened on our watch. As a matter of fact, I think we need to talk. Maybe this level of live-in care wasn't appropriate for Rose, given her level of confusion. Maybe we should rethink our priorities, and –"

Paula launched herself at Claire with all the ferocity of a mama grizzly bear. Her fingers dug into Claire's arm. "Are you crazy? This isn't the time or place to talk about this. Come see me in my office later, if you want. We can talk after work, in private."

Claire pulled away, out of her boss's grasp. "You're right, I'm sorry." She rubbed her arm, aware it would probably bruise.

Barbara appeared in the archway. "I hope I'm not interrupting anything. Sorry I sort of fell apart back there for a few minutes."

"No need to apologize," said Claire. "It's perfectly understandable."

Paula had stiffened at the sound of Barbara's voice, and now she was sending Claire frantic signals with her eyes, pursing her lips in a silent "Shhh."

"This came as such a shock," said Barbara, "but I'm feeling better now. I just wondered who you've notified."

"I called Dr. D'Attilio, and when I left the police with your mother, they were about to call the coroner."

Barbara paled visibly. "The coroner? What's he going to do?"

Probably as little as possible, thought Claire. She had encountered Herbert Davidson on a couple of previous occasions, and she remembered being decidedly underwhelmed by his forensic skills and motivation. "He'll probably want to see your mother's body before we move her," she told Barbara. "But it's basically a formality. This was obviously an accident, and as soon as we have his okay, I'll call the funeral home and have them come for her."

"Good." Barbara shuddered delicately, and a little color crept back into her face. "I hate to think of her lying out there alone. Are the police still with her?"

"Yes, they'll be there until the coroner comes." Claire paused a moment, trying to read Barbara's mood. "Did you change your mind about wanting to see your mother?"

Barbara blanched again. "I don't think I could take it. I'd rather wait."

"Okay. I just thought I should ask. Sometimes it helps in terms of closure –"

"What would help me in terms of closure is to make all the arrangements and have the funeral as soon as possible. As soon as we know the details, I can FAX the obituary to the newspapers."

Claire was taken aback. Barbara's mood was flipping back and forth so fast, it was hard to keep up. Grieving daughter one minute, self-possessed businesswoman the next. But she'd been with enough bereaved family members over the years to know that when it came to predicting behavior in the aftermath of death, all bets were off.

"All right," she told Barbara. "That sounds like a plan."

Just then the doorbell chimed and the door burst open to reveal Herbert Davidson, the aging gentleman who had been elected county coroner some three years ago. Before that, he'd been in the insurance business, Paula had told her. Short and pudgy with a deeply tanned face and shock of snow-white hair, he was expensively dressed in a rust-colored V-neck sweater, heathery wool pants, and shoes of soft caramel-colored leather with mahogany saddles. Obviously he had just come from the golf course.

"Good morning, ladies," he boomed. "I'm Herb Davidson, the coroner."

Claire crossed the room and extended her hand. "Claire Lindstrom, nursing supervisor with Compassionate Care." Since he showed no signs of remembering her, there was no point in trying to trigger his memory and embarrassing him in front of the others.

He smiled. "Magnificent morning, isn't it?" Then he sobered abruptly. "I understand a woman died on these premises this morning."

"Yes, in the woods. The police are with her. Would you like me to take you there?"

He glanced down at his shoes. "I suppose so. This won't take long, I hope. I was in the middle of a meeting, and I told them I'd be back by noon."

Never fear, Claire wanted to say. You'll be back at the clubhouse for the second round of martinis, if not the first. "No problem," she said instead.

Barbara sidled over and took his hand. "I'm Rose Dobson's daughter, Barbara Whitman."

His smile crept back. "How do you do."

"I just want to tell you how concerned I am about preserving my mother's reputation. She's lived in this town all her life, and she knew everyone for miles around. Before her illness, she was active as a board member with the historical society and a number of other local organizations. You may well have heard of her."

His eyes darted away from Barbara's as he extricated his hand from hers. "Now that you mention it, maybe I have."

"Anyway, Mr. Davidson –"

"Please, call me Herb."

"All right. Anyway, Herb, she'd be mortified if people knew she died in such a pathetic, undignified way. For the obituaries, I'm going to tell the papers that she died peacefully at home after a long illness. I hope I can count on you to back me on that."

Clasping her hand in both of his, he leaned in a little closer. "I understand she was suffering from Alzheimer's?"

Barbara nodded.

"In that case, I'd say those are the appropriate words to describe the situation." He was murmuring now, like a priest in the confessional. "A ghastly disease. I think you can take comfort in the fact that your mother's suffering is over, and that she's gone to a better place."

"Thank you, Herb. I'm so glad you see it that way." Leaning a little closer, Barbara smiled into his eyes. "My mother wanted to be cremated, by the way. You won't have to put her through an autopsy or anything like that, will you?"

"We try to abide by the family's wishes in that respect. In this case, from what you tell me, an autopsy wouldn't be called for." He glanced over at Claire. "You may as well call the funeral home. Tell them to come in about an hour. That should be more than enough time."

Chapter 10

*T*he funeral home was in dire need of a makeover, Gabriel decided as he stashed his dripping umbrella in the tarnished brass stand in the corner of the lobby. With its overstuffed baroque furniture and walls of faded red brocade, the place looked like a second-rate Italian restaurant, the kind that makes most of its money from Chamber of Commerce breakfasts and farewell employee lunches. But if the crowded parking lot was any indication, the Parker & Newell Funeral Home was just fine for his purposes.

In a way, he was here to make amends. Athena had been royally pissed when he phoned in Saturday morning. He'd gone overboard, played it too close to the edge when he'd carried Rose Dobson out to the woods and staged that picturesque streamside tableau. His contact didn't appreciate his spur-of-the-moment improvisation, and now that he'd had a couple of days to cool off, he could see her point. The police had been called, even the coroner, and it was sheer luck that aside from the obituary, the case hadn't made the papers. Too bad, in a way – the reporters could have had a field day, and he would have loved reading about it, maybe starting a scrapbook. But she was right: the publicity could have been a disaster.

Now, thanks to his creative zeal, he was virtually on probation. Stick to the plan, Athena had told him, or else. Or else what? He had no desire to find out. Better save the artistic license for his painting. In the meantime, digging up some new referrals for the organization might win him a few brownie points.

A young woman stood at the bottom of the central staircase, next to an enormous urn overflowing with dusty silk flowers. Her expression was carefully neutral, with the slightest hint of a smile. With straight chestnut hair and elegant features, she was a lot classier than her surroundings. Her velvet suit was the color of old pewter, and it set off her gray-blue eyes.

"May I help you?" she asked.

He donned a suitably somber expression. "I'm here for the Rose Dobson viewing."

She gestured to her right. "That's in the east parlor, through the double doors. Please sign the guest book on your way in."

"Of course. Thank you. So you have two viewings today?"

"Yes. You wouldn't believe how busy it's been. For some reason, more people seem to die in the fall. I don't know why." She stopped abruptly, an embarrassed flush on her face. Obviously she wasn't as sophisticated as she looked.

Narrowing his eyes, he zapped her with a penetrating stare. "That's interesting," he murmured. Her blush deepened. Back off, he reminded himself. Damp down the charm. You're not here to score, you're here on business. Better not make yourself too memorable. "I'd better get going, pay my respects. Thanks again."

Regret flickered in her eyes as he moved toward the open archway she had indicated. Intricately carved Victorian doors stood propped open on either side. The soft hum of voices beckoned him forward. Standing on the threshold, he contemplated the room. At least two dozen people, some middle-aged, but most of them elderly. The majority were tastefully, expensively dressed. Good – there was plenty of money here.

He smoothed down the jacket of his navy pinstripe suit, stepped into the room, then paused to sign the padded leather guest book that lay atop an old gilded lectern. Who should he be today? He scrawled something illegible, squinted with satisfaction at the signature. Distinguished, like a doctor's.

Rose Dobson lay in state at the far end of the room. Too bad her casket was closed. He would have liked to see her one more time, but maybe he'd done too much damage when he dropped her face-down on the rocks. Probably the resulting trauma was too much for the undertaker's art.

Dozens of pale pink roses blanketed the coffin, and floral arrangements hung on stands to either side. Roses, mums, glads – the room was sickeningly sweet with the scent of flowers already past their prime. He stood a moment, committing the tableau to memory in case he decided to paint it sometime. Then he started across the room to pay his respects, aware of the many eyes following his progress. Near the casket, Barbara Whitman sat on a gilded dining chair, her eyes downcast, her hands wringing an embroidered handkerchief.

He felt a hand on his arm. "I don't believe we've met," said a female voice. "Are you family?"

He turned to confront a slender woman with elegant features and straight, silvery hair. "No, just an old friend."

"Well, it's nice to see you here," she said. "I hope you don't feel too out of place in the midst of all us old folks."

"Not at all. I love being around older people. Benefiting from their life experience."

"A shame about Rose, isn't it? Although all things considered, maybe it's for the best. Alzheimer's is a horrible disease. Not as bad as Parkinson's, though. That's what my husband has."

Gabriel suppressed a grin. *Like lambs to the slaughter.* "I sympathize," he said. "I have first-hand experience with Parkinson's, because my mother died of it. I spent a lot of time caring for her in her last years, and believe me, I wouldn't wish the experience on anyone." *Let's hope she doesn't call my bluff and try to talk symptoms. I'm a little rusty on the particulars.* "Are you the main caregiver?"

"Oh, God, no, I couldn't handle it. Actually, he's my ex-husband. We got divorced ten years ago. Until recently, he was staying with my son and daughter-in-law, but the situation was driving everyone up the wall, so now he's back in his own house. He's got live-in help from the same agency that was with Rose Dobson."

"Compassionate Care?"

"Yes, that's the one."

Gabriel leaned in closer, lowered his voice. "They're a fine agency, but aren't you a little worried about their quality of care, given what happened to Rose?"

Her eyes flickered. "From what I understand, it was an accident. Even the best care in the world can't help when someone's time has come. As I said, maybe it was for the best. Sometimes people outlive their usefulness, don't you think?"

An open invitation if he'd ever heard one. He decided to play it cool, let her talk. "Hmmm," he said. "I haven't given it much thought."

"Well, I have." She grasped his arm, steered him away from the coffin and back toward the double doors. "Out of respect for Rose, I shouldn't be talking like this in here, but I get really incensed when I think of all the money that George is shelling out for round-the-clock care, money that by all rights should go to our children and grandchildren. My son has no idea how he's going to pay for college for his three kids. He was counting on George's help, and now everything is just dribbling away."

"I can see how that would be upsetting. But you're right, this probably isn't the best place to talk about it." He tossed her his most disarming grin. "Obviously you're in need of a good listener, though. When we've finished paying our respects, maybe I could treat you to coffee? There's a diner near here that has some dynamite cheesecake."

"The Acropolis? I know it well. But personally, I'm partial to their chocolate seven-layer cake."

"You're on. My name's Gabriel, by the way. What's yours?"

"Ruth Cropsey."

———

Paula Rhodes huddled beneath her black umbrella the next morning. She stared down at the dark brown water that ran alongside the brick office building. Cold rain had been falling for over a day now. It pelted the brackish surface of the watercourse, sweeping red and yellow leaves into the swollen stream. The string of gorgeous Indian summer days had been swept away in the storm, and she felt November waiting in the wings. Shivering, she pulled her trench coat tighter against the chill.

She glanced at her watch: ten o'clock. Rose Dobson's funeral would be starting right about now, but she and Claire had agreed to pass on this one. Rose had been a client for barely a week, so it wasn't as if they were close to the family. In fact, they were damn lucky Rose's daughter hadn't said anything about suing the agency for negligence. It could still happen, of course, but Paula had a gut feeling it wouldn't. To be on the safe side, she had already touched base with her lawyer. They had gone over the live-in contract for the umpteenth time, and he had reassured her that they couldn't be held liable.

A wave of nausea swept over her. God, had she fallen this far? Was the death of a defenseless old lady nothing more than a potential lawsuit? She hated to admit it, but the loss of income bothered her more than the actual death. Just when the caseload was on an upswing and they were actually pulling ahead, another client died. She had barely banked the check for the deposit and first week's service, and now she would have to write Barbara Whitman a refund check for practically all of it.

She patted the box of donuts, snug and dry inside its paper bag. In the office, Claire and Maria would have been hard at work for a good two hours already. High time to furl her umbrella, put on her game face and march inside, radiating confidence to cheer them on, although in truth she felt more like turning tail and heading home to curl up in bed for the day.

Her eyes fell once again to the water. The renovated factory building formed a U-shape around a courtyard, with a paved walkway leading across a small bridge to the entrance in the center. Below the bridge, the swollen stream flowed rapidly, bearing leaves in a rainbow of fiery autumn colors. How long would it take the fallen leaves to travel downstream from one side of the bridge to the other? She focused on a cluster of scarlet maple leaves, checked her second hand, then crossed to the other side and waited. Thirty-three seconds before the leaves reappeared. She watched as they continued their journey through the open stretch of water, then beneath the west wing of the building into blackness.

A dingy beige glob floated from beneath the bridge into her field of vision. A dead animal, perhaps a body part? No, just a plastic bag. She shuddered. The building had once been a shirt factory, she'd been told, and they used to dump industrial waste into the water. How deep was it? What if someone fell, a poor swimmer, or someone weak or infirm, someone like Rose Dobson? Swept beneath the building, trapped against the rusty old iron bulkheads that supported its structure, they might never be seen again.

She shivered and stepped away from the iron railing, back to the center of the bridge. This morbid fantasizing wasn't like her at all. Get over it, Paula, she told herself. You've got a business to run. Gulping a lungful of cold, moist air, she headed resolutely for the warmth and dryness, the fluorescent brightness of the building.

Watching from her office window, Claire saw Paula collapse her umbrella and enter the lobby. She'd been spying on her boss for several minutes now, seen her climb out of her Prius and head for the building, then stop and stare at the water. Normally Paula came charging into the office; her dawdling didn't augur well for the day ahead.

But regardless of their respective moods, Claire was determined to confront Paula about the agency's admission criteria. Claire had broached the subject the morning of Rose Dobson's death. Paula had been right in warning her to stifle her comments when others were within earshot, but they'd both been avoiding the issue ever since. It hung in the air between them like a noxious cloud. Now it was high time to clear the atmosphere.

Hearing Paula's mumbled greeting to Maria, her footsteps in the hall, Claire shoved up from her chair and crossed to the doorway to intercept her boss. "Paula, I need to talk to you. How about right now, before we both get distracted with other things?"

Paula scowled. "Jesus, can't I even make it into my office without somebody hassling me?" Then she stopped short and forced a smile. "I'm sorry, Claire. I didn't mean to inflict my nasty mood on you." She shrugged out of her trench coat. "This coat is soaked through. And look at these shoes. The first time I've worn them, and they're probably ruined."

Claire glanced obligingly at Paula's feet. The leather looked expensive, and their light mocha color had turned a deep muddy brown around the edges. "Take them off and dry them as best you can," Claire suggested. "Then stuff them with paper towels but keep them away from heat. A little saddle soap, and they'll probably be fine."

Paula gave a begrudging grunt. "Madame Nurse to the rescue. What would I do without that down-to-earth practicality of yours? Just give me some time to get toweled off and check my messages, then come to my office. Say, fifteen minutes?"

"You've got it."

Facing Paula across the expanse of her golden oak desk the requisite quarter hour later, Claire wrapped both hands around her coffee mug for warmth. The emotional climate had turned decidedly chilly.

"There's no way I'm going to have you turning down perfectly good cases," Paula said between bites of her donut. "Imagine what that would do to our reputation. Our referral sources love the way we bend over backwards to open cases quickly, at their convenience. If we start communicating the message that we can't handle the clients they send us, pretty soon they won't refer anyone at all."

"Imagine what it will do to our reputation if our clients keep dropping dead," Claire retorted. "I don't think we should accept intakes for people who are at serious risk of wandering off and falling the way Rose Dobson did. We can't provide nonstop eyeball-to-eyeball supervision at this level of care, Paula. Much as I hate to admit it, clients who need to be watched every minute of the day should probably be in nursing homes. Either that or on rotating eight-hour shifts, and you know how hard it is to staff cases like that."

Paula sighed. "I know. Not to mention how hard it is to find families willing to pay that kind of money. We've established a really strong market niche with these live-in aides. We're fulfilling a genuine need, and now you're threatening to undercut everything we've worked so hard to build."

Claire shoved back her chair and stood, propelled by an adrenaline rush of rage. But why this sudden fury? Paula didn't deserve it. Maybe Claire was angry at death itself. In the end, no one escaped. Not in a nursing home, not in their own homes, not anywhere. Ministering to the ill and the elderly as they did, death loomed inexorably over the landscape. If Claire couldn't cope with it, she had no business working with such a vulnerable population. All she was doing was tilting at windmills, trying to postpone the inevitable.

"I can't talk about this any more," she told Paula. "The issues are too complicated, I need time to sort them out." She turned and headed for the door. Better to leave now, before she said something irrevocable.

———————————

Minna Schatz sat in the big wing chair in her living room, watching the rain outside. Maizy curled at her feet, snoring softly. The wind whipped the branches of the enormous maple in the front yard, stripping the bright orange leaves and strewing them all over the grass. The lawn was practically buried in leaves, but would Dahlia rake them up? Not on her life. The leaves were clogging up the gutters on the roof, too – Minna could tell by the way the water ran off midway across the eaves instead of flowing to the corners where it should. Usually Lester swept them out, but this year he couldn't be bothered. Climbing the ladder made his arthritis worse, he claimed, and his balance wasn't what it used to be. He had Jack Daniels to thank for that, but Minna knew better than to say anything. His temper was getting worse by the day, and for the first time in her life, Minna was actually afraid of him.

They had called the agency about the leaves, but the nurses backed Dahlia a hundred per cent. It wasn't in the care plan for the aide to rake leaves, much less climb a ladder and sweep them out of the gutters. Dahlia's job was to care for Minna, to do the basic cooking and light cleaning. Even waxing the floors was above and beyond the call of duty. With all the money Minna was shelling out, you'd think the agency could bend the rules a little, but no. They could send over their driver Stephen to do some yard work, but it would cost extra.

Let it go, Lester had said. Before we know it, the leaves will be buried in snow, and we'll have to pay someone for shoveling. But damned if it will be Compassionate Care. We're paying through the nose already.

Minna hated the rain, although she had to admit upstate New York was better than California, where they had all those wildfires. She'd seen it on TV, all those houses going up in smoke, the families standing outside the ruins in tears, like refugees in some God-forsaken war zone. But at least they had their health. They were young, they could rebuild. The insurance would cover it. But what did Minna have? This big old house, but aside from that, nothing.

Through the rain she made out the shape of a black sedan crawling slowly past her house. Creeping along, probably casing the place. And in the yard across the road, some black forms hanging from the trees, flapping back and forth like gigantic, broken-winged crows. Her heart lurched into her throat. She grabbed her silver bell, shook it frantically. "Dahlia! Dahlia, come here, quick!"

Dahlia hurried into the room, her outstretched hands covered with something stringy and red. "What is it, Minna? What's wrong?"

"Someone is watching the house. A black car went by really slowly. I'm positive they were looking in the windows."

Dahlia's lips twitched. "Why would anyone do that?"

"Damned if I know. Probably looking to rob the place. Can you turn on some more lights? Let them know we're home, in case they come back. And what are those black things flapping in the yard across the street?"

"Probably witches. I saw the kids out there with their mother a couple of days ago, decorating for Halloween."

"Well, I don't like it. I think they're sending me a message, trying to frighten me. They're probably in cahoots with that driver, too."

Dahlia sighed. "Stop vexing yourself, Minna. Anyone out driving today would have to go slow, because of the rain. All those leaves on the road make it real slippery. I'm sure they weren't paying any attention to this house."

"Easy for you to say. You're not the one they're after."

All at once Minna caught sight of orange circles of light shimmering through the rain. There were dozens of them, dancing on the wind. "What's that?"

"They just turned on the lights on the porch. I think they're little pumpkins."

"See, what did I tell you? They're signaling the driver, telling him to come back."

Dahlia wiped her hands on her apron, then strode to the window and pulled the cord to close the drapes. "I'll get us some privacy. Night comes so early now. This way no one can see in."

Minna shivered. "They'll see if they want to. Nothing we can do to stop them. What's that stuff on your hands? It looks like you've been butchering some poor defenseless animal. Some kind of Jamaican voodoo, I'll bet."

"Just meat loaf, Ma'am. I'm making it for dinner." Dahlia turned tail, disappeared back into the dark corridor that led to the kitchen.

The nerve of the woman! Probably she was in on the plot as well. Might as well call the agency. Most likely it wouldn't do any good, but there was no one else Minna could turn to.

Chapter 11

Claire suppressed a yawn. "Minna, I'm positive you have nothing to worry about. Dahlia's the most honest, caring person I know. I'd trust her with my life."

The phone line crackled. Then Minna Schatz's voice came through again, scratching through the static. "That's easy for you to say. You're probably in cahoots with them too."

Claire glanced at her watch. Five thirty, and the rest of the staff had left. She kicked off her shoes, tilted her chair back, then rested her stockinged feet on the files crammed into the bottom right drawer of her desk. She'd discovered this posture back in her first nursing job. Not as comfortable as her aunt's old recliner at home, but a good way to relax her spine after hunching over charts for hours. "I'm sorry, Minna, but I'm still not clear exactly who these people are that you're so worried about."

"My son Lester, for starters. I've seen the way he looks at me. There's something different about him lately."

"How do you mean?"

"Well, he always had a short fuse, but it's getting shorter. Practically every time he comes over, he blows his top about something. Mostly the money it's costing to keep your people in here. He'd like to see me dead, I'm sure of it."

"Has he said anything specific to give you that idea?"

"Not in so many words. But he's my only child. I've always been good at reading his mind."

Claire sighed. She'd been on the phone with Minna for a good twenty minutes, and nothing she said seemed to calm the woman. "I'll give Lester a call," she said for the umpteenth time. "He may be under stress, but he shouldn't be taking it out on you."

"Why not just stop in and see him?" Minna cackled. "Then you can report back to me on his housekeeping. I'll bet his place is a pig sty."

"I do want to see him in person, but I'd rather phone ahead first."

"See him tonight. Don't let him weasel out of it. This is important."

More important than Claire's workout at the Y? Unfortunately, yes. "I'll do what I can, Minna."

"That's a wishy washy answer, but all right. If it's the best you can do."

Even through all the static, Minna's voice brimmed with emotion. Hurt, anger, suspicion – no wonder poor Lester had high blood pressure. Claire thought longingly of the Y. A run on the treadmill, a circuit on the weight machines, the sauna, then a plunge in the pool, followed by a quiet evening at home – that was all she was up for tonight.

"Claire? Did you forget about me?"

"No, Minna. I'm here."

"Had a long day, huh? I imagine you went to poor Rose Dobson's funeral."

"No, as a matter of fact, I didn't." Too late, Claire realized she'd slipped. Now Minna would realize she knew Rose.

"Your agency had people in with her too, didn't they?"

"I'm not at liberty to say."

"Well, I know the truth. I have my sources. And I have my suspicions about who did her in."

This was entirely too much. "Minna, I'll get back to you tomorrow, after I've talked to Lester."

"But what about the black car? And the people signaling me with those orange lights from across the street?"

"We'll discuss all of that tomorrow."

"And what about this phone line? Somebody's bugging it. I can tell because of the static."

"That's probably because of all the rain we've been having. My phone at home gets that way too sometimes."

Minna's paranoia was definitely getting worse. Claire flipped her calendar to the next day's page, jotted down a note: call D'Attilio, review Minna's meds. Maybe get him to prescribe something to take the edge off. "Sorry, Minna, but I've really got to go."

Claire set the receiver gently in its cradle, silencing the angry squawks that were still slicing through the static. Then she bit the bullet and dialed Lester Schatz's number. His machine picked up. "Lester, this is Claire Lindstrom," she told it. "I'd like to get together with you to discuss some concerns about your mother. I believe –"

She heard a click. "Yeah, hi, Claire," the live Lester said. "What's up?" There was a clatter and what sounded like shattering glass. "Shit!" he shouted. Silence, then, "Sorry, I dropped the phone."

"Did I catch you at a bad time? Because I was wondering if I could drop by to see you for a few minutes."

A long, resonant belch, then, "Sorry, no can do."

It took all her powers of persuasion, but at last he agreed to meet her at three o'clock the next day. His house, so they could talk privately.

By seven thirty, Claire had put in her time on the treadmill and was halfway through the Cybex circuit. She positioned her feet on the rubber footrest of the leg-press machine, straightened her legs and pushed forward. A new personal best – 180 pounds and twelve reps. She felt the strain in her thighs, but it was a wholesome strain, easily within her capabilities. She decided to try for another set.

"Hmmm, nice quadriceps! You work out here a lot?"

Startled, she glanced up at the man looming over her. Sexist pig, horning in on her workout! As she struggled to frame a suitably withering response, she recognized the tail end of the mermaid tattoo on his forearm, but for a moment she drew a blank.

"Rick Kozlowski. We met at Tanya's remember?"

"Right, of course." She felt suddenly, absurdly vulnerable, picturing herself as he must see her: scantily clad, practically on her back, legs splayed as if awaiting a gynecology exam. Hurriedly she sat up and swung her legs to the floor. As she stood, a wave of dizziness swept over her.

He reached out a hand to steady her. "You all right? Maybe you had the weights set too high."

"I'm fine, thanks."

He was wearing a skimpy black tank top, satiny shorts in gunmetal gray, and an impressive variety of tattoos. He flexed ostentatiously, showing his body to maximum advantage. It was obvious he'd put in a lot of time developing his muscular physique, but the tattoos were unnerving. Grotesque gothic images snaked over and around the exposed flesh that would normally be covered by clothes. She couldn't help staring in spite of herself.

He grinned. "Like the artwork? It represents years of investment."

"Years of pain, it looks like."

"It's not that bad when you get used to it. Hey, want to grab some coffee when you're done with your workout?"

"No thanks. Working out gets me revved up enough. The last thing I need is caffeine at this hour of the night."

"Maybe a drink then? I could meet you at Tanya's."

She stepped to the side, edged toward the next machine in the circuit. "Look, Rick, no offense, but I'm not feeling sociable tonight. It's been a rough day."

"Yeah, I understand your agency lost another client. The funeral was today, right?"

"Who told you that?"

"I have my sources." He moved closer, stared down at her with his chocolate brown eyes. "Meet me at the tables near the vending machines, and I'll treat you to a Gatorade. I have some information I think you'll find interesting."

How did he know Rose Dobson was their client? In the interests of due diligence, she supposed it was her obligation to find out. "Make it cranberry juice and you're on," she said. "But I want to finish my circuit first."

Fifteen minutes later, he was waiting in the lounge, bottles at the ready. "So how's it going at Compassionate Care?" he asked as soon as she sat down. "You guys keeping your heads above water?"

Claire unscrewed the cap from her bottle, took a long swig of cranberry juice as she glared at Rick. Except for them, the lounge area was deserted. "You were supposed to share information with me," she said. "Not vice versa."

"All in good time. You go first."

What a weird, exasperating man. She decided to play along, see where this went. "We're doing very well, thank you."

"It can't be easy for a small, local agency like yours, competing against the big chains like ours. I'm surprised you've hung in there as long as you have. What's the secret of your success?"

A mental image of Dahlia flashed before her eyes. It's the live-ins, she almost said, but she caught herself in time. No need to share trade secrets. "We pride ourselves on providing really personalized service."

"You must have a lot of private-pay clients, right?"

"Why do you ask?"

"Never mind." He sipped his chartreuse sports drink. "Okay, I'll stop picking your brain. My turn to share. The reason I'm so curious about Compassionate Care is that I've heard some scuttlebutt around the office. Did you know my boss tried to buy out your boss?"

Claire felt the bile rise in her throat. "When was this?"

"Oh, a couple of years ago, I think. Your boss turned down the offer. But the mucky mucks in the corporate headquarters weren't happy about it. I wouldn't be surprised if they try again one of these days."

"Why are you telling me this?"

"Damned if I know. Maybe it's because Tri-County hasn't treated me all that well, or maybe it's just this gut feeling I have." He leaned closer, lowered his voice. "We nurses have to stick together. Health care can be a cutthroat business, but there's no reason we have to buy into all the backstabbing. I don't know about you, but I got into this business to help people."

"So did I, obviously." She shoved back her chair. "So, Rick, was this the interesting information you wanted to share? Because it sounds like old news to me. If you'll excuse me now, I still want to get in a swim."

"Okay, I'll let you go. I confess, the main reason I wanted to talk with you was to tell you I understand how hard it is when you lose a patient. They say it comes with the territory, that we nurses should take it in stride, but it really never gets any easier. Especially when it's unexpected. What was the cause of death in this case, if I may be so bold?"

Claire stood. "It's confidential. Just like the last time you asked."

"I thought you'd say that. I also thought we might be able to help each other if we share. Tri-County has had several clients die unexpectedly in the past couple of months, and I was wondering if there might be a correlation."

"How do you mean?"

"I don't know, maybe some kind of pattern we haven't discovered yet. But we'll never know if we don't share any data."

A pattern? What was he talking about? She felt a sudden queasiness, decided she wasn't up for this particular conversational journey. Rick was too weird, too gossipy. "My clients aren't data, they're human beings," she said. "Individuals, each with their own unique set of circumstances."

"Have it your way. But Claire, let me give you a little unsolicited advice that I had to learn the hard way. Watch your back. Be careful the powers that be at Compassionate Care don't start blaming the deaths on you."

———————

Stephen McClellan couldn't believe his good fortune. Here he was, lounging with his back up against the jets of the Y's whirlpool, when who should come sauntering toward him but Claire Lindstrom. Well, not sauntering, exactly. Her walk was straightforward, business-like, the same walk he saw every day on the job. But that swim suit! The legs were cut high, revealing the long thighs and elegant hipbones he'd only imagined till now.

"Hey, Claire! I didn't know you go to the Y."

She stopped short, startled. "Stephen! I didn't see you there!"

"Care to join me? This whirlpool feels fabulous. We can pretend we're in the tropics, forget about all the rain we've been having."

She pulled her beach towel protectively around her shoulders in a futile effort to hide everything he'd already seen. "Not right now, thanks. I just got out of the sauna, and now I'm going to swim some laps."

The sauna – so that was why her skin had that rosy glow. He'd been hoping it was due to his effect on her. "Good way to unwind, right?" he said. "This has been a hell of a week, what with Rose Dobson and –"

"Sssh!" She stepped to the edge of the whirlpool, squatted down close beside him with her finger to her lips, looking like some dame in an old-time beer commercial.

He grinned, let his body float lazily to the surface. "Sorry, I forgot. Confidentiality and all that good stuff. So, you a member here?"

"Yes, but I'm afraid I've been wasting my dues. In the summer I do all my swimming in the lake. Not to mention kayaking. But now that it's cold, I'll probably be spending more time here. I finally got back on the Cybex machines today. I need to build more lower body strength to get ready for ski season."

"You ski? No kidding! Cross country or downhill?"

"Both." She glanced around nervously, then stood. "I'd better go do those laps."

"You do that."

He stretched his arms lazily skyward, then clasped his hands behind his head and arched his back. He knew the pose showed the muscles of his chest to maximum advantage. Was it his imagination, or did Claire's face turn a deeper shade of rose? Other women admired his buff physique, Maria especially, but it was hard to tell with Claire. She was acting dodgy, her eyes darting every which way to avoid meeting his. She wanted him, he was virtually positive, despite that line she'd given him about maintaining professional distance. She might be frightened, maybe fighting her feelings, but she'd come around eventually. Women generally did.

She made him feel awkward, insecure. It was an unaccustomed feeling, and he didn't like it. They were acting as edgy as strangers who'd just met at a singles bar. Speaking of which – "I'm going to Tanya's after I finish up here," he said. "Why don't you meet me there?"

She stood there thinking, her hips canted to one side, driving him crazy. "I'm tempted," she said at last. "But I think I'll pass. After my swim, I'm going home to work on my jewelry."

Stephen pictured her hunkered over an anvil, hammering away at a slab of silver like some kind of Nordic goddess. The image was oddly intriguing, but not half as intriguing as the way she looked in that swimsuit. He wanted her more than ever.

Chapter 12

*N*ext morning, Claire was at her desk, sipping coffee and staring balefully at the stack of charts in her in-basket, when she heard the clomping of Paula's shoes down the hall. Her stomach lurched at the thought of yesterday's talk, when she had stormed out of her boss's office. *Not another argument about our quality of care,* Claire thought. *I'm not up for it, not when I have to confront Lester Schatz in a few hours.*

Fortunately, Paula was smiling when she materialized in the doorway. "Morning, Claire. I just wanted to check – have you cleared your calendar for tomorrow?"

"You mean for that caregivers' conference at the Empire Inn? Absolutely. I'm looking forward to it."

"You and me both. I can't see my way clear to a vacation in the foreseeable future, but at least this will get me out of the office. The way I've been feeling, if I don't get a break, I'm liable to harm myself or others."

Claire felt a stab of anxiety. "Better not put it like that," she said. "I know someone who used that phrase once to a cop who pulled her over for speeding, and it took half an hour for her to convince him not to have her committed. He wouldn't believe she was kidding."

"Well, I am. Don't worry, I'm not about to go postal."

Judging by the dark circles under Paula's eyes, the nervous tic at the corner of her mouth, Claire wasn't so sure. She'd been thinking of asking about the buy-out rumors Rick had brought up, but that seemed needlessly sadistic. And the notion of bringing up the unexpected deaths at Tri-County was just as bad. She settled for some innocuous chitchat instead. She and Paula had unfinished business, but their differences were too profound to settle over a single morning's coffee. Besides, Paula's mood swings were becoming more volatile lately. Might as well enjoy her sunny side while it lasted.

For the next few hours Claire zeroed in on her paperwork, breaking every so often to phone clients' homes and touch base with the aides, then documenting the conversations in progress notes. *All's well,* she thought. *Almost too well. Maybe too good to be true?*

At three on the dot, she was standing on the cracked concrete stoop outside Lester Schatz's cottage, knocking on a dirty yellow door. The ramshackle one-story structure was nestled alongside a lake a few miles from her own. The dark brown siding and yellow trim reminded her of the color scheme at Minna's house, and she wondered how much maternal influence was involved in the look of this small, dumpy place.

No answer. She knocked again. Still no response, so she ventured around the outside of the house. She found Lester out on the back deck, cleaning a rifle. The wood on the deck was splintery, in need of restaining, and littered with empty beer cans. "Deer season will be here before you know it," he said. "I can't wait. The buggers are all over the place, acting crazy. Almost hit one with my Explorer last night. Rutting season, you know." He leered. "Mating, I mean."

His beefy hand caressed the polished wood stock. Then he hoisted the gun to his shoulder and zeroed in on a Canada goose that was swimming close to shore, a good twenty feet from its flock.

Claire gasped. "Please don't shoot it!"

Lester cackled. "Scared you, did I? Don't worry, I won't. I'd love to, but the neighbors wouldn't approve. I hate those damn geese. Their honking keeps me awake at night, and they're always crapping all over my lawn."

Claire loved Canada geese, but she decided to keep her opinion to herself. This was definitely not an auspicious beginning for a discussion of his mother's paranoia. "Maybe we should talk inside," she said.

"Out here's better."

"It's kind of chilly, don't you think?"

"Only if you're not dressed for it." He eyed her trench coat, her ankles in their sheer panty hose. "We can go in if you want, but I warn you, housekeeping's not my strong point."

That was the understatement of the century, Claire thought as he ushered her inside and into the kitchen. The place reeked of mold, mildew, and the oily smell of a heating system probably long overdue for a tune-up. Empty beer cans, liquor bottles and pizza cartons littered every available surface, and the sink was piled high with encrusted dishes, no doubt rife with unsavory new organisms. Minna would be mortified if she knew.

"So what do you want?" he asked. "From what you said on the phone, my mother's been filling your head with all kinds of bullshit about me."

"She's expressed some concerns, yes." *She thinks you want her dead. Is that true?* "She seems to be growing more suspicious about a variety of things, some of them probably groundless, but I thought it would be good if we got together to clear the air."

His already ruddy face turned a deeper red, and a vein pulsed in his forehead. "She's getting senile, that's all. It comes with the territory, doesn't it? All this paranoid crap?"

"It's not a normal part of aging, no. In her case, I've noticed a change for the worse since we began services, and her suspiciousness seems to be getting a little out of hand. I've been thinking of contacting Dr. D'Attilio, maybe suggesting he prescribe a mild tranquilizer to take the edge off."

"Whatever you think. You're the professional, that's what we pay you for." He turned away, rummaged in a battered knotty pine highboy and extracted a bottle of bourbon. "You want a drink? I don't have any clean glasses, but there are some paper cups around somewhere."

"Thanks, but I'll pass. Lester, maybe it's none of my business, but are you doing okay living here on your own? It looks as though you could use some help. And how long has it been since you've had a thorough medical work-up? I have some concerns about your blood pressure. "

He slammed the bottle onto a chrome and Formica table, spilling the contents of an overflowing ashtray onto a stack of unopened mail. "You're goddamn right it's none of your business. Except that your business is ruining me. My mother's sitting pretty, being waited on hand and foot, and it's still not enough for her. It's never enough, never has been. Ever since I was a kid, she's been dumping on me. No matter how hard I try to please her, I can never do anything right. I swear she's going to drive me to an early grave, if something doesn't kill her first." His eyes bulged wider, as if aghast at his own words. "I didn't mean that the way it sounded. But you better get out of here."

Gladly, Claire thought. Lester's hair-trigger temper was making her uneasy, and the rifle didn't help. Driving to Minna's house, she kept punching buttons on the car radio, looking for something soothing, but to no avail. The music just jangled her already frazzled nerves. As she slowed for the turn into Minna's driveway, she had the sudden impulse to drive on by. What on earth could she say to reassure the woman? That her son was living in unbelievable squalor, that he had practically blown a gasket? Never mind, she would think of something. She had promised Minna they'd talk, and talk they would.

Dahlia had other ideas, though. "Minna's napping," she said when she opened the door. "I would have had her stay up if I knew you were coming."

"I'm sorry, I should have phoned ahead."

Dahlia crinkled her forehead and shot Claire a look of reproach. "I'd better not disturb her. She woke up at three last night and never got back to sleep. I stayed up with her, and we're both exhausted."

"Better let her sleep, then. When she wakes up, tell her I visited with Lester. If she wants to talk, call me on my cell, and I'll come back over."

"Thanks, Claire. Talking about Lester gets her all riled up, but I'll give her the message."

There was no call from Dahlia or Minna that night. Claire hated to admit it, but she was secretly relieved.

Next morning at the Empire Inn, Claire took an experimental bite of her Danish. Much too sweet, she decided. The sticky raspberry filling practically made her teeth ache. She returned it to its paper plate and abandoned it on the serving table next to a glass bowl full of used creamer containers.

Paula stared at her, aghast. "You're not throwing that away!"

"It's so sugary, I'm afraid it'll make me sleepy during the presentations."

"You could have given it to me. Never mind, I'll get one of my own. If I'm going to sit through hours of Power Point lectures, I need to fortify myself."

Claire suppressed the urge to lecture Paula on rapid-cycling blood sugar. "Maybe we'd better find ourselves some seats. It looks like they're about to start."

"All right, but let's sit separately. It's better for networking." Paula grinned. "We can work different parts of the room."

Claire smiled back. She was here at the hotel's conference center to learn about the latest developments in research and treatment of Alzheimer's disease, but the networking was important too. There must be a couple of hundred family caregivers here, along with dozens of professionals. Who could resist a free conference, especially when lunch was part of the deal? It was a golden opportunity to escape the relentless pressures of day-to-day care.

Paula leaned in close. "Don't look now," she said in a conspiratorial whisper, "but there are a couple of guys over there checking us out. I think they're heading our way."

Ignoring her boss's advice, Claire wheeled and found herself facing two men. Both were slim, dressed in expensively tailored suits. One was young, blond, with green eyes and the clean-cut, all-American looks of someone who'd aged gracefully out of a boy band. The other, a little older and taller, had dark wavy hair and eyes the color of faded denim. Out of the corner of her eye, she caught sight of Paula's predatory smile. This was shaping up to be an interesting day.

Claire glanced from one man to the other and back, unsure where to focus first, till the boy-band guy took the decision out of her hands. Stepping forward, he extended an open palm. "I'm Patrick Delafield."

"Claire Lindstrom." As she grasped his hand, Claire felt a charge of warmth. She was glad she'd worn the black ultrasuede dress, glad it worked for something besides funerals.

He was too relaxed, too self-assured for a caregiver, she thought as she reclaimed her hand from his. Maybe a rep from the drug company that was underwriting the conference?

His smile was quirky, a little crooked. "I'm an attorney specializing in elderlaw. And this is my associate, Justin Greylock."

The taller man stepped forward and extended his hand. His grasp was a little cooler, his gaze more guarded. "Pleased to meet you."

Claire smiled. "Are you an attorney too?"

"No, I'm an account executive."

Patrick inserted himself back into the space between them. "We're with a firm called Oaktree Associates. We specialize in helping people cope with issues of later life. Not just the legal issues, but the emotional and psychological ones. We have social workers and psychologists on staff, and we help families confront end-of-life issues."

"You mean like Hospice?" Paula asked.

"No, we're not involved in the hands-on or medical aspects of care, although we do work with Hospice. We get a lot of our referrals from them, as well as from other kinds of health care agencies, both proprietary and not-for-profit."

Paula smiled. "And which are you?"

Patrick returned the smile with interest. "Oh, strictly not-for-profit, both in terms of our legal structure and in terms of our financial ambitions. Our founder, Nathaniel Gebhardt, is a true visionary. Perhaps you've read some of his articles? Because if not, I can refer you –"

Paula cut him short. "I don't have much time for articles. Running an agency keeps me too busy. Have you heard of Compassionate Care?" She put down her plate, then fiddled with the clasp on her Dooney & Burke bag, displaying the leather logo to maximum advantage. She pulled out a fistful of brochures. "We specialize in round-the-clock live-in services, and we have special expertise with Alzheimer's. Isn't that right, Claire?"

Claire nodded, at a momentary loss for words. She was acutely conscious of Justin, who was standing just to the left of Patrick, studying her with his faded blue eyes. If only she were as glib as Paula in these situations. She'd have to remember to practice her thirty-second sales spiel.

Paula patted Claire's arm. "Claire is our nursing supervisor. I'm grateful to have her; she's second to none."

Patrick studied Claire with a look of pleased concentration, as if he were reading a particularly delectable dinner menu. She was relieved when an amplified voice instructed everyone to take their seats. And she was even more relieved when Patrick headed off toward a row near the back of the room, and she ended up next to Justin.

"That was fascinating," Justin said as they rose to leave hours later. "I can't believe it's already four o'clock."

Claire glanced around, feeling a little spinny. "I know Paula had to get back to the office, but where's Patrick? I haven't seen him since the last break."

"He went back to work too. I guess some people are just workaholics. I have to confess I'm not one of them. How about you?"

"Today I feel like one. I haven't taken so many notes since I was in nursing school."

"Yes, I saw you scribbling away. I admire your powers of concentration, Claire, but it's not like you'll have to take a final exam on everything you heard today."

Her heart rate accelerated at the thought of his eyes on her. "Sometimes I feel like every day is a final exam. At least I picked up a few new facts that might come in handy when I'm talking with the families of my Alzheimer's patients."

"Think you'll try out that new medication they were hyping all day?"

"That would be up to the patients' doctors, not me." She grabbed the complimentary canvas tote bag that had been nudging her feet all afternoon, hoisted it onto the table. "Jeez, this thing weighs a ton. I got some extra copies of the handouts for the physicians I work with. Not to mention enough pens and note pads to last me a year."

He laughed. "That's one of the perks of these conferences. Personally, I like the Post-It pads. I must have half a dozen stashed away in here." As he stooped to retrieve his own bag, his hand brushed her thigh. Intentionally? From the way his skin flushed, she decided it was an accident.

"Sorry," he murmured. "Kind of close quarters."

Claire had been acutely aware of that fact all day. She had been glad the seating arrangements turned out as they had. Patrick was too pushy, too overbearing for her taste, while Justin, even though he was in sales, had a relaxed, laid-back quality that piqued her interest. But his physical proximity had been a powerful distraction; she had taken all those notes in large part as an exercise in concentration to keep from dwelling on the attractive man at her side.

"What struck me most," she said, "was that new study about the feelings of people who care for family members with Alzheimer's. I forget the exact figures, but wasn't it seventy per cent who admitted they were relieved when the person died? And ninety per cent believed the person with Alzheimer's would rather die than go on suffering?"

"Something like that." His blue eyes darkened. "And that was just people who were interviewed after the victim died. Imagine what it's like for people who have to go on living with the illness day after day, year after year. Especially in the advanced stages, it has to be a living hell for everyone involved."

They stood silent between the rows of narrow burgundy-clothed tables, gazing at their purple tote bags with the logo of the conference sponsors emblazoned in white. Justin would have to move first. Either that or she'd have to edge past him, and she wasn't up for that degree of intimacy. Not yet, anyway.

"Excuse me," he said. "I didn't mean to trap you."

He was picking up on her thoughts again. Surprisingly sensitive for someone in sales. "Care to stop by the cocktail lounge before we head home?" she asked impulsively.

His eyes lightened again, to a color she'd seen once in a Siberian husky. "I'm tempted," he said, "but I'd better take a rain check. I told Patrick I'd meet him back at the office, touch base about some marketing plans."

So much for her powers of persuasion. What had gotten into her, anyway?

Chapter 13

A s Claire strode through the hotel lobby, she kept her eyes focused resolutely forward. She resisted making a detour into the cocktail lounge, resisted turning to see if Justin was by any chance watching her. A tingly sensation at the back of her neck gave her the feeling he was.

In the parking lot, she zapped the lock on her Focus and climbed in. What next? Justin might not be up for cocktails, but she had the makings for a Bloody Mary at home. On the other hand, she really ought to drop in on Minna Schatz. She pulled out her cell, punched in the number.

Dahlia picked up on the third ring, sounding slightly breathless.

"Did I catch you at a bad time?" Claire asked.

"No, that's okay, but Minna's napping again. She seems to be turning night into day."

"I should probably come by anyway."

"If you want. But Allyson Quigley's coming in a little while."

That was news to Claire, but then Allyson pretty much set her own schedule. "In that case, maybe I should put off my visit till tomorrow," she said.

Dahlia laughed. "That makes sense. Minna's been acting so paranoid, having two nurses here at once might really freak her out."

Claire mixed herself a Bloody Mary as soon as she got home. Celery stick, Tabasco, Worcester sauce, and a twist of fresh-ground black pepper from the foot-tall wooden mill she kept on the counter near the stove. She took a large gulp, nearly choked. She ran tap water into a second glass and slugged it down to dilute the impact.

"What is it with me, Freia?" she asked her dog, who was bouncing and whining to go out. "Not only would I make a lousy bartender, but I finally meet a man I might actually be interested in, and he ends up blowing me off." She crouched down to doggy level and exhaled full-blast into Freia's face, which always got her mutt wildly excited. "Do I need a new mouth wash or something?"

Freia took a deep sniff and sneezed. Then she licked Claire's cheeks, her chin, with frenetic enthusiasm.

"At least you love me. Either that or you're just telling me you want your evening walk."

Cautiously she took a few more sips of Bloody Mary, poured in some water, stirred, then sipped again. Now it was drinkable.

She was heading for the door with Freia when the phone rang. She checked the caller ID: Angelo Giordano. Her heart sank as she thought of Regina, but his voice was cheerful. "Hi, Claire, I just saw you pull in a couple of minutes ago. You want to come over for dinner? I made a beef stew with everything orange, in honor of Halloween. Carrots, winter squash, yams. Full of beta-carotene, good for what ails you, and beautiful to boot. It's too much for me and Regina to eat all by ourselves, especially since she's got hardly any appetite these days."

"Thanks, Angelo, I'd love to. I'll just change and walk Freia. Then I'll be right over."

"Bring the pooch too. I cooked a few scraps of beef separately just for her. Besides, I had an interesting experience today, and I'm anxious to get your opinion."

Suddenly ravenous, Claire cut the walk short. When she and Freia arrived, she was shocked at the change in Regina. She was markedly more haggard than she'd been on Claire's last visit, and her skin had a yellowish, waxy cast to it. *It won't be long now*, Claire thought as she gazed at the woman she'd known practically all her life. The cancer had metastasized, and its ravages were obvious. Her shiny scalp was visible through the wisps of baby-fine white hair that had grown in since the last round of chemotherapy. Regina's luxuriant mane of hair, once chestnut brown, then silver, had been a source of enormous pride to her. Claire could only imagine the pain of its loss, along with all the other losses Regina was confronting now. First and foremost the impending loss of life.

They'd scarcely started their supper when Regina braced both hands on the table and pushed back her chair. "I'm stuffed, I can't eat another bite. I think I'll turn in for the night."

Angelo looked stricken. "But Regina, you've barely eaten a thing. You've got to keep up your strength."

"What's the point?" Regina's sigh was so deep, it seemed wrenched from her very soul. "It's just postponing the inevitable."

Angelo turned to Claire. "You're a nurse. Can't you talk some sense into her? Tell her how important it is to keep up her nutrition?"

"That would be presumptuous, Angelo. Regina has the right to decide what's best for her."

"But she's wasting away before our eyes!"

Cachexia. Weight loss and malnutrition, part of the cancer's inexorable progress. "Yes, I know," Claire said. She reached across the table, laid a hand on each of theirs. "It's associated with the illness. There can be many reasons for it."

Regina's eyes were wet with tears. "I feel nauseous half the time, and food doesn't taste good any more. Angelo just can't accept what's happening, Claire. Maybe you can help him understand."

Claire was close to tears herself. "Maybe I'm not the best person to do it. You two are like family to me, the closest family I have, and it's hard for me to be objective. Have you thought of calling in other professional help?"

"You mean like your agency?" Angelo asked. "We had visiting nurses and aides after Regina's last surgery, but right now I'd rather care for her myself."

"I was thinking more of people who could talk things over with you, help you confront the issues you're facing."

"Like the fact that I'm dying," said Regina.

"Yes." *Why can't I say the word? Why does Regina have to bear the burden of honesty?*

Angelo coughed. "Maybe now's the time to tell you about my experience today."

"I've heard this already," said Regina. "Angelo, could you be so kind as to escort me to bed? Then you can come back and talk Claire's ear off into the wee small hours. Give her some of that nice brandy we've been saving. Or we've got some crème de menthe."

Ever the gracious hostess, Claire thought. Even now. She hoped Regina didn't see the tears filling her eyes.

"So today I went to this outfit called Oaktree Associates," Angelo said as he topped off Claire's brandy. Regina was in bed, settled down for the night.

"That's a coincidence. I met some men from Oaktree at a conference today. How did you get involved with them?"

"Father Julian at St. Paul's suggested I give them a try, so I went to a meeting last week, and again today."

"What kind of meeting?"

"It's a caregivers' support group, for people whose loved ones are seriously or terminally ill. George Cropsey's son Paul showed up too."

"Good for him. It sounds like something that family could really use. And you too. Who facilitates the group? Do you feel good about them? What are their qualifications?"

Angelo chuckled. "I'm glad you're looking out for me, Claire. It was a social worker named Gloria Wallender. She seemed okay, if you go in for that kind of stuff."

"How do you mean?"

"Well, all this sharing and self-disclosure. She kept stressing how important it is to be honest and open about our feelings, even the negative ones. Maybe it's the generation gap, but I don't feel comfortable spilling my guts to a bunch of strangers I've never met before. I'm still a good Catholic, and I'd rather save it for confession."

"Even so, maybe you should give it some time before you decide whether to stick with it or not. Is that their main service? What else do they offer?"

"Oh, a bunch of things. Legal consultation to help deal with living wills and estate planning, and individual counseling. After today's session, Gloria Wallender pulled me aside and told me she thought I could benefit from some individual sessions. But my insurance won't cover it unless I get a referral from a psychiatrist. They've got one on staff, and Gloria took me over to a gal in the office to see about making an appointment, but I felt like they were trying to railroad me into something. I told them I needed time to think it over."

"What about the support group? Is that covered by insurance?"

"It's free for the first four weeks. After that they move you into other groups depending on your needs, and you have to go through the same referral rigmarole. I guess the support group is kind of a loss leader, a way to lure you in so you'll spring for the paid services. As a businessman, I can respect that; they can't be expected to do this purely out of the goodness of their hearts. It's the psychological stuff I object to. In all my seventy-eight years, no one's ever suggested I need my head shrunk, and I don't see why that should change now."

"I see your point." Claire drained the last of her brandy. "Tell you what, Angelo. I'm curious about this Oaktree organization. Before it gets too late, why don't I go home and Google them? I'll let you know what I find out."

"Excuse me?"

"Google them – oh right, I always forget you're still resisting going online. I'll type Oaktree Associates into the Google search engine, research them and see what turns up."

Angelo grinned. "Isn't technology wonderful! Maybe I'll give in and try to get computer-literate one of these days. Thanks, Claire. I don't know why, but something just strikes me as odd about that place. The first time I was there, a guy was coming out of one of the offices, and he looked furious about something. His face was red, and he was muttering under his breath. So they've got at least one unhappy customer."

Claire rose, planted a kiss on Angelo's forehead. "Well, they don't need another one. I'll check it out and tell you what I find."

———————————

A few miles away, Minna Schatz edged forward on her couch and glowered at the dumpy woman standing in front of her, holding a Tupperware cake container. The other nurse – Allyson Quigley, her name was, if Minna wasn't mistaken. Dahlia stood nearby, twisting her hands nervously. Maizy was looking bristly, standing at full alert as her eyes darted between the woman's face and the cake in her hands.

"Where the hell is Claire Lindstrom?" Minna demanded. "She was supposed to come by and see me yesterday, and I haven't heard a word."

"She phoned while you were napping," Dahlia said. "Remember I told you?"

Minna felt a rush of anxiety. "You told me no such thing."

"Sorry, Minna, but I did. Maybe you forgot." The aide moved closer, patted her shoulder. "Claire phoned again late this afternoon. She wanted to come over, but when I told her Allyson was coming, she said she'd visit tomorrow instead."

The dumpy woman smirked. "Ms. Lindstrom was at a conference today, and I guess it ran longer than she expected. I'm Allyson Quigley."

"I know who you are, damn it! You've already been here a couple of times. You can't fool me. I don't have Alzheimer's or anything."

Allyson smiled. "I know you don't, Mrs. Schatz. You're sharp as a tack."

Minna sighed. The smile struck her as phony, but what choice did she have? Claire had already explained how Allyson would be doing some of the nursing visits, how experienced and caring she was. They were treating her like a sack of potatoes, passing her back and forth between the two of them. She'd told Claire she didn't like it, but Claire had insisted. Allyson was on call after hours, she'd said, and it was better to have two nurses familiar with her needs. "I'm sharp enough to know I didn't ask for a visit from you," she told Allyson. "What's the occasion?"

"I don't need an occasion, do I? I just wanted to see how you ladies were doing, and to bring you a little treat."

Minna eyed the container in Allyson's hands. Through the cloudy plastic, she could make out what looked like chocolate frosting. Her favorite. It was a couple of hours past dinner, and she hadn't eaten that much. She felt her stomach growl in anticipation. "What's in there?"

"A Halloween cake. I made it myself. How about we go to the kitchen, and I'll cut you a piece? You too, Dahlia."

Minna pushed off from the sofa, stood tottering a moment. "Get me my walker, would you Dahlia? She's twisted my arm."

Dahlia rushed to her side with the tubular aluminum contraption, made sure she was safely stabilized. Then Allyson headed through the dark corridor and into the kitchen. Minna hobbled slowly after her with Dahlia hovering protectively behind, as Maizy bounced back and forth and generally got in the way.

As they settled around the Formica table, Minna realized she was glad of the extra company. Dahlia wasn't much of a conversationalist. "So you say Claire was off at a conference today?" she asked the nurse.

Allyson's mouth twisted in a grimace. "Yes, something about Alzheimer's, I believe. Her and the head of the agency."

"So that's why she didn't have time to drop in on me. Must be nice, gallivanting around like that."

"She's entitled, seeing as she's nursing supervisor. She's just lucky she has me to do the hands-on care." Allyson snapped the latch on the lid of the cake container. "I don't know if she told you, Mrs. Schatz, but I used to be nursing supervisor for Compassionate Care until Claire Lindstrom came along."

Minna leaned forward. This was getting interesting. "You mean she took your job?"

"I guess you could say that."

Dahlia shoved her chair back and stood. "I'll get some plates and a cake knife." Maizy began to whine, and Allyson forced a smile. "It's all for the best, really. I was never big on all that administrative claptrap. I much prefer the actual nursing. Being with my families, helping people. Dahlia, don't forget the forks and napkins."

Damn that Dahlia! She'd gone and distracted Allyson just when the gossip was getting juicy. Probably did it on purpose. But Allyson had more going for her than Minna had realized. Maybe she should tell the nurse about her suspicions of Lester, since Claire didn't seem to give a damn.

Allyson removed the plastic lid with a flourish. "Ta da!"

Chocolate layer cake, just as Minna had hoped. Or at least the frosting was chocolate. "Is the inside chocolate too?" she asked Allyson.

"Oh, absolutely. Dahlia told me chocolate's your favorite. You're so slender, you could stand to gain a little weight. And you don't have diabetes, so the indulgence won't hurt you any."

The frosting was kind of amateurish, with orange loops and squiggles around the side. Minna could have done better herself, once upon a time. The witch in the middle was professional looking, though. Crossing in front of a full moon on a broomstick, a cat arching behind. Probably something ready-made she'd bought at the store and stuck on later. Amazing what they came up with these days. But the witch gave her the shivers. It reminded her of those ghastly black apparitions the neighbors across the street had put up to scare her. Maybe Allyson was part of the same plot.

On second thought, maybe Minna wouldn't tell her about Lester after all.

Chapter 14

*O*aktree Associates brought up over four thousand hits on Google. Claire stared at the computer screen in disbelief, then started scrolling down. Many of the entries were duplicates, but even so, who would have believed so many people were so enamored of oak trees? There were real estate developers, financial planners, furniture makers, and innumerable consultants in all manner of fields. Obviously oak trees had some kind of primordial appeal. Tall, strong, long-lived – Claire thought of her Nordic ancestors, who worshipped in sacred groves and built Viking longships out of oak wood.

She retreated to the kitchen, where she downed two tumblers of water to dilute the brandy still in her system. Then she headed back to the computer to dig deeper. She typed "eldercare" and "consulting" into the advanced search box, and in a few seconds, she zeroed in on a likely candidate: a web site for Oaktree Associates, specializing in consulting services for adults, based in New York City.

Adult? The word conjured up a whole range of pornographic possibilities, but Claire decided to give it a try. She clicked on the bold, blue underlined link and brought up an elegant home page. Forest green print on a pale gray marbleized background, understated and easy on the eyes, with a series of choices embedded in gold-tone ovals running down the side. "Our Mission," "About Our Services," "What Our Clients Are Saying," "Articles," "Office Locations."

Her eyes went blurry. This could take awhile. She bookmarked the home page, then clicked on locations. Albany headed the list. She jumped up, retrieved her handbag from its customary spot near the recliner, and rummaged through it until she found the business card Patrick Delafield had given her that morning. Yes, the phone number and street address were the same. Maybe she'd pay them a visit one of these days. Or still better, visit the New York City office, and get together with some of her old friends while she was there. For now, though, she would let her fingers do the walking. She arrowed back to the home page, then clicked on "Our Mission."

At last she shut down the computer and dragged herself to bed. As she drifted into sleep, images of Angelo and Regina swirled through her mind, mingled with visions of oak trees. Their huge limbs were gnarled and twisted, disfigured by cavernous holes, and their dying leaves blew in windswept drifts that threatened to bury her.

Something was wrong with Maizy, Minna was sure of it. Instead of bounding up onto Minna's bed the way she usually did, Maizy had dragged herself up slowly and painfully, acting twice her natural age.

It was the damn cake, it had to be. Chocolate was bad for dogs. They were allergic to it, Minna had read some place, and she had told the nurse, but by the time she thought to mention it, Allyson had already given Maizy a gigantic piece. And you didn't dare take food away from Maizy when she was in the middle of eating; she was liable to snap at you.

Minna rolled over and stroked the sleek fur of the dog lying beside her. "Are you all right, sweetie?" Maizy sighed deeply, stretched her legs, then curled back into a ball. She seemed comfortable enough, but she should have opened her eyes.

"I'm going to call the vet," Minna told the dog. "Just to be on the safe side." She reached for the silver bell on the bedside table, rang it as hard as she could. But a wave of weakness swept over her. The bell slipped from her hand, onto the floor.

Damn! What was happening to her? It must be the cake. Too much sugar – she shouldn't have had two pieces. Or maybe the nurse had slipped something into it. She wouldn't put it past her. Maybe she and Lester were part of the same plot.

"Dahlia!" she screamed. "Wake up! I need to call the vet and the doctor. Somebody poisoned Maizy and me!"

There was no answer from the room down the hall. That wasn't like Dahlia; she usually showed up on command, regardless of the hour. Was she in on it too?

Minna screamed again. Still no reply. She tried again, but she felt sleep stealing over her, enveloping her like a warm down comforter.

———— — ————

Gabriel gazed down at the old woman. In the cold light of the full moon, her skin was pale and blue. She had thrown off the covers, and her body was skinny and angular. Like Picasso's Blue Period, he thought. The pose was interesting – awkward, graceless, as if she'd been trying to get out of bed. The dog lay curled at her feet. He wished he'd brought a sketchbook, or maybe a camera, but Athena had made it clear: keep it simple. No delays, no improvisations, no extracurricular excursions into the woods. Follow instructions precisely, or you're out.

There wasn't a peep out of the aide down the hall. It was Dahlia Douglas, the one who'd been with Harriet Gardener, but he still didn't know whether she was involved with the organization. He felt a rush of anger as he thought of the phone call from Athena. Don't concern yourself with details, she'd said. Everything will be ready for your arrival; that's all you need to know. Less chance of a slip-up that way. He could see her point, but either they didn't trust him or they took him for an idiot. Either way it was insulting, but he supposed he'd have to live with it. For now anyway.

The little terrier was so quiet, for a moment he had thought it was dead, but then, to his relief, he'd seen its flank rising and falling with the rhythm of its breaths. Athena had warned him there would be a dog, said they would put it out of commission, but she hadn't said anything about killing it. If they had, he would flat-out quit. Snuffing dogs was definitely not part of his game plan. Their lives were short enough already; they didn't outlive their usefulness the way people did.

For that matter, why did they want him to off this old lady? She didn't have Alzheimer's or a terminal illness. She was recovering from a hip fracture, Athena had said, and she was pretty paranoid, but aside from that she was fairly healthy and totally with it.

But if she wasn't suffering, wasn't in imminent danger of death, then how did this particular killing jibe with the alleged mission they'd told him about? He had known better than to ask. If they refused to tell him who knocked out the old lady before his arrival, or exactly how they did it, they certainly wouldn't share all the whys and wherefores of their operation.

What was the saying? *Even if you're paranoid, it doesn't mean people aren't out to get you.* Ours not to question why, he thought as he readied the injection. There must be a valid reason. This time he would administer the shot, then leave her to die peacefully in bed, as he should have done with Rose Dobson.

Minna scarcely stirred, just whimpered a little as the syringe found its target in the carotid artery. The dog whined once, then began paddling its hind legs in a silent dream of running.

Good. The dog's not dead. Maybe she'll survive.

Claire woke to the sound of Canada geese flying low over the house. Their haunting cries drew her out of bed to the window, where she caught sight of the last of the flock silhouetted against the full moon.

Where were they going this time of night? Something must have disturbed them, she thought as the trill of the phone cut through their calling. How long had it been ringing? She heard her own voice click on, inviting the caller to leave a message. A pause, then the sound of Dahlia's frantic voice. "Claire, pick up. Please! It's Minna. She's not breathing!"

Claire stood rooted to the spot. The chill from the hardwood floor rocketed up through her body, stole her breath away. Surely she couldn't have heard right. Her answering machine had crummy sound quality, and those geese had raised such a ruckus, she must have misunderstood.

She could still hear the raucous honking of the geese, fading into the distance. Maybe their calls were all she had heard, and the terrifying phone call was nothing but a nightmare or hallucination. But no, here was Dahlia's voice again.

"Claire, are you there? Wake up! There's something wrong with Minna. I think she's dead!"

On the braided rug beside the bed, Freia stirred and stretched, giving Claire a sleepy-eyed stare. Claire padded toward the phone in the living room, grabbed the receiver. "I'm here, Dahlia. What did you say?"

"Minna's not breathing, and I can't get a pulse. I already called 911. Should I start CPR?"

Had Minna signed her advance directives? Claire willed her groggy brain to wake up. Now she remembered. The woman had refused to sign a health care proxy or living will. From the outset, she'd been far too paranoid to discuss the possibility of her own death, or whether she wanted extreme measures in the event of an emergency.

"Do you have any idea how long she's been unresponsive?"

"No, but her skin is still warm."

"Then start CPR immediately. If you possibly can, keep it up until the EMTs get there. I'll throw on some clothes and be right over."

"Please," Dahlia said in a strangled tone. Then there was a click and the line went dead.

Please let this be a nightmare. Claire ran back to her bedroom, stood immobilized. Minna Schatz, dead? It didn't make sense. She'd been making a good recovery from her hip fracture, getting around with her walker, and she had the kind of feisty, domineering temperament that augured well for survival into a cantankerous old age.

Unless Minna was right, and someone wanted her dead. Someone like Lester. The guilt hit Claire like a low punch to the gut. She shouldn't have let Dahlia brush her off for two days in a row; she should have insisted on visiting Minna today, after the conference. If she had, maybe she would have picked up some warning signs, some physical symptoms. Something Allyson Quigley had missed.

She threw on an ultrafleece pullover, a pair of corduroy pants, as her dog stood staring, waving her plumy tail in puzzlement. "Want to go for a ride, Freia?"

Freia bounced an enthusiastic yes. Claire knelt, wrapped her arms around the dog's broad shoulders and squeezed, grateful for the one friend who wouldn't pass judgment.

The scene outside Minna's house was eerily brilliant yet silent. As Claire stared through the windshield at the ambulance, the police car flashing its red and blue lights, she had an odd feeling of detachment, as though she were watching a TV crime show with the sound on mute. And the actors were all off screen.

Beside her, Freia sat panting, eager to jump out and explore. Claire ruffled the dog's curly hair. "You'd better stay here, baby. Guard the car." As she opened the door and climbed out, Dahlia emerged through the red door onto the front steps. Her shoulders sagged, and she descended the steps slowly, like a runner who'd hit the wall and dropped out of a marathon. Administering CPR could do that to a person. Even someone young and in good shape, which Dahlia was definitely not.

Claire threaded her way between the ambulance and the squad car, opening her arms to the aide. They hugged for a long, silent moment. Claire felt the aide's chest heaving raggedly against her own. They pulled back and looked at each other. Gazing into the liquid pools of fathomless brown that were Dahlia's eyes, Claire read the answer she dreaded. It was all over for Minna Schatz.

Even so, she had to ask. "What did the EMTs say? Were they able to save her?"

Dahlia shook her head. "Too late. They used those paddle things, gave her some kind of shots, but nothing worked. She's gone."

Claire hit the Indiglo button on her watch: 3:35 a.m. "How did you happen to look in on Minna? Did she call out? Was she in some kind of distress?"

"Something woke me, I don't know what. Maybe an owl." Dahlia shuddered. "Those birds are evil. They give me the creeps. Anyway, I decided to check on Minna. That's when I discovered she wasn't breathing. I called 911, then you." She gulped twice, convulsively. "Maybe I should go back to the city. I shouldn't be working for you people; I bring some kind of jinx on these poor ladies."

"No, you don't, Dahlia. Please don't blame yourself. It's not your fault."

"But I had evil thoughts about Minna. She vexed me something awful. Many times I told myself I couldn't take it much longer, and now look what's happened."

Claire draped her arm around the aide's shoulders. "Minna would vex anyone, even a saint. You had every right to think negative thoughts about her, as long as you kept them to yourself."

"Yes, but I didn't have love in my heart for her. Not like with Harriet Gardener. I treated Harriet the way I'd treat my own mother, but she died even so. I'm no good for this work. Maybe I go back to Jamaica."

"Please don't, Dahlia. Give it some time, let us figure things out. Take a break if you need to, but in the meantime –"

A police officer materialized on the front steps, cutting short Claire's train of thought. She recognized Officer Frances Milgrim at once. The small, compact build, the hazel eyes. Strangely enough, Claire was glad of the interruption. It spared her from having to come up with an insightful comment to lighten Dahlia's load.

"I remember you," said Milgrim. "You're the nurse who found that victim out in the woods last month. Tough break, having two deaths on your watch, one right after the other." She tossed Claire a cryptic half-smile, then fell silent, fixing her with an expectant gaze.

Claire was suddenly self-conscious. What did the woman want? An explanation? An apology? A "comes with the territory" brush-off? Maybe Dahlia was right: at the moment, a trip to Jamaica seemed like an excellent idea. Maybe they could go together.

Nothing rang true but the truth. "Yes, it's terrible," she told the officer, trying to maintain eye contact and project a stoic professionalism she was far from feeling. "Now if you don't mind, I need to go inside and see Mrs. Schatz. Is she still in her bedroom?"

"Yes, my partner is up there securing the scene. The rescue squad people should be just about finished. There's a dog in there too. She didn't want to leave the body."

"My God, Maizy! I'm surprised she let them in."

"That wasn't a problem. Anyway, they couldn't resuscitate the woman, and they declared the death right before I got here. Any preexisting conditions you can think of?"

Sergeant Milgrim's hazel eyes were narrowed, studying Claire intently. *Waiting for me to crack, to confess. But confess to what?* "No, nothing obvious comes to mind." She sidestepped the officer, headed for the front door. "I'd like to examine her now."

Milgrim took a step forward, blocking her way. "Not a good idea. We want to keep the scene intact until the coroner gets here."

"Herb Davidson? You called him already?"

"I thought it best, given the circumstances."

Claire waited for her to elaborate, but she didn't. Fill in the blanks: given your agency's abysmal track record lately, given the uproar surrounding Rose Dobson's death – Claire could almost read the officer's mind. In a way, it was a relief. Lester could yell bloody murder – she winced at the unintended irony – but at least

Claire wouldn't bear the brunt of the blame for calling in the authorities.

"You're probably right," Claire said. "But Davidson won't be able to tell you anything. He has no medical training; he's just a retired insurance executive. I'll bet he wasn't crazy about being dragged out of bed in the middle of the night, either."

Milgrim's mouth twitched in the hint of a smile, but she sobered instantly, then overcompensated with a glare. "He should be here within the hour."

"In the meantime, can I go upstairs and see Minna?"

"I guess so. Just don't touch anything."

Officer Stan Ormsbee wheeled as Claire entered Minna's bedroom. "You can't come in here."

"Officer Milgrim told me it would be all right."

He grunted, scrutinized her with squinty eyes. "Well, I suppose it's okay. The scene's chaotic enough already. If there was anything to find, the EMTs probably screwed it up when they were trying to resuscitate her."

Anything to find? Like what? Claire sidestepped Ormsbee and made her way toward Minna's bedside. The two medical technicians stood silent guard as she stared down at the frail body. A small blue-shaded table lamp beside the bed threw off a feeble glow that combined with the cold bluish light of the full moon to illuminate the woman's bony torso. Claire thought she glimpsed dusky areas of discoloration where the futile attempts at resuscitation had left their marks. There was a bruised area on her neck as well, just over the carotid artery. Or were the marks just shadows of the narrow bands of cloud that scuttled across the moon? She wasn't sure; she couldn't see clearly, maybe because of the tears that filled her eyes.

A sudden whine cut through the stillness, a mournful, uncanny sound. Startled, Claire focused for the first time on the tangled mound of bedclothes beside Minna's body. There, snuggled up against her mistress's side, lay Maizy. In her white coat with its scattering of black spots, she blended almost seamlessly with the sheets. But her huge brown eyes were alight with anguish.

Chapter 15

*T*he sight of Minna's dog triggered more tears, and soon they were flowing down Claire's cheeks. She was relieved she had her back to the cop and the EMTs; it would have been embarrassing for them to catch her crying. The reaction caught her by surprise. Usually she was more professional, more self-possessed. She hadn't even been that fond of Minna. Closing her eyes, she turned inward and tried to sort out the contradictory mix of emotions swirling inside her. Sadness, yes, but mingled with guilt, anger, frustration. Like Harriet Gardener's death, this one made no sense.

She wiped her eyes furtively on her sleeve, then turned to face the three men. "Any ideas yet as to the cause of death?" she asked.

Ormsbee shrugged and glanced pointedly at the two medical technicians.

"Hard to say," said the older one, whose gaunt face had the haunted look of someone who'd seen too many deaths over the years. "By the time we got here, she was completely unresponsive, and I couldn't get a pulse. We tried anyway, but I called the death at 3:05 a.m. Maybe the coroner will have a better idea as to the cause."

I doubt it, Claire wanted to say, but she bit back the words. The coroner's competence wasn't the issue here. It was her own ability, hers and the agency's. And maybe Dahlia's. *A pattern is emerging here*, she thought. *If only I could decipher the design.*

Crouching down, she reached toward the dog. Maizy recoiled, growling softly.

"She was that way with us too," said Ormsbee. "Better leave her alone. You shouldn't touch anything anyway."

"I know."

Feeling worse than useless, Claire excused herself and headed down to the kitchen to call Lester. His machine picked up, and his recorded message was terse, to the point. "I'm not available. You know what to do." No name, no number, no conventional niceties. Just that rough, blustery voice with its typical edge of anger.

"Lester! Are you there? It's about your mother." Claire waited, then tried again. "Lester, please pick up. It's Claire. I need to talk to you. I'm at your mother's house."

She was talking to a vacuum. She pictured all the empty bottles she'd seen strewn around his cabin. He was probably sprawled somewhere, semicomatose with a blood alcohol that was through the roof. Even if he did pick up, he'd be in no shape to drive anywhere.

Deciding to try again later, she was on the verge of hanging up when she heard a click, then his voice. "Yeah? Claire? What's happening?" His voice was heavy and slurred, as if he was slogging his way through molasses.

Break it to him slowly. Remember his blood pressure. "Lester, I'm afraid I have some bad news. Some very bad news."

"So? Spit it out. It's four in the morning, for Christ's sake."

"I'm sorry to have to tell you this, but your mother passed away suddenly during the night. I'm at the house now."

Utter silence at the other end, then a muffled thump. She pictured his face flushing, his blood pressure rocketing skyward. "Lester? Are you all right?"

"Damn, my hand hurts like hell. I shouldn't have hit the table so hard. Yeah, I'm okay. I mean, hell, I'm as well as can be expected, considering the news you just dumped on me."

"Would you like me to come get you, drive you over here?"

"What's the point of that?"

"I thought you might want to see her."

"Thanks but no thanks. I'll see her soon enough at the funeral home." He paused. When he spoke again, it seemed to Claire that he was choking on his words. "Look, I'm not good at this shit, uh, I mean stuff. Do what you have to do. That's why you people are in there."

"Okay, Lester. We have everything under control. The coroner should be here any time now, and I'm going to call Dr. D'Attilio. I just wanted to tell you first."

"Thanks. But why is the coroner coming? Isn't the doctor enough?"

"The EMTs notified the police after they failed to revive your mother. Then the police called the coroner's office."

"Jeez, are they going to make a federal case out of this? She's just a poor old lady, for Christ's sake. Can't they let her rest in peace?"

Just then the doorbell rang in a cascade of incongruously cheerful chimes. A shrill salvo of warning barks sounded from upstairs, and Claire sighed in relief. Maizy was back on the job.

"Is that the dog?" asked Lester.

"Yes. I think the coroner's at the door. I'd better go."

"Wait a minute. What's going to happen to the damn dog?"

"I hadn't thought about it. I could bring her over to stay with you."

"Naw, Maizy and I don't get along that great. Could you take her over to your place? The bitch really likes you."

"I don't know, Lester. I already have a dog."

"It's that or the pound."

"Well, there may be other options if we –" But Lester had already hung up.

As she headed toward the front door to admit the coroner, Claire flashed on the fact that Lester Schatz hadn't asked so much as a single question about the cause of his mother's death. *Weird,* she thought, and shelved the information at the back of her mind for future consideration.

Herb Davidson looked every bit as confused and disgruntled as Lester Schatz had sounded, but the coroner's social façade was comparatively intact. "So, we meet again," he said, extending his hand. "Miss . . . sorry, I remember your face, but your name slips my mind."

"Claire Lindstrom. I'm the Nursing Supervisor with Compassionate Care."

"Yes, of course. You're the one who found that unfortunate Alzheimer's victim in the woods."

She nodded. Why couldn't his memory lapse have included Rose Dobson's death? "Unfortunately, yes," she began, but her words were drowned out by Maizy, who was barking frenetically as she scrambled down the stairs into the front foyer. Her hackles were up, her eyes bulging wildly as she confronted the stranger in the doorway.

Davidson took a step back. "You'd better do something about the dog," he snapped. His blue eyes were almost as bulgy as Maizy's. His hair was as prickly, too; he must have forgotten to comb it.

"Stay right there. I'll get a leash." Claire identified with the scrappy little terrier. Why did this pompous, pudgy old man have to intrude on the sanctity of Minna's deathbed scene? It wasn't as if he had the competence to shed any light on the cause of death. For that, they would need an autopsy. And this time there'll be one, she vowed as she stood rooted to the spot.

"Miss Lindstrom?" Davidson was glaring at her. "If you can't get that dog under control, I'll have to leave. It looks vicious, and the last thing I need tonight is a dog bite."

"Sorry." Claire hurried to the kitchen, where she found Maizy's leash hanging on its accustomed hook. The dog stood wild-eyed and trembling as she approached cautiously and snapped on the leash. She coaxed the dog through the back door and into the yard. Maizy squatted efficiently, taking care of business, then let Claire hook her by the collar to her outdoor chain. With her front paws, she made a few tentative digging motions, then circled three times and flopped down on the grass, looking utterly exhausted.

Claire stooped down to stroke her silky ears. "Are you all right, girl?" Maizy might seem ferocious to Davidson, but to Claire, she seemed unusually subdued, especially considering the fact that she'd recently been lying snuggled up against the body of her dead mistress. "You poor thing," Claire murmured. "You're probably suffering from post-traumatic stress. Don't worry, I'll take you to my house. Freia doesn't know yet, but we'll confront that hurdle when we come to it."

As Claire stumbled through the hours that followed, she was thankful Lester hadn't wanted to come over. The house was electric with tension, swarming with strangers, and it was easy to picture him blowing his stack. *Minna would have hated this,* she thought. *People rummaging through her room, snapping her picture. Talk about paranoia! Maybe she was right after all: maybe someone was out to get her.*

Neil Portman had shown up soon after Davidson arrived. The patrol sergeant quizzed the EMTs, conferred in hushed tones with Milgrim and Ormsbee, then with the coroner. As if by mutual consent, they excluded Claire from their deliberations.

As Davidson headed up the stairs to view the body, Claire started after him, but Milgrim thrust out an arm to block her. "You're not needed up there."

"There might be some medical questions I could help with," Claire protested.

The officer smirked. "If I were you, I wouldn't bother."

Five minutes later, Davidson was back down. Claire intercepted him as he was heading for the front door, about to make his escape. "I assume there'll be an autopsy," she said.

He made a harumphing sound. "What are the family's wishes in that respect?"

"I'm not sure. I talked to the son, Lester Schatz, but he was so shocked that he wasn't in shape to discuss any details. I'll talk with him again later today. I'll discuss the situation with Dr. D'Attilio as well."

"You do that." Davidson let loose a gigantic yawn, and Claire thought she caught a whiff of bourbon on his breath. Funny she hadn't noticed it earlier. Could he have been carrying a flask? "Now if it's all the same to you," he said, "I'm going home to bed."

She felt her adrenaline rise. It was never all the same, she wanted to scream. Every death is different. Every death deserves respect and attention. But what was the point? She couldn't make him care if he didn't already.

Dr. D'Attilio took his own sweet time returning the answering service's page, and he sounded half-asleep when he finally called. He was all too ready to pronounce the death over the phone, no questions asked. "Call me during office hours," he repeated at the end of each exchange. She might as well have been talking to a recording.

The police took photos, the funeral home people came for the body, and at long last Claire was alone with Dahlia in the kitchen. The aide slumped over the Formica table with her head cradled in her arms, sound asleep as Claire gazed out the window. How could she possibly sleep, now of all times? Claire decided it was probably a stress reaction. No need to wake her up.

To the east, at the very bottom of the black sky, faint bands of dusky rose hovered over the black silhouettes of the trees. She stared transfixed as the bands broadened into lurid crimson swaths. Red sky in the morning, sailors take warning. Did the red signify a storm on the way? She hoped so – anything to distract her from the storm clouds within.

An hour later the red was gone, swallowed by clouds of that deep, turgid gray that presaged a storm on the way. Gabriel swore softly as he wiped off his brush and plunged it into the can of paint thinner. He'd been trying to capture the sunrise over the lake, but the light was totally shot. He remembered reading how Monet did multiple versions of the same scene, kept several canvases going – haystacks, cathedrals, whatever – so he could switch from one to another when the light changed. But Gabriel wasn't that dedicated, and there was nothing he could imagine creating out of this murky gray. Too depressing.

He kept picturing Minna Schatz the way he'd found her, lying defenseless on the bed, her body in its threadbare nightgown, exposed in the blue light of the full moon. He'd thought of Picasso, but actually the image reminded him more of photos he'd seen of Nazi concentration camps. Minna had no way of knowing, but she'd been every bit as doomed as the victims of the Holocaust.

For some reason, maybe because Minna didn't seem all that ill, her death bothered him more than the others. He had followed orders: didn't speak, didn't move her body. Athena had been pissed about the last time, when he'd engineered that accident in the woods. Much too risky, too exposed. This wasn't like painting or jazz, she said. Creativity wasn't welcome, and improvisation was permitted only as a last resort. He had bought into the company line, but what did that make him? A good Nazi?

He was feeling far too wired to sleep, but he didn't want to take anything to dull the edge. Soon it would be time to check in with the powers that be. He would need all his wits about him, and God forbid he should fall asleep and not make the phone call at the appointed time.

The wind was picking up now, tossing the branches around, flinging red and yellow leaves through the air. Maybe he should start a composition that focused on the bare trees. They had interesting, contorted contours. He could try to capture the turbulence, make it kind of an homage to Van Gogh. He was reaching for a new canvas when a flash of viridian green caught his eye through the window. A car, creeping along the road that hugged the shoreline. Could it be? He hurried to the window, adjusted his telescope. Yes, it was Claire Lindstrom's Focus hatchback. She was probably just getting back from Minna Schatz's house.

He lost sight of the car as it pulled behind a stand of spruce, but he knew she would be pulling into her driveway momentarily. He refocused the telescope on her house, with its lawn leading down to the lake. Knowing Claire, since she'd been away for the past few hours, she would probably come out to walk her dog.

Sure enough, here was the dog now. It came bouncing out onto the lawn, a giant blond fur ball. It hunkered down to make a turd, then ran back toward the house. Now Claire came into view. She walked slowly, head down, her blond hair whipped by the wind. And at her side – no, it couldn't be, but it was – the little terrier bitch from Minna's house. Claire had it on a leash, and now her own dog was bounding up to them, bowing, inviting the terrier to play. The terrier wagged stiffly, nervously, and through the telescope, Gabriel could see its mouth open and close. The view was so good, he could almost hear the barks.

He felt a surge of relief. The dog had been so out of it earlier, he'd been afraid it might not survive. If the dog had died, he would definitely have had some serious decisions to make about his role in the organization.

How easy it would be to stroll along the lakeshore over to Claire's. He would love to sit down with her over some morning coffee, play with the dogs, get her talking about the horrific events of the night she'd just endured. Their views of the situation might not be all that different, he suspected. They'd already talked quite a bit, after all – enough for him to realize how much they had in common. They were both nurses, for starters, although they used their expertise in rather different ways.

But no, it was out of the question. Claire Lindstrom would be a powerful distraction, and he couldn't afford any distractions right now. He had too much work to do. Speaking of which, he'd better make that phone call now. Check in with Athena, see what she had in mind for him next.

Chapter 16

*S*tephen killed the radio as he eased the Taurus into Minna Schatz's driveway, parked and switched off the ignition.

Unnerved by the sudden silence, he sat a moment, trying to psych himself up to enter the house. There were no cars around, so most likely Dahlia was the only one left. They'd probably taken the body away hours ago. At least he hoped so.

This part of the job gave him the creeps. He liked schmoozing with the old people, working his charms on them to coax a smile or a laugh, but he didn't like thinking about how sick they were, and how they could actually die. Maria said he was in denial, but he'd been over this territory with Claire, and on the whole, she was okay with the way he related to the clients. Socialization was good for them, she'd said not long ago, and his presence had a normalizing, therapeutic effect. "I'd like to try some of my therapy on you," he'd replied. "I bet you'd feel better too." He'd gotten a gratifying blush out of her, but that was it.

Claire had called him an hour ago, woken him out of a hung-over sleep to tell him about Minna and ask him to take Dahlia to the Amtrak station. She'd told him to hurry; the aide was freaked out about Minna's death and anxious to get back to New York. He couldn't blame the poor woman. She'd had a run of abominable luck, with two old ladies croaking on her watch in barely a month. First Harriet Gardener, and now Minna Schatz. Weird.

His head felt like shit, and as he climbed out of the car, he barely stifled the impulse to barf. He glanced at his watch: eight twenty. He hadn't expected to be working so early, but hey, he shouldn't complain. At least he had a job, unlike Dahlia, who would probably have to go on unemployment until they found her another live-in.

He climbed the front steps to the barn-red door and rang the bell. No reply. He waited, staring down at the grungy pumpkins that flanked the door. Dahlia's concession to Halloween, he guessed. She hadn't bothered to carve them. He rang again. Still no answer. Something was wrong, it was too quiet, and suddenly he realized why: Maizy wasn't barking. Maybe someone had taken the dog and it was safe to let himself in. He tried the door. It opened easily, and he stepped inside.

"Dahlia? Are you there?"

No reply, but then he heard a faint sound coming from upstairs. A woman sobbing – it had to be Dahlia.

Damn! He hated dealing with weepy women, but he might as well get it over with. Resolutely, he crossed the foyer, headed up the stairs. He paused at the top. The crying was louder now, coming from down the hall. He padded in the direction of the sound to an open door, where he came to a screeching stop, aghast.

Dahlia was huddled on the floor in the middle of a round braided rug, with her knees pulled up and her arms wrapped around them. Her shoulders shook convulsively, in rhythm with her sobs. Her head was down, and he couldn't see her face. Across the room, under the window, was a makeshift altar. A red and blue cloth with an African-looking design in gold was draped over a carton. Three fat candles stood burning on top, giving off a pungent odor that reminded him of pot. Along both sides and over the window, a string of miniature Christmas lights blinked in a crazy, random rhythm. A ceramic rooster stood watch in the center, surrounded by small fabric bags tied in twine. Half-dead plants were draped over everything.

"Holy shit! Dahlia, what the fuck is all this stuff?"

Slowly, she extricated her head from her arms and scrunched around on the rug to face him, still sobbing. "Thank God you're here," she stammered at last. "Stephen, please take me away from this place!"

"Okay. But what's with the candles and everything?"

"Those are to ward off evil, and to cleanse the aura of the house."

He advanced cautiously into the room. "A little late for that, isn't it?"

She buried her face in her hands, sobbed harder.

"Sorry," Stephen said. "I didn't mean that the way it sounded." He stepped onto the bedraggled old rug, feeling as skittish as if he were crossing a stream on a string of unstable rocks. He crouched down and gave her shoulder a tentative pat. "What do you say we get out of here? If we hurry, you might make the 9:50 train."

"Bless you, Stephen." She struggled to her feet. "I'm almost ready to go. Just give me ten minutes."

He rose. "You got it. I'll wait for you downstairs. Just don't forget to blow out the candles." Turning to leave the room, he stopped short in shock. Tacked above the door was a bow of black ribbon, with something grotesque and twisted dangling beneath it. Jesus – it was the foot of a large bird.

———— ———

Claire was in her office, trying to maintain her tenuous grip on the day, when Stephen burst in, looking uncharacteristically flummoxed. "I've got to talk to you about something really weird," he said.

And I've got to talk to Paula and Allyson, she thought. And phone Lester about the autopsy. But the prospect of spending a few minutes with Stephen was more alluring than the items she had on her plate. "Come on in," she said.

"I don't think this is the right place," he said, rolling his eyes toward the door. Maria was standing there, hips akimbo, striking a seductive pose. "You guys want some coffee?"

Claire forced a smile. "No thanks, Maria. I've already got some. Now if you'll excuse us, Stephen and I need to discuss something."

Maria pouted prettily. "Very well. I just wanted to find out more about Minna Schatz. I helped set up that case, you know, with Dahlia and everything."

"I know you did," said Claire. "But this isn't a good time to discuss it."

"Whatever. I also wanted to tell you that Paula called to say she'll be in around eleven. And Allyson called in sick. Now I'll leave you guys alone together." Maria made her exit, closing the door with unnecessary vigor.

Stephen winced. "Like I was saying, this isn't a good place. How about we touch base at Tanya's after work?"

"Is it about Maria?" Claire mouthed the words in a whisper, gesturing at the door.

"No, it's about Dahlia."

"Dahlia? Did she make the train all right?"

"Yes, she's off, safe and sound on her way back to Brooklyn. And a good thing, too."

"How do you mean, Stephen? What's wrong?"

He tossed her an impudent smile. "Later, my little chickadee. At Tanya's."

"Wait a minute! I didn't say I'd go."

"Come on Claire, give yourself a break. You look exhausted, and the day's barely begun."

"I beg to differ. For me it began at three this morning."

"All the more reason you'll need to unwind."

She sighed. "All right. See you at Tanya's, a little after five."

As he left, Claire felt the wind go out of her sails. A little diversion would have been welcome. Now she had no choice but to begin dealing with the confusing aftermath of Minna's death. Should she call Paula at home? Her boss didn't know yet, and she wouldn't be happy. Claire decided to procrastinate and tell her in person.

But there was no excuse not to call Allyson Quigley. Sick or not, the nurse could damn well answer some questions. Claire had her finger over the phone, poised to punch in Allyson's speed-dial number, when suddenly it hit her: officially, Allyson had been the nurse on call last night. By rights, Dahlia should have paged Allyson instead of calling Claire. In the heat of the crisis, the aide could hardly be blamed for forgetting the proper pecking order, but Allyson probably wouldn't see it that way. Worse, she'd blame Claire for leaving her out of the loop. But the nurse's insecurities were the least of her concerns right now. She took a deep breath and punched the number.

The nurse was every bit as grouchy as Claire had expected. "You woke me up just when I'd finally gotten to sleep," she grumbled. "I've got some kind of intestinal virus. It hit me around midnight, and I was up all night with vomiting and diarrhea."

"I'm sorry to hear it, but I thought you ought to know: Minna Schatz died last night."

There was a sharp intake of breath at the other end. "I don't believe it! What was the cause of death?"

"I don't know. I'm hoping there'll be an autopsy. I understand you visited last night."

"Yes, I thought I'd better, seeing as how you were off at that conference."

Please, Allyson, spare me the attitude. "Was Minna feeling under the weather? Did you notice anything unusual?"

"No, nothing except her usual paranoia. You're right, it does seem to be getting worse." Allyson coughed. "Did, I mean. I still can't believe she's dead."

"Did you take her vital signs?"

"No, it didn't seem necessary, since we've been mostly concerned about her mental status. I didn't want to make her more suspicious."

Claire was surprised. It wasn't like Allyson to neglect the basics. Pulse, blood pressure, temperature – they were a routine part of the standard nursing visit. Better not push it, though – Allyson sounded defensive enough already.

"I decided to make it more like a social call," Allyson continued. "I even brought them a nice Halloween cake I baked myself."

"Really? I didn't see any cake when I was there. Not that I would have noticed, with everything that was going on." An idea struck Claire with a jolt. "Is there any cake left? If so, we should probably get it analyzed."

More silence, then an explosion. "Are you critiquing my cooking now? It's bad enough having you constantly on my case about my nursing skills."

"Calm down, Allyson. It's just a strange coincidence, with you getting sick the same night Minna dies. Did you use any ingredients that could have been contaminated, maybe in the frosting? Raw eggs, say, or mayonnaise?"

"Jesus, Claire, that sounds vile. Remind me not to try your cooking." There was a pause. "I do have some of the cake here at my house. I brought the leftovers back here."

"Hang onto it, just in case. Come to think of it, you should probably get checked out by a doctor too. I'm sure you've heard of those fast-acting, lethal viruses that crop up every so often."

"I'll keep that in mind, but it feels like the worst of this bug has already passed. Honestly, Claire, I think you're going overboard, grasping at straws. I'm sure they'll find some logical explanation for Minna's death, most likely some kind of cardiac event. Something that has nothing to do with my transitory tummy problems."

"You're probably right. By the way, Allyson, I know you were on call last night, and Dahlia should really have called you first, but –"

"No big deal. Most likely I was puking my guts out right around then anyway. Dahlia prefers dealing with you; I can live with that. You know, I'm realizing my symptoms are just about gone. I could probably come in later today if you need me."

"That's okay, Allyson. I'd rather you take the rest of the day off, just to be sure."

Claire let out a huge sigh of relief as she hung up the phone. Talking with Allyson was always like tiptoeing through a minefield. There were drawbacks to working in a small agency. She missed the collegial, bantering relationships she'd enjoyed with her fellow nurses back in the city. There, she'd always had someone to bounce her ideas off when she needed a second opinion or simply some good old-fashioned reassurance. She wished she knew another nurse she could vent to, someone who could understand her fears and frustrations. A peer, not an underling.

With a start, she realized she knew such a person – Rick Kozlowski. When she'd seen him at the Y the other day, he'd said several clients from his agency had died unexpectedly in recent months. There was something unnerving about him – for one thing, he was too damn inquisitive. But even if they weren't destined to become best buddies, perhaps he could come up with some useful insights.

First, though, she ought to call Lester Schatz to see if he'd consent to an autopsy. She sighed as she popped a Tum. Might as well get it over with. She punched in his number before she had a chance to chicken out.

He was even more vehemently opposed than she'd feared. "Are you kidding? You want my permission for them to carve up my mother? What kind of monster do you think I am? Fuck no, she's suffered enough. Let her rest in peace."

"But Lester, her death was so totally unexpected. Aren't you curious to know the cause?"

"Why are you butting in about things that are none of your business? The coroner already called me this morning, and I told him the exact same thing I'm telling you. No autopsy."

"Herb Davidson called you?"

"That was the guy's name, yeah."

"And he went along with your wishes?"

"Yeah. And unlike you, he had the courtesy to mention that I'd have to foot the bill if there was an autopsy. And it's not cheap. Anyway, she was seventy-eight years old, for Christ's sake. The Good Lord decided to call her home."

Claire had never heard him invoke the almighty before. His tone had a phony ring to it, but who was she to say? This was hardly the moment to confront him about the depths of his religious convictions. She took another tack. "Lester, an autopsy could be important in terms of shedding light on your own health, and the risk factors you might face as you get older."

"Who gives a shit? The doctor's already read me the riot act. I smoke, I drink, I'm overweight, I have high blood pressure. I don't expect to make it to anywhere near my mother's age, and when my time comes, I hope it's quick and painless, the way my mother went."

"But we don't know the way she went. That's exactly why an autopsy would –"

"Will you get off my case? I don't know how I can make it any clearer: no god- damn autopsy." There was a click, and the phone went dead.

Claire cradled her head in her hands. Now what? Without an autopsy, she'd never know why Minna Schatz had died. Maybe Lester could live with that, but Claire couldn't. Minna's death was one too many. Something was very wrong.

Logically, her next step should be to call Herb Davidson, but she wasn't up for that quite yet. Maybe she'd call Rick Kozlowski first, get some moral support. He'd given her a business card the night they'd first met at Tanya's, and it was probably still in her handbag. Paula wouldn't be crazy about her touching base with a nurse from a rival agency, but her boss wouldn't be in for another hour.

Claire rummaged around in her bag, found a business card wedged down deep next to a pocket pack of tissues. Patrick Delafield. She really ought to call him. She'd rather talk to Justin Greylock, his crony at Oaktree Associates, but a lawyer would be more relevant than someone in sales. Maybe later.

She resumed her fishing expedition. Ah, here it was: Rick Kozlowski, RN, BSN, at Tri-County Home Care. No title beneath his name, but with a bachelor's in nursing, he had the right background. Better than most.

The woman who picked up at Tri-County sounded so chipper, Claire could picture her sitting there with flipped up hair, grinning like Doris Day. But that changed when Claire asked for Rick. There was a long pause. "Rick Kozlowski?" the woman asked finally. "He hasn't worked here for over a year. May I connect you to the nursing supervisor?"

"No thanks, that won't be necessary."

Judging by the abrupt chill in the woman's voice, Rick's departure hadn't been a happy one.

Chapter 17

*C*laire took two gulps of tepid coffee, winced as the acid attacked her stomach. The Tums weren't cutting it any more. At the rate her stress was escalating, she'd have to switch to stronger medicine.

So what was up with this Rick Kozlowski, anyway? The other day at the Y, he'd seemed so knowledgeable about all the goings on at Tri-County, so eager to dish the dirt about both their agencies, and now it turned out he'd left the agency over a year ago. But then why was he so preoccupied with home care?

The way he'd quizzed Claire about the case load at Compassionate Care, it had occurred to her that he might be some kind of corporate spy, out to steal some of their clients. Now she wondered if he'd been putting out feelers to see if they had any nursing jobs available. But then why hadn't he come right out and asked? Probably because he knew even the most cursory reference check would turn up a glaring hole in his resume.

And what about the unexpected deaths he'd mentioned at Tri-County? Was he talking fact or fiction? He'd suggested possible patterns, correlations, but how would he know about the deaths if he was no longer working there? He could still have an inside source. On the other hand, he could have invented the whole thing. He seemed unusually preoccupied with death. Even fascinated.

Maybe she could ask Herb Davidson whether there had been an upsurge in deaths at Tri-County. He'd probably blow her off, but it couldn't hurt to try. She needed to discuss Minna's autopsy anyway. Now was as good a time as any to confront the coroner.

As Davidson's wife summoned him to the phone, Claire took a deep breath, exhaled slowly. *Honey, not vinegar. Keep it cool. Don't alienate him.*

But judging by the gruff edge in his voice, he was already alienated. "I got off the phone with Lester Schatz less than an hour ago," Davidson said. "The man was vehement. He doesn't want an autopsy."

"Vehement's putting it mildly," Claire said. "He swore and hung up on me when I tried to get him to change his mind."

Davidson made a choking sound. "You called him? Why? You had no business getting involved."

"Well, when I talked to you at Minna's house, it sounded as if you were going to go along with the family's wishes. And knowing Lester, I thought he would probably refuse, so I –"

"As next of kin, he has every right to refuse."

"Can't you override his decision, in view of the circumstances?"

There was a long pause. "What circumstances are you talking about?"

"The fact that there was no obvious cause of death."

"The woman was almost eighty years old, for Christ's sake. She was receiving round-the-clock care. Any number of conditions could have caused her death."

"But we don't know which. She was making a good recovery from a hip fracture. She was becoming increasingly paranoid, but there weren't any other problematic medical conditions that I'm aware of."

Davidson chuckled. "That you're aware of. Ah, there's the rub. Perhaps your agency overlooked some preexisting medical condition. As nursing supervisor, you could be held accountable for the oversight, isn't that right?"

An ominous pulse began throbbing in her temples. "I suppose so, especially since I did the initial nursing assessment. But that's all the more reason I'd want to know if there's something I overlooked."

"Take my advice, Ms. Lindstrom. Leave it alone. I don't think your boss would appreciate your stirring up controversy about your agency's quality of care. And think of the tremendous drain on public resources if we autopsied every old person who died peacefully at home."

"But Lester said you told him he'd have to pay for it."

"My conversation with Lester Schatz is privileged information." Davidson was practically shouting now. Claire yanked the receiver away from her ear. "Minna Schatz was under a doctor's care," he continued. "She saw Mike D'Attilio ten days ago. Her orthopedic surgeon too. I saw nothing suspicious at the scene, and I'm ruling this a death from natural causes."

At least he's done his homework, Claire thought. Maybe I underestimated the man. "I see your point," she said. "One more question. Have you by any chance noticed an increase in unexplained deaths at any of the other local home care agencies?"

Silence at the other end. "What's this, a conspiracy theory?" he said at last. Talk about paranoia. "Off the record, I can assure you there's no such trend. Officially, on the record, information like that is confidential, and I'd be out of line if I told you a goddamn thing."

The phone went dead. Herb Davidson had left Claire with her stomach in knots, and far more questions than answers. Her eyes fell on the ecru linen business card she'd extracted from her handbag when she'd been looking for Rick Kozlowski's. Patrick Delafield, Attorney, Oaktree Associates. Maybe he could give her some perspective, even some suggestions for getting around Lester Schatz's refusal and Herb Davidson's stonewalling.

Delafield picked up on the second ring. No secretary, she noted. This must be his direct line.

"Patrick, this is Claire Lindstrom. Remember, we met at the Alzheimer's conference last week?"

"Claire! Yes, of course I remember you. I've been meaning to call, but things have been hectic."

His voice had a warm lilt to it, and suddenly she pictured his face. The green eyes, the crooked smile – the memory had almost faded from her mind's eye, but now it was back with a rush. And miracle of miracles, he actually sounded happy to hear from her, which was a definite improvement over the other people she'd phoned so far. "I've got a couple of questions, if you have a minute," she said.

"Why not? My next client isn't due for half an hour. How can I help you?"

"This is strictly confidential. I normally don't discuss our clients with anyone outside the agency, but I'm at my wit's end. A woman died unexpectedly last night." Omitting the names, she proceeded to give him the bare-bones version of Minna's death and her calls to Lester Schatz and Herb Davidson.

"If the family refuses to consent to the autopsy, and the coroner already declared it a death from natural causes, there's really not a lot you can do," Patrick said once she'd wound down at last. "You'd have to jump through all kinds of legal loopholes to override the decision, and there'd have to be a damn good reason."

"But I don't think the coroner knows what he's talking about. Herb Davidson's not an MD, let alone a medical examiner, and he's pretty squeamish when it comes to confronting the details of an actual death. I clocked him when he went up to the dead woman's room last night, and he spent less than five minutes there. He's a retired insurance executive, and he's okay at making nice with people, maybe pushing papers around. But I get the feeling this job is more than he bargained for."

Patrick laughed. "I've heard about him. It's peculiar that some counties still have that archaic system of electing coroners the way you'd elect someone to the school board or the town council. They should all be qualified physicians, in my opinion. But maybe there just aren't enough of them to go around. So Davidson didn't go for the idea of an autopsy, huh?"

"That's putting it mildly."

"And why do you think there should be an autopsy? Do you suspect foul play?"

Do I? Maybe Davidson is right; maybe I'm just conjuring up conspiracy theories. "I don't know, but this is the third unexpected death we've had in the last few weeks, so I'm getting concerned. The police wouldn't let me examine her at close range, and the light wasn't good." Suddenly the image came flooding back, bright as the cold full moon. "I saw some marks where they'd done CPR, and an area of discoloration on her neck, a slight bruising. It barely registered at the time, but it occurs to me - maybe it was an injection site."

"What would someone inject her with? And why?"

"I have no idea. If someone wanted her dead -"

Just then the door flew open to reveal Paula Rhodes. Her face was flushed, and her hands were shaking. "Claire, Maria just told me about Minna Schatz! Why didn't you call and tell me sooner?"

"Patrick, I've got to go," Claire murmured into the phone. "Thanks for the advice." She placed the receiver in its cradle, swiveled to face Paula. "I'm sorry, but I didn't see any point in disturbing you at home. There wasn't anything you could have done, and I knew you were coming in soon."

A tic surfaced at the corner of Paula's eye, and her mouth twitched as she struggled for composure. "Is that by any chance the Patrick we met at the conference?"

"Yes, as a matter of fact."

"How nice for you that you have time to cultivate your social life in the face of everything that's going on."

"I'm not cultivating my social life. This was strictly business. I wanted his opinion on whether we could override Lester's opposition to an autopsy on his mother."

"Claire, are you out of your mind, blabbing about a client's death to someone outside the agency? What are you trying to do, torpedo our reputation? It's halfway down the tubes already, or it will be if word of this latest death gets out."

"You're exaggerating, Paula. But Minna's death is so unexpected. It came totally out of the blue, like Harriet Gardener's. For my own peace of mind, I want to get to the bottom of it. Maybe there's something I overlooked, or –"

"Damn it, Claire, don't go pulling that *mea culpa* shit! That's the last thing we need right now. Save it for the next Quality Assurance Committee meeting. There's one coming up soon, isn't there?"

"Not till the first Thursday in December. Maybe we should convene it sooner. I could call Dr. D'Attilio and see if he has time this week or next. We should take another look at these recent incidents. Harriet Gardener, Rose Dobson, Minna Schatz – I'm not comfortable with all these deaths happening on my watch."

"And I'm not comfortable with the way our caseload is plummeting. Mike D'Attilio and the other doctors in his practice are our best referral source, and he schmoozes with the discharge planners at all the hospitals. Make a big deal out of a couple of unfortunate incidents, plant the suggestion in his mind that we're somehow at fault, and we can kiss all those referrals goodbye."

Claire felt a surge of anger. "Is that all you care about? Our image? Maybe we shouldn't be accepting new referrals anyway. Not until we get to the bottom of this."

"Claire, are you crazy? Without new cases, I might as well cut my losses and quit. Refer our clients to another agency. Hell, I could send the staff along with them for good measure, maybe negotiate some kind of finder's fee. Or sell the agency outright." Paula's face came alight with a mischievous Cheshire smile.

"You're not serious, are you, Paula?"

The smile reverted to a grimace. "Damned if I know. But I do know one thing. If my nursing supervisor is afraid to open new cases, she's the wrong one for the job. But luckily Allyson Quigley is waiting in the wings. I'm sure she'd be delighted to have her old position back."

That afternoon, staring down at the murky watercourse outside the office, Claire reflected that maybe Paula was right. *Maybe I'm the wrong one for the job. Let Allyson have it; she's welcome to it.*

She walked alongside the building, scuffling dead leaves out of her way. The office had been making her claustrophobic, but this break wasn't helping. She glanced at her watch: three fifteen. Just under twelve hours since Minna's official time of death, but it felt like an eternity. And just two hours till she met Stephen at Tanya's. She could barely wait for that drink.

Death from natural causes: the words kept ringing through her mind. A Teflon phrase, glossy and reassuring, with a slick, non-stick surface that repels all questions. All at once Angelo Giordano's face flashed before her mind's eye. What was it he'd said the night she had told him there would be no autopsy on

Harriet Gardener? *People don't just up and die of old age. There's always a reason.*

Angelo was right: no death should be brushed aside as insignificant, no matter the person's age. Call me paranoid, she thought, but something's off-kilter and I'm going to find out what it is, with or without my job. I owe it to Minna, and to Harriet and Rose.

———————

That evening at Tanya's, smiling across the table into Claire's eyes, Stephen decided she was as stressed out as he'd ever seen her. He'd ordered a big basket of Buffalo wings in honor of the happy hour get-together he'd engineered with her, but Claire was having none of it.

"Come on, these wings are good for what ails you," he said. "The spices are better than Claritin for clearing the cobwebs out of your head."

She forced a smile. "I don't need my head cleared, Stephen. If anything, I need the opposite. Tonight, a little consciousness blurring would suit me just fine."

"Then let me buy you another Pinot Grigio."

"I think I'll switch to red – it's better for my heart. Maybe some Merlot."

"You got it." He signaled the waitress, ordered another round.

With any luck, tonight could be the night. There was something lost and vulnerable about her, and she'd made it plain she wanted company. But so far all she'd wanted to do was talk about Minna and Lester Schatz, how she must have missed something, how guilty she felt about blowing off Minna's paranoid ramblings. Stephen had let her rant.

"So what did you want to tell me about Dahlia?" she asked when the fresh drinks had arrived. The house Merlot for her, Sam

Adams dark for him. "This morning it sounded super-urgent, but you haven't said a word."

"I wanted to give you a chance to unwind first. This could be kind of upsetting."

He laid out the scene – the altar, the candles, the Christmas lights, Dahlia sobbing on the floor. "And there was some kind of bird's foot over the door, hanging from a black ribbon bow. It looked like some kind of voodoo shit, maybe black magic. I mentioned it to Maria today. Because of her being Latino and all, I thought she might know something about it. She got all uptight about me thinking in stereotypes, but once she calmed down, she said it sounded like stuff they use in Santeria."

"But that's Puerto Rican, right? Dahlia is Jamaican."

"It's still the Caribbean; they're probably related. She said most likely it was a chicken foot. They use it to cast spells, or to hang over doors for protection."

"Maybe Dahlia was just protecting her own space, or trying to summon strength for herself. She had an awfully hard time putting up with Minna and Lester, their nastiness and paranoia." Claire's eyes brimmed with sudden tears. "I should never have let her stay there. I was dubious from the beginning, but Dahlia really wanted the job, and I knew she needed the money for her kids in Jamaica."

Stephen reached across the table, patted her hand. "Don't lay another guilt trip on yourself, Claire. Dahlia's an adult; it was up to her to decide whether she could handle it. But maybe she finally flipped out and decided to try a little black magic. Maybe it worked better than she thought, or maybe she put something weird in the food –"

Claire jerked back, away from his outstretched hand. "Stephen, stop! I can't stand to listen to any more of this crap! Dahlia's very possibly the most gentle, caring soul I've ever known." Her blue eyes darkened. "But I admit it bothers me that she told me two nights in a row not to visit Minna. Almost as if she was concealing something."

"See, what did I tell you? You've got to check her out, before –" Stephen stopped abruptly at the sight of the guy looming over their table. Damn, it was Rick Kozlowski.

"Check who out?" Rick asked with a cocksure grin. "Sorry if I'm interrupting anything."

"Yeah, you look real sorry," Stephen said. *Shit! Just when Claire has her guard down and I'm in a position to score, this creep has to show up and ruin everything.*

Claire set down her glass so abruptly, the wine sloshed onto her place mat, creating a bloody stain that defaced the ad for Al's Auto Repair. She glared up at the man. "Well, if it isn't the elusive Rick Kozlowski. What a coincidence. I tried phoning you at Tri-County Home Care this morning, and they told me you hadn't worked there in over a year."

"I can explain." Without waiting for an invitation, the intruder yanked over a chair from the adjoining table and sat down.

Claire's eyes took on a predatory sparkle. "This had better be good," she said.

Chapter 18

*I*n the dim light of the bar, Rick Kozlowski's dark brown eyes looked to Claire like the muddy loam in her garden after a week of rain. Folding her arms, she fixed him with a confrontational stare. "Well, I'm waiting. Why did you lie to me about working at Tri-County?"

His eyes darted away, then refocused on hers. "It wasn't a lie, exactly. I worked there for over a year."

"Then why not come right out and say you weren't there any more?"

He had the good grace to look sheepish. "I guess I just wanted to impress you."

Stephen's grin had all the sociability of a shark. "Guess you can forget about that. Looks like you've blown it, Kozlowski."

Rick turned toward Claire, pointedly ignoring Stephen. "I can explain. I was embarrassed – my unemployed status isn't exactly something to brag about."

"So you've been unemployed for a year?" She studied him with unabashed curiosity. He was personable, attractive, and given the region's chronic shortage of nurses, he could have waltzed into a new job in a day or two max, unless his closet was harboring some truly horrendous skeletons.

"I was getting unemployment insurance until four months ago." His voice had a defensive edge. "See, I was badly burned out. I needed to step back and get away from nursing for awhile. In fact, the longer I'm away from the field, the more I wonder if I even want to get back to it. I'm just not good with end-of-life issues. I saw too many people die on my watch at Tri-County, and it got to the point where I couldn't hack it anymore."

Claire's breath caught in her throat. If she was going to learn more about his peculiar conspiracy theories, now was the time. "I understand how you feel," she said. "As nurses, we're trained to cope with whatever comes our way, but sometimes it gets overwhelming. Especially when people die with no rhyme or reason. We had a situation like that last night at Compassionate Care."

Rick edged his chair closer to hers, and she caught a whiff of lemony cologne. "Maybe it would help to talk about it," he said.

"Strangely enough, that's why I tried calling you at Tri-County this morning. As nursing supervisor, I pretty much have to keep my feelings to myself. I miss having other nurses to network with."

"Well, now you have me."

Stephen shoved back his chair abruptly. "This is my cue to split. Today was a bummer, and I'm in no mood for more talk about death. I'm going to find myself some company that's a little more upbeat. Claire, just remember what you're always telling me, about keeping stuff confidential. You don't know this guy from Adam, and he already conned you about his nonexistent job."

Rick clenched his jaw, and his whole body went tense. Claire was acutely aware of the corded muscles in his neck and forearms. He glared at Stephen, then turned to Claire. "Speaking of con artists, I could tell you a thing or two about this guy."

Stephen rose. "Go ahead, gossip all you want. I've got nothing to hide." He headed for the bar, where two women of dubious drinking age were casting welcoming glances his way.

"So, Rick," Claire said once Stephen was out of earshot. "What's the deal with you and Stephen McClellan? Obviously there's no love lost between the two of you."

"We go back a way. I'd just as soon not talk about it."

"I'd like to know. Especially if it's anything that might impinge on his work at Compassionate Care."

"No, it's nothing like that." He looked around. "Where's the waitress? I could go for some beer. Oh, hell, you might as well know. I'm gay, in case you haven't already guessed."

"Somehow I'm not surprised." Claire smiled, let her eyes linger on his well-toned body, the long lines of his thighs in his faded jeans. She thought back to the way he had looked at the Y. All those tattoos, hidden tonight beneath another flannel shirt. Now that he was officially out of reach, he seemed suddenly less threatening.

"It's ancient history now," Rick said, "but I came on to Stephen once. Who wouldn't? He's absolutely gorgeous. But it totally freaked him out. He's homophobic in the extreme."

"So that's all it is between you?"

"That's it. So, girlfriend, now that you know my back story, are you ready to dish some dirt?"

In the hours that followed, Claire did her best to draw him out. She didn't quite trust him, so she was stingy with her revelations. Unfortunately, so was Rick. But he was an empathic listener, a witty conversationalist, and there was something about the warm, liquid pools of his eyes that drew her in.

Her gaze kept drifting to the tattoo on his muscular forearm, the way it snaked beneath the flannel sleeve, and she couldn't help remembering the way he'd displayed his body so brazenly at the Y. "Mind if I see your tattoo?" Surprised at herself, she instantly regretted the question, but he obediently pushed up his sleeve like a patient prepping for a blood test. Against the pallid skin of his inner elbow, the curving lines of the design looked almost black.

"A mermaid, just as I remembered." Looking more closely, she could see its crudity compared to the tattoos she'd seen at the Y. And it was monochromatic, the lines all carved in a deep ballpoint blue. She'd seen tattoos like this before, when she worked in ERs in the city. They were the kind men made in prison.

Feeling a sudden chill, she glanced at her watch. "Eleven thirty! I'd better go." She'd learned next to nothing, but that wasn't likely to change. Not tonight, after all the wine she'd been drinking. Suddenly claustrophobic, she rummaged in her purse, slapped a ten-dollar bill on the table and rose, eager to escape the beer-soaked, testosterone-laden atmosphere of the bar and breathe in some cold night air.

She was in no mood to confront the office, Claire realized when she awoke the next morning. Her mouth tasted like recycled cardboard and her head was pounding, but the hangover wasn't insurmountable. No, it was the thought of Paula Rhodes that triggered thoughts of evasive action. Paula and her lust for new cases, her preoccupation with image and spin control. So what if a few clients died unexpectedly? As long as there were more in the pipeline, who cared about quality assurance? To Paula, the concept of risk management had little to do with providing an adequate level of care, and everything to do with the bottom line. Kowtowing to their precious referral sources, like the almighty Dr. Michael D'Attilio.

At the thought of D'Attilio, Claire's heart did a skip and jump. What if she were to play hooky and pay him an unscheduled visit to talk about the recent deaths? She'd met the good doctor a few times, at the Quality Assurance Committee meetings and doing intakes on the patients he referred at the local hospitals. But he was always in a rush, always glancing at his Rolex with a vaguely abstracted air that conveyed his message loud and clear: he was far too important, with far too much on his mind, to waste time hobnobbing with a mere nurse. She'd met plenty of doctors with that attitude, and she had even less respect for them than they had for her, but she was generally careful not to show it.

She'd never get anything out of him if she waited for the next QA meeting, but maybe she'd learn something if she bearded him unexpectedly in his office. Paula would have a fit if she knew, but right now Paula seemed more like part of the problem than part of the solution. Yesterday she'd actually had the gall to tell Claire her job was in danger. Her boss was probably bluffing when she talked about giving Allyson Quigley her old job back – she'd complained over and over about the woman's abysmal managerial skills. But Paula's threats to close or sell the agency were all too plausible. In her position, Claire might very well have felt the same.

If the agency was about to go down the tubes, taking her job with it, Claire might as well be proactive. Stripped of her current title, she wouldn't have a chance of getting through to D'Attilio. Today she might.

She dragged herself to the kitchen, where she tossed down two aspirins in a glass of V-8. Two tumblers of tap water, a long hot shower, and she felt almost human again.

The digital clock on her dashboard read 8:11 as Claire pulled into the lot at the medical practice. She gave herself a mental pat on the back. Especially considering the hangover, she'd gotten out of the house in record time, hoping to intercept the doctor before his daily routine kicked in. There were just a few cars, one of them a black BMW sedan with MD plates. D'Attilio's car? The aristocratic, Germanic vibes gave her a feeling it was, but there were several doctors in the group. Well, she'd see soon enough.

She caught the receptionist off-guard, emerging from the back hallway clutching a ceramic coffee mug. A twenty-something woman with an angular brown bob, she glared at Claire with undisguised annoyance. "You don't have an appointment? Then there's no way you can see the doctor. He's already fully booked."

"I'm not a patient. It's professional business, it'll only take a few minutes."

"We only see drug reps on Thursday mornings, and even then, you need an appointment."

Claire laughed. "I'm not a drug rep. My name is Claire Lindstrom. Nursing supervisor with Compassionate Care." She could understand the woman's mistake. Claire had dressed for maximum impact, in a fitted red suit with a kick-pleated skirt that just grazed her knees. Higher than usual pumps, and she'd even blow-dried and artfully tousled her hair. Never let it be said she couldn't relate to doctors.

"Why, Claire, what a pleasant surprise. What brings you here so bright and early?"

Startled, Claire spun around and found herself facing the object of her fishing excursion. "Dr. D'Attilio! I'm so glad I caught you in. Forgive me for not calling ahead, but do you have a few minutes to talk?"

He studied her a moment. His eyes did a vertical sweep, top to bottom, then slowly back up to her face. "Sure, why not?"

Her instincts had been right on. The red suit was perfect.

Your best's just not good enough, she was thinking a half-hour later. She had gotten nowhere with the doctor, never managed to break through his proclivity for platitudes and generalities. She'd shared her misgivings about the deaths of the three women, but he brushed her off. Normal process of aging, inevitable deterioration of the organ systems, allotted life span – he meandered through a virtual forest of clichés and double-talk. It all boiled down to the same thing: sometimes nobody knew why old people died, and it wasn't worthwhile finding out, especially when it meant such pain and aggravation for the families. Not to mention the expense.

"I'll put the three cases on the agenda for next month's QA meeting," Claire said at last. "The Health Department's regulations specify that we examine any unusual incidents, and the deaths of Harriet Gardener, Rose Dobson and Minna Schatz certainly qualify. If we try to gloss over them, there could be hell to pay at survey time."

A look of alarm flitted across his round face, and his mouth twitched in disgust. "Those damn regulators! If they had their way, they'd drive all of us out of business. It's hardly worth practicing medicine anymore, what with the skyrocketing malpractice rates, the lousy insurance reimbursements and all the other hoops they make us jump through. Sometimes I think I should take early retirement, just cash it in and move to Costa Rica or Mexico."

Claire thought of Paula's diatribe yesterday, and decided she didn't want to hear any more. At this rate, soon there'd be no one left to work for. She smoothed her skirt, which had crept halfway up her thighs. "Don't give up, Dr. D'Attilio. You're providing a much needed service. At least that's what people are always saying to us at Compassionate Care."

He forced a smile. "Thanks. And please, call me Mike."

"Okay. One favor, Mike. Paula Rhodes didn't know I was coming here. I'd appreciate it if you don't mention our little visit. She has more than enough to worry about already."

"No problem. I can understand your needing to touch base with another professional. The bean counters just don't understand." He took off his glasses, extracted a handkerchief and polished them, fixing her with a myopic brown stare. "Perhaps we could get together for lunch sometime. Talk this over some more."

Talk what over? I thought your mind was already made up, she thought, then reminded herself not to burn any bridges. "I'd like that," she said. "I'll have to check my schedule."

"I'll look forward to it. So are you still accepting referrals, despite these unfortunate recent events?"

"Oh, of course. And we've got some wonderful aides who can use the work." *Now why did I go and say that? What happened to all my convictions about quality of care? Maybe I'm just a sales rep after all.*

"Good, because I think you've got a fine agency. And I've got a couple of patients in St. Francis Hospital who are going to be discharged in the next few days. They'll both need round-the-clock live-in care."

Late that afternoon, Gabriel felt his heart swell in his chest as he sighted the flash of green along the lakeside road. It was Claire's Focus, he was sure of it – that viridian shade was unusual; Ford wasn't making it anymore. Too classy for the hoi polloi, and it probably hadn't sold well enough, but it suited Claire.

He'd researched the color – Gofer Green was the official name, and some people would call it emerald, but as a painter, he knew it as viridian. He liked the sound of the word. It was the clear, deep green of spruce trees. Hunter's green, they called it sometimes, and that suited him too – after all, he was a hunter of sorts.

The car disappeared behind the trees, and he refocused the telescope on the house and lawn. Tonight he'd have a jazzy new toy to play with: yesterday he'd sprung for a night-vision scope that would enable him to watch Claire after sunset and whenever he damn well pleased. He'd tried it out last night, and it gave her and the dogs a ghostly green tinge, but hey, it was better than losing sight of her for long stretches of time.

His cell phone trilled suddenly, startling him. His hand jerked, and the lens swung sideways on its tripod. Damn! It must be the agency; no one else had the number.

"Gabriel, this is Athena. There's been a new development you should know about."

"Yeah? What is it?"

"The nurse with Compassionate Care, Claire Lindstrom, has been nosing around asking questions, especially about your most recent assignment. She suspects something out of the ordinary."

Gabriel forced a laugh. "I can't imagine why. Who's she been talking to?"

"That doesn't concern you, Gabriel, except insofar as we may need you to take some action."

His heart lurched. "What kind of action?"

"Stage an accident. The sooner the better."

Gabriel gulped down air, stalled for time. "Not a good idea," he said with all the cool he could muster. "It would be too obvious. She can't have proof of anything. Or does she? Are you holding out on me, Athena?"

Silence at the other end. Good, he had her on the defensive – Athena or whatever her real name was. He wished he knew her true identity, could talk with her face to face. That way he'd have more control.

"No, I'm not withholding any information, Gabriel," she said at last. "There have been no autopsies, and the two previous bodies are already cremated. The police aren't pursuing any leads, and aside from Claire Lindstrom, nobody has suggested anything out of the ordinary."

"Well, then doing away with her would raise a red flag for sure."

"You have a point. But perhaps you're getting too emotionally involved. You may not be seeing things clearly."

"On the contrary, Athena. I pride myself on my clarity of vision." He smiled at the irony as he adjusted the telescope with his free hand. Claire was just coming into view, onto the lawn with the dogs, the little one still on a leash. Later than yesterday, and the light had almost faded from the sky. She had turned on the spotlights above the deck, and they cut conical swaths across the lawn, throwing her and the animals into high relief, like prisoners in a courtyard. Even without the night-vision scope, she was far too visible against the encroaching blackness of the night. He wished there were some way to warn her, but that was absurd. After all, he was the enemy.

She was running a terrible risk by questioning the deaths, sharing her suspicions with all and sundry. She struck him as strong-willed and outspoken, and she probably didn't have the foggiest notion that her curiosity was putting her in danger.

Athena's throaty voice cut his thoughts short. "Gabriel? You live right near Claire Lindstrom, don't you."

"Yes." He hadn't given them this address, but he wasn't surprised they knew.

"Keep an eye on her and give me a call if you notice anything out of the ordinary. Any company she has, or any unusual comings and goings."

"It'll be my pleasure."

"Not to belabor the point, but are you positive you're not developing any kind of emotional or sexual attachment? She's an attractive woman."

He manufactured another laugh. "You've got to be kidding! You put me through a lengthy interview and ran that exhaustive psychological profile on me. You know getting emotionally involved isn't my style; that's one reason you hired me."

"Yes, but the testing isn't infallible. And people with the kind of clinical detachment we look for sometimes have the smarts to outwit even the most sophisticated protocols."

"Well, I don't. I'm just a lowly RN, remember? My psychological savvy is limited."

"That's not the way we see it. True, your experience may not be as extensive as some of our people's, but you have a lot of potential. We placed you in one of our smaller markets as a trial run, with Compassionate Care and those other agencies, but if things work out, we have every expectation you can move on to bigger and better things."

"Where did you have in mind?"

"New York, maybe, or Los Angeles. When it comes to eldercide, the sky's the limit. But you have to follow procedures. So far as Claire Lindstrom is concerned, it's okay just to keep an eye on her for now. But be prepared. You may have to take more aggressive action any day now."

Chapter 19

"Good morning, Paula. I've got a surprise for you!"
Paula Rhodes glanced up from her desk to see Allyson Quigley standing in the doorway, holding a paper plate with an enormous slab of chocolate cake. "Oh, no, Allyson! Don't tell me you're trying to sabotage my diet again!"

The nurse smirked. "I'm so proud of this recipe, I just had to share it."

"You mean you're still baking from scratch? I thought maybe you'd given it up – you haven't brought anything in for ages."

"Oh, I could never give up baking. It's one of my favorite hobbies. I've just stopped bringing my creations in here because Claire always gets on my case about it, and I know you're trying to stick to your diet. How's that going, by the way?"

Paula groaned aloud, hoping the sound would drown out the rumbling of her stomach. God, that cake looked good. "It could be better. I've been stuck at a plateau for awhile."

Allyson laughed and patted her ample stomach. "I can relate. I've been stuck at a plateau for, oh, something like five years."

What had gotten into the woman? Allyson hadn't been this cheerful in ages. "Oh, what the hell," Paula said. "I'll try a piece. But only if you have some too. We deserve to celebrate. We've got four new live-in referrals."

Allyson's eyes widened. "Paula, that's fantastic! But will we be able to staff them?"

"We'd damn well better – we need the business. I want to sit down with you and Claire and go over our roster of aides as soon as she gets in. But first, let's you and me have some cake."

"Okay. I'll just scoot over to the lunchroom and cut us a couple of pieces. Be right back."

"Better hurry, Allyson. We don't want Claire to catch us in flagrante delicto - or delicioso, rather. She'd have a hissy fit."

Allyson shot her a complicit grin, then disappeared down the hall as Paula silently berated herself. Why had she made that catty remark? She knew better than to pit her two best nurses against each other; the tension between Allyson and Claire was sky-high already. But she had to admit it: she was mightily bugged with Claire's pie-in-the-sky idealism, the way she harped on everything that went wrong, her complete and utter disregard for the bottom line. True, Paula had gone overboard the other day, threatening to fire Claire and give Allyson her old job back. She'd blurted it out in the heat of their argument, in the aftermath of Minna Schatz's death, but maybe it wasn't such a bad idea at that. At the very least she needed to come up with some way to get Claire to back off, rein her in before she did irreparable harm to the business.

"Ta da! I'm back!" Allyson padded across the carpet to the coffee table, where she deposited two plates of cake. "Should we sit on the sofa?"

"Yes, that would be fine." Paula settled herself, then took a bite. "Mmm, Allyson, this cake is to die for."

"Thanks. The recipe's called Death by Chocolate." Allyson's face reddened. "Sorry. I guess under the circumstances, that isn't the best name for it."

"That's okay. I've seen all kinds of things called Death by Chocolate. Yogurt, ice cream, even low-carb diet bars." Paula took a few more bites, savoring the sensation of the flavors melting in her mouth. Fat, sugar, chocolate – a potent combination that unleashed sensations almost as pleasurable as sex, or so she had read somewhere. She wouldn't know about the sex part – these days, she couldn't care less. Probably it was the Zoloft and the other meds she was taking to control her mood swings.

"This is the same recipe I used for the Halloween cake I brought to Minna Schatz's house the night she died," Allyson said. She gazed down at her plate, shoved the few remaining crumbs around with her fork. "I have to admit, that's one reason I wanted you to try some. Claire was giving me a really hard time about that cake, as if she thought it was tainted or something. She was way out of line, in my opinion. Not to mention off the wall. No recipe could possibly –"

"Excuse me, ladies. Did I hear my name?" Claire stood in the doorway, gazing down at the empty plates. She was wearing that black ultrasuede outfit again, looking disgustingly svelte. But Paula would have to broach the subject of Claire's expanding her wardrobe a little. She looked as if she were headed for a funeral. Then Paula realized she was: services for Minna Schatz were today at eleven, and Claire had already announced her intention to go.

Paula dropped her paper napkin over her plate in a futile effort to conceal the evidence of her unexpected pig-out. Why did Claire have this infernal way of making her feel guilty, without even saying a word?

"You want some cake?" Allyson asked. "It's a special recipe. I made it myself."

Claire shot Allyson a startled look, almost a look of horror. How pathetic, Paula thought. She's so terrified of gaining weight, she acts as if cake is a mortal enemy. But then Claire surprised her. "Thanks, Allyson, I'd love some," she said. "But just a tiny slice."

A few minutes later, Claire was looking a lot happier. The cake had helped, Paula thought, but so had the mention of the four referrals. To her surprise, Claire had given her less resistance than she'd expected.

"We'll be stretching our live-in staff awfully thin," Claire was saying now, "but maybe we can pull it off. Dahlia needs a new case, and –"

Paula coughed, trying to dislodge a cake crumb caught in her throat. Here it was, the moment she'd been dreading. She choked out the words. "I'm afraid Dahlia's out for now."

"What do you mean?"

"I've suspended her, in light of recent events. Sorry I didn't tell you sooner, but I'm sure you can understand."

Claire stiffened, and her mouth went taut. "I've had some concerns about Dahlia too. But since I'm her immediate supervisor, I'm the one who should deal with her. You should have consulted with me before taking such drastic action."

Allyson's jowls crinkled as she suppressed a grin.

"Under normal circumstances, yes," said Paula. "But it's hardly normal for her to be practicing some kind of voodoo or witchcraft right in a client's home. A client who just happens to die mysteriously on Halloween night."

"I gather Stephen's been talking to you," said Claire.

"Yes, and thank heavens somebody does. Were you going to share this little time bomb with me, or were you just going to wait for it to blow up in our faces?"

"I certainly didn't intend to conceal anything from you, Paula, but I was going to talk with Dahlia first, find out the facts before I brought it to your attention. I haven't had the chance yet, since she went back to New York City."

"Well, you can talk with her, but I don't want you assigning her any more clients until we've conducted a thorough investigation, and maybe not even then."

Claire's eyes flashed. "As nursing supervisor, I should be the one to make that decision. Besides, I know Dahlia a hell of a lot better than you do." Her face fell. "She'll be devastated. She's saving to bring her daughters up from Jamaica, and she really needs the work."

"She should have thought of that before she started building altars and burning candles in her room. And chicken feet! Give me a break!"

"We don't know for sure what she was doing. We just have Stephen's word for it."

"Because you didn't take the time to track what was really going on. That's another thing that concerns me, Claire." Paula felt her pulse hammering in her neck. Soon, if she didn't cool it, she would start hyperventilating. She tried to breathe slowly, deeply, but the cake crumb still tickled her throat. "You've been stretching yourself too thin, and I hold myself partially responsible. I'd like to redistribute the work load by having Allyson open two of the new cases."

Allyson threw Paula a startled look. *I should have discussed it with Allyson first,* Paula thought. *But hey, this is seat-of-the-pants management.* "Don't worry, Allyson, I'll make sure your compensation is adjusted accordingly."

"Okay, thanks," Allyson said. "Which cases would you like me to open?"

"Why don't you take the two from St. Francis Hospital, since they were referred by Dr. D'Attilio. You've worked with him for years, so there shouldn't be any glitches. Claire, you take the two from Oaktree Associates."

Claire's eyes lit up. Thank God she was resilient enough to muster some enthusiasm, Paula thought. She hadn't meant to stomp quite so heavily on Claire's ego; when it came to marketing, she was vastly superior to Allyson.

"Who's the contact person?" asked Claire. "Is it one of the men we met at the conference?"

"No, although I did have lunch with Patrick Delafield yesterday. He set the wheels in motion, but the person who handles the referrals is a social worker. Gloria Wallender."

The light in Claire's eyes dimmed again. So it wasn't the new cases that got her enthused – it was the men. At least Paula didn't have that problem with Allyson.

"All right," Claire said. "I'll give her a call before I head over to Minna Schatz's funeral. After the service I'll start following up on the new intakes. If there's time, I'll phone Dahlia, then drop in on George Cropsey to see how he and Errol James are getting along."

"That's Dahlia's cousin, right?"

"Yes."

"Better make it a surprise visit. See if you catch him burning any candles. And watch out for chicken feet."

———————

Paula was right, Claire mused as she sought shelter in her office minutes later. Maybe I've been slacking off on my day-to-day involvement with our ongoing cases. And maybe I was wrong to trust Dahlia so much. How well do I really know her?

The speculation could wait for now. She picked up the business card Paula had given her, punched in Gloria Wallender's number. It was a direct line.

"I've already heard about you from Angelo Giordano," Claire said by way of breaking the ice. "He's been going to a support group you facilitate at Oaktree."

Silence at the other end. "I can't comment on that," the woman said at last.

What did she think this was? A press conference? Then Claire remembered. "Of course. You're right. Angelo and Regina Giordano are close friends and neighbors of mine, but they're not clients of Compassionate Care, so I understand why you can't share any information."

"I'm glad we understand each other," Wallender said. Her tone was cool, formal. Odd, for a social worker.

"We do have a client in common, though. George Cropsey. I understand his son Paul has been going to Oaktree as well."

Silence again. "Ms. Lindstrom, I don't mean to sound abrupt, but I'm scheduled to lead a group in a few minutes, and I'm concerned about these new referrals. Will your agency be able to staff them?"

Talk about cutting to the chase. "We'll do our best. Why don't you give me the details, and I'll get right on it." Right after the funeral, that is.

Claire checked her watch as she pulled into the parking lot at the Parker & Newell Funeral Home. Good – five minutes to spare. She recognized Lester Schatz's battered red Chevy truck. And she remembered the white hearse and the two matching white sedans from Harriet Gardener's funeral procession. Aside from that, the place looked practically deserted, with only a handful of cars.

Something was off kilter. Did she have the right date and time for Minna's funeral? Maybe this was just the viewing, and the funeral was tomorrow. She rummaged in her handbag, extracted the obituary she'd clipped from yesterday's paper and double-checked the information at the bottom. Wednesday, November 3rd at 11 a.m. Yes, she'd gotten it right.

In the lobby, a young woman stood at the bottom of a staircase next to an urn of silk flowers. "May I help you?" she asked.

"Yes, I'm here for Minna Schatz's funeral."

The woman flashed a smile and gestured to her right. "How nice of you to come. It's in the east parlor, right through the double doors. Please sign the book on your way in."

"Thank you." Claire crossed the lobby to a pair of ornately carved golden oak doors. Early twentieth century, arts and crafts period, she decided. No doubt the funeral home had been a private residence at one time, and it still had the original woodwork. The red brocade wallpaper could go, though. It reminded her of a discount steak house.

Stepping through the doorway, she was struck by a sense of abandonment. At the far end of the room, the casket lay in solitary splendor, flanked by two modest flower arrangements. On either side of a central aisle, chairs of walnut-colored wood stretched in both directions, but there was scarcely anybody in them. Claire counted seven people, all elderly and all virtually motionless. Lester wasn't among them.

She had an eerie feeling of disorientation, as if she'd stepped into a wax museum. Stifling an irrational impulse to flee, she stepped over to the gilded lectern with its white leather guest book. The book lay open to the first page, the signatures filling less than half the ivory vellum sheet. Hadn't there been viewing hours? Shouldn't there be more signatures? She flipped to the next page, and the ones after that, but they were totally blank.

How could anyone slip so quietly out of the world, with so few people to mourn her passing? Had Minna Schatz outlived most of her friends, or had she never had friends to begin with? Had she always been as cantankerous as she was in her last months? If so, maybe she'd alienated everyone she'd come in contact with. And as far as Claire knew, there were no close family members except for Lester. As for the people in the wooden chairs, they might well be funeral groupies who studied the obituaries and came to services for strangers, either for the illusion of companionship in sorrow or for the refreshments that often followed in the wake of these events.

She flipped back to the first page. Who were these people? Would she have time to copy down the names, check out their relationship to Minna? She was peering at the scrawls, trying to decipher them and see if any looked familiar, when a hand clamped down hard on her shoulder. "Can't you leave us in peace? Haven't you had enough?"

She wheeled to face Lester Schatz, who was looming over her, exhaling hot blasts of bourbon-scented air like some fire-breathing dragon. "Lester! I was wondering where you were!"

His fingers tightened their grasp. "What are you doing, snooping in the guest book? Looking for more poor old people to sink your claws into?"

"Actually, I was just about to sign my name. I was figuring out what to say."

I hate lying. She knew she was blushing, but he was probably too drunk to notice. His speech was badly slurred. She'd never seen him this smashed before. Still, he was entitled, given the circumstances. She twisted out from under his grasp. "I just came to pay my respects, and to tell you how sorry I am."

"No, you came to hound me." He summoned up an impressive belch. "Speaking of hounds, how the hell is my dog?"

"You mean Maizy? She's doing great." Since when was she Lester's dog? Whenever Claire had seen them together, Lester and the little terrier had barely tolerated each other. She hoped he didn't intend to lay claim to Maizy. Releasing her to his care would be tantamount to animal cruelty.

"Glad to hear it. You wanna hang onto her awhile?"

"Yes, I'd be happy to. She gets along really well with my dog Freia."

"What kind of name is that?"

"It's a Norse goddess. She's a Labradoodle."

"What the fuck kind of dog is that?" He belched again, then glanced around wild-eyed, as if suddenly remembering his surroundings. "Anyway, you're probably here about money, right? Although God knows we paid you people enough."

"That's not why I'm here. You're already paid up. As a matter of fact, you might have a refund on your security deposit coming. I'm here because I wanted to pay my respects to your mother. She was quite a lady. Feisty, opinionated. I know it couldn't have been easy, but –"

"That's enough!" Lester's bulging eyes brimmed with sudden tears. "You've paid your respects. Now leave."

"I'd like to stay for the service, if that's all right with you."

"It's not."

Claire's heart went out to the man. Despite all the bluster, his hard shell had developed a crack. He gave every sign of feeling genuine grief for his mother, but this wasn't the time or place to reach out, lest he shatter completely. Besides, from the looks of him, Lester was on the brink of that long-overdue circulatory disaster she'd been dreading ever since she met him. She didn't want to be the one to push him over the edge.

Gently, she touched his arm. "All right, Lester. If that's what you wish, I'll leave. But call me if you want to talk, okay?"

His reply was a phlegmy grunt.

Chapter 20

*K*icked out of a funeral! This was a new low, Claire reflected as she trudged down the steps to the parking lot. But at least now she had time for the intakes from Oaktree Associates. Both clients were in desperate need of live-in care, and the sooner the better, according to Gloria Wallender.

Claire detoured to the nearest Subway and fortified herself with a low-carb chicken wrap, then headed out to evaluate the two clients. She decided to visit Louella Marcovicci first. Gloria had said the woman had diabetes and congestive heart failure, but the social worker had neglected to tell her that Mrs. Marcovicci weighed well over 250 pounds. Interviewing her was like pulling teeth, but Claire soon realized that the primary challenge would be to keep her as active as possible in order to preserve what little mobility she had left. The family lived out of state, and there seemed to be no friends or neighbors involved. Small wonder – the woman had all the warmth and personality of yesterday's mashed potatoes. A good client for Sharon Westerly, Claire decided – not medically complicated. But she could picture the two of them hanging out together, watching TV hour after hour. She'd have to stress the importance of getting their butts off the couch on a regular basis.

Compared to Louella Marcovicci, Ray Rienzi was a whirlwind of energy. A tiny widower with mid-stage Alzheimer's, he circled the dining table a dozen times within the first five minutes of the intake interview.

"He's a regular Energizer bunny," his sister Peggy said with a sigh. "He's been staying with me the past three months, but he's been turning night into day. Last week when he took his latest midnight jaunt outside in his pajamas, I decided I just couldn't take it any more."

Claire flashed on the image of Rose Dobson lying face down and bloodied beside the creek. *Not again. Paula would kill me for saying this, but I've got to be honest.* "Have you considered nursing home placement? There are some local facilities with excellent Alzheimer's units."

Peggy frowned. "And astronomical prices. Anyway, Ray would be happier here at home. I've heard good things about your live-in care, and it strikes me as the perfect solution."

"I'm not so sure. Our live-in aides stay in the home nonstop, but they don't provide constant one-on-one supervision, and they need downtime for a normal night's sleep. From what you tell me and what I've already observed, Mr. Rienzi may need a more intensive level of care."

Peggy's face reddened. "Are you telling me your agency's people are too incompetent to care for my brother?"

"No, not at all. It's just that –"

"I don't know why Gloria Wallender recommended you. What's your boss's name? I've got a mind to call her right now and straighten this out. She might be interested to know you're sabotaging your own agency."

Paula would hit the ceiling, but so be it. This man's safety was too important to base his care on a snap decision. Claire tried for a confident tone. "Why don't I take a walk with Mr. Rienzi? I'll get a better feel for his personality, finish the assessment, then go back to the office and discuss the situation with my boss. It might be possible to provide care for a few days as a trial run, then make a decision as to whether live-in care is feasible."

Peggy grasped Claire's hand in both of hers. "Oh, that would be great! I didn't mean to dump on you, but I'm at my wit's end."

Ray Rienzi shot Claire a flirtatious grin, then scuttled to the foyer. A blast of November air rushed in as he pulled the knob, flung open the front door and disappeared outside into the dusk.

Back at the office later, Paula slammed both palms down on the desk. "What do you mean we can't take the case?"

Claire sighed. She'd already explained ad nauseam, but her boss just didn't get it. "Paula, please. For his own safety, Ray Rienzi needs to be in a locked facility. He's hyperactive, always on the go. He'd run our aides ragged."

"So get someone young and energetic, like Tanisha Clarkson."

"I'm sorry, it won't work. I spent two hours with him, and I was absolutely exhausted by the time I left. And his sister says the nights are even worse. He sundowns."

"Can't you adjust his medication? Mellow him out a little?"

"Turn him into a zombie, you mean?" *Cool it, Claire. Paula has a point.* "I could review his medications, discuss the situation with his doctor, but it would take time."

"Fair enough. Meanwhile, how soon can we get an aide in there?"

"Paula, I just don't feel comfortable –"

Paula shoved away from her desk, stretched her arms skyward and clasped both hands behind her head. "Never mind, forget it! I'll give Allyson Quigley a call. I'm sure she'll be delighted to open the case."

———————

Claire was in no mood to confront the office the next morning, but her to-do list was running off the page of her planner, so she determined to give it a go. Heading across her living room, she hunkered down to dog level and gave Freia and Maizy a farewell scratch behind the ears. "Goodbye, ladies. Be good to each other, and guard the house!"

Two tails wagged half-heartedly, and two pairs of liquid brown eyes gazed up, reproaching her for their impending abandonment.

"Give me a goodbye kiss," she coaxed Freia, and the dog gave her a sloppy lick on the cheek while Maizy nuzzled her hand.

Claire hadn't quite reached the kissing phase with Maizy. The little Jack Russell was too high strung to invite that kind of intimacy yet, but all in all, she had adapted amazingly well to her new surroundings. Claire couldn't take all the credit. Freia's sweet Labrador temperament and poodle intelligence had a lot to do with it. Far from being jealous of the new arrival as Claire had feared, the Labradoodle had taken to Maizy immediately. Her maternal instincts had kicked in, and by now she seemed to regard the smaller dog as her very own puppy and playmate.

"You like having a little sister, don't you, Freia," Claire said. "It must beat hanging out alone all day while I'm at work."

Thank God Lester Schatz hadn't asked to take Maizy back. She'd thought he was about to yesterday, right before he kicked her out of the funeral, but fortunately he'd dropped the subject. He could still change his mind, though. The companionship of dogs was infinitely superior to complete solitude, and his mother's passing must have left an enormous void in his life, no matter how problematic their relationship had been. But she decided not to dwell on the subject of Maizy's future. She had more pressing things to think about, like orienting Sharon Westerly to the

Louella Marcovicci case. And she still had to call Dahlia and drop in on George Cropsey and Errol James. Her confrontation with Paula had left her too wrung out to do either yesterday.

Stepping onto the porch, she closed the door on the two pooches. She inserted the key in the lock, started to turn it, but it wouldn't budge. Damn! The lock had been getting steadily worse. She'd kept meaning to do something about it, kept putting it off, and now it was completely impossible. Was it fixable? Did it need a new cylinder? She hated to spring for a locksmith. Maybe she'd stop by the hardware store after work, see what they had to suggest.

She extricated the key and went back inside, to the dogs' overwhelming delight. "Thanks for the welcome, guys, but I was only gone half a minute, and I'm not staying." She locked the deadbolt that was mounted above the malfunctioning lock. She headed through the house to the door that led onto the rear deck, repeated the farewell ritual with Freia and Maizy, and made her escape. This door was newer, and it locked automatically. One of these days she supposed she should get a deadbolt installed on this one too, but the neighborhood felt so secure that she'd never gotten around to it.

Twenty minutes later, as she turned into the parking lot at Compassionate Care, she caught sight of Stephen's red Mustang in her rear-view mirror, roaring up on her. He loomed alarmingly close, then swerved and peeled into the space alongside. Climbing from his car, he executed a sweeping bow and grabbed hold of her door handle. It didn't budge.

"It's locked," she mouthed through the glass. Then she clicked the unlock button and let him complete his chauffeur ritual by ushering her out. He was looking especially striking today, in a beige shearling coat that complemented his blond hair.

She clicked her key fob, heard the locks in the Focus click into place. As the car beeped and flashed its lights in farewell, she had a burst of inspiration. "I couldn't lock my front door this morning. The key wouldn't turn, and I didn't want to break it by trying too hard. I suppose I'll have to call a locksmith."

"Don't do that." His green eyes took on a mischievous gleam. "I'm pretty good at that kind of thing. We could go take a look at it now, if you want."

"I've got too much to do. It'll be okay for the day. I locked the house from inside and went out the back. But if you've got time after work, I'd really appreciate it."

"You're on. You were right not to force the key in the lock. It's probably just rusty. I've got something I can squirt in there, give it some lubrication."

The gleam in his eyes grew positively predatory, and he threw her a wicked grin that told her he was thinking about more than locks. *I'm pretty rusty myself,* she thought. *Extremely rusty, in fact.*

Once inside, she felt a twinge of guilt as she stopped at Maria's desk. *Your boyfriend's coming over to work on my lock tonight.* She smiled, hoping Maria wouldn't pick up on her X-rated thoughts. "I just stopped in to pick up a couple of charts," she told the coordinator. "Then I'm off to open a new case."

"I know. Louella Marcovicci, right? Lucky Sharon Westerly is available. I'm having a hell of a time staffing the Rienzi case, though."

Claire stiffened. "When's the start date?"

"Today if possible. Allyson's already over there doing the intake. She got here bright and early. You don't have to worry about Paula, though – she won't be in till later."

Why would I worry about Paula? What does Maria know? "I've got to go," Claire said. "I'm stopping at George Cropsey's house, too."

Maria grinned. "Say hi to Errol for me. He's really hot, don't you think?"

Errol James was hot in more ways than one, Claire reflected as she sat across from him at George Cropsey's kitchen table three hours later. A magnificent man, yes, but he was also hot under the collar, or at least he would have been if he hadn't been wearing a collarless Henley shirt. The black knit showed his muscular build to intimidating advantage. He was hot to trot, too.

"I want out by the weekend," he said with a glower. "I've been here three solid weeks, and Maria keeps giving me the runaround. An agency your size, you've got to have some relief aides available."

"We do, but –"

"But, but, but. Don't hand me that crap. It's what Maria keeps saying." He leaned forward, crossing his mahogany arms for maximum definition. "What about my cousin? I bet she could use the work."

"Dahlia? I'd like to get her a new assignment, but I need to talk to her first."

"So what's keeping you? Do it! I don't want to leave George in the lurch, but . . ."

There it was, that word again. *But* – just three little letters, but with the unspoken overtones of an ultimatum.

Back at the office, Claire phoned Dahlia Douglas. A man with a thick Jamaican accent answered.

"Why you treat my wife this way?" he asked with a plaintive lilt to his voice. "Dahlia is a good woman, and she is deeply hurt that your agency treat her so shamefully."

"I understand how she feels. I'd like to get her back working again, but I have to talk to her first. Can she come to the phone?"

"One moment, please. I'll ask her."

Claire heard the clatter of the phone being put down, silence, then a muffled conversation. She couldn't make out a word, but with each exchange his voice grew louder and angrier.

"Sorry," he said when he came back. "She won't talk to you. Can't you hear her weeping? You have wounded her pride, and she say she won't work for you again. Also, she feels terrible about these women who died."

"I know she does." *Maybe for good reason.* Claire kept her tone light. Sharing doubts and accusations over the phone couldn't possibly do any good. "Do you think she would talk to me if I came down to see her in person?"

"She might." He chuckled. "I have my ways. Maybe I can persuade her. My wife is a good woman and a hard worker, and I know she liked the job."

I'll bet you liked it too, Claire thought. A regular weekly paycheck - what's not to like? I wonder if you contribute even half as much. "Why don't I come down?" she asked impulsively. "Tomorrow's good for me - I could use a day in the city."

"All right. I'll soften her up a little, make sure she's around when you come. What time you be here?"

Claire thought a moment. Maybe she could drop in on one of the training schools, recruit some new aides. "How's early afternoon?"

"Sounds good. I won't mention you're coming, though. Better it should be a surprise. My name's Peter, by the way."

"I know, she's told me about you."

He laughed, deeply and sensuously. "I hope it was nice, what she said. It was a pleasure speaking with you. Call me when you're in the city, and I'll give you directions."

A surprise home visit. Not necessarily the way Claire would have engineered the meeting, but it might be better this way. Maybe Dahlia would have her guard down, and Claire would actually learn something.

Night had fallen by the time Claire ushered Stephen up the steps to her front door. Inside, both dogs were barking up a storm.

"They're not used to visitors," she said.

"Why not? You mean you're a total recluse?"

"Something like that."

His smile gleamed in the darkness. "We'll have to remedy that situation." He raised his hand, displayed a dusky canister with a tapering nozzle at the tip. "Let me get right to work. Like I said, a little lubrication will probably do the trick. Open this baby right up."

She felt a sudden clenching deep inside, and she took a step back.

He whistled a snatch of something familiar, then began to sing. "Open up and let me come inside . . ."

She giggled, a little hysterically. "No fair singing Rod Stewart songs."

His laugh was throaty and deep. "Aha! Got to you, did I? I've got quite a repertoire. I can entertain you later."

The barking escalated, and Claire heard the scrabbling of both dogs' nails on the door. "We're driving the dogs crazy," she said. "You'd better get to work. In the meantime, I'll go pick up today's mail."

She retreated back down the steps, onto the gravel driveway. Heading toward the mailbox, she felt unexpectedly giddy, in a way she'd forgotten existed. *Is tonight the night? Could be – no, wait a minute, Claire. Don't be ridiculous.*

The mailbox was wooden, shaped like an old-fashioned red barn. Battered and kitschy, and the door didn't close properly, but it reminded her of her Aunt Alice, so she'd never had the heart to change it. She reached inside, came away with the usual fistful of bills and catalogues. Glancing up at the porch, she saw that Stephen had gotten to work on the lock. Better not distract him.

She strolled toward the nearest streetlight, a good fifty feet away, and rifled through the mail. Bills and catalogues, just as she'd thought. A nursing trade magazine. And at the bottom of the stack, an ivory envelope. Heavy stock, squarish, like a greeting card or wedding invitation. No stamps or address, just her name in block letters.

Odd – her birthday was months away, and no one she knew was getting married. She tore open the flap, pulled out a sheet of paper. Standard office stock, nothing fancy. She unfolded it, squinted in disbelief at the neat lettering in navy ink:

CLAIRE,
YOU HAVE BEEN STIRRING UP TROUBLE, ASKING TOO MANY QUESTIONS ABOUT MATTERS THAT DON'T CONCERN YOU. BACK OFF NOW! CEASE AND DESIST, OR YOUR LIFE WILL BE IN JEOPARDY.

> SINCERELY,
> A FRIEND

Chapter 21

Claire trembled as she stared at the letter in her hands. "Stephen! Quick, come here!"

"What's the matter?" He was off the steps, at her side in a matter of seconds.

"Look at this note. Someone's threatening me."

He squinted down at the paper, studied it in silence. "Warning you is more like it," he said at last. "Not necessarily threatening."

"That's splitting hairs."

"No, it isn't. This person has no intention of harming you. They're just telling you someone else might. They want to keep you safe."

She shivered. He wrapped an arm around her shoulders, pulled her close. In his free hand, he was still holding the canister. Oily goo dripped from its tip.

"Stephen, how on earth do you know what this person has in mind?"

"Maybe I'm just putting myself in the guy's shoes. But regardless, I want to make sure you're safe. I don't think you should be alone tonight."

You're right. Stay with me, she almost said, but she bit back the words. What if Stephen had dropped the note in her mailbox today? She'd been vehement in resisting his come-ons. Maybe the note was his way of getting a foot in the door.

"I'll be fine," she said. "I won't be alone – I have two dogs."

"Sorry, but I'm not buying it. The lock is almost fixed. At the very least you can invite me in and feed me some dinner."

"I'm afraid I don't have anything to offer you except a couple of frozen Healthy Choice dinners."

He grimaced. "Yuk! Let's order in pizza instead."

To Claire's amazement, her stomach growled. How could she think about food at a time like this? Easily, it appeared. Some other appetites were stirring too. "Okay," she said. "Let's go around to the back door. I can let you in that way, order the pizza and walk the dogs while you finish up with the lock."

"Sounds good to me." He began singing again, channeling Jim Morrison this time. "Back door man . . ."

Throughout their impromptu dinner, by unspoken consent, they avoided discussing the note. Stephen broke first. "Let's cut to the chase. Who do you think could have sent that thing?"

They were sitting side by side on the sofa, warmed by wine, tossing pieces of pizza crust to the dogs. Speculations and suspicions had been swirling nonstop through Claire's mind since she'd opened the letter two hours ago. She'd been determined not to share them with Stephen, but she was still at a total loss. Maybe he could help.

"Strangely enough, Paula seems like the most obvious culprit," she said. "She has a flip side. I suspect she's bipolar, although she hasn't come right out and said it. The comment about my stirring up trouble sounds just like her. She hates the fact that I keep raising questions about the adequacy of our level of care. She was furious with me for wanting to turn down the Ray Rienzi case, and she had a fit when I suggested discussing the three ladies' deaths with Dr. D'Attilio. She's always accusing me of trying to sabotage our referral sources."

"And are you?"

"Of course not. But all our referrals lately have been for live-in care. It's what we're best known for, and people like it because it's more economical than split shifts. But it isn't always the best option, because it doesn't involve eyeball-to-eyeball supervision. Take Ray Rienzi. What if he slips out of the house in the middle of the night while the aide is asleep? He could be out on the Thruway hitchhiking to New York City before anyone knows he's missing. Live-in care is fine for someone like Harriet Gardener or Minna Schatz, but –"

"But they died anyway."

"Yes." Claire leaned forward, buried her face in her hands.

"Home care is risky business, Claire. You're dealing with old, sick people. There are bound to be some losses."

"True, but we can minimize them by being more careful about who we accept for live-in care. Paula doesn't see it that way, though. She's too caught up in her never-ending panic about the cash flow."

"I can't say as I blame her." Stephen edged closer on the sofa. "Maybe Rick Kozlowski sent the note."

"Why on earth would he do that?"

"Who knows? He's a kinky guy, and he seems obsessed with you and the agency. He's on kind of a death trip, too."

"That seems far fetched, but I'll take it under consideration." Claire leaned back, laced her fingers together and stretched her arms skyward, palms up. "I'm glad I'm going to New York City tomorrow. Maybe the distance will help me put things in perspective."

Stephen's eyes took on a sudden gleam. "When did you decide to go to the city?"

"This afternoon when I talked to Dahlia's husband. I'm going to make a surprise visit to her place in Brooklyn, ask her some questions."

He grinned. "At least you can be sure she didn't send the note."

"You mean because she's in New York City?"

"No, because she's not literate enough. That note is grammatically correct, with no misspellings. Somebody reasonably intelligent wrote it."

"Stephen, what a nasty, bigoted thing to say!"

"I just calls 'em like I sees 'em."

She punched his arm. "Now who's being grammatically correct! But I admit I've got some concerns about Dahlia. She was with Harriet Gardener and Minna Schatz the nights they died. Hopefully I'll be able to get her back on the active roster, but I need to make an objective assessment before I decide."

"So you're going to the Big Apple on company business, huh? Is Paula picking up the tab?"

"Yes, to my amazement. I'm also going to visit a training school to see about recruiting some new aides, and I'll drop in at Oaktree Associates' New York office. Paula loved the idea of my schmoozing with the higher-ups at our newest referral source. Told me it was cost-effective to combine three things in one trip, and that I was thinking like a manager for a change. Actually I think she just wants me out of the office. We've been at each other's throats lately."

Stephen slid closer to her on the sofa, draped his arm casually over her shoulders and pulled her close. "So at least you're not running away from me. That's good."

She scrunched out from under his arm. "Why on earth would I run away from you?"

"Damned if I know." Leaning forward, he cupped her face in his hand, kissed her slowly and searchingly.

Deep inside, some impish inner critter started turning somersaults. She had known this was coming, known it ever since she'd first laid eyes on him. It took every ounce of willpower she possessed to draw away from him. "This isn't right," she murmured.

"Why not?" His voice was husky with desire.

She hadn't felt these cravings in ages. Not since Mark. She remembered Angelo's face in the fading light, the evening he told her she was too young to stay a widow. What was it he had said? *You should be out on the town with some handsome young gentleman.*

On the town? Maybe. In bed? No way. At least not with Stephen. "I don't jump casually into relationships," she said. "And we work too closely together. I can just picture the office politics – it's a recipe for disaster." She reached up to run her fingers through his hair, caressed the strong contours of his cheekbones, his jaw. He was so beautiful, like some kind of magnificent young god, straight out of an Old Master painting at the Metropolitan Museum. Maybe that was one of the things that scared her.

"No one has to know," he said. "We can be discreet."

"But how do I know I can trust you? It sounds crazy, but it occurred to me that you could have placed that note in my mailbox today, to scare me into letting you spend the night."

He narrowed his eyes. "You're right, that does sound crazy. Not only that, it's insulting. Let's say for the sake of argument I did want to spend the night with you. I can think of all sorts of ways to convince you that would work a hell of a lot better than an anonymous note." He leaned closer, his lips inches away from hers.

"I'm sure you can." She launched herself off the sofa, away from him. "I confess I'd feel better if you stay over. That note really unnerves me. I think I'll take it to the police tomorrow, before I leave for the city. But if you stay, you have to promise to sleep on the sofa."

———————

Lester Schatz stared down at the wet ring he'd just made on his mother's banged up Formica table. The highball glass left a donut-sized impression on the pockmarked surface. When he was a child, he'd loved the random pattern of the yellowing plastic; it always reminded him of the craters of the moon, and he used to pretend his milk glass was a lunar module coming in for a landing. Even though the wet rings never hurt the tabletop, his mother used to yell at him anyway. *You careless slob,* she'd say. *Can't you do anything right?*

Amazing the way her voice still echoed in his head. Even now, almost a week after her death, it felt as if she was in the same room with him, running him down, just like she always did. *Can't you do anything right?*

He grabbed the bottle of Jack Daniel's, sloshed a couple more ounces into the glass. *No, Mother, I can't do anything right. I'm a loser, now and forever.*

He'd thought her death would make things better, but instead they were getting worse. Here he was, in the house he had wanted for so many years, and it already looked like a dung heap. Pizza cartons, empty bottles, overflowing ashtrays littered every available surface, and if he didn't do something soon, they'd be spilling onto the floor. But somehow he couldn't summon the energy to take out the garbage or do much of anything else. If he wasn't careful, he'd end up on the local news, one of those dingbats who filled their houses with floor-to-ceiling garbage until the stuff spilled over into the yard or the stench got so bad the neighbors called the cops. Then the TV crews moved in like turkey vultures. "How could someone live like this? How did things get so bad before anyone noticed?"

It got so bad because no one gave a shit, he thought as he slugged down more of the whiskey. The liquid burned, sent shock waves through his stomach, and he almost retched. *Watch it, Lester. You're drinking too much.*

Damn! His mother's voice again! He grabbed the glass, threw it at the sink. Crystal splinters flew in all directions, and the pungent smell of Jack Daniel's filled the room. What a waste of good booze.

Slumping onto the table, he cradled his head in his arms and let out a low moan.

He hadn't expected the guilt. His mother was old, over the hill, in chronic pain. For years she'd been complaining about every damn thing, saying her life wasn't worth living. All he'd done was take her at her word and help her along a little. He'd thought he was doing her a favor. They would both be better off, he'd been convinced of it. How could he have been so stupid?

The fear was the other problem. He'd had practically no contact with that weird organization, paid them in cash so there was no paper trail. Old people die all the time, they'd said. No questions asked. But they hadn't bargained on Claire Lindstrom. Even at the funeral, she'd been in his face, asking intrusive questions, snooping in the guest book. She was probably still bugged that he hadn't allowed an autopsy. Now it was too late; his mother had been cremated and they'd never turn up anything incriminating. But what if he was wrong? What if there was some detail he'd overlooked that would come back to haunt him?

Curiosity killed the cat. His mother's voice again, one of her favorite sayings. She never wanted him to ask questions or take any chances, but Claire Lindstrom was doing plenty of both. She was kind of catlike, too, with that slim figure and those big blue eyes that stared at him so coolly, like a god damned Siamese.

She'd even taken away his dog. Or his mother's dog, to be exact. True, it was his idea, because the yappy little bitch got on his nerves something fierce. But the silence in this big house was freaking him out, and right now the idea of Maizy's company didn't seem all that bad. It had been just a few hours after his mother's death when he'd asked Claire to take the dog. She should have realized he was still in shock, should have offered to give Maizy back when she saw him at the funeral home.

He felt a surge of adrenaline rage so strong, it jolted him out of his chair and sent him lurching toward the mudroom at the back of the house. He had brought the rifle with him when he'd moved. And here it was, right where he'd left it, all cleaned and shiny, ready for action.

Still two weeks till deer season, but maybe he wouldn't wait that long to use it.

Chapter 22

*G*abriel slowed to a walk, gasping for breath as he glared at the red Mustang parked in Claire Lindstrom's driveway next to her green Focus. The contrast of the two complementary colors set up an interesting vibration, especially with the morning sun glinting off the metal, but the color scheme was too raucous, too Christmasy for his taste. And the fact that Claire's gentleman caller had spent the night triggered a rage that stunned him with its intensity.

He extracted a stopwatch from his jacket and clocked his pulse as it descended back toward normal. He'd really pushed the envelope on his run this morning in hopes of bleeding off the excess energy he'd been feeling since last night, when he'd sighted Stephen McClellan through Claire's window. What the hell was she doing with the damn driver? She was way out of his league; she should have known better.

Who are you kidding, Gabriel? You know damn well what McClellan is doing there. You brought it on yourself by leaving her that stupid note. Athena had been right to warn him: he had let his personal feelings for Claire sabotage his professional judgment.

His plan had backfired bigtime. He was positive she'd shown McClellan the note; he'd glimpsed it through his binoculars, lying in plain sight on the dining table while the two of them wolfed down pizza and sat talking on the sofa.

Like an idiot, he'd pushed them into each other's arms. He could picture the driver, painting himself as a knight in shining armor, insisting on spending the night, pumped and primed to protect her from the big, bad bogeymen who might be lurking outside her cottage in the night. Preying on her fears, taking advantage. That kiss - he'd seen her draw away, but soon after that, they'd closed the curtains, and for all he knew -

Chill out, Gabriel. It's none of your business who she fucks. He picked up his pace as he passed her house. Before him, the road rose in a slow, steady climb as it curved away from the lake, then back down again. He'd done some casual running since moving to this neighborhood, but until yesterday, he'd avoided Claire's house. But so what if she saw him? She'd been friendly enough when they met; for all he knew, she might even have the hots for him. There was something a little guarded and standoffish about her, or so he'd thought, but maybe he was wrong. If she was screwing Stephen McClellan, she had to be a slut. And if she was a slut, that changed everything.

Again his inner critic kicked in, warned him to drop it. This kind of speculation distracted him from the big picture. Claire Lindstrom's depravity had no bearing on his mission. Still, it was an area of vulnerability, worth filing away for future reference. One way or another, it might come in handy.

If he continued in this direction, he could make a complete circuit of the lake and end up back at his house. How long a run would that make? Probably well over three miles. He'd have to check it out on his car odometer later, after Claire left for work. He was so involved in his painting lately, he'd been neglecting his physical side. But staying in shape was important. Take the night he had carried Rose Dobson into the woods. She was a frail, diminutive woman – she'd felt feather-light in his arms. If he hadn't been working out regularly, her body would have been more of a burden.

———————

As Stephen drifted slowly into consciousness, he heard baroque chamber music in the distance. There were scuffling and jingling noises too. Now he remembered: he was on the sofa at Claire's house. The music was coming from her clock radio, he realized, and the weird noises must be the dogs waking up. Cautiously, he opened his eyes a crack and let them adjust to the brilliant sunlight pouring through the curtains.

He rose and padded into the bedroom to look at Claire. She seemed so angelic, so innocent lying there on her side, her face cradled atop one arm. He couldn't resist: he reached out to stroke her hair, the delicate contours of her neck and shoulder.

Her eyes flew open. "Oh, my God, what time is it? I've got to stop at the police station and then catch the train."

"Why take the train? I can drive you to New York. I could use the break."

"That's okay, Stephen. It's no problem, I like the train."

"But why blow the money on Amtrak when you can have free door-to-door service with me?"

She studied him silently, considering, then shook her head.

"Come on, Claire! We don't have to be joined at the hip all day. I could just drop you off wherever you want and pick you up a few hours later. I could find lots of stuff to do there. I have friends I could see. I could pick up the new *Variety* and see if there are any casting calls –"

"Please, Stephen, I need the solitude."

"You had an entire night of solitude. Although let me tell you, it wasn't easy staying out there on the sofa."

"I just need some time to myself. It's got nothing to do with you, believe me."

"Yeah, right. I've heard that line before." *Except I'm usually the one who says it, and usually after I've fucked the woman.*

Driving to the police station, Claire kept picturing Stephen as he'd looked in the morning sunlight when he stroked her hair. Half asleep, her defenses down, she'd been tempted to invite him into her bed. Her superego had kicked in with seconds to spare. A good thing, too. A casual friends-with-benefits arrangement wasn't her style, and anything heavier would be a disaster. Besides, she had a lot on her plate today.

First, the police station. She felt an almost physical urge to rid herself of the threatening note. It lay beside her on the front seat, secure in its gallon-sized freezer bag. She'd thought of the baggie too late; the paper was already contaminated with her prints and Stephen's. But from the malevolent aura it gave off, it might as well have been harboring Anthrax.

The female officer at the front desk was inscrutably cool. "There's no one around with the expertise to examine it now," she told Claire, "but we'll get on it later today." She asked Claire a few questions, jotted down notes, and sent her on her way. Just as well – Claire was eager to get out of town.

An hour later, she gazed out the train window and watched the river slide by. There were so many waterfowl in this stretch of the Hudson, south of Albany. Canada geese, mallards and teals, sea gulls – and all of them paired off or in flocks. They're smarter than I am, she thought. They know it instinctively: they need each other. None of this Garboesque "I vant to be alone" crap.

A day in the city with Stephen would have been fabulous. A night, a weekend, would have been even better. But forget about business or sight seeing. They could check into a hotel, spend the whole time in bed. Someplace elegant, like the Algonquin, where they could order room service in between bouts of love making. But a dumpier hotel would be okay too – they could always send out for pizza again.

Get real, she told herself. It's not going to happen. He's beautiful, yes, but a boy toy is the last thing you need right now, and it wouldn't be fair to Maria. Outside the train window, she caught sight of a great blue heron standing alone in the shallow marshland that ran alongside the river. Still as a statue, until all at once his head shot down like lightening into the water, then reemerged with a fish trapped in his long, lethal bill.

Mercifully, the train shot past before she could see him swallow his prey. He knows his business, she thought. And he's alone – no mate to distract him. For that matter, how do I know it's a he? It could be a female, fishing. Just like me. Speaking of which, I think I'll start with the training school, then Oaktree Associates. That should leave ample time to call on Dahlia in mid-afternoon.

———————

The bronze plaque was so tastefully understated, Claire had to mount the broad stone steps of the brownstone building before she could read it. *Oaktree Associates* was engraved in an ornate, old-fashioned typeface next to the stylized tree logo she recognized from the web site. She'd had no trouble finding the building. After all, she had lived in Manhattan for years, but she had called up the address on MapQuest and printed out the directions just for the hell of it.

The East Seventies between Madison and Park – definitely an upscale neighborhood. The organization had to be doing pretty well. Either that, or there was big money behind it. Some of the elegant town houses that lined the block were still home to Manhattan's wealthy, but others had been taken over by foreign embassies and medical groups.

She had no particular game plan in mind. The idea for this excursion had come to her in a flash of inspiration late yesterday afternoon, and by then it had been too late to set up a formal appointment. Paula had been surprisingly supportive of the idea, with just one caveat. "Do me a favor," she'd said. "Don't wear that black ultrasuede outfit. It's too funereal."

Actually, black would have been perfect for the city, where the more stylish denizens seemed to dress in perpetual mourning, but in deference to Paula, Claire was wearing her red wool suit again. After all, it had worked wonders with Mike D'Attilio, and maybe it would prove equally effective if she encountered any of the higher powers at Oaktree.

The phone was ringing as Claire walked into the lobby. "Please hold," the receptionist said as she jabbed a button with a fuschia fingernail. She punched another button, looking frazzled. "Oaktree Associates." She glowered up at Claire, then turned her attention back to the phone. "Sorry, he's not available, and his secretary is out. Can you hold a minute?" She jabbed again, then held up her hand and studied her nails. They were long, square-cut with silver starbursts atop the fuschia. No doubt quite an investment; no wonder she didn't want to sully them with work.

She glanced up again. "May I help you?"

Claire smiled. "I can wait till you're off the phone."

"That isn't likely to happen any time soon."

"I can wait. I'm in no hurry."

"Thanks, I appreciate it. Have a seat."

Claire crossed the room to an armchair upholstered in dusty rose velvet, settled in and took advantage of the opportunity to study her surroundings. They were opulent, with dark, rich woodwork and walls papered in a subtle gray-green brocade and hung with pseudo-impressionist paintings. Originals, but in the derivative, production-line style she'd seen in the lobbies of chain hotels.

The brass nameplate on the receptionist's desk identified her as Penelope Cerutti.

"I'm sorry, Ms. Cerutti, it looks like I've caught you at a bad time," Claire said when there was finally a break between calls.

"Oh, I'm not Ms. Cerutti. Penny's on vacation. Las Vegas for two weeks – I should be so lucky. My name's Jennifer. I usually work upstairs, but the secretary who's been covering for Penny called in sick. Sorry if I was rude, but I'm not that familiar with the phone system."

"That's okay. I'm Claire Lindstrom from Compassionate Care in upstate New York. I don't have an appointment, but I wonder if it would be possible to see one of the executives here."

Jennifer furrowed her brow and played with a strand of her long brunette hair. She was a pretty young woman, but if she kept making that face, she was going to need Botox before she hit thirty. "I'm sorry," she said, "but I don't think that's possible. Everyone's really booked up today."

"That's okay. I know I should have phoned first, but I just decided to drop in on the spur of the moment. Your Albany office referred two clients to us for live-in care, and I was curious to learn more about your organization."

Jennifer smiled. "That's great! I know Jeff Livingston, our vice president of marketing, would love to talk to you. He's out in the field today, but I could set up something for next week."

"I'm not sure of my schedule. I'll have to get back to you on that."

"Okay. In the meantime, if you want, I can give you some materials about Oaktree to take back with you."

The phone trilled again. "Oh, shoot!" Jennifer exclaimed, with another brow furrow. "Excuse me!"

"While you get the phone, is it okay if I use the facilities?"

"Sure, I guess so." The receptionist waved vaguely toward a large mahogany doorway. "Right through there."

"Thanks." Claire opened the door and found herself in a long, dimly lit corridor carpeted in a floral oriental pattern. Doors on either side led to half a dozen offices, but the area was eerily silent. At the far end she came to a doorway with a white marble sill. She tried the door and stepped into a white tiled room with imposing old porcelain fixtures, including a gigantic clawfoot bathtub. The sheer scale of the room, the unrelieved whiteness, conjured up images of Germanic matrons giving vigorous massages and enemas.

She finished her business, checked her makeup and was headed back down the hall when she heard the trill of a phone coming from one of the offices. Two rings; then a recorded message kicked in. "Hello, this is Nathaniel Gebhardt. I'm not available right now, but leave a message and I'll get back to you."

Nathaniel Gebhardt? She remembered the name from the Oaktree web site. She followed the sound to its source, an office with its door standing ajar. The call was none of her business, but the opportunity to eavesdrop was too tempting to pass up.

The machine gave a long electronic beep. Then a masculine voice kicked in. "Nathaniel? Herb Davidson here. I need to touch base with you about our arrangement. Give me a call when you get a chance."

Herb Davidson, as in Herb Davidson the coroner? Unlikely. It was an ordinary name; this had to be some other Herb Davidson. Still, the voice was familiar.

Then he left the number, beginning with the 518 area code. The Capital Region! Claire mouthed the numerals, committing them to memory as she rummaged in her purse for a pen. She jotted the phone number on the back of an old sales receipt.

I'll try the number when I get home, she thought. Even with the same area code, it could still be a different Herb Davidson. But the soft voice with its boozy overtones called up a vivid mental image of the coroner's ruddy face, his thatch of white hair, his stylish golf togs.

What business could Oaktree Associates possibly have with an upstate coroner? Her heart was beating faster as she shoved the paper back in her purse.

A door creaked open somewhere close behind her. "Can I help you?" A masculine voice, and this time it wasn't electronic.

"No, thank you." *Cool it, Claire. You've got nothing to act guilty about.* "I was just using the bathroom."

"Are you here to see anyone in particular?"

"No, not really."

"Then let me escort you out. This isn't a public area."

She felt the sudden touch of a hand on her elbow, wheeled to find herself face to face with Patrick Delafield. "Claire!" he exclaimed, looking almost as startled as she felt. "What a pleasant surprise! I had no idea you were coming down to corporate headquarters."

"It was a spur of the moment decision. Paula and I are so appreciative of the referrals Oaktree has sent our way, and I was going to be in the city anyway, so I thought I might as well stop in."

"Want me to show you around?" His green eyes were studying her intensely.

Enough evasion, she told herself. Get to the point. "You know, the weirdest thing happened just now. I was on my way back from the bathroom when I heard a phone ring and Herb

Davidson left a message. Our county coroner. What a coincidence!"

His mouth tightened. "Talk about synchronicity! So you were back here eavesdropping?"

"No, of course not, but I'll admit I'm curious. He was asking for Nathaniel Gebhardt. That's your director, right?"

"Yes. But look, Claire, you're way out of line here. Our business dealings are strictly confidential, as you of all people should understand."

"Of course. I'm sorry." *Sorry my diplomatic skills are so primitive. He probably won't tell me a damn thing now.* "Actually, I've got to get going. I'm on my way to Brooklyn to see one of our aides."

"Then you could certainly use some sustenance first. Want to grab a quick lunch? Or at least some coffee?"

Hadn't she wanted more information about Oaktree? This could be her chance. A few minutes ago, she would have jumped at the invitation. But Patrick Delafield's eyes had turned icy, and she was feeling defensive. Time to get away, before this conversation turned into an interrogation.

"Thanks, Patrick. Let's make it some other time. See you in Albany."

Chapter 23

Claire flinched at the feel of Patrick's fingers pressing into her arm. As he escorted her past Jennifer's desk, the receptionist held out a manila envelope. "Here's some information about Oaktree for you."

Patrick thrust out a hand as if to grab the envelope, then stopped short. "What are you giving her, Jennifer?"

"Just the standard information folio."

"Oh, all right."

Claire took the packet, trying not to squirm as Patrick's arm snaked around her back. He propelled her toward the door and out onto the stoop. As she descended the steps and turned east toward Lexington Avenue, she sensed his eyes drilling into her back. *Walk, don't run.* She turned to look over her shoulder, raised her hand in a cheery wave.

His scowl morphed into a charming smile as he returned the gesture. "Let's get together soon. I'll give you a call."

"Great, Patrick. I'll look forward to it."

Like it or not, she'd take him up on his invitation. This peculiar excursion had whetted her appetite for more information about Oaktree Associates, and who better than Patrick to fill her in on the subject? But she needed time to marshal her thoughts and plan her strategy.

She sighed in relief as she left the deserted side street and rounded the corner onto Lexington. The avenue was alive with people: expensively dressed women window-shopping, nannies pushing prams, elderly ladies walking dogs, tradesmen and messengers hurrying to unknown destinations.

She headed north toward the subway entrance and down into the darkness. After the posh, moneyed atmosphere of Oaktree Associates, the descent into the bowels of the Lexington Avenue local was a rude reminder of the New York Claire knew all too well. The noise, the dirt, the chaos – she'd made the right choice in leaving it behind.

The subway car was cleaner, better maintained than she remembered, and half empty in the mid-day lull. She found a seat, did a quick scan to insure there were no unsavory occupants close by, then opened the manila envelope. She extracted a forest-green folder, embossed with the Oaktree logo in gold and crammed full of papers printed on heavy, expensive stock. Brochures described their legal services, their counseling and mental health offerings. There were article reprints, testimonials from satisfied clients, but nothing to explain the organization's professional ties to an upstate coroner.

The train pulled into the Union Square station just as she finished rifling through the pages. She crossed the platform, waited what seemed an eternity until the Brooklyn train rumbled into the station. Once aboard, she settled in to continue her research. The atmosphere was more distracting now. Black and Hispanic families conversed in animated tones. Groups of teenagers paced restlessly through the aisle, and just across from her, a disheveled junky nodded off. The subway car was older and scruffier, the windows scratched and clouded and the seats covered with graffiti. Evidently the residents of the outer boroughs didn't rate spiffy new cars like the one she'd just transferred from.

But the subway was pure luxury compared to Dahlia's neighborhood. Half the storefronts were abandoned and boarded up. Others still had metal security gates pulled down, even though it was early afternoon. The sidewalks were teeming with people, which should have been reassuring, except that hers was the only white face in sight.

She paused outside a fried chicken establishment, fished her cell phone out of her bag and punched in Dahlia's number.

Peter answered on the second ring, and she told him where she was.

"You're almost there," he said. "Look across the street, half a block down. You see a store with a big white sign up above, red letters saying Caribbean Specialties?"

She scanned the street in both directions. "I see it."

"Go in there and tell the lady you're waiting for me. I'll come get you, five or ten minutes tops." He clicked off.

Claire could have crossed mid-block, but the traffic was unpredictable, nonexistent one minute, insanely zippy the next, and the thought of jaywalking ratcheted up her already high anxiety. She retraced her steps to the corner and crossed obediently with the light, then doubled back to the storefront. Young men in low-slung hip-hop pants stood in clusters, watching her progress with hooded eyes.

From the outside, the place looked like an average convenience store, but she smelled the difference the moment she stepped over the threshold. A riot of spicy scents assailed her nostrils, and she was suddenly ravenous. She made her way to the deli counter toward the rear, where an enormous woman stood stirring a huge stockpot. She stopped when she caught sight of Claire. "May I help you?"

"I'm here to meet Peter Douglas. He told me to mention his name."

"Ah, Peter!" The woman flashed a gold-toothed grin. "He is my cousin. My name is Yvonne. You want anything while you wait? Knowing Peter, he may be awhile." The melodic lilt to her voice sounded just like Dahlia's.

"What are you cooking?" Claire asked. "It smells delicious."

"Jamaican jerk chicken. Here, try some." Before Claire could protest, the woman scooped a generous sample into a white Styrofoam bowl, then handed it to her along with a paper napkin and plastic utensils. "Sit and enjoy. There's room over there."

Claire followed her gaze to a spindly café table and two matching chairs. She settled in, draped her coat over the back of the chair, took a bite. The spicy sauce brought tears to her eyes.

Yvonne chuckled. "Too hot for you?"

Claire took another bite. "It takes getting used to, but I like it."

"I got the recipe from Peter's wife, Dahlia. She comes from Montego Bay, same part of Jamaica as me."

"Really? She's actually who I came here to see."

"Ah, I knew it. You must be the nurse from the agency."

"Claire Lindstrom, yes."

"She has spoken highly of you, many times. And now you have come to give her her job back."

"Did Peter tell you that?"

"He didn't have to – I know. We have our ways." She gestured to the glass display case adjoining Claire's table. The shelves were crammed with jars and vials, mysterious pieces of plant material, small burlap sacks tied in ribbons of varied colors. And near one end, a selection of bird claws in graduated sizes.

Claire had been so ravenous for food, she hadn't noticed the display. So this was what Stephen had been talking about! She felt suddenly queasy.

Yvonne grinned. "Don't worry, nothing here will harm you."

Somewhere behind Claire's back, a bell tinkled, and she heard a door creak open. "Ah, here is my cousin now," Yvonne said.

Claire swiveled and found herself confronted by an enormous hulk of a man. Peter Douglas was built like the pro football players on the TV at Tanya's, with mahogany skin and luxuriant dreadlocks that hung midway down his chest. "So you're Claire," he said with a golden grin a lot like Yvonne's. "It's a pleasure to meet you. Won't you come up to our place?"

After the squalor of the neighborhood and the dingy stairwell, Dahlia and Peter's fourth-floor apartment was an inviting oasis, full of warm colors and a melange of spicy scents reminiscent of the store downstairs. Claire had an immediate impulse to kick off her black pumps, which were killing her by now, and pamper her feet on the burgundy carpet. But Dahlia was decidedly less welcoming than her apartment. She emerged from the kitchen exuding a chilly formality, glanced briefly at Claire, then averted her eyes in silence.

This visit was going to test all Claire's diplomatic skills. "What a fabulous place," she said. "I really appreciate your seeing me."

"That's all right." Dahlia's voice had an edge that told Claire it was anything but.

Might as well get to the point. "It wasn't my idea to suspend you, Dahlia. As a matter of fact, I told Paula I didn't approve of the way she handled it. I'm your immediate supervisor, and she shouldn't have gone over my head."

"Yes, I was surprised when she called me. But I figure she runs the agency, she has a right to do what she wants."

"Well, I came down to see about getting you back to work. But I do have some concerns. We need to talk."

Peter moved toward his wife, draped an arm around her shoulders. "There's nothing to talk about. Dahlia and I already decided she should go back to work." He gave her a squeeze. "Right, baby?"

Dahlia winced. "I don't know. It depends."

Peter was practically a foot taller than his wife, and a good hundred pounds heavier. How did Dahlia hold her own with him? Probably she didn't. No wonder she liked working upstate. "I appreciate your interest, Peter," Claire said carefully, "but Dahlia and I should talk privately, since it's company business."

He shrugged, crossed the room and clicked on a gigantic flat-screen television. "Fine with me. You ladies go in the kitchen, and I'll watch TV. I'll just get a beer first."

Dismissed to the servant's quarters, Claire thought. But at least he hadn't asked Dahlia to bring him the beer.

"So Dahlia, tell me about the altar in your bedroom," Claire said when they were settled in the kitchen. "I never saw it, I only heard about it from Stephen."

"I didn't set out to make an altar, you know? At first I just had a couple of candles, for the aroma. No matter how I clean, that house still stink of urine. And I could always smell the dog. I added things bit by bit. I wanted it to look nice, make it more like home."

The sweet smell of marijuana wafted in from the other room. Talk about aromas! Maybe this was why Dahlia favored scented candles. Had she been trying to mask the unmistakable odor of pot? "I have to ask, Dahlia. Do you smoke marijuana too? Or is it just Peter?"

Dahlia's eyes darted to the floor, and she grimaced. "I don't like weed. It makes me lazy and paranoid, and I eat too much. I haven't smoked in years, and even if I did, I'd never do it on the job. I take my work too seriously."

Her answer had the ring of truth, Claire decided. "Okay, well what about the chicken foot? If that's what it was?"

"A chicken foot, yes. Yvonne give it to me last time I was down here on break. She say it keep evil away from my door."

Claire flashed on the memory of Herb Davidson's voice on the machine at Oaktree. "Were you worried about some kind of evil in particular?"

"Kind of. Ever since Harriet died, I've been sick at heart. Her death stole up on her so suddenly, it seemed all wrong. If death could take her that way, so fast and quietly, it could take me too."

"But it took Minna Schatz instead."

"I know, that's been vexing me. I was selfish, thinking only of myself. Maybe I could have done something to protect her."

"Like hang a chicken foot in her bedroom? I don't think she would have gone for that. Besides, it would have driven Maizy crazy."

Dahlia recoiled. "It's not good to joke about these things. It could bring bad luck."

"I'm sorry. I don't mean to make fun of your beliefs. Let's talk about getting you back on the job. As far as I'm concerned, you have a right to observe your own customs and beliefs in the privacy of your own room, and I think I can get Paula to agree on that. What's really bugging her is that you happened to be in the house when two different ladies died unexpectedly, and that their deaths were so similar. I'll admit it bothers me too."

"I don't blame you. What's weird is that both times I slept so soundly, I didn't know anything was wrong. Usually I take a long time falling asleep. And I have a weak bladder. I get up and use the bathroom two or three times in the night. When I do, I always look in on the lady, make sure everything is okay. But on the nights those ladies died, I didn't get up at all. It was like I was drugged or something."

Claire's stomach turned over. "Drugged? Can you be more specific?"

"Well, the night Minna died, I got feeling kind of woozy right after dinner. I thought I might be coming down with the flu or something. I was anxious for Allyson to leave, so I could go to bed."

"That's right, Allyson Quigley made a home visit, didn't she? I remember she brought you some cake."

"Yes, and I had two big pieces. So did Minna, and Allyson gave some to the dog. Minna had a fit about it."

Claire's heart thudded in her chest. She remembered arguing with Allyson about the infamous cake. Could the nurse have laced it with a sedative, or something toxic? That might explain Maizy's lethargy as well.

"Dahlia, do you remember what happened the night Harriet died? Did Allyson come over that night too?"

"I don't know. She makes a lot of visits, so I wouldn't have any special reason to remember." The aide's eyes widened. "Why? You think she put poison in the cake?"

"I wouldn't say that." *I might think it, though.* Claire made a mental note to check the nursing notes for Harriet Gardener, to see if Allyson made a house call that day. Rose Dobson too, for that matter.

"Dahlia, if I can talk Paula into it, would you consider coming back to work for us?"

Dahlia glanced uneasily into the living room, where Peter was watching TV, his feet up on the coffee table. "I might. I don't like being idle. Do you have a case for me?"

"I probably will, but in the meantime I need you to provide relief for George Cropsey. I think you'd be terrific with him, although it wouldn't be easy. He has Parkinson's disease and diabetes. He's basically bed bound, and there's a lot of hands-on physical care."

"I know my cousin Errol's with Mr. Cropsey, but Errol hardly told me anything about him. You think he would like me?"

Claire could read between the lines. *Is he racist? Will he treat me like dirt, the way Minna and Lester did?* "He's depressed, and he can get grouchy at times, but that's common in Parkinson's patients. At heart he's a true gentleman, and I'm sure he'd like you."

And Oaktree Associates is involved, so he bears especially close watching, she wanted to add. Should she confide her newly roused suspicions to Dahlia? Better not – the aide was skittish enough already.

"I'll think about it," Dahlia said.

"Okay, and I'll talk to Paula first thing tomorrow morning about getting you back on the active roster. If she gives me the okay, could you come up tomorrow afternoon? Errol's threatening to walk."

Chapter 24

*P*aula's head felt ready to explode. Where the hell was Claire, anyway? Already nine fifteen – she should have been in by now. Paula should never have let her go waltzing off to New York City yesterday, not with these new cases to worry about. She grabbed a second donut and glared at Maria. "What do you mean you can't find anyone to relieve Errol James?"

The coordinator glared back. "I've been telling you we're stretched too thin. With four new cases opening in the last week, we're using some of the relief aides as primaries. I called everyone who might conceivably be free, but no luck. The only ones left are the absolute dregs. People on probation for disciplinary problems, or whose skills aren't up to par. Claire doesn't want me calling them unless I check with her first."

"She's right – you shouldn't." Paula massaged her temples, but the pain only got worse. "Give me a minute to think."

Staffing was absolutely the worst thing about running an agency. To open new cases, you needed good aides, but you couldn't keep good aides unless you already had the cases to offer them. It was a vicious circle. If you couldn't give them work the instant they wanted it, they would jump ship and go to another agency. Or at least that was true of the aides who lived locally. The live-in aides from New York City were a different story. They were reasonably loyal, in part because they didn't know the area or the other agencies, in part because of their liking for Claire. But they were all prima donnas with tunnel vision, all looking out for Numero Uno. They didn't give a shit about the agency.

Claire materialized in the doorway, looking unusually haggard. "Sorry I'm late."

"It's about time," Paula snapped.

Maria narrowed her eyes and gave Claire the once-over. "How was your day in the city?" Her tone had a sarcastic edge to it.

"Interesting, but too frenetic for my taste. I'm glad I don't live there any more."

Enough chitchat, Paula decided. "How was Dahlia? Did you counsel her? Can we feel okay about using her?"

"I think we can," Claire said. "She's willing to give George Cropsey a try. She should be home now, waiting for my call. She can't come up till Sunday, though."

"Damn!" Maria rolled her eyes skyward. "Errol's been climbing the walls. He said he wants out today whether we can relieve him or not. I begged him not to leave us in a bind, but he said if worst came to worst, the family could take care of George for the weekend. Then Errol would come back Monday morning."

The words hit Paula's head like a sledge hammer, doubling the pain. She winced. "No way!" she exclaimed. "We'll lose the case if he pulls that. I'll fire his ass if he walks out today."

"Please don't, Paula! We need him. I'll call and see if I can sweet-talk him into staying." Maria turned to leave and collided with Stephen, who was on his way in. "Oooh, sorry!" She threw him a startled look. "I didn't see you coming!"

"That's okay." He edged past Maria into the office, his eyes on Claire.

"I was just talking about Errol," Maria said. "He's probably so hot to get out because it's payday, and he wants to go cash his check and start partying. I have to convince him to stay with George for the weekend – that's all I meant by sweet-talking. I don't want to make you jealous."

Oh yes, you do, Paula thought. She knew Stephen and Maria had something going on; you'd have to be blind to miss it.

"I'm not jealous," Stephen said, his eyes still on Claire.

Claire closed the door to her office, leaned against it to catch her breath. *Deliver me from office politics,* she thought. *There's nothing going on between me and Stephen.* If only he wouldn't look at her that way. Maria would have to be blind not to notice.

She hoped Maria's wiles were more effective with Errol than they'd been with Stephen. Otherwise Claire could very well find herself playing personal care aide with George Cropsey till Dahlia arrived on Sunday. Strangely enough, the idea had a certain appeal. Caring for George would be more stimulating than a weekend alone with the dogs.

Down to business. She decided to pull Harriet Gardener's and Rose Dobson's charts to see whether Allyson Quigley made any nursing visits right before they died. Then she would check the number for Herb Davidson she had jotted down at Oaktree. And she should call the police to see if they had any new information on the threatening letter, but not while Paula was in the office. Her boss was still her prime suspect, after all.

The files for the closed cases resided in a locked cabinet in the copy room down the hall. She retrieved the charts, brought them back to her office. Within ten minutes, she found what she was looking for: Allyson Quigley had visited both Harriet Gardener and Rose Dobson in the evening, hours before they died. Ever the conscientious nurse, she had documented both visits in the progress notes and signed off on them. They were routine drop-in calls, unannounced so as to catch the aides off-guard. All the better to monitor their performance.

Both women were healthy, with no abnormal physical findings. Nothing out of the ordinary, except that they were both dead mere hours after the visits.

Claire recalled going through the charts before, closing them out after the clients' deaths. On one level, she had known about Allyson's visits, but on another level, they had slipped under the radar of her consciousness. She hadn't been looking for anything suspicious, but here it was, an obvious pattern. The question was what to do about it.

Might as well get all the bad news at once. She retrieved her handbag from under the desk, found the scrap of paper where she'd jotted down that number yesterday. Then she reached for her planner, flipped to the "C's." There it was, under Coroner: Herb Davidson.

The number was the same.

———————

Tonight was the night, Lester decided. Assuming Claire Lindstrom was home, of course. He'd scoped out her house last night, but her car wasn't there. Just as well. He hadn't been in shape to pull it off. With all the alcohol in his system, it would have been just his luck to get pulled over and charged for DWI, and he would have had a hell of a time explaining the rifle stashed behind the bench seat of his truck.

He was relatively sober now. Not completely – he felt like shit and his hands shook too badly when he tried laying off the booze completely. No, he'd been drinking just enough to maintain a nice little buzz, and to damp down his mother's voice. She still yammered at him all hours of the day and night. *You idiot! What the hell do you think you're doing?*

I'm going to get your dog back, Mother. Maizy belongs here in this house. And I'm going to put a stop to Claire Lindstrom's snooping once and for all, so I can sleep soundly again without worrying that she's out to get me.

The rifle was ready, lying in wait beneath a blanket on the floor of the truck. The night was fairly clear, with a brisk breeze whipping the clouds in front of a half moon. Enough light to see by once his eyes adjusted to the darkness, not enough to make him too conspicuous. He had dug out his old duck-hunting get-up; the drab brownish camouflage was perfect for early November. The pants didn't fasten at the waist the way they used to, so he had to belt them low, below the belly. And the zipper on the jacket was broken. But hey, it wasn't like anybody was going to see him.

He splashed some more Jack Daniel's into his glass, just enough to steady his nerves.

Lester, are you crazy? You never do anything right. You'll never get away with this.

Shut the fuck up, Mother!

He gulped down the whiskey and shoved back his chair. Time to get the show on the road.

———

Claire stirred restlessly as she dreamed of barking dogs. Freia and Maizy were running free, in hot pursuit of prey. She caught sight of a doe and two fawns leaping through the woods. The trees were green, dappled with summer sun, and Stephen was at her side, laughing as the deer bounded out of range. The dogs doubled back, still barking excitedly.

Gradually she swam to the surface of consciousness and opened her eyes to the cold light of the moon slicing through her window and across her bedroom wall. She snaked an exploratory arm across the bed, but of course it was empty. Her body was aroused, eager, but whatever X-rated scenario she'd been playing out in her unconscious mind, it was shattered beyond recall, thanks to the dogs.

They were barking for real. "Quiet, ladies!" she called, although she knew they wouldn't obey. Even before Maizy's arrival, Freia had indulged in occasional bouts of nocturnal noise making, and now, with Maizy to egg her on, the barking had gotten more frequent. Claire wasn't alarmed by it; in fact, she found it oddly reassuring. The neighborhood was rife with animals, both wild and tame, and somehow, maybe by smell, the dogs sensed their presence. Tonight's visitor could be a wandering raccoon or possum. Or maybe a dog or cat had decided to take a midnight ramble through the yard.

Whatever it was, Freia and Maizy were on the job, warning the trespasser to stay away or face dire consequences. "Good girls," Claire murmured. Then she rolled over and fell back to sleep.

A few houses away along the lakeshore, Gabriel came suddenly alert to the sound of barking. It had to be Claire's dogs – he could tell by the direction. Besides, he'd learned to recognize their voices. If you really listened, dogs communicated in tones that were just as distinctive as people's.

They sounded unusually upset tonight. He slipped out of bed, padded to the living room, and peered through his night-vision scope. He saw nothing at first. Then a flash of movement caught his eye near the grove of trees at the edge of Claire's lawn. Light tones among the dark trunks of the spruces and maples. Something big – a deer, maybe?

He hunched closer, squinted hard through the eyepiece. Too blotchy, too random for a deer. Then, slowly, the shapes resolved into a recognizable pattern: the interlocking amoeba design of military camouflage. He was looking at a man, and the man was heading for Claire's house. Holding something long and dark – maybe a rifle.

Gabriel's heart began slamming against the wall of his chest. No time to waste. Should he drive? Run? Could he reach the house in time? The possibilities raced through his mind as he pulled on his running clothes, his sneakers. He grabbed his gun, shoved it in the waistband of his pants. Then he crossed to his closet, rummaged on the shelf beneath the sweaters for the soft leather pouch that held his medical essentials.

He unzipped the pouch. Better prepare it now – there might not be time at the scene.

The moon was half full and he knew the road well, so it wasn't hard driving without headlights. As he neared the grove of spruce, the same one he'd watched Claire's car disappear behind so many times, he saw a truck parked off the road just ahead – a battered Chevy truck. In the cold light of the moon, the color was a washed-out black, but he recognized it instantly: the truck belonged to Minna Schatz's son.

What the hell was Lester doing here? Gabriel had never met the man, but he'd seen him from a distance a couple of times, seen enough to know he was a hothead. That and a chronic drunk.

This could get dodgy, but if the man was after Claire, he had to be stopped. Gabriel killed the engine, climbed out and stood silently, getting his bearings. The stand of trees was thick, with no discernible paths, and he couldn't see through to the other side. On the other hand, Schatz couldn't see him either. Gabriel took a deep breath and stepped cautiously into the woods.

The moon through the trees cast crazy, disorienting shadows, jagged and menacing, like something out of an expressionist movie. He took a mental snapshot in case he decided to paint it sometime, then crept forward. There was just enough light so that he could see his way, avoid fallen branches that might snap noisily, vines or prickers that might trip him up. The ground was perfect: soft and moist with recent rain. No dry leaves to crackle and give him away, not mushy enough to suck and squish underfoot.

The dogs had gone silent, but why? Was the man still here? If he had made it to the house, surely they would have raised a ruckus.

Gabriel was almost through the clearing when he caught sight of Schatz. He was sitting on the ground, his back against the trunk of an enormous maple, snuffling softly. The rifle lay on the ground beside him.

Jeez! What the hell was going on? Gabriel reached for the leather pouch, extracted the hypodermic and stashed it in his jacket pocket. As he crept closer, he heard Schatz belch, then utter a strangled sob.

The man was blind drunk, a sitting duck. Gabriel flew at him broadside, got one arm around his throat and the other over his mouth. Then he eased down onto his knees and leaned toward the man's ear. "This is Claire Lindstrom's property. What are you doing here?" he murmured.

"Mmmph." Lester thrashed in his grasp, struggled to face him.

"I've got a couple of things to ask you." Gabriel grabbed the pistol, jammed it into Schatz's temple. Against his arm, he felt the man's throat straining, his pulse fluttering wildly like a trapped bird. "I won't shoot as long as you speak very, very quietly. In a minute, I'm going to take my hand off your mouth. But one yell and you're history. You got that?"

The man bobbed his head.

"Good. Now tell me: what the fuck are you doing, trespassing on Claire Lindstrom's property with a rifle? Have you got it in your head to kill her?"

"Yes. I mean no. I don't know." Schatz's voice gurgled in his throat. "She kept hounding me, always on my case. I just wanted her to stop meddling in things that are none of her goddamn business."

As do I. That's exactly what I told her in my note. "So which is it? Do you want her dead? Yes or no?"

"I thought I did, but I changed my mind. I could never hurt anybody. I'm not a killer."

"Oh no? You could have fooled me. You killed your mother, didn't you? Maybe not directly, but you set the wheels in motion." He nudged the pistol harder against the skin of Schatz's face. "Didn't you?"

The man let out a low whine, and his eyes rolled skyward.

All the answer I need. "Your mother didn't need to die, not so soon. She wasn't in unbearable pain. No terminal disease, no cancer, no Alzheimer's. You wanted her out of the way for your own selfish reasons, didn't you? Tell the truth."

Schatz's mouth gaped open, and tears trickled from his piggy little eyes. "Please don't kill me," he rasped.

A pathetic, disgusting excuse for a man. He doesn't deserve to live. "Don't worry, I'm not going to shoot you," Gabriel said. "I have something more merciful in mind. It's actually better than you deserve. You'll go swiftly and painlessly, the same way your mother went. Call it poetic justice if you want. As you experience your own death, you'll be reliving what you put her through in the most intimate possible way."

He gave Schatz another warning jab with the pistol. The man whimpered softly as Gabriel reached for the syringe. He uncapped it, plunged it swiftly and decisively into the carotid artery, pushed the contents home. Then he withdrew the needle, placed two fingers gently on the injection site and waited until the fluttering ceased.

Chapter 25

The cold, wet sensation against her cheek startled Claire out of a deep sleep, and she shot bolt upright in panic. Her eyes flew open and met the deep brown pools of Maizy's. The terrier's nose nuzzled her cheek again.

"Jesus, dog! You scared me half to death!"

The dog stood her ground, looming over Claire, whimpering. Her nails dug into the soft down comforter. Claire shoved her gently away. "Get down! Maybe Minna let you sleep with her, but in my house, dogs don't sleep on the bed."

Maizy gave her a reproachful look and hopped down, still whining. At the bedroom door, Freia stood wagging eagerly.

Claire glanced at her clock radio. Almost nine – no wonder the dogs were restless.

She rarely slept this late. No doubt the frazzling events of the past few days had left her in a state of severe sleep deprivation. But the dogs could care less that it was Saturday morning.

"Okay, guys, hold on while I get dressed." She climbed out of bed, pulled on jeans and a microfleece top. By the time she had laced her hiking boots, the dogs were bouncing off the walls.

"I know, I know. It's hard when you really have to pee."

She shrugged into her jacket, snapped on Maizy's leash, and they were out the door. Freia paused on the deck, pointed her whiskery muzzle skyward and sniffed the air, then bounded onto the lawn and streaked toward the grove of trees at the far side of the property. Maizy tugged at her leash, desperate to follow.

Claire thought back to the wild spell of barking that had awakened her in the night. Did the dogs remember too? Were they eager to track down the phantom intruders that had gotten them so excited? Or was this a whole new ball game, a whole new batch of fresh scents to explore? "It's hard to fathom the depths of the canine mind," she told Maizy as the little dog yanked her forward.

Across the yard, Freia let out a salvo of high-pitched yips, the "Eureka!" bark that announced she had found something truly exciting. Please, God, don't let her corner a skunk, Claire thought. Or any other critter, for that matter. The barks had a frantic overtone that set her teeth on edge.

She was halfway across the lawn when the camouflage pattern leapt out at her. Near her favorite Norway maple, the one she'd always thought would make a perfect tree house, something large sprawled on the ground. A heap of fabric, she thought at first, but from the way Freia was acting, she knew it was more than that. She yanked back on Maizy's leash. "Heel, Maizy!"

She moved slowly and stealthily the rest of the way. Why, she wondered. For fear of waking the dead? Because she already sensed the truth: this wasn't a random pile of cloth, it was a human body. Freia circled warily, pawing the ground around the fallen figure.

Even before she saw the face, the bloated, lumpish contours of the body told her it was Lester Schatz. *Damn it, I warned him! I knew he was going to stroke out or have a coronary one of these days!*

She rushed to his side, knelt on the mushy carpet of brown maple leaves and placed two fingers on his carotid artery. Just as she'd expected, there was no pulse.

He was lying sprawled on his back with his arms outstretched. Blood pooled in the parts of the body closest to the ground: postmortem lividity. The dark, dusky color of the blood, the way it had settled in the back of his neck and in his hands where they touched the forest floor, told her he had been dead for hours. His skin was cold, but that was to be expected – the outside temperature must be in the low forties.

It would take a medical examiner to determine the exact time of death, as well as the cause. True, Lester Schatz had obvious health problems that had probably done him in, but he was still in the prime years of middle age, much too young to write off his death as attributable to normal aging. This time she wanted a good look at the body. This time there would be an autopsy, and she wanted to be there to witness it.

She should call 911, but there was no rush. First she would take a closer look, commit the scene to memory. She should have done that with the three women, but she'd let herself get shunted aside. That wouldn't happen again.

Hunkered down at her side, Maizy growled softly. With Minna, she'd been whimpering. "You poor girl, you've seen more than your share of death lately," Claire said as she rubbed the dog's ears. Then she bent closer to study the body once more. The face was swollen, the mouth agape, the eyes staring fixedly at the treetops. The cords of the neck distended, the skin – could it be? There on the carotid artery, near the place where she'd taken the pulse, was a definite bruising, a puncture mark like the one she had seen on his mother's neck. In Minna's case, Claire had only a vague impression of the strange lesion. The room had been dark, and they hadn't let her stay long. But here in the light of day, there was no doubt.

She rocked back on her heels, struggled to her feet in shock. What had happened here? She reached for Freia, buried her hands in the dog's thick, curly coat. It was only then, glancing around, that she noticed the hunting rifle lying in the leaves a few feet from the body.

"I recognize that man!"

At the sound of the unexpected voice, Claire let out a shriek. Whirling, she found herself face to face with Angelo Giordano.

"Angelo! You shouldn't have snuck up on me like that!"

"Sorry. I heard the dogs making an uproar, so I came out to see what was going on. What was this guy doing here, anyway?"

Good question, Claire thought as she stood waiting for her pulse to descend to normal. "I haven't had time to think about that. As soon as I saw him, I went into automatic overdrive. I've been doing my nursing thing, checking his vital signs and trying to figure out what happened to him."

"He doesn't look too vital now. What do you think killed him?"

"My first thought was heart attack or stroke. But then I noticed that little mark on his neck. See right there on top of the carotid artery?"

"You mean that little blue bruised area? I've gotten similar marks occasionally when a lab technician takes blood. Sometimes they get clumsy and don't hit the vein right."

"Exactly. Except maybe this time they were giving something instead of taking it."

Angelo's eyes widened. "You mean someone injected him with something?"

"I certainly intend to find out. This time I'm not going to leave it up to that incompetent clown, Herb Davidson." At the thought of Davidson, her pulse started climbing again. How was she going to cope with the coroner? The same way you cope with a porcupine: very carefully.

All at once she remembered Angelo's first comment. "This man's name is Lester Schatz," she told him. "You said you recognized him?"

"I don't know him personally, but I've seen him before. Remember when I was telling you about my visit to Oaktree Associates, and I saw someone stomping out of one of the offices? A guy who seemed furious about something?"

Claire nodded.

Angelo nodded back. "This is the guy."

───────

Gabriel smiled as he gazed through his binoculars. This was the first time he'd had a ringside seat for the aftermath of one of his killings, and it was unexpectedly satisfying. He was pleased with his handiwork, as usual, but always before he had left the scene well before the discovery phase. It was nice to have an appreciative audience for a change, especially when that audience was Claire Lindstrom.

But he shouldn't make light of the problems. For one thing, she was taking too damn long about everything. She should have called 911 by now. Instead, she'd spent a long time studying the body, and now she was standing there talking with the old man from next door.

He thought of the note he'd left in her mailbox. *There you go again, Claire. Stirring up trouble, asking too many questions. I tried to warn you – too bad you didn't take me seriously.*

He'd seen her peering at the neck, and he wondered if she'd noticed the injection site. Gabriel had been careful, precise as always, and he didn't think he'd left any telltale marks, but it had been so dark there in the woods that he couldn't be positive. If she saw anything, she would certainly point it out to the crime scene people. But by then the potassium levels in the body would already be skewed, and they wouldn't be able to detect a thing on autopsy. Even if they did, there was nothing to tie him to the scene. He was virtually home free. Even so, he would feel better once they took the body away.

The other problem was that this had been a spur-of-the-moment extracurricular activity. The higher powers didn't like surprises or improvisation, Athena had made that abundantly clear. There was no reason they should tie this death to Gabriel, and he certainly wasn't about to bring up the subject. On the other hand, the death happened on Claire's property, and he was supposed to be keeping an eye on Claire. And since Lester Schatz's mother had been one of his assignments . . .

Cut it out, Gabriel! You'll drive yourself crazy with all these "what if's" and "on the other hands." Why keep obsessing about something he couldn't do anything about? The deed was done. He couldn't take it back, nor would he want to. Lester Schatz was a despicable creep who deserved to die. And by intervening when he did, Gabriel might well have saved Claire Lindstrom's life last night. Too bad she didn't know it - maybe he would find a way to tell her one of these days.

What else would he do the next time they met? He felt a rush of edgy energy course through his body. *Hard to say.*

Maybe a little art therapy would help him chill out. He flashed on the memory of the trees last night, with all those weird shadows cast by the half moon. The image was vivid in his mind's eye, and he congratulated himself - his powers of observation were definitely improving. What if he tried a landscape with some expressionistic figures? The man lying lifeless on the ground, the woman kneeling at his side, maybe even the dogs. The subject might incriminate him, but hey, no one ever saw his work anyway.

I need an audience. I'm tired of anonymity.

Now Claire and the old man were walking toward her house, the dogs hot on their heels. Soon the cops and the EMTs would be on the scene. Better not watch – he shouldn't risk being seen.

A good time to start a painting.

─── ─── ───

Officer Frances Milgrim got to her feet and stripped off her purple nitrile gloves. "You were right," she announced to Claire. "This guy has definitely been dead awhile."

Her partner, Officer John Thorne, stood immobile at her side, his round face revealing nothing. Their interaction had been the same the last time Claire had seen them together: minimal. Easy to guess who was the top dog in this relationship.

Milgrim folded her arms and fixed Claire with a penetrating stare. "So here you are again, at yet another death scene. Peculiar, don't you think?"

"Yes, it's really bizarre."

"How do you mean, bizarre?"

"Isn't it obvious? Finding Lester Schatz out here in my woods. I mean what on earth was he doing here?"

The officer took a step closer, but she was three inches shorter than Claire. Evidently she realized the difference in height didn't work in her favor, because she stepped back again. "I was hoping you could tell me."

"I have no idea. Hunting, maybe?"

"In the middle of the night? I don't think so. Anyway, it's not deer season yet, and I noticed three *Posted* signs near the road on your property." Milgrim glanced over Claire's shoulder. "The EMTs are here. We'll continue this discussion later."

"Wait a minute," Claire said. "Did you get the message I left yesterday, about the anonymous letter? No one ever got back to me."

Milgrim scowled. "You'll have to take that up with my supervisor. He should be here soon." She brushed past Claire and headed across the lawn toward the medical technicians. "There's no rush," the officer said. "In my estimation, it appears he's been dead a few hours already."

Claire felt a rush of annoyance. *That was my estimation, not yours, lady. I told you at the outset.* But what did it matter who took credit for the judgment call? Lester was indisputably dead.

"Let's have a look," said the taller of the two EMTs. As he strode past her, Claire recognized his gaunt, angular face. He'd been there the night of Minna's death. Relief washed over her; she remembered him as reasonably caring and sympathetic.

"There's something I want you to see," Claire said as she hurried to catch up with him. They reached Lester's body simultaneously, and she crouched down. "Look right there on his neck, at the carotid artery? See the discoloration?"

"You mean that bluish area?" He squatted down beside her. "Yes, I see what you mean."

"It looks like an injection site to me."

He raised his eyes to hers. In the light of day, they looked even more haunted and sorrowful than she remembered. "Hmmm, could be," he said.

Officer Milgrim hunkered down beside them and glared at Claire. "Why didn't you point this out to me?"

Turf battles. Just what they needed. "I would have, but you started asking all kinds of questions."

"Count on it, there'll be more. You're not going to be able to brush this one off so easily."

"Brush it off? I never wanted to brush anything off. On the contrary –"

Claire stopped short at the feel of a hand on her shoulder, wheeled to face Angelo. Thank God he was back; he'd gone home to check up on Regina. "No need to use that tone with Ms.

Lindstrom," he told the officer. "She's been through enough already this morning."

Milgrim ignored him. "As I was about to say, Sergeant Portman should be here soon, and I'm sure he'll have some questions for you. I know he'll call in the crime scene technicians. The homicide detectives too."

"Good, I'm glad." *Glad I won't have to deal with you.* "I really want to get to the bottom of this," Claire said.

"So do I, believe me." Milgrim turned to her partner. "Thorne, you stay here and keep watch. This is a crime scene, and I don't want anyone messing with it." She glared at Claire. "You and your friend, step back and away."

"Are you going to check for footprints?" asked Claire. "See if anyone else was at the scene?"

Milgrim sniffed. "Too many cop shows on TV. Everyone thinks they're an expert. Matter of fact, the first thing I'm going to do is go to the car, make a couple of calls. Sergeant Portman asked me to notify the coroner."

"Herb Davidson? On a sunny Saturday morning? You'll probably have to page him on the golf course."

No sooner were the words out of Claire's mouth than she flashed on the Oaktree connection. "I'll be extremely interested in what he has to say," she told the cop.

Chapter 26

"*F*reia! Maizy! Down! Quiet!"

Blowing off Claire's command, the dogs kept hurling themselves at the dining room windowsill, raking the paint with their nails. Now she saw why: Herb Davidson was crossing the lawn, and sure enough, he was dressed in his golf gear. "It's about time," she told the detective seated across the table. He'd introduced himself as Stan Kupcinek, and he had a squarish, Slavic-looking face to go with the name.

He gave her a cryptic half-smile, glanced at his watch, said nothing. As the minutes ticked painfully by, their exchanges weren't getting any more comfortable.

"I should really get out there and talk to the coroner," she said.

"It's not necessary. My partner will handle it."

"But I want to make sure Davidson takes his time and sees everything he should. Including that mark on the neck I showed you."

"Relax, Ms. Lindstrom. That's not your responsibility."

Relax? How could she relax with all these strangers milling around her yard? Detective Kupcinek's partner was out there, along with Milgrim and Thorne, their supervisor Sergeant Portman, the EMTs and several others she guessed were crime scene technicians. One was taking photos, and others were scouring the ground.

"They must be looking for trace evidence," she said. "Footprints, fibers, that kind of thing. Right?"

The detective smiled and nodded, like an old-school shrink who believes less is more and measures out his words as if every one is golden. Using silence as a tool, hoping she'd open up. But she was too savvy to fall for that game.

She stood. "I'm going to get some more coffee. Would you like a cup?"

"Thanks, that would be good. Milk, no sugar."

As soon as Milgrim had shooed her away from the body, she'd headed for the house and brewed a full carafe of coffee, and now she was on her third cup. As if she needed anything extra to jangle her nerves. But the familiar morning ritual was comforting, and it gave her something to do with her hands.

She returned with the two mugs, set them down on the table, then settled herself across from Kupcinek once more. "It's ironic what a difference twenty or thirty years can make."

His blue-gray eyes glittered, then went flat. "How do you mean?"

"When our client Rose Dobson died, no one took photographs or called in the crime scene technicians. It was just written off as an unfortunate accident. She was a good thirty years older than Lester Schatz, and I'm wondering how much her age had to do with it. Some people might call it age discrimination."

"There are some other key differences. She was on her own land, for one thing. And no one suggested foul play."

"So you're familiar with that incident, Detective?"

"I was informed of it, yes."

"Good, because I have some serious questions about what happened to Rose Dobson. Specifically in regard to a nurse at our agency, Allyson Quigley. I checked the charts yesterday, and she made a home visit to Rose the night she died. She also visited Lester Schatz's mother, Minna, and another client of ours who died in early September, Harriet Gardener. A few hours after her visits, all three ladies were dead."

Kupcinek was silent, scribbling on his steno pad. Then he raised his eyes to Claire's. "Why did you happen to check the records yesterday? Doesn't the timing seem strange to you?"

"How do you mean?"

"You uncover these supposedly questionable visits, and a man turns up dead in your yard the next morning."

Claire's stomach began churning. "I don't see how one thing relates to the other."

"I was hoping you could tell me." His gaze narrowed. "We'll be looking into it."

Her hand shook, and her coffee mug chattered against the table. She let go the handle, clasped both hands in her lap out of sight. "Actually, I can explain why I checked the records yesterday. On Thursday, I visited Dahlia Douglas in New York City. She was the aide on duty with Minna Schatz the night she died. Dahlia mentioned feeling unusually sleepy that night, almost as if she was drugged. And Allyson Quigley had brought over some cake. Dahlia said she felt the same way the night Harriet Gardener died, so I decided to see if Allyson had been there as well. I checked Rose Dobson for good measure."

"So this same aide was on duty all three times?"

Damn! He was like a football player on the opposing team, intercepting the ball, then zigzagging in some unexpected direction. "No, another aide was with Rose. Sharon Westerly."

"Do you have an agency roster, with names and numbers of all your staff?"

"Yes, but it's confidential. I'd have to check with Paula Rhodes, the agency owner, before I give it to you."

"If she refuses, we can always get a warrant. Do you have any idea what Lester Schatz was doing outside your house?"

"None at all."

"How well did you know the victim? Did you have any arguments or disagreements with him?"

Where was he going with this? Should she get a lawyer? There was no point in whitewashing the problem; if he had a mind to, Kupcinek could probably dredge up witnesses, especially from that final exchange at the funeral home. "I wouldn't call them arguments, exactly. But I think he felt I was too intrusive, both in regard to his mother's care and in regard to his own health."

"Intrusive – that's basically what that anonymous note said about you too."

"Oh good, you've looked at it! Did you dust it for prints? Have you reached any conclusions yet?"

He gave her another flat stare. "I can't comment on that, but given these new developments, we'll be looking into it further. Now, you were telling me about your relationship with Lester Schatz."

"Right. In my professional opinion, he probably had a variety of physical problems, especially hypertension. When I broached the subject of his health, he accused me of meddling and told me to back off. But the circulatory problems may have brought about his death. Most likely he threw a clot or had a myocardial infarction."

"Awhile ago you were talking about suspicious needle marks. Which is it? In your professional opinion, of course?"

She didn't like the sarcastic spin he put on the word *professional.* "I honestly don't know. That's why there should be a thorough and competent autopsy. You're not going to have Herb Davidson just sign off on this death, are you? Because more than likely he'll blow it off, the way he did the other ones."

"You have a beef to pick with him too?"

Claire fell silent. Should she tell the detective about the call she'd overheard at Oaktree? Better not. He was already twisting everything she said. Apparently he didn't buy into her suspicions of Allyson, and she had nothing concrete to incriminate Davidson. By slinging vague accusations around, she might dig herself into a deeper hole than she was already in.

"He's not an actual medical examiner," she said at last, in the most neutral tone she could muster. "I just wouldn't want you to miss anything important on autopsy. There will be one, won't there?"

"Yes, definitely. The fact that the victim was trespassing on your land, apparently armed with a rifle, makes this death highly suspicious." He looked toward the window. Following his gaze, she saw the men stringing yellow crime tape from tree to tree at the edge of the grove.

"Don't go anywhere near the scene," he said gruffly. "That goes for your dogs too. Be sure to keep them leashed."

She attempted a smile. "You don't have to worry about that. I wouldn't want them making any more grisly discoveries."

The detective didn't smile back.

What seemed an eternity later, Claire sat at her dining table, nursing a glass of Merlot and watching the dregs of the day drain from the sky as the dogs slept at her feet. Across the lawn, the grove of trees loomed dark and forbidding. The branches of the Norway maple looked like the limbs of an arthritic witch, and she knew she would never again lounge lazily against its enormous trunk. The image of Lester Schatz's body sprawled beneath the tree was printed indelibly in her memory, poisoning the beauty of the place.

In the fading light, the yellow crime scene tape gave off an eerie glow. She rose, drew the draperies against the encroaching night. *I shouldn't be alone, not tonight.* She crossed to the phone, punched in Angelo and Regina's number. But they were in no shape for company, he said. The day's events had upset Regina badly. Not the actual sights and sounds – she had been well insulated from those – but the thought of someone dying in the night, so close to home. She needed peace and quiet tonight.

Claire wished Stephen would call. She could hardly blame him for avoiding her after the way she'd blown him off. Why not take the initiative, call to apologize? She was a liberated twenty-first century woman, after all – no need to pine away by the phone. But his machine picked up.

"Hi, Stephen, it's Claire. Call me when you get a chance."

As she hung up, she realized he had no way of knowing what had happened since they'd talked yesterday in the office. He'd know tomorrow, though, if he checked the Sunday paper or the TV news. By the time they carted Lester's body away, the local media had descended on her yard like a coven of ravenous crows. Or was it a murder of crows? She seemed to recall that term from somewhere. Probably *Jeopardy.*

Maybe Stephen would be at Tanya's. Come to think of it, she could use some of their barbecued ribs, with a side of sweet potato fries. She hadn't eaten all day, and the wine, superimposed on too many mugs of coffee, was burning a hole in her stomach. Besides, the thought of staying home alone terrified her far more profoundly than she wanted to admit.

Tanya's Sports Club was packed to the gills, but Stephen was nowhere in sight. Oh well, she was here for the food anyway.

They had a hostess on duty tonight. "Just one?" she asked.

"That's right." Why did they always have to say "just," with that edge of pity in their voices?

The woman led her to a table against the far wall, perilously close to a dartboard. Claire would have to move if a game got going, but it would do for the time being. She summoned the waitress. "I know what I want." She ordered, then settled in and let the sound of rock wash over her. Ironically enough, she recognized Counting Crows.

"Hey, Claire! What a pleasant surprise! Mind if I join you? Or are you saving this seat for someone?"

She looked up to see Rick Kozlowski grinning down at her. There it was again, this assumption that there was something weird about her venturing out without a man at her side. Or maybe she was just projecting. "No, I'm alone, despite the fact that it's Saturday night," she said. "I had an overwhelming urge for baby back ribs tonight. That's why I'm here."

He slid into the chair across from her. "When you came in, it seemed like you were looking for someone. I thought maybe your friend Stephen."

The realization that he had been watching her gave her the creeps. "Since when are you keeping tabs on my social life?"

"Whoa, don't get so defensive, Claire. I just happened to be facing the door when you came in. It's not like I'm stalking you or something."

"Funny you should say that. If I seem skittish, it's because someone actually was stalking me, or at least it looks that way." She paused, suppressing a shudder as she remembered Stephen's words. Could Rick be the one who sent her that note? For all she knew, he could even have murdered Lester. Well, here he was, and escaping him would be awkward. She might as level with him, watch his reaction.

"My dogs found a body in the woods near my house this morning," she said. "The man was dressed in camouflage, and he had a rifle. I have a hunch he was on a hunting expedition, and I was the intended prey."

Rick's eyes lit up, and he leaned closer. "Get out of here! You're putting me on, right?"

"Unfortunately not. No doubt it'll make the eleven o'clock news tonight and the papers tomorrow, so I guess it's okay to tell you about it."

"God, it must have been horrible for you. No wonder you wanted to get out on the town." He reached a hand across the table as if to clasp hers, then withdrew it again. "You poor thing, you're probably suffering from post-traumatic shock, but it'll do you good to talk about it. Tell Uncle Rick. He wants to know everything."

Uncle Rick? He was giving off strange emanations tonight. Acting excited and fluttery, as if eager to share some particularly juicy gossip over the water cooler. Camping it up, playing against type. He was wearing the faded jeans again, with yet another plaid flannel shirt that showed off the blue mermaid on his forearm. Macho Man meets Richard Simmons. But he was right: she did need to talk.

"So? Out with it," he said. "When I was active in nursing, I prided myself on my listening skills, and I might as well keep in practice, in case I get desperate for cash and have to jump-start my moribund career."

She laughed in spite of herself. "So you see this as some kind of in-service refresher session? I don't think so."

"Touché. Sorry, that did come across as a tad too self-serving. And I know I must sound like a vicarious thrill seeker, because I've never had the experience of finding a body in my yard. But in all sincerity, I believe it would do you good to talk. Let me buy you another drink."

He couldn't have sent the note, she reflected. *He loves gossip too much, and my anonymous pen pal hates it.* Her eyes scanned the room once more. Still no Stephen. "Okay," she said. "You're on. Let's see, where should I start?"

"How about cause of death? Did he screw up and shoot himself by mistake?"

"No, there were no obvious signs of violence. My first guess was heart attack or stroke. Maybe a ruptured aneurysm, something like that. He was obese and he had obvious health problems, but he refused to do anything about them."

"Oh, so you knew the man?"

"Yes." She nearly blurted out Lester's name, caught herself just in time. The case would be public knowledge soon enough, but in the meantime, out of respect for Minna, she might as well cling to the vestiges of confidentiality. "He was the son of one of our clients."

They paused to order their drinks. Then she embarked on a capsule summary of the saga of Minna and Lester Schatz.

"So you think his circulatory problems finally did him in?" Rick asked when she finally wound down. "If he was really out gunning for you, the timing couldn't have been better. How weird – somebody else's heart attack might have actually saved your life."

"Yes, that would be ironic, wouldn't it. But I noticed something odd. An area of bruising and a little mark, right above the carotid artery. It looked like an injection site, and I'm wondering if someone else could have shot him up with something."

He leaned forward, his dark eyes rapt. "You mean earlier, or right there at the site?"

"Either one, but right there seems more likely. I pointed out the mark to the police and the EMTs, and within an hour the place was swarming with crime technicians, so hopefully they're taking me seriously. Maybe something will show up on autopsy."

"What kind of injection, do you think? Any ideas?"

"Something fast acting. Maybe insulin or potassium."

His voice dropped to a whisper. "Potassium would be better. It's really fast, and soon after death, the blood cells start to hemolyze and the potassium levels get all out of whack. It would be difficult, almost impossible to detect on autopsy."

His intensity unnerved her, and she leaned back, away from him. "How do you happen to know so much about this?"

"It's common knowledge for nurses – you thought of it too. But I confess I have kind of an extracurricular interest in the subject. I like true crime stories, especially ones involving medical crimes. Another one made the news just recently – a male nurse who killed upwards of forty nursing home patients. Somewhere in New Jersey, I believe. He said he was putting them out of their misery."

"Yes, I remember that too."

The waitress brought her baby back ribs just then. Claire realized she'd lost her appetite in the course of her conversation with Rick, but she dug in anyway. "What do you say we change the subject while I eat?" she asked. "Something innocuous, like what's your least favorite month? I vote for November."

He laughed. "February. Sorry if I got a little carried away there."

"I asked for it. Want some of my ribs? I'll never get through all these."

"No thanks, I've got to get going." He reached in his pocket, pulled out a twenty and slapped it on the table. "This should cover the drinks. I just remembered some calls I have to make. But I have one question before I leave."

"What's that?"

"If someone did kill this guy in your yard, what do you suppose the motive was?"

"I have no idea."

"I do. It's pretty far out, but what if you had two stalkers? The guy who died and the one who killed him? Maybe the second guy was hung up on you and just happened to be watching when the first one waltzed onto your property with a rifle. So the second guy took him out in order to save your life. If that's how it happened, you owe him a debt of gratitude."

Far out was putting it mildly. It occurred to Claire that what Rick had just said was tantamount to a confession.

Chapter 27

C laire's heart lifted at the sight of the black Taurus in George Cropsey's driveway. Nothing to do with Stephen's presence, she told herself. No, it was the fact that Dahlia had made the train, and Errol hadn't walked as threatened. Maria must have done a good job of cajoling him into staying. Could she have used a little friendly persuasion above and beyond the call of duty? Maybe a drop-in visit to keep him company? Claire wouldn't put it past her, but some things were better left unexplored.

To be on the safe side, in case Dahlia didn't show and Claire had to play personal care aide, she had packed an overnight case, but evidently she wouldn't need it. Too bad, in a way. She'd been looking forward to the prospect of spending the night with George; it would have beat another night at home with only the dogs to help fend off the fears that threatened to overwhelm her. Talk about Gloomy Sunday – the one she'd just endured had been pure hell. Her usual diversions hadn't worked. The Sunday Times, a long walk with the dogs, a frustrating couple of hours in her jewelry studio all failed to banish her dark ruminations over the recent deaths.

Errol James was out on George Cropsey's front porch, suitcase in hand, by the time Claire was halfway up the walk. "Hey, Claire, good thing you got here – I'm more than ready to split. Can you tell Stephen to drive me to the train? He's been giving me a hard time."

Claire found it difficult to believe anyone would give Errol a hard time. In his black jeans and leather jacket, his expression unreadable behind dark glasses, the aide projected an intimidating image. But come to think of it, Stephen had been giving her a hard time, too. Where the hell had he been all weekend?

"What's he been doing?" she asked Errol.

"Waiting on you. I introduced Dahlia to George, went over the Hoyer lift and everything else I could think of, but he wanted to make sure I gave you my report in person and that you're okay with everything."

"That sounds reasonable enough." Nice, but not mandatory. Claire had already confirmed she'd be stopping in tonight, and with aides of Errol's and Dahlia's experience, the nursing visit didn't have to coincide with the aide change. Maybe Stephen had wanted to hang out in hopes of seeing her.

"I know you've been doing a great job with George," she told Errol. "Is there anything new I should know about?"

The aide cocked his head, looked momentarily pensive. "No, nothing special. Can we get this over with? With any luck, I can still make the five o'clock train."

Stephen was waiting for her in the hallway outside George Cropsey's room. His smile was beatific, radiant. "Claire, I'm so glad to see you," he said. "Want to get something to eat after you're done here?"

She flashed on the last time she'd seen him at George's house. Same narrow hallway – she wondered if he intercepted her there on purpose, to insure maximum physical proximity. Same invitation, except maybe this time she'd take him up on it. Now more than ever, she was squeamish about solitude.

"Maybe," she said. "It'll be awhile, though. I need to spend some time with Dahlia and George. At least half an hour."

"Want me to meet you later at your house? I could drive Errol to the Amtrak station, then pick up a bucket of KFC."

"That sounds like a good idea. Having you there might make me feel better about being there."

"You mean because of that anonymous note? Did the police have any ideas about it?"

"No, but it's not only that." He was looking cheerful, expectant, like a puppy waiting for a Milk-Bone. Was it possible he didn't know? "I gather you didn't see the news or buy this morning's paper?"

"No, I went down to the city Friday night, and I got back barely in time to pick up Dahlia this afternoon. I guess thinking about your trip got me in the mood for the Big Apple. I'm not big on the news anyway. Did I miss something?"

"Lester Schatz. Maizy and Freia found him dead on my property."

Stephen's eyes widened in shock. "Then I'm definitely coming over. No way you should be alone, not after something like that."

What was it Rick Kozlowski had said last night? *What if you had two stalkers, the guy who died and the one who killed him?* She'd thought he might be confessing, but what if Stephen was the second stalker, the one who'd killed Lester? That was ridiculous, wasn't it? Stephen was no murderer. On the other hand, he'd been upfront about his strong feelings for Claire, and if he'd been there and seen her in danger, all bets were off. But even if Rick's harebrained theory was right, the second guy was out to save her. Either way, Stephen wasn't out to harm her. Keeping a respectful distance, she edged past him into George Cropsey's bedroom.

Claire could sense it as soon as she saw Dahlia Douglas with George: they were going to be fine together. As she walked in, Dahlia was at the head of the hospital bed, massaging his bony shoulders with her strong brown fingers.

George sighed with contentment. "I like this lady already," he told Claire. "She obviously knows her stuff."

Claire smiled. "You're lucky to have her. Dahlia's a topnotch aide, and she's got a wonderful heart. If I ever needed home care, she's the one I'd want taking care of me."

"How long can she stay?" he asked. "Errol's got a lot on the ball, but I've got to admit I'm partial to women."

"It's a good sign he's feeling so talkative," Claire told Dahlia a few minutes later. They were settled in the kitchen, drinking Constant Comment tea they'd found in the cupboard. "Like many Parkinson's patients, he's clinically depressed, and he's frustrated that his speech isn't as clear as it used to be. I think that's one reason he gets so withdrawn at times. If you encourage him, I'll bet he can do a lot better."

"I will. He's a gentleman, just like Errol said." Dahlia placed both hands on the table, began studying her nails intently. They were bitten to the quick. "Errol told me about Lester Schatz. He left the newspaper in the living room for me to read later. Said he thought I had a right to know what's going on."

Thanks a bunch, Errol. Remind me to strangle you next time I see you. "We don't really know what's going on," Claire said in what she hoped was a judicious tone. Then she realized Errol was right: Dahlia did have a right to know. "I don't think you and George are in any danger," she said. "But to be on the safe side, I'm going to handle all the nursing visits. If Allyson Quigley shows up, call me immediately. Don't let her anywhere near him, or for that matter, into the kitchen or near his meds. And for heaven's sake, don't eat any food she brings over!"

Dahlia's eyes widened. "So it was true, what we were talking about at my place? She put poison in the cake at Minna's?"

"I don't know. But I checked the records, and she did visit Harriet Gardener the night she died. Rose Dobson too."

"Have you told Paula?"

"Not yet. As we were saying in Brooklyn, Allyson makes a lot of nursing visits to a lot of clients. It could just be coincidence. But I'll talk with Paula tomorrow."

"What about Lester Schatz? What did he die of? Errol said the paper didn't say."

Claire was silent. Should she share her suspicions with Dahlia? If she did, the poor woman might very well hop the next train back to New York. Besides, Lester's death didn't have anything to do with Dahlia - it was clearly about Claire. "They don't know yet," she said at last. "But this time there'll have to be an autopsy."

"Good. Do me a favor, Claire." Dahlia reached across the table, grasped Claire's hands in both of hers. "Tell me when they find out the results. I didn't like the man, but I swear I didn't have anything to do with his death. I didn't put a hex on him or anything."

"Dahlia, it never occurred to me that you did."

"I'm glad. Everyone was so uptight about my candles and everything."

"Not everyone. The way you explained it to me, you were just creating a safe space for yourself." Claire withdrew her hand from Dahlia's, sipped her tea in silence. Should she ask? What the hell, why not? "Dahlia, did you by any chance bring any of that paraphernalia with you this time?"

The aide gave her a blank stare. "Para what?"

"The candles, the herbs, all that stuff."

Dahlia's eyes darted nervously away. It was answer enough for Claire, but what to do about it? She searched her soul, realized the main thing she feared was fire. "Okay," she said, "I won't say anything to anybody, because I realize it's important to you. I'm not much of a believer when it comes to any kind of formal religion, but it can't hurt to cover all the bases. If you do happen to light any candles or whatever, light one for George. And for me too. But promise me you won't leave them unattended, even for a minute, and put them out the minute you feel sleepy. I'll check to make sure the smoke alarm in your room is functioning. We don't want you setting fire to the place."

Later that night, Claire gazed across her dining table at Stephen. Illuminated from below by the three fat candles she'd placed there, his angular face took on unfamiliar and vaguely sinister overtones. Should she tell him about her conversation with Dahlia? Better not – not the part about the candles anyway. Stephen's religious tolerance left something to be desired. But she did need to talk about this whole crazy situation. For that, she wanted privacy. That was why, despite her suspicions, she'd agreed to invite Stephen back to her house instead of going to Tanya's or another of his hangouts.

"That Rick Kozlowski gives me the creeps," she said as she reached into the bucket of fried chicken for the last drumstick. The motion brought Freia and Maizy to their feet, wagging expectantly. "Oh, okay, girls, I'll give you some more skin." Claire stripped the crusty coating from the chicken, divided it equally and tossed it to the dogs. "I'm sacrificing the best part. Anyway, I ran into Rick last night at Tanya's. He plied me with drinks and managed to get me talking about Lester Schatz's death."

"I've been telling you all along there was something weird about him," Stephen said.

"I know, but I didn't take it all that seriously. I thought maybe you were just homophobic."

"Me? No way." He grinned. By candlelight, his smile was especially devilish. "I used to be, but I had to get over it. I could never work in the theater otherwise."

Claire suppressed a sudden longing to run her fingers through the gold waves of his hair, trace the line of his cheek. "You're so scrumptious, I imagine lots of gay men have hit on you."

"Occasionally, but I've developed a sixth sense about these things. Gaydar, as a friend of mine calls it. Like radar. He's fine-tuned his so he knows who to hit on, but I use mine as a way of knowing when to be on guard. And I've learned how to let people down diplomatically. But back to Rick Kozlowski. What did he say that freaked you out? Anything in particular?"

"He said he has a special interest in true crime stories, especially medical crimes involving nurses who kill their patients. He knows an awful lot about lethal injections. But the most unnerving thing was when he suggested maybe I had two stalkers – Lester Schatz and the man who killed him. He said maybe the second guy was hung up on me and just happened to be watching when Lester trespassed on my property. That this guy killed Lester to save my life, and I owe him a debt of gratitude."

"That's bullshit. You don't owe anybody anything, except maybe me for bringing you this fried chicken dinner." He edged his chair closer to Claire's. "But I've got an easy way for you to repay me. Later for that, though. You think there's any truth to this two-stalker theory?"

"I have no idea. Maybe he was just picking up on what I said about noticing a possible injection site. But he came up with this notion of a second stalker awfully quickly. It occurred to me he might be describing himself." *Or you, Stephen.* She kept the thought to herself.

"You think he's hung up on you? Even though you get gay vibes from him?"

"I'm not talking sexually. He seems more interested in my role as a nurse, and the clients who've died on my watch. I lay awake most of last night thinking about it."

Stephen draped an arm around her shoulder. "I should have been here for you. I'm sorry."

"You have nothing to be sorry for. You had no idea what was going on. Besides, I pretty much blew you off the other day."

"Even so, I should have called you from the city instead of just going AWOL."

"I trust you weren't totally AWOL, and that you kept your cell phone on in case Maria needed to reach you."

He grinned. "Don't worry, I checked my messages every so often."

How often was that, and what was he doing in the city anyway? Claire realized she had no right to ask. He'd been off the clock, after all.

"Anyway, I'm here now," he murmured. "And I'm not going to let you out of my sight."

"That's fine with me." She nestled closer. Then, with no premeditation and to her total amazement, she kissed him on the mouth. His lips tasted of secret spices.

Chapter 28

"Gabriel, this is Athena."

Gabriel put down his brush, took a long slow breath to steady his nerves. Damn! He'd been up painting since before dawn, was really on a roll till this call shattered his concentration.

"Yeah, Athena. What's up?"

"I was hoping maybe you could tell me."

He'd known they would call sooner or later. He double-checked his watch: 8:15 a.m. He was surprised she'd waited till Monday morning. "I'm not sure what you're referring to," he said carefully.

"The fracas at Claire Lindstrom's place, obviously. Where you live, you must have had a ringside seat, even if you missed the newspaper and TV coverage."

"Oh, you mean the Lester Schatz incident? Now that you mention it, I did read about it in the paper yesterday."

"Come on, Gabriel, don't act so blasé. Did you have anything to do with it?"

"Of course not. I only carry out the assignments you give me."

"But one of those assignments was to keep an eye on Ms. Lindstrom and report anything out of the ordinary. Surely you must have seen some police action over there on Saturday morning. Wasn't that worth reporting?"

"Yeah, I was just about to call you. Didn't feel it was worth bothering you over the weekend."

Silence on the other end. Probably she was wondering exactly how to hang him out to dry. He could hardly blame her. Lester Schatz's death had made a big splash in the media, and Gabriel's end of this conversation was pathetic.

"Ah, Gabriel, what are we going to do with you?"

She was toying with him now, and it made him furious. Still, she didn't sound as angry as he might have expected. "Give me more assignments, I hope," he said in a conciliatory tone.

"We will, on one condition. In the future, keep us posted on everything the instant it happens. You can reach me twenty-four seven."

"Of course. You have my word on that."

Just then he caught a flash of movement along the lake shore, on Claire's land. He didn't need the scope to verify what he already knew – Stephen McClellan had spent the night again. Now the two of them were out walking the dogs. "Matter of fact, Ms. Lindstrom has a visitor right now," he said, hoping his voice didn't betray the rage that was rocketing through his body. "The same guy I called you about last week, Stephen McClellan. Looks like he spent the night."

"The agency's driver? Okay, no problem."

Oh, but it was a problem – an enormous one. *Forget it for now, Gabriel. You can deal with it later.*

Watching Claire walking with Stephen, Gabriel had trouble concentrating as Athena nattered on. "If you did have anything to do with Lester Schatz's death, I don't want to know about it," the woman was saying. "But it's only fair to tell you it solves some problems. Mr. Schatz wasn't entirely happy with our services. He was a potential trouble maker, and coincidentally, we had been thinking of getting in touch with you about handling the situation."

Synchronicity! He felt a rush of adrenaline at how perfectly things were coming together. As if he were part of a plan so potent even the Powers couldn't fully comprehend it. No, not just part of a plan - a plan in which he was the Mastermind. "I'm glad you have faith in me, Athena," he said. "I promise you, your trust isn't misplaced."

"I hope not, for your sake as well as ours. We have some more assignments for you, at Compassionate Care and the other agencies. Are you ready for the particulars?"

He ripped a sheet from his sketchbook, grabbed a 3B drawing pencil. "Fire away."

He scribbled furiously for the next couple of minutes, agreed to do his usual reconnaissance. He reached for the paintbrush even before he heard the click that ended the conversation. Far from ruining his concentration, the call had actually energized him.

He gazed at the landscape on his easel, the grove of moonlit trees with the lifeless body below. He had roughed out the composition Saturday, and it was coming along well. Time to add the woman and the pooches. That would be tricky; he might have to check out some art books or magazine photos for reference, so he could get the poses right. On the other hand, Claire Lindstrom was still out there with the dogs. His muse, his inspiration.

He grabbed the sketchpad and a brick-red Conte crayon, headed for the window. If he hurried, he might be able to get down some quick gesture drawings. Leave out Stephen McClellan, though. He didn't belong in the picture.

He'd better work on developing a speedier style. With all the assignments Athena was giving him, he'd have no time to waste.

————————

Paula Rhodes was ready to explode. She paced from her desk to the window, skirted the edge of the glass-topped coffee table, practically collided with the desk as she started the circuit again, scattering maple cruller crumbs in her wake. At the rate she was going, she'd grind them all into the carpet, but what the hell – the cleaning crew could vacuum them out tonight.

Maria peered in the doorway. "Good morning, boss. Is everything okay? You look uptight."

Paula flung her arm at the newspapers that lay strewn across the desk. "Damn straight I am! Did you see the *Times Union*? Lester Schatz's death is big news. Yesterday's story was bad enough; it mentioned Claire as the owner of the property where he was found. But today's is even worse. There's a sidebar that explains her connection to Compassionate Care, along with the fact that Lester Schatz's mother died while under our supervision. I've been here since six a.m. trying to figure out how to do damage control."

"Calm down, Paula. Don't freak out."

Paula smiled in spite of herself. "Don't freak out" was one of Maria's favorite phrases, but with her Puerto Rican lilt, it came out sounding like "Don' frick out." Paula had taken to saying it herself, complete with accent, though out of Maria's hearing, of course. "You're right, Maria," she said. "This too shall pass. Or at least that's what I keep telling myself."

"It's true. That nasty man's death has nothing to do with our agency, and besides, things are going really well." Maria's mouth twitched in the suggestion of a smile. "Stephen called me yesterday from George Cropsey's house. The switch happened right on schedule. I called Dahlia last night to see how things are going.

She and Mr. Cropsey really hit it off. She plans to stay till Friday when Errol comes back. Then she'll relieve him again over the Thanksgiving holiday."

"That's good." Paula felt her eyes glaze over; she hoped it wasn't too obvious. The minutiae of scheduling bored her to tears, but that was precisely why she had to listen to Maria, give her some strokes to keep her happily doing her job so Paula wouldn't have to think about it. "How's the staffing for Thanksgiving coming?" she asked dutifully.

Maria beamed. "Excellent. Twelve live-in clients, and I've got them all covered already. Offering double the usual pay rate worked wonders."

"Double? We've always paid time and a half."

"No, remember when we talked after Labor Day, after we had that crisis? You said double would be okay for the major holidays."

I must have been in some kind of fugue state, Paula thought. The payroll is going to be horrendous that week, and I can't pass it on to the clients, not without a change in the contract. And it's too late for that. Maybe in time for Christmas . . .

"Shit!" Maria exploded.

Paula practically choked on her cruller. "Jesus, Maria, don't scare me like that! What's wrong?"

"Come quick and see for yourself. God damn that bitch! I could kill her!"

Paula hurried to the window, followed Maria's gaze. In the parking lot below, Claire was climbing out the passenger's side of the agency's Taurus. Stephen stood close by, extending his hand. She grasped it, rose to meet him. They stood close as they talked. With their blond hair, their lean good looks, they could have been modeling for a fashion shoot. Something disgustingly classy but wholesome, like Ralph Lauren.

"I knew he had the hots for her," Maria said. "But I thought she had enough sense not to mess with him. She's going to be sorry!"

Paula glanced at Maria, then quickly away. Spare me the drama, she thought. I don't have time for this.

"He stood me up yesterday," Maria continued. "He was going to come over after he dropped off Dahlia, I had a nice dinner all ready for him, and he phoned and said something had come up. Now I see why. Something came up, all right. He probably spent the night with that slut."

Slut? Claire Lindstrom? Somehow the words didn't compute. "You don't know that for sure," Paula said.

"Then why did she show up with him in the agency's car?"

"I don't know. Maybe she had car trouble."

"Yeah, right." Maria's dark eyes were venomous, her lips quivering. Poor creature, she's on the verge of a total meltdown, Paula thought. "Come, sit on my sofa," she said. "Have a donut and pull yourself together. You don't want Stephen to see you so upset."

Maria snuffled. "I shouldn't, I'm too fat already. That's probably why he likes her better."

"Fat? Are you kidding? Maria, you have a figure to die for. You probably weigh 120 pounds soaking wet."

Maria smiled. "Closer to 130. But thanks, Paula. I guess one donut wouldn't hurt."

———————

One look at Paula and Claire could tell this wasn't an auspicious time to broach the subject of Allyson Quigley. And Maria was even worse. The boss and the coordinator were seated side by side on the sofa, a Dunkin' Donuts box on the coffee table in front of them. They were both chowing down on donuts and glaring bullets at Claire.

As she crossed the threshold into what felt like a den of vipers, she caught sight of the newspapers scattered across Paula's desk. No surprise there. No doubt Paula was perturbed about Lester's death and its handling in the media. But what was up with Maria?

Claire had a sudden urge to turn tail, but she decided to tough it out. "Good morning, ladies. Paula, when you've got a chance, there's something I need to talk with you about."

"Likewise. Why don't you go hang up your coat and then come back?"

"This involves Allyson too. Is she around, by any chance?"

Paula frowned. "You should know - you're her supervisor."

She wasn't going to make it easy. "Right," Claire said. "As I recall, she was going to make some home visits this morning, but I thought she might have touched base here before she set out."

"Why should she?" Maria asked. "She popped in Friday afternoon to grab some progress notes and assessment forms. She told me she'd be in the field all day today. What with all the cases she has, she's really overwhelmed with work."

Since when had Maria become Allyson's advocate? "Allyson's work load isn't your concern, Maria," Claire said. "If you don't mind, I need to speak privately with Paula."

Maria flounced up from the sofa, stormed to the door. "Fine! Shut me out, treat me like shit. See if I care." Crossing the threshold, she yanked the doorknob as if about to execute a grand slam, then made a mocking curtsey instead. She closed the door with exaggerated politeness.

Claire crossed to the sofa, plopped down in Maria's place. If Allyson was already out on the road visiting clients, there was no time to waste. "Paula, I'm concerned about Allyson Quigley. I believe she may have been involved in Minna Schatz's death. Perhaps Harriet Gardener's and Rose Dobson's as well."

Paula inched away from her on the sofa. "Claire, are you out of your mind? What in God's name are you talking about?"

"She visited all three women just a few hours before they died. Dahlia was with Harriet and Minna, and she mentioned feeling unusually sleepy after Allyson's visits, as if she'd been drugged."

"Come on, give me a break! How can you believe a word she says? The woman's Jamaican; she's probably stoned half the time. She wouldn't know the difference."

"That's not fair, Paula. You're just slinging stereotypes around."

"Bullshit! If she's into voodoo, why shouldn't she be into drugs as well? I bent over backward to give her another chance at your request, but maybe I made a mistake. I think you're losing your grip. Gallivanting around with Stephen McClellan, for example."

"What do you mean?"

"Isn't it obvious? Maria just saw you drive up with him. She was practically in tears watching the two of you down there in the parking lot."

So that's what Maria was so steamed about! Claire felt the blood rush to her face. It had taken all the will power she possessed not to invite Stephen into her bed last night, but she realized how easily the coordinator could have misinterpreted the situation.

"We were just talking," Claire said. "Stephen's concerned I might be in danger. He didn't think it was safe for me to be alone last night, so he stayed over, but it was strictly platonic. That's why he drove me to work as well." To her chagrin, she felt her eyes welling with tears. "It would be nice if you felt even a fraction of his concern. I see by the newspapers on your desk that you're aware of what happened over the weekend. You could have at least given me a call."

Paula's eyes strayed to the donut box on the table. She lifted the lid, peered inside, then closed it again. "I thought about it, but I was so upset, I couldn't think of anything reassuring to say. I know it probably sounds callous, but do you realize what this Lester Schatz fiasco will do to our reputation?"

Claire rose. "You're right, it does sound callous. I don't think there's any more point in our talking right now. You don't take me seriously about Allyson, but the first thing on my agenda is to protect the welfare of our clients. So I'm going out to make some home visits of my own, starting with Louella Marcovicci. Sharon Westerly's there, and she was on duty the night Rose Dobson died."

Paula glared up at her. "Don't go planting any crazy conspiracy theories in people's heads. If you do, you're out of a job."

"Paula, if you can't trust my judgment, I might as well quit anyway." Claire headed for the door, yanked it open.

She found herself staring into the square, stolid face of Detective Stan Kupcinek.

Chapter 29

*D*etective Kupcinek's tall, stocky frame loomed in the doorway, blocking Claire's escape. He gave her a cryptic half-smile. "Good morning, Ms. Lindstrom. Glad I caught you in."

"Actually I was just leaving." She took a step forward, but he didn't budge, just gazed down at her with that inscrutable look she found so unnerving. "I'm going to see some clients," she added. "It's fairly urgent."

He stood his ground. She fought the urge to scream at him, to drum at his chest with her fists – he probably wouldn't feel a thing. Defeated, she backed into Paula's office again. He followed her in, trailed by his partner. "You remember Jean Renshaw from the other day," he said.

"We didn't meet, but I saw her around." Claire gestured toward her boss. "This is Paula Rhodes, Director of Compassionate Care. Paula, this is Detective Kupcinek."

Paula heaved herself out of her chair, extended a hand. "Pleased to meet you, Detective."

Now that this travesty of a social call was out of her hands, maybe Claire could make a halfway graceful exit. "If there's anything I can help you with, I'll be back this afternoon," she told the detective.

"It would be better if we talk now," he said. "I've got a few questions for you, some loose ends to tie up. It shouldn't take more than an hour."

"Sorry, but my clients take priority." *I need to get to them before Allyson Quigley does.*

Maria edged into the room, insinuated herself between Claire and Kupcinek. "Is everything okay, Detective? I see you found Ms. Lindstrom."

"Yes, thank you. Do you have a spare office my partner and I could use? I'd like to speak with you and Ms. Rhodes, as well as any other staff that might be around."

Maria tossed him a coquettish smile. "Our driver just came in; you'll probably want to talk to him. Paula and I should go first, though. Our schedules are more demanding. The conference room would be perfect, wouldn't it, Paula?"

"No problem," Paula said. "Maria, can you go ask that new receptionist to make sure the room's straightened up? Have her put on a fresh pot of coffee too."

In the space of a minute, Maria had managed to shut Claire out of the loop. "Maybe I can make time too," she told the detective. "If it's that important."

"No, this afternoon will be okay, Ms. Lindstrom. But come down to the station. We'll have more privacy there."

————   ———

This detective character was really getting on Stephen's nerves, and the cramped space was making him claustrophobic. "Conference room" was kind of a grandiose name for this windowless, sheet-rocked cubicle that felt more like a storage closet. The oblong table hogged most of the room, and as the detective stared him down across the expanse of fake oak veneer, Stephen was acutely aware of the guy's massive shoulders, his chest development. The detective was around Stephen's height, six feet give or take an inch, but he was easily fifty pounds heavier, most of it muscle. Not a man to mess with.

Kupcinek leaned forward. "So did you ever witness an altercation between Claire Lindstrom and Lester Schatz?"

Get out of my face, Stephen wanted to shout. "No, I've already told you. I never saw her act anything less than professional."

"What is your relationship with Ms. Lindstrom, exactly?"

"She's the nursing supervisor, I'm the customer service representative."

"The driver, in other words?"

Now the guy was belittling him. Stephen felt a flash of annoyance. *Cool it, Stephen.* "Among other things."

Kupcinek had been coming at him for half an hour already, peppering him with questions, trying to make him blow his cool. To incriminate Claire, it sounded like, but why? It wasn't like she'd planned to discover a corpse on her property.

"Are you and Claire Lindstrom romantically involved?"

Don't I wish. Where did the cop get that idea? Maria, probably. Oh well, eat your heart out, you pathetic prick. Stephen grinned knowingly. "Why is that important?"

"I ask the questions here, Mr. McClellan." Kupcinek shoved back his chair. "A gentleman never tells, right? Never mind, I've already got what I need. I guess that's it for now. Give me a call if you think of anything else that might be relevant."

Fat chance. "You got it, Detective."

Back in the hallway, Stephen exhaled slowly as he watched the detective walk to the lobby. He could use a cigarette right about now.

He smelled Maria's musky perfume, felt her hand on his arm. "Hey, Stephen. We have to talk," she said breathily into his ear.

"About what?"

"About why you stood me up last night, and why you drove Claire to work this morning."

He heard Allyson Quigley's voice. "Maria, wait up," she called. "Did you meet with the detective? What did he –" She rounded the corner, bit back her words as she saw Stephen. Her piggy face looked even puffier than usual.

"Yeah, I met him," Maria said, grinning up at Stephen. "He's kind of cute, isn't he? Looks like he must work out a lot, to get a body like that."

Jeez, how pathetic. If Maria was trying to make him jealous, she wasn't succeeding. "Hey, Allyson," he said, grateful for the interruption. "I thought you were going to be out making house calls all day."

"I am, basically. I just stopped by to touch base with Paula about something." She favored him with a condescending smile. "The last thing I expected was to get waylaid by a homicide detective. Maria, can you come in the conference room a minute? I need to talk with you about something."

Maria rolled her eyes at Stephen. "Give me a few minutes, okay, Allyson?"

"That's okay," Stephen said. "I've got to get going anyway."

"Where to?" asked Maria. "There aren't any aide changes on the schedule. Come to think of it, why are you here, anyway? I don't remember assigning you anything today. Did you just come to drop off Claire?"

Oh no you don't, Maria. We're not going there, not now. "If you have problems with my schedule, talk to Paula about it," he said. "You're not my supervisor."

Maria's face contorted in anger. Thank God for Allyson, who was wearing a look of mild expectation, like a referee waiting for the next round. If not for the nurse's presence, Maria would have cut him a new asshole.

"Come on, girlfriend," Allyson said, wrapping an arm around Maria's shoulders. "He's not worth the aggravation."

To Claire's relief, Louella Marcovicci and Sharon Westerly had turned out to be a decent match. Louella was flabby, phlegmatic, content to lie in bed and channel surf for hours on end. Her deep chestnut skin aside, Sharon could have passed for Louella's daughter, they were so alike in their passivity, their flat expressions, their puffy bodies. In her aqua sweat suit, Sharon looked as if she'd been fathered by the Michelin Man. The aide had been here less than a week, but Claire could swear she'd already put on a few pounds. Temperamentally, the two seemed to be well suited; the challenge was to keep them from succumbing to terminal sloth.

"Louella, have you been out of bed yet today?" Claire asked.

Client and aide exchanged a heavy-lidded, guilt-laden look. "I was about to get up," Louella said. "But I feel so achy all the time."

"Staying in bed all day won't help. And changing position every so often is important for your circulation. So are the sponge baths. Sharon, you've been giving them every day, right?"

Sharon nodded wordlessly.

Louella narrowed her eyes, squinted at Claire. "Sharon is a sweet girl. We're getting along wonderfully together." Her voice had a belligerent edge.

"I'm delighted to hear it," Claire said.

Summoning every bit of positive energy she could, stressing the importance of purposeful activity, she went over the plan of care with them. It took all her strength to resist the pull of their lethargy, sucking her down like a swamp full of quicksand. At last, satisfied she'd done all she could, she took Sharon into the kitchen.

"So, Sharon, do you remember Allyson Quigley's visit the night Rose Dobson died?"

The aide looked down at her lap. "Maybe. I guess."

"In particular, I'm wondering if she brought you anything special to eat. A cake, maybe."

"Meatloaf, I think. Yeah, that was it. I remember, because I was kind of surprised she'd go to all that trouble."

Claire felt a surge of excitement. "Did you and Rose both eat it?"

"Sure. It was pretty good. Allyson kept talking about the recipe, how she'd added bran for regularity. That was a little gross, talking about that at the dinner table." She raised her eyes to Claire's. "What's this about, anyway?"

"I'm just checking out something." Claire's cell phone chimed, and she fished it out of her purse. "Claire Lindstrom."

"Claire, this is Patrick Delafield from Oaktree Associates. Remember me?"

"Of course. As a matter of fact, I'm at the home of one of the clients you referred. Louella Marcovicci."

"Excellent. How's it going?"

"She's doing fine. So is George Cropsey." As for Ray Rienzi, she couldn't say. Not since Paula assigned him to Allyson and said he was none of Claire's business. On the positive side, at least he hadn't run away yet.

Fortunately, Patrick didn't ask about the little man with Alzheimer's. "Glad to hear things are going well," he said. "I called to see if by any chance you're free for lunch today. There are a couple more referrals I'd like to discuss with you."

His timing was odd, she thought. Hadn't he read the papers? Well, Paula would be delighted to know at least one referral source wasn't scared off by the negative PR surrounding their nursing supervisor. And Claire had been wanting to infiltrate Oaktree, to explore the Herb Davidson and Lester Schatz connections. This was the perfect opportunity. "I'm pretty booked up with home visits, but I might be able to spare an hour or two," she said.

"Great! Why don't you stop by our office? Noonish, or whenever you can get away. I'll be here. We can order in."

"Thanks, I'm looking forward to it."

She clicked off, refocused her attention on Sharon. The aide was huddled in the corner of the sofa, picking nervously at her cuticles. Looking guilty as all get out.

"Sharon, don't worry. This isn't about you, it's about Allyson. Do you remember if you felt strange after you ate the meatloaf? Unusually sleepy, maybe?"

"I don't remember. I always get sleepy after dinner. It's annoying, because I always fall asleep half way through the ten o'clock shows, and those are my favorites. Stuff like CSI and Law & Order."

Obviously Sharon wasn't going to provide the thunderbolt of illumination Claire was hoping for. "Okay, Sharon, thanks. Just one more thing. Since I'm handling the case management for Louella, I'm the only nurse authorized to come here. Not Allyson Quigley."

"That's cool. I like you better. Allyson reminds me of this nasty teacher in fifth grade who always dissed me."

Claire suppressed a smile. "If Allyson comes here, I want you to notify me right away. Don't eat anything she might bring over, and that goes for Louella too."

Sharon's flat brown eyes lit up. "Is Allyson fired or something?"

"No, and this conversation is just between you and me, okay? It doesn't concern anyone else at the agency."

"Okay, whatever. Can I get back to Louella now? We always watch The View."

———————

As Patrick Delafield clasped her hand and zapped her with his spring-green eyes, Claire felt a surge of nervous energy course through her system. After the lethargic atmosphere at Louella's house, it felt like a jolt of espresso.

"Claire, it's great to see you again." He took hold of her arm as he ushered her through the lobby to his office, and she flashed back to their encounter at Oaktree's New York office. His grip had been a lot tighter that day. "I'm glad you made it back safely from the wilds of Brooklyn," he said. "Venturing out of Manhattan – I was worried about you."

"Oh, I can look out for myself. I lived in the city for years."

"Do you ever regret moving up here? It must seem pretty boring by comparison."

Boring? Was he putting her on? Or didn't he follow the news? "Not really," she said mildly. "I guess I'm a country girl at heart."

She scanned the office as she waited for him to get to the point. Good quality but generic furnishings, with teak-toned veneers and that sea green and dusty rose color scheme that seemed practically inescapable in professional offices these days. The wall behind his desk was hung with plaques and certificates, his law degree centered prominently behind his head. The rest appeared to be certificates for seminars and in-service trainings.

He chuckled. "Checking out my credentials? You want a closer look?"

"No, that's okay. I see you went to Ohio State."

"Yes, I'm relatively new to the Northeast." He tilted back his chair, laced his fingers behind his head. "I know you're busy, so let's get down to business. This guy you found dead on your land Saturday morning – was he by any chance the same one you called me about recently? The one who refused to consent to his mother's autopsy?"

"Why do you ask?"

"Just curious. Judging by the newspaper coverage, I'm guessing he was." He unclasped his hands, leaned forward and stared into her eyes. "I know you're concerned about confidentiality. So am I, but as professional colleagues, I think it's legitimate for us to share. Lester Schatz was an Oaktree client."

So Angelo was right – he *had* seen Lester here. "What kind of services was he receiving?" she asked.

"He was in a support group for clients coping with seriously ill family members. Similar to the one your neighbor Angelo Giordano attends."

Claire's breath caught in her throat. How did he know they were neighbors? And why was he bringing it up? "I don't see what Lester Schatz has to do with Angelo Giordano," she said after a moment.

"More than you might imagine. Mr. Giordano is still a little resistive in coming to terms with the severity of his wife's illness and the need for our services. Lester Schatz was in denial as well, and he terminated right after his mother died. I believe he could have benefited by continuing on in grief counseling. If he had, perhaps he'd still be alive today."

"How do you mean?"

"I was hoping you could tell me. When an Oaktree client dies, our staff generally does some group processing around the issue, both to resolve our own feelings and to see if there's anything we could have done differently. I'm sure you do the same at Compassionate Care."

Not as much as we should. Paula keeps us hustling too fast and furiously. "Mmm hmm," she murmured.

"Since you provided round-the-clock care for his mother, you probably got to know him better than we did. And I wonder if you have any idea how he happened to be on your property, and what actually caused his death. The news stories weren't clear –" He stopped abruptly, glared over Claire's shoulder. "Justin, what the hell? This is a confidential conversation. Why didn't you knock?"

"The door was open. I didn't realize you wanted privacy."

Claire swiveled in her chair. Justin Greylock, Patrick's confederate from the Alzheimer's conference, was already halfway across the room.

"And I didn't realize you were here." Patrick's tone was decidedly chilly. "We didn't have an appointment, did we?"

"No, I thought I'd just drop in." Justin's tone was cavalier, almost insolent. Clearly Patrick's displeasure didn't faze him in the least.

Claire stood, found herself gazing into the Siberian husky eyes she remembered from the conference. The ice blue irises were even more striking than the green of Patrick's eyes, and the jolt when Justin took her hand was more electric by far. The tactile memory brought up a wealth of sensations from the day they'd spent in close proximity at the Empire Inn.

"Good to see you again, Claire." He pressed her hand harder. "I was sorry to read about that ordeal you went through. It must have been pretty traumatic, finding a dead man on your property bright and early in the morning."

"Yes, it was. Thanks for your sympathy." She glanced pointedly at Patrick, who had been notably unsympathetic. Callous, even. Suddenly the prospect of lunch with him seemed unappetizing. "I should be going," she said. "You two seem to have some private business to discuss."

"No, stay," said Patrick. "I still want to discuss those referrals with you, and Justin's about to leave." He edged out from behind his desk, patted Justin's back. "Excuse us both a minute."

Justin let go of her hand, shot her a look of resigned complicity. As the two men left the room, she let out a sigh of relief. The testosterone levels had been escalating so fast, she felt like throwing open a window to air out the room. Office politics – the last thing she needed after this morning with Paula and Maria. Amazingly, the men were actually worse.

As their voices faded into the distance, her eyes strayed around the room. She longed to snoop around a little, but she didn't dare. Patrick had practically caught her red-handed in their New York office; she couldn't let it happen again. Even so, her gaze lit on the day planner he'd left open on his desk. It was Franklin Covey, the same brand she used herself, but in the jumbo executive size. She focused on the To Do column, began reading upside down. Lucky she was far-sighted. CALL HERB DAVIDSON, he'd printed in compulsively tidy caps. Then, further down: SCHEDULE G.C. AND R.R.

G.C. and R.R., she thought. George Cropsey and Ray Rienzi? Schedule what?

Murder came to mind.

Chapter 30

---

*T*he sound of Patrick's footsteps was so soft, Claire heard nothing until he was back in the room. He laughed. "Did I startle you? Sorry about that."

She was glad he couldn't see her face. Guilt must have been written all over it. "A little. The plush carpeting in here really deadens the sound."

He studied her so quizzically that her jitters skyrocketed. *Chill out, Claire. You didn't do anything wrong.*

"How about that lunch I promised you? I'll have my secretary order in. You've got a choice: Thai, Chinese, or all-American deli."

Right now her stomach couldn't handle anything exotic. "Deli sounds fine."

Half an hour later, they were seated at a chrome and glass table in the company lunchroom. Sea green and dusty rose again, with a few Impressionist posters – the room had the stereotyped touch of the same designer who'd done Patrick's office. They'd both settled on turkey triple deckers, but Claire was finding it hard to swallow.

Patrick was having no such problems. "Sorry about the interruption earlier," he said between bites. "Justin's a brilliant account executive, but sometimes he gets too gung ho for his own good. As I was saying, I have some referrals to discuss with you, but first let's talk about Angelo and Regina Giordano. They could really benefit from our services, but he has to overcome his resistance. I'd like to enlist your help."

"In all honesty, I wouldn't feel comfortable getting involved unless I know more about Oaktree. That's one of the reasons I'm here."

He narrowed his eyes. "Didn't you read all the hand-outs the receptionist gave you in New York?"

"Yes, but that's not the same as knowing your staff personally. I'd like to meet your social worker, Gloria Wallender, for example. Angelo Giordano told me he's seen her a couple of times, but I've only touched base with her by phone in regard to the referrals. Actually, I should think she'd be the one to discuss your clients' social and psychological needs."

"And I should avoid those areas, is that what you're saying? True, I'm a lawyer, but strange as it seems, I have some sensitivity to our clients' needs."

"I didn't mean to imply otherwise, Patrick, but I'd still like to meet Gloria. Is she around today, by any chance?"

"No, she's out of the office."

His tone was cold, dismissive. She could feel the conversation degenerating, and she knew she bore part of the blame. In her mind's eye, she pictured them: two dogs circling stiffly, checking each other out. Friend or foe? The jury was still out on that one, but she couldn't forget those two entries in his day planner. CALL HERB DAVIDSON. SCHEDULE G.C. AND R.R. She couldn't think of any reasonable way to ask about the coroner, and Paula had told her to stay clear of the Ray Rienzi case. But George Cropsey was another matter, if in fact that's who the initials stood for. Maybe the notion of murder was far-fetched, but what could the note possibly mean?

Suddenly she knew how to frame the question. "Do your therapists ever make home visits?"

Patrick looked momentarily startled. "Occasionally. Why do you ask?"

"I was thinking about Angelo and Regina Giordano, but George Cropsey also comes to mind. It's obvious he and his son have a lot of unresolved issues. They could probably benefit from some family therapy sessions, but he's in no condition to travel. Maybe Gloria Wallender or another therapist could come out to his home."

"They may have already, but I'll make a note to check." He reached for his palm pilot. "I couldn't live without this baby. My secretary's a little old fashioned, insists on keeping up the day planner, but it's degenerated into a to-do list. Her version of post-it notes, reminding me how she thinks I should spend my time." He gestured dismissively at the bound planner on his desk, then began jabbing at the tiny keyboard with a metal pointer.

Claire watched intently. Maybe he hadn't written those notes after all. She knew the body language for lying, and he wasn't displaying it. No telltale nose rubbing, no furtive glances. He looked sincere enough, but how could she tell? The man had the slick demeanor of a consummate salesman. In his own way, he was as inscrutable as Stan Kupcinek. Speaking of which, she had promised to pay the detective a visit.

Might as well get it over with, she decided. She put down her third quadrant of turkey club, snapped shut the clamshell box. "Sorry, Patrick, but I've got to run. I just remembered an urgent appointment."

How odd, she reflected as she left the office. She'd rather be down at the police station, submitting to grilling at the hands of a homicide detective, than spend another minute dining with Patrick Delafield.

The referrals! It wasn't until she was snugly ensconced in her Focus with the smooth jazz station soothing her tattered nerves that she realized Patrick had never gotten around to discussing the promised new cases. Should she go back? She gazed across the parking lot at the building that was home to Oaktree Associates. It was part of a business park that housed insurance groups and high-tech start-ups. Low and rambling, its charcoal gray surface textured like rough-hewn rock, the structure looked as cold and phony as Oaktree felt.

All at once it dawned on her: this hadn't been a casual invitation. Patrick had been checking her out, taking her measure, probing to learn what she knew about Lester Schatz's death, what she thought about Oaktree. She strongly doubted there would be any new referrals.

———————

Detective Stan Kupcinek was a big bear of a man, but from the beginning, Claire had never mistaken him for the warm fuzzy teddy bear type. Now, in the cramped interrogation room, wedged in next to his partner, Jean Renshaw, he was cooler than ever. *Something's changed,* she thought. *Is it my imagination, or has something happened to turn him against me?*

It had to be Paula and Maria. Claire should never have cut out this morning when he wanted to talk with her at the office. She'd left him in the clutches of the two women. Stephen too, for that matter. She was pretty sure she could trust him, but how well did she know him, really?

"I had some illuminating talks with the staff at Compassionate Care this morning," the detective said.

Claire's stomach clenched. Her mouth went dry, and words wouldn't come.

Kupcinek smiled at his partner. She nodded, and they both turned to Claire. Watching, waiting.

I've seen this scene a million times on TV, Claire thought. Now's the time I should talk about lawyering up, but I can't think of any lawyers to call, except Patrick Delafield, and the thought of him makes me nauseous.

"I'm free to leave, aren't I?" she asked. "You can't keep me here against my will." She knew that from TV too.

"Yes, but why would you want to leave?" Kupcinek asked. "Is there something you're not telling us?"

"I've got nothing to hide. But I do want to tell you about Oaktree Associates. I was just over at their office, and I came across some information that concerned me."

She proceeded to tell them about Patrick Delafield's date book, the one he claimed his secretary kept. They listened impassively, saying nothing, exchanging a cryptic glance from time to time. "You don't believe me, do you," she said finally. "You think I'm just spinning conspiracy theories when I say someone may be out to kill George Cropsey and Ray Rienzi."

Kupcinek permitted himself a wry smile. It was the most emotion he'd shown all afternoon. "You said it, I didn't. I may as well tell you, people have expressed some serious concerns about your mental health."

"That's absurd! What people are you talking about?"

"I'm not at liberty to say."

"I'll bet it was Maria Gonzales, or maybe Allyson Quigley. They're probably in cahoots together." *Or Paula, or Stephen. It could be anybody. Or everybody.*

"We interviewed people independently. I don't think they were plotting against you, if that's what you're thinking. Do you believe they are?"

Easy to see where this was going. *Back off, Claire, or it's going to be loony tunes time.* "No, of course not."

"There does seem to be a pattern here," the detective said. "I'm no shrink, but you apparently see people as out to get you, or to harm your clients."

"What about that anonymous note? Whoever wrote it certainly believes I'm in danger, but you seem to be blowing it off."

"Not at all. We're still looking into the matter. Including the possibility that you wrote it yourself."

"That's utterly absurd!" Claire practically choked on the words.

The detective leaned forward. "Do you believe Lester Schatz was out to harm you too?"

"It certainly looks that way. He was in my woods with a rifle."

"And you already suspected him, so you were ready and waiting."

"What do you mean?"

Kupcinek leaned back in his chair, folded his arms and focused on her eyes. "The autopsy's scheduled for 4:00 p.m. today in Albany. Matter of fact, I've got to get going soon, because I don't want to miss it. But the medical examiner already alerted me to some preliminary findings. You were right about that mark on the neck. He agrees it looks like an injection site."

Claire felt a fluttering in her chest. "So he didn't die from natural causes? Somebody murdered him?"

"We don't know for sure yet, but it's a strong possibility." He leaned forward, and his eyes drilled into hers. "If so, it was subtle. Would have taken someone with some pretty slick nursing skills to carry it off. Like you, for example."

The fluttering escalated to a frantic thumping. "But if I did it, why in God's name would I bring it to your attention? Why not try to pass it off as a heart attack or something?"

"Maybe that was your original intention, but when you looked at the body in the light of day, the mark was more conspicuous than you realized. You figured someone would notice it, so you decided you'd better mention it yourself. Trying to cover your tracks by deflecting suspicion, the same way you did with that note. Unfortunately it didn't work."

"Am I under arrest?" She couldn't believe she was saying it.

"No, but don't go anywhere. We'll be in touch."

Don't go anywhere - how ironic, she thought as she walked out of the police station. Where could she possibly go? Not back to the office - she couldn't stand the thought of facing Paula and Maria. Not home - she'd have to go back to walk the dogs before long, but right now the thought of being home alone was terrifying. What if Lester Schatz's killer was still out there watching, stalking her, waiting to strike?

Where was Stephen? Would he stay with her again tonight, or was he too tired of her diversionary tactics? In the parking lot this morning, they had agreed to talk later, but then the day had spiraled out of control, and she hadn't seen him since. With a jolt, she realized she didn't even know where he lived. She could call him on his cell, but what if he was still on the clock for Compassionate Care? Now that Claire was persona non grata at the agency, her call might just embarrass him. He valued his job; for all she knew, he could have thrown in his lot with the others by now. He might even be with Maria.

Could he be at Tanya's? Probably too early. Even so, she could take refuge there, calm her nerves with a glass of wine or two. But drinking was a terrible idea right now - she needed to stay alert and think clearly, not fog her consciousness with alcohol.

Approaching her car, she punched the fob to spring the lock. The hatchback sprang open. Damn, she'd hit the wrong button! She flung up the door, prepared to slam it shut when she caught sight of her gym bag nestled in the corner of the cargo compartment. She thought longingly of the Y – a good long swim was exactly what she needed to clear her head. But later for that. She knew exactly where she should go: George Cropsey's house.

———————

Dahlia Douglas winced as she massaged her abdomen. "I don't know if I can stay here, Claire."

"Are you sick, Dahlia? You keep patting your stomach."

"I'm afraid my ulcer may be coming back."

Claire's own stomach clenched. "I'm sorry. What can I do to help?"

"Maybe go to the drugstore, get me some medicine. But it's not just that. Maybe it was a mistake, me thinking I could take care of Mr. Cropsey."

"Dahlia, I know this is a difficult case, but I have every confidence in you. You were terrific with him yesterday during the orientation."

"That part is okay. I'm just so jumpy. I didn't sleep at all last night. I kept going in to check on him, make sure he was breathing all right."

Unnerving as she'd found her visit with Patrick Delafield, he'd been right about one thing: it was crucial to help staff work through their feelings when a client died. We haven't done nearly enough of it, Claire thought. No wonder Dahlia's upset. "This has to be hard for you," she said. "Maybe it's too soon after Minna Schatz. Do you feel up to sticking it out, or should we try to get someone to relieve you?"

"I can probably make it till Friday. But it doesn't help that George is so paranoid. He even has me watching for strange cars in the road. Last night I looked out around two a.m. and saw a black one cruising by real slow, just like Minna saw before Halloween." Dahlia shivered convulsively, as if in the grip of a fever. "For a minute, I thought it was a hearse. I thought Minna was just paranoid, but maybe she had special powers. Maybe she was predicting her own death."

Claire was silent, racking her brain for words of comfort and reassurance, finding none. What if Dahlia was right? "I don't know what's real and what isn't," she said at last. "But if you feel you're in danger for any reason, call 911 immediately. Don't worry about being logical or believable; just do it." *And don't mention my name – it won't help your cause. The police think I'm a suspect, and crazy to boot.*

George Cropsey was depressed as all get out. In the space of ten minutes, Claire learned that no one from Oaktree had ever visited. Not Gloria Wallender, not anyone.

"Why the hell should they?" he asked. "Paul mentioned something about going to see them once, but it has nothing to do with me."

"On the contrary, George, it has everything to do with you. They're supposed to help families deal with the changes surrounding late-life issues and –"

He hunched forward in bed. "Bullshit! They just want me to kick the bucket as expeditiously as possible, so they can get their hands on my money."

"What gives you that idea?"

His face reddened alarmingly. "Stands to reason. Why else would Paul be in cahoots with them? He doesn't give a shit about me, never has."

"Has he been by to see you?"

"Not since your agency has been in here. His wife came by a couple of times to go through the mail, but that's it." His eyes welled with tears. "I'd be better off dead, I really would, but I'll be damned if I give them the satisfaction."

———

Gabriel drew the grubby blue drapes against the darkness, then turned on the fluorescents. He'd installed the fixtures this morning, intending to paint tonight. Lately he'd taken to working till two, even three in the morning. But the corkscrew shaped energy-saving bulbs he'd been using distorted the colors. By lamp light, the reds and oranges were glowing, radiant, but when he looked at the work in the morning, the colors were flat and lifeless, as if some anti-art vampire had crept in and drained away their life's blood while he slept.

He'd done some internet research, learned these top-of-the-line lights were designed to eliminate the distortion. The eight-foot tubes had a special frequency that supposedly mimicked daylight. The quality of the light was even supposed to ward off depression during the dark winter months, but depression wasn't his problem. On the contrary, he was climbing the walls, psyched up to take care of the next clients as soon as the people at Oaktree gave the okay. He knew it wouldn't be long – he'd already scoped out the locations.

He didn't like what the new lights did to his painting. Despite all the hype on the web site, they stripped away the warmth. Even the reds took on a cold, bluish cast. That was unacceptable, especially now that he was ready to paint Claire. They hadn't talked for long today, but the impression she'd made on him had been so vivid, so visceral, that it was more than enough. In his mind's eye, he could still picture her delicate features, the elegant lines of her body.

He narrowed his eyes as he stared at the painting on the easel. When his eyes were practically closed, the details blurred and the underlying structure of the composition stood out better. He was pleased with the leafless trees, the lifeless body on the ground, but what pose should he use for Claire? Maybe he should try more than one. He could paint her in three poses, dancing over the corpse like the three graces in that Botticelli painting he'd studied in art history. Primavera – springtime. She had Botticelli looks, blond and willowy.

Was Athena right? Was he getting too emotionally involved? It wasn't like him to obsess about a woman this way. It was a sign of weakness he couldn't tolerate, much less afford in his current line of work. *I gave you a reprieve, Claire. I saved your life and you don't even know it. But I could take your life just as easily. I may have to if you keep tormenting me this way.*

He glanced at his watch. He could keep painting, but he needed to get away from the work, give it a break. He decided to take a stroll up the road. Check out Claire's house, see what she was up to.

Chapter 31

Claire lingered at George's house far longer than she'd intended. He needed the chance to talk, she rationalized, but she needed the company every bit as badly. Depressed as George was, giving him the opportunity to vent was vastly superior to facing her own demons at home. But the dogs needed her, so she finally said her farewells.

Now she shivered against the chill night air as she yanked back on Maizy's leash. "No, girl! Don't go there! That goes for you too, Freia!"

Her Labradoodle stopped short, shot Claire a questioning look. The little terrier kept on tugging.

"Not the woods!" Claire glanced toward the water. Across the cove, an eerie blue glow caught her eye. Funny she'd never noticed it before. She shuddered, conjuring up images of cinematic space aliens. Was it a will of the wisp, or was she losing it completely?

"Let's go down to the lake!" she exclaimed with phony enthusiasm. Who was she kidding with this display of bravado? Not the dogs. The yellow tape was gone, but they were all too aware of the crime scene. Tense, quivering, they kept glancing at the stand of trees where Lester's body had lain two days before. No doubt they longed to explore the terrain, sniff the ground for unfamiliar scents.

"If only you guys could talk. Maybe you could say who's been here that shouldn't have been. Help get me off the hook. Would you believe I'm actually a suspect in Lester's death?"

Both dogs gazed up at her. In the darkness, the spotlights from the deck ricocheted off the black pools of their eyes. "You try so hard to understand, don't you," Claire said. "You have such utter faith in me. I wish the people in my life felt the same way."

As she fell silent, the stillness of the night wrapped around her like a shroud. She had always loved the solitude of this place, found tranquility in its isolation. Until now, fear had never been a factor, but Lester's death had shattered the fragile illusion of safety. Could she ever regain the old sense of security? Right now she had her doubts.

Flanked by the dogs, she walked slowly to the shore and stared out across the water. The view was black on black. The vacationers had shut down their cottages for the winter, and only a handful of houses still had lights. As she stared out across the cove, the strange blue glow swam into focus. It wasn't a chimera, merely a picture window with closed draperies. Someone must have installed fluorescent lights.

"I wonder if one of our neighbors is suffering from seasonal affective disorder?" she asked the dogs. "Full-spectrum fluorescent lights are supposed to be good for that, and we're entering the darkest time of the year."

Freia bounded into the water, returned with a soggy piece of deadwood clamped in her jaws. She dropped it at Claire's feet, then snatched it up and shook it violently, daring Claire to take it. Maizy yipped excitedly. Clearly both dogs still had energy to burn.

"Sorry, girls, I'm in no mood to play," Claire said. "In fact I'm not in the mood to stay out here at all. Tell you what, though. I'll take you for a walk on the road."

A few hundred feet up the twisting lakeside road, the solitude felt even more foreboding than on her own familiar turf. She had thought to follow the fluorescent glow to its source, to see which neighbor had found a new way to fight the darkness of impending winter, but halfway there she realized how pointless the excursion was. She had no idea who lived there, and she could hardly knock on the door and introduce herself at this hour of the night.

"Let's turn around, girls. Time to go home."

No sooner had she said the words than both dogs began growling softly. Claire stared at the road ahead, saw only blackness. Then all at once a silhouette loomed into view. She crouched down, reached out to Freia and Maizy. Both dogs were trembling, their hackles bristling.

"Cool it, guys, I'm just out for a walk. I won't hurt anybody."

Claire froze. The deep male voice was familiar, but she couldn't quite place it. She grabbed Freia's collar, pulled up on Maizy's leash. "They won't hurt you either, unless you try anything weird," she said.

"Claire?"

The dark silhouette refused to resolve into anyone recognizable, but she suddenly knew the voice. She'd heard it today at Oaktree. "Justin? Is that you?"

"Yes, it's me. Unbelievable, isn't it?"

She went limp with relief. "I knew your voice was familiar. What are you doing here?"

"I live just up the road, and I was out for a walk."

"What a coincidence. Where do you live? Not the house with fluorescent lights, by any chance?"

Long silence, then "Yes, as a matter of fact."

"Are they new? I never noticed them before tonight."

"I just installed them today. I'm an artist of sorts, and I'm hoping they'll give me more accurate color when I paint at night."

"An artist! That's amazing. I'm into jewelry myself. I'd love to see your work sometime, and you can see mine."

"I'd like that. You'd have to leave your dogs at home, though. I'm allergic."

He wasn't coming any closer, she noticed. Maybe he was phobic as well as allergic. Or just sensibly cautious – Freia and Maizy were still growling. "Sorry the dogs are acting so unfriendly," Claire said. "They're not usually like this."

"It's understandable, considering what you've been going through. They probably feel it too." Another pause. "I'd better go. My painting was at an impasse; that's why I went out for a walk. But I feel revitalized all of a sudden. With any luck, I can still get in two or three hours of work tonight."

The silhouette shifted shape, becoming a slender profile, then shrinking back into the blackness as if it had never been. "See you around, neighbor," Claire called. He didn't answer. All at once she wondered: why hadn't he been more surprised to see her? It was almost as if he knew she lived here.

Heading back home, she realized the prospect of solitude was even more frightening than before. Beyond her house, she caught sight of the lamp in Angelo and Regina's living room window, a welcoming beacon in the cold November night. "Come on girls, I'm taking you in now," she told Freia and Maizy. "Then I'm going to pay our neighbors a visit."

I shouldn't have come, Claire thought as Angelo opened the door and ushered her inside. His craggy face was drawn and haggard with fatigue. Being Regina's primary caregiver was obviously taking its toll, and the last thing he needed was a neighbor unloading still more upset on his already fragile shoulders.

"I'm sorry I didn't phone first," she said. "Is this a bad time?"

He sighed. "These days, no time is exactly good. But come on in. Misery loves company."

"I'm pretty miserable myself. Maybe I shouldn't inflict my problems on you." Tears came to Claire's eyes, and she felt her face crumpling.

Angelo draped one arm around her shoulder and squeezed as he led her into the house. "Come in and tell me all about it. Maybe it'll take my mind off Regina for a few minutes."

"How's she doing?"

"She just drifted off to sleep. She's sleeping more and more these days. I, on the other hand, seem to be sleeping less and less. But I'd rather hear about you. Why are you so upset?"

"Well, for starters, I paid a visit to the police station this afternoon. Detective Kupcinek seems to think I could have murdered Lester Schatz."

"Claire, that's crazy!"

"Excellent choice of words. Thanks to my cronies at Compassionate Care, he evidently thinks I'm losing my mind."

He guided her into the kitchen. "This calls for a stiff drink. What's your pleasure?"

The kitchen was warm, but she shivered. "Do you have any brandy? I feel like a traveler marooned in some God-forsaken mountain pass. I need rescuing before I'm swallowed in an avalanche."

"I'm no St. Bernard, but I've got some Courvoisier. It's not in a keg, though, just a plain old bottle."

"That's fine with me."

He pulled out one of the spindleback maple chairs from the kitchen set she remembered from her childhood. "Have a seat."

As she sank onto the cushion, she felt the vibration of his trembling hands through the wood of the chair. He brought over the bottle, two tumblers and a cut crystal pitcher of ice water, poured them each a double. The liquor burned her throat, but soon the chill began leaving her body. She launched into a rambling account of her day, touching on the office politics at the agency, her visit to the police station.

At last she circled back to her visit at Oaktree. "I had lunch with Patrick Delafield at Oaktree Associates, and he wanted me to talk with you about your situation. Yours and Regina's."

Angelo scowled. "What about it?"

"He says you don't understand the benefits you could derive from their services, and he wanted me to help show you the light. I told him I don't feel comfortable doing that unless I know more about them myself."

"Good for you, Claire! I don't trust that guy. He says he specializes in elder law, but he seems more like a snake oil salesman to me. And he looks barely old enough to have graduated college. What could a kid like that possibly know about the concerns of the elderly?"

"Good question. I wouldn't necessarily hold his age against him, but I agree he comes on like a salesman. Anyway, he seems to feel you're in denial about the severity of Regina's illness."

Angelo slammed down his glass. "That's bullshit! I'm well aware my wife is dying; it's practically all I think about, night and day. I just resent the idea of a bunch of strangers prying into what should be a private matter between Regina and me. This whole issue of pain management, for example. It's up to Regina to decide how much she can stand, and for how long. No one else has the right to make that decision for her."

"I agree. Did anyone suggest otherwise?"

"Not in so many words. But I had another one-on-one session with Gloria Wallender. She got to talking about how it might be more humane, both for Regina and me, if we could somehow speed up the process."

"Like euthanasia?"

"She never used the word. She just kept spouting these generalities about how modern medicine forces people to outlive the life spans nature intended, and how much senseless pain and suffering we endure as a result. How unfair it is that the caregiver suffers as much as the patient. Sometimes more so, as in the case of Alzheimer's patients."

"She talked about Alzheimer's?"

"A little. She was saying how in the advanced stages, the person with the disease just lives in the present and doesn't have the mental ability to process what's happening, whereas the caregiver is forced to endure an eternity of torment. I remember that phrase – an eternity of torment – because it sounded so melodramatic. It conjured up these old master paintings of Hell, like Hieronymous Bosch."

"She sounds awfully opinionated and outspoken for a social worker."

"Yeah, she really got on a soapbox. She kept saying how I have to nurture myself, look out for my own needs as well as Regina's."

"She has a point, Angelo."

"Maybe. But what really ticked me off was when she started talking about conserving our resources so we wouldn't deplete our estate. I told her to mind her own business. Both our sons are out of state, and they don't expect or need our help. Unlike George Cropsey's son Paul. That kid is a money-grubbing bastard. If I were George, I'd write him out of my will."

"I gather you and George are pretty close?"

"Sure, I've known the family for probably forty years. I used to sit on some boards with George before he got Parkinson's and retreated from the world. I'll never forgive that bitch of a wife for divorcing him when he started going downhill. And I've known Paul since he was a child. Haven't seen him in so long, I didn't recognize him at first when he showed up in that support group at Oaktree."

Claire hesitated. Should she burden Angelo with her worries? He was her oldest friend, her staunchest ally, and she sorely needed his perspective. Was murder a possibility, or were the police right to question her sanity?

"I'm worried about George," she said. "Do you think you could stick it out at Oaktree a little while longer? Maybe you could help me find out –" She stopped short at the sound of her dogs next door, barking up a storm.

"What do you suppose they're so upset about?" asked Angelo. "You think there's some animal in the yard?"

"No, that's their people bark."

Just then the doorbell chimed.

Angelo frowned. "Who on earth could that be at this ungodly hour? It's after eleven o'clock."

Claire rose. "You stay here. I'll go see."

"Don't let anyone in unless you know them."

She edged into the darkened corridor that led to the front of the house. The bell chimed again, and she stiffened. The light in the vestibule was on, but as she gazed at the oval glass pane of the front door, she saw only blackness beyond the frosted floral motif. No curtains, of course – Angelo and Regina had never seen the need to shut out the world. She wondered if that would change, and hoped the door was locked.

———————

Gabriel yanked the chain on the fluorescent lights so forcefully that he set the fixture swaying as the room plunged into darkness.

He must have been out of his mind, talking to Claire Lindstrom. The night was pitch black, especially on that tree-lined road, and he could easily have turned tail and disappeared. But no, he had to go blow his cover, let her know he was her neighbor. What in God's name had possessed him?

He tried telling himself it didn't matter. She knew him as Justin, not Gabriel. Not that it mattered, since both names were pure fiction. Justin Greylock, his alter ego, was a nebbish. An account executive – a glorified salesman, in other words. She had nothing incriminating on him. Let her come see his paintings, invite her for high tea – she wouldn't find anything to tie him to the killings. Even so, a protective barrier had been irrevocably breached. He had violated his word to Athena, become dangerously involved at an emotional level. Any way you cut it, that wasn't good.

It was Claire's fault. She was a siren, a regular femme fatale. Maybe not intentionally, but she had an uncanny power to send his self-control plummeting into free fall whenever he was in her presence. He hated losing control. On the road, thanks to the dogs, they'd been fifteen feet apart, unable to see clearly. Face to face at close range, her effect on him could be lethal, destroying everything he'd worked so hard to build. He couldn't let that happen.

The walk had revitalized him, he'd told her. Understatement of the century. He had come back totally wired, painted for hours, and what did he have to show for it? A turgid mess.

Sometimes it was better to shift gears. He checked his watch; the dial glowed aqua. Three fifteen: an ideal time to take one last sweep past the homes of his latest clients.

Chapter 32

*P*aula woke to the sound of her cell phone trilling the first bars of a Mozart sonata. She peered at the digital clock beside her bed. Seven fifteen. Who could be bugging her at home at this uncivilized hour? They ought to know better.

She scrambled out of bed as the cell sang out the melody again. She should really change the ring one of these days; she couldn't abide Mozart. Too insipid.

Leaning against the dresser, she took the call.

"Paula, it's Allyson. Ray Rienzi is missing. What do you want me to do?"

The words hit like a jab to the solar plexus. She was silent a moment, processing the information. "Why are you calling me?" she asked. "Why not Claire?"

"You told me to keep Claire out of the loop on this case."

Paula's stomach started to roil as she remembered. Claire had been dead set against using live-in rather than hourly staff to care for Ray Rienzi. Maybe she should have listened. "That's right, I did. So what happened? How long has he been missing?"

"We're not sure. Tanisha paged me about ten minutes ago, and I'm going to head over there now. She went to check on him around six thirty, and he wasn't in his bed. She looked everywhere she could think of, all over the house and yard, but he hasn't turned up. She says he was okay when she checked on him at midnight, but he could have gotten up and wandered away anytime during the night. He has a history of doing that, you know."

The roiling intensified. "I thought he was doing better since we opened the case. Didn't you increase his meds or something?"

"Well, yes, but –"

"Never mind, we'll discuss it later. You'd better call 911. Tell them we need to start a search, STAT."

Silence at the other end. "Are you sure?" Allyson asked at last.

"Yes, why wouldn't I be?"

"You didn't like it when Claire did that for Rose Dobson."

"This is different." *Different because I screwed up big time. Claire was right: some clients are too damn risky for live-in care. I made a crappy judgment call, but this isn't the time for guilt tripping.* Paula took a deep breath, tried to project a tone of calm confidence. "Allyson, you call 911, and I'll call Claire. Then I'll head over to help you look."

———————

Claire padded barefoot to the dining room window, pulled back the drapes and peered outside. The day was gray and drizzly.

Stephen moved close, wrapped both arms around her and nuzzled the back of her neck. "You look gorgeous this morning," he said. "Like a maiden in a Victorian painting I saw at the Metropolitan Museum one time."

Claire shivered at the feel of his warm breath on her ear. I'm acting like a Victorian maiden, too, she thought as she tightened the cord of her ice blue fleece robe. Why does Stephen put up with it?

"This morning-after stuff is getting ridiculous," he said. "Especially since there wasn't a night before."

"I beg to differ. We were up talking till practically two in the morning."

He grasped her by both arms, turned her around to face him. "That doesn't count, especially since we spent half the time hanging out and chewing the fat with your neighbor Angelo."

She smiled. "I'm glad the two of you hit it off so well. It's a point in your favor."

"Anyway, Claire, I woke up early. Horny as hell, and with all kinds of kinks from sleeping on your sofa again. But I came to a decision. I'm going to have a talk with Maria today after work, make a clean break once and for all. Thing aren't right between me and her. They never were, even aside from my feelings for you. Once that's settled, maybe you won't have so many scruples about getting involved."

Claire felt a flood of warmth. Was this what she wanted? "I don't know," she began, but the ring of her cell phone cut her short.

Stephen's fingers tightened on her arms. "Ignore it," he murmured.

She was tempted to obey, but she was still half asleep, feeling far too fuzzy to converse rationally with Stephen about the bombshell he'd just dropped. "I'd better get it," she said. "It might be important."

Important was putting it mildly. Ray Rienzi gone AWOL! As she listened to Paula's rant, she clutched her cell phone so hard, her knuckles went white. It took all the strength of will she possessed not to scream at Paula. "I was afraid of something like this," she muttered.

"That's beside the point." Paula's voice crackled with tension. "It's probably a false alarm. For all I know, he's back home by now, safe and sound. Even so, I thought you'd want to be kept informed. After all, as nursing supervisor, you have the ultimate accountability."

Was that true? Probably. Claire racked her brain, trying to conjure up the relevant paragraphs from the policies and procedure manual. She had voiced her objections to taking the case, but she should have taken a stronger stand. At the very least, she should have documented her concerns in writing, limited her own liability.

Cut it out, Claire. What's wrong with your priorities? "We can worry about accountability later," she said, trying to keep the angry edge out of her voice. "The point now is to find him."

Thirty minutes later she stood in Ray Rienzi's bedroom, grasping Freia's leash.

"Take a good sniff, girl," she said. "We're going out to find the guy who sleeps in this room."

Allyson Quigley edged through the doorway. Her face was dead white, and she was trembling. "Why did you bring the dog?"

"I figured at this point, we've got nothing to lose. She might help."

"Is she specially trained to track people?"

"No, but she's half poodle and half Labrador retriever. Poodles are extremely intelligent, and they use Labs to sniff out missing persons, so I'm hoping she might be able to pick up Ray's scent." Claire glanced across the room to a ladderback chair, where Tanisha had laid out his clothes for today. Khakis, a sweater and shirt, neatly folded and probably too clean for her purposes. "Is there anything he wears all the time? Something that hasn't been washed recently?"

Allyson stood petrified, clearly terrified of Freia. "You'd have to ask Tanisha, and she's outside waiting for the police."

Claire caught sight of a bentwood coat rack in the corner. A scruffy gray cardigan hung from one peg. She took down the sweater, inhaled cautiously. The wool was musty, redolent of stale tobacco. "This might work." She held it out to Freia, who gave it an experimental sniff, then sneezed.

The squad car pulled up just as Claire was heading out the front door with the dog. Milgrim and Thorne clambered out. About time, Claire thought. I wonder what took them so long? She retraced her steps back into the foyer and turned to glance at Allyson, who was lagging halfway down the stairs.

"Come on, let's go meet the cops," Claire said. "Then I'm going to leave you to deal with them, since you're the case manager here."

"I'd rather you handle it. You've dealt with them more than I have."

"That's exactly why I shouldn't be the one they focus on. Last time they saw me was the morning I found Lester Schatz's body in my yard, and my presence here will raise all sorts of questions in their minds. Better they should concentrate on looking for Ray Rienzi."

She turned away from Allyson, who was still immobilized between floors, clinging to the banister. Tightening up on Freia's leash, Claire headed out the door to meet the two officers.

"Thank goodness you're finally here," she said to Milgrim. *Take the offensive, before she can dump all over you.* "It took you long enough."

Milgrim drew herself erect, stared at her watch. "Just twelve minutes since we got the call. I'd say that's a reasonable response time."

"If you say so." When did Allyson get around to calling 911? It must have been just before Claire got there. Why did she wait so long? "Allyson Quigley is the nurse assigned to Ray Rienzi, so I'm going to let her fill you in on the situation," Claire said. "She's right inside. And the aide, Tanisha Clarkson, is over there." She pointed across the lawn toward Tanisha, who was pacing near some rhododendrons, then held out the ratty gray cardigan for Milgrim's inspection and gestured to Freia. "My dog and I are heading out to look for Ray."

Freia wagged at the two officers, then sniffed the flagstone walkway and tugged Claire in the direction of the driveway. *Good girl! Let's hope you know what you're doing, because I certainly don't!* Milgrim and Thorne watched in bemused silence, then headed for the house.

The drizzle turned to serious rain as Claire and Freia headed down the driveway onto the blacktop road. Freia veered to the left. "I've never been this way," Claire told the dog. "I don't know the road." But she'd seen no sign of Ray when she'd driven here from the other direction, so she might as well follow Freia's lead.

Before long Claire's windbreaker was soaked, and she was shivering uncontrollably in the chill November air. But Freia was bred for water, and the raindrops merely beaded on her curly coat. Every so often she stopped and shook, the spray flying in all directions, then dropped her nose to the ground and took off again.

"Are you actually tracking anything, girl? I wish I could read your mind." For all Claire knew, this was just an ordinary walk for Freia. Every few feet she stopped to sniff, but that was her standard operating procedure. What scents was she picking up? Squirrels, rabbits, cats, dogs – Claire had no way of knowing. Had Ray actually walked this way? If so, the rain could well have washed his scent away by now.

They came to a fork, and Freia tugged to the right. The blacktop gave way to dirt, and the road narrowed. Bare branches arched overhead far into the distance. The filigree pattern of black tracery against gray sky was gothic, hypnotic, and Claire felt as though she was walking down the central aisle of a skeletal cathedral.

All at once Freia jerked to a stop, her hackles bristling. The dog whimpered, growled softly, sniffed the dirt. Where the road crested at the center, an expanse of rusty reddish brown glistened in the rain. Huge, amorphous, with raggedy edges, like a Rorschach inkblot but asymmetrical. An explosion . . .

Blood, she was sure of it. A collision? Maybe a deer? She scanned the area, looking for road kill, found nothing.

She yanked Freia's collar, pulled her away from the scene. "Come on, girl. We're going back to get the police."

Gabriel snapped on a fresh pair of purple nitrile gloves, reached out to reposition the hand. It didn't move.

Damn! The rigor mortis was advancing more rapidly than he'd expected. A good thing he'd started sketching as soon as he brought the body back to his studio. He'd been working feverishly in the hours since, and the floor around him reflected the fruits of his labors. He gazed down at the figure studies. Crap, most of them, but a few were pretty good, especially considering he'd never drawn directly from a cadaver before.

Following the Old Master tradition. DaVinci, Rembrandt, countless great painters had studied anatomy by working directly with the dead. The practice had long since fallen by the wayside, and it was sheer synchronicity that had given Gabriel the opportunity to revive it.

There was a downside, though. As he recalled from his reading, the rigor would last a day or so, then wear off again as the muscles began to decompose. He would be able to reposition the limbs and change the pose once more, but soon the body would begin to ooze and stink. The very thought made him gag.

Thirty-six hours at most, a few more figure studies, and then he would dispose of the body. Tomorrow night would be perfect. Any longer, and the stench would become unbearable. *I'm a nurse, after all. Not a necrophiliac.*

As he stood peering down at the drawings, a sensory memory came flooding over him. The heavy thud of impact as his car rammed the body on the dark, wooded road. There had been no warning; he hadn't seen a thing. At first he thought he'd hit a deer, and he'd almost driven on by. Some sixth sense made him stop, walk back to the crumpled form on the road's shoulder. An old man, skinny and small, lay curled in a fetal posture. Beneath the overhanging trees, Gabriel couldn't see the extent of his injuries. He squatted, reached down. His fingers touched the chest, came away sticky. The sharp tang of blood assailed his nostrils as he heard the man's last rasping breaths fade into silence.

Grasping a wrist, probing for a nonexistent pulse, he felt the cool metal links of a chain, a flat disc the size of a fifty-cent piece. An ID bracelet, maybe? He rose, walked back to his car. He retrieved the Maglite from under his seat, returned to the body, aimed the beam at the medallion.

Ray Rienzi! The name was engraved into the metal in block letters, along with the address and phone. A dog tag of sorts, for a man who couldn't reliably find his way home or tell others how to take him there. A man with advanced Alzheimer's. Gabriel already knew the bare-bones facts, since Ray Rienzi was the next victim on his list. Gabriel had been checking out the house, cruising the back roads of the neighborhood when Rienzi came flying out of the night like a dark angel, offering himself up for sacrifice on the hood of the car.

Now, in the studio, Gabriel's breath came faster as he fingered the silvery medallion. Synchronicity didn't begin to explain what had happened in the pitch blackness back on that road. *A miracle is more like it.*

Mission accomplished. Should he report back to Athena? No, not yet. Let things play out for a day or two. For all practical purposes, Rienzi would disappear from the face of the earth, and Compassionate Care would bear the brunt of the blame. Oaktree wouldn't even enter into the equation. So much the better: he could move on to his next assignment that much sooner without arousing suspicion.

If he even wanted a next assignment. Maybe he was destined for something greater.

Everything is different now. I'm coming into the height of my powers, and I've got the upper hand. Over Athena, over Claire, over everybody.

Chapter 33

*T*his day from hell was about to get even worse, Claire reflected as she hunkered down at her desk listening to Dahlia's plaintive voice on the phone. Late afternoon, and still no trace of Ray Rienzi last time she'd heard. Milgrim had banished Claire from the scene soon after one. His disappearance was a police matter now, and Claire was persona non grata.

Paula had no use for her either. Claire's very presence antagonized her boss; she'd seen it in Paula's eyes every time they'd encountered each other as this endless day slogged along. Displacement, Claire thought. A classic defense mechanism. Somehow Paula had found a way to blame her for Ray's disappearance. And now Claire was intellectualizing – another defense mechanism, but it wasn't helping. She still felt like shit.

"Claire, I can't stay another night, I'm sorry," Dahlia was saying. "My stomach pains me so bad, I'm afraid it may kill me. I saw the black car again last night, too. If I see it a third time, I swear it'll be the end of me."

Claire felt a pang deep in her own innards. Not again! Visiting Dahlia at George Cropsey's house yesterday, listening to the aide describe her symptoms, she'd felt the same sympathetic lurch. Somehow this phone call didn't surprise her.

"Maybe Errol could come back early to relieve you," Claire said.

"I already called him, and he flat-out refused to come back before Friday. Said he'd rather quit."

"I don't know who we can get this late in the day." Claire glanced at her watch: ten after four. "Tell you what, I'll consult with Maria and see if she can work something out. Sit tight. I'll get back to you as soon as I can."

Claire found Maria at her desk, squinting into a makeup mirror and refreshing her mascara.

"Dahlia's sick, and she needs to come out tonight. Can you think of anyone to relieve her?"

Maria yanked the mascara wand away from her eye and waved it breezily, like a film noir siren brandishing a cigarette holder. "You've got to be kidding, Claire."

"I wish I were."

"Well, it'll have to wait till tomorrow. I'm just winding up for the day."

"You're here till five, right, Maria? That's plenty of time to make a few calls."

"You don't get it. There's no one to call. Everyone on our roster is either working or unavailable. I know because I've spent all day on the phone firming up the staffing for the weekend." Maria reached into a floral makeup bag, extracted a lipstick. She unscrewed it and leaned toward the mirror, lips pursed.

Claire resisted the impulse to snatch the lipstick out of her hands. "There's got to be something we can do. I'm really worried about Dahlia; she wouldn't complain unless it was serious."

Maria began stroking the fuschia cylinder over her lips. Suddenly she stopped short. "I know! I could call Tanisha! They haven't found Ray Rienzi yet – maybe she'd like a new case."

God, Maria! How could anyone be so crass? Claire took a deep breath to calm herself. "I don't think that's wise. She was awfully upset when she left Ray's house early this afternoon."

"So? She's a good aide. She'll get over it."

"Sorry, but I veto the idea." Claire fell silent as an inspiration began to take shape. What if she spent the night at George's house? He was better company than a lot of men she could think of.

"You know what, Claire? You need to stop being such a bleeding heart. Toughen up a little. It makes life a lot easier." Maria scrutinized her lips in the mirror. They were now a lurid, bruised purple. She smacked them. "I already told Paula, I'm leaving a little early. Stephen's taking me out to dinner."

Claire smiled sweetly. "I thought it might be something like that, since you're taking such care with your makeup."

Could Maria really have no inkling she was about to get dumped? Claire managed to dredge up a tinge of pity, but only a tinge. Maria was remarkably insensitive; Stephen deserved better. "Oh, by the way, Maria," she said. "Never mind about finding someone to replace Dahlia. I'll go there myself and play aide for the night. I've been wanting a chance to get better acquainted with George Cropsey."

Back at home, Claire's spirits were oddly buoyant as she tossed clothes into her old overnight bag. She hadn't spent a night away since the last time she'd filled in for an aide more than two months ago. George Cropsey's house wasn't the most exotic destination in the world, but it beat staying home alone and awaiting the outcome of Stephen's rendezvous with Maria. And she had told the coordinator the truth: she genuinely welcomed the opportunity to get better acquainted with George. Perhaps she could learn more about his family's involvement with Oaktree as well.

She scrounged up some old polyester pants and smocks from her hospital nursing days, then decided they looked too institutional and opted for a few tees and the lightweight velour pants and jackets she wore to work out at the Y.

How long would she stay? At worst, she might be stuck till Friday, when Errol James was due back, so she packed accordingly. She wouldn't be surprised if Maria left her marooned there deliberately, especially if Stephen actually broke up with Maria. The idea of being out of the office had a certain appeal. This afternoon, Paula had been as close to hysteria as Claire had ever seen her, and Maria would be impossible if Stephen followed through on his plan.

The worst thing about round-the-clock live-in care was the enforced inactivity. Even with a client like George, with his multiple needs and complicated plan of care, there would be long stretches of utter tedium. He had an enormous library, so there would be plenty to read, but the passivity would drive her up the wall in no time.

Jewelry – that was the perfect solution. She wouldn't have the time or tools for anything too complicated, but she could pack some beading supplies. And she could make some wire-wrapped pendants – she'd picked up some beautiful turquoise and malachite stones at a gem show a few months back, and she had several coils of sterling silver wire.

She finished packing her suitcase, zipped the canvas overnight bag closed, then headed for the door. Freia and Maizy trailed after her, their tails wagging tentatively. Both dogs radiated the same kind of crackling tension they showed when a thunderstorm came rolling in from the west.

"You girls know something's up, don't you?" she asked. "Don't worry, I'll walk you before I leave, and then Angelo will take over for the duration. But right now I'm heading for the garage to pack my toolbox. I'll be right back."

At the door, she flipped the switch for the floodlight at the apex of the garage roof. It flared, then fizzled into blackness. Damn! No time to change it now. Retrieving a flashlight and her keys, she made her way across the bluestone pavers to the garage. At the side door, acutely aware of the surrounding darkness, she focused the beam on the padlock and began fumbling with the key chain. She found the right key, inserted it into the padlock, twisted.

A car peeled past as the lock fell open. She heard the squeal of brakes, saw the car back up and stop. The headlights illuminated her mailbox, and "Lindstrom – 21" gleamed black on silver.

What the hell? She didn't recognize the maroon sedan, wasn't expecting anyone. She switched off the flashlight, popped the padlock off the hasp. Then she opened the garage door and sidled inside and out of sight, all the while realizing the futility of her actions. It was too late to hide. Whoever he was, he'd already seen her.

Inside the house, the dogs barked frenetically as the car pulled into the driveway and stopped. Her heart in her throat, Claire waited as the door opened. By the glow of the dome light, she could barely make out the hulking male silhouette. Then the door slammed and the driver disappeared once more into darkness.

"Claire? Is that you out there?"

The voice was soft, insinuating, and she knew it at once – Rick Kozlowski. Her pulse began its descent to something approaching normal, but then the memories came flooding in. The way he'd lied about his work, his obsessive talk of stalkers and bizarre medical murders. She had to get rid of him. Now, before his weird talk turned to action.

She edged out onto the walkway. "Yes, Rick, it's me."

"Why are you skulking around in the dark at this hour of the night?"

"The spotlight on my garage blew out, and I just wanted to get some –" She stopped short. She didn't owe him any explanations. Quite the reverse, in fact. "What are you doing here?" she asked. "And how do you know where I live?"

"I called the office this afternoon. They said you were tied up, but Maria gave me your home phone and address."

"She had no right to do that." Claire switched her flashlight back on, aimed at his face. It looked disembodied, ghoulish in the pale circle of light.

"Jeez, Claire, you don't need to jump down my throat. And don't blame Maria. I leaned on her a little, said I was worried about you. How are you holding up, anyway? I've been thinking about you ever since we talked at Tanya's on Saturday. You were certainly right about the story getting a lot of media coverage. Do the cops have any idea who did it yet?"

Yeah, they think I did. I'm the prime suspect. "I don't have a clue. To be honest, I'd rather not talk about it."

"Come on, Claire, you'll feel better if you talk things out. Aren't you at least going to invite me in?"

"Sorry, not tonight." She saw his mouth twist in a scowl, refocused the flashlight at the ground so she wouldn't have to look at him.

He reached out, touched her arm. "How come you're so hostile?"

She pulled away, edged toward the road. "Sorry, Rick, it's not you personally. I'm just stressed out."

"I can tell."

Far up the road in the distance, she saw a sudden glint of light as a door opened, then closed again. Justin's house. *Wonder how he'd like an unexpected visitor?* He'd been strangely standoffish when she'd encountered him on last night's walk. On the other hand, he was certainly preferable to Rick.

"Actually, I'm meeting a friend," she said. "A neighbor. See that light over there? He's waiting for me. I'd better go, I'm running late."

"Why didn't you say so? Want me to walk you over?"

"No thanks, I'll be fine. Do me a favor, Rick. Next time you want to see me, please call ahead. Right now my life is too chaotic for unexpected visitors." She stepped onto the road and headed into the darkness.

Justin's yard was as dark as her own. Wielding her flashlight, she saw that he'd left his garage door open, a black Mazda parked inside. She walked to the side door where she had seen the light, jabbed at the doorbell, heard nothing. The bell was rusty, probably hadn't worked in years. She made a fist, hammered on the door. "Justin! It's Claire! Open up!"

Dead silence. But his car was there; he had to be home. She grabbed the knob, turned and pushed, but the door held fast. "Justin!" she called again.

She heard a faint scuffling sound, like dry leaves blowing in the wind, then his voice at the door. "Claire? What are you doing here?"

"I'll explain if you let me in."

"Just a sec." The metallic thunk of a bolt being thrown, a creak, and the door opened a crack. Behind him, the room was bathed in the cool glow of fluorescent lights. His ice blue eyes glared out at her, more piercingly intense than ever. "What's wrong, Claire? You look frazzled."

"An unexpected visitor showed up at my house, and I'd rather not see him. It's probably silly, but he gives me the creeps."

His gaze hardened. "Was it someone you know? Did he give you a hard time?"

"He said he just wanted to talk, but I get strange vibes from him, and I don't want to let him in. Not after everything that's happened. Can I come in?"

Justin opened the door wider. Claire took a step forward but he planted his feet and folded his arms, blocking entrance. "Look, Claire, we hardly know each other." His voice was low and gruff. "This isn't a good time, and I have no interest in the details of your personal life."

Why the hostile reception? This wasn't the caring, sympathetic man who'd greeted her at Oaktree yesterday. But then Justin hadn't been exactly sociable on the road last night, either. She stared at the man before her. Barefoot, in faded jeans and a black sweatshirt, he looked as if he'd just climbed out of bed and into the nearest clothes. Suddenly it dawned on her: he probably had company. "Sorry to disturb you," she said. "The guy's probably gone by now. I should go."

He smiled unexpectedly. "Forgive me, I'm the one who should apologize. You caught me by surprise, that's all. I've been drawing and painting all day, and when I'm really into my work, I go into a different zone. Come on in."

"Oh, you weren't at Oaktree today?"

"No, I had the day off."

"Then you probably haven't heard about Ray Rienzi."

"What about him?"

"He's been missing since early this morning."

Justin frowned. "That's terrible. Where do they think he's gone?"

"The police are investigating a possible hit and run. My dog and I found a big stain in the road that I thought might be blood. They confirmed I was right, but they clammed up after that. They don't want Compassionate Care involved."

His mouth tightened. "Like it or not, I'd say your agency is already involved."

"Yes, as the responsible party." Claire felt her eyes tearing up and hoped he didn't notice.

"You'd better come in. Maybe I can help you place things in perspective."

"I'd like that, but I only have a few minutes. I'm due at a client's house."

"You work too hard." He placed a hand gently on her shoulder and ushered her into the room. The rich, resinous smells of turpentine and oil paints invaded her senses. Canvases stood on the olive green sofa, the battered beige recliner, against the walls. Landscapes, from the looks of them. Figure studies littered the floor – male nudes, brown Conte crayon and charcoal on paper, looser and sketchier.

"You're really good," she said. "You obviously like Van Gogh."

"Yes, and Munch, the Fauves, the German Expressionists. Artists who value passion over technical precision." He strode toward the massive oak easel that dominated the room, grasped a large canvas by its stretcher bars and hoisted it off the easel, then carried it toward the kitchen.

Claire started after him, eager to see the front of the canvas. "Is that your latest? Can I take a look?"

His eyes darted away from hers. "Sorry, it's not fit for viewing. I'm afraid I screwed it up royally."

"I know what that's like. I work in silver, and it's really frustrating when I mess up a piece. Sometimes the only solution is to melt it down for scrap."

He met her gaze once more, but his eyes had a glazed, far-away look. "This work may have some redeeming features. I just need to chill out, give it some time. See if it's worth salvaging."

"It probably is," she began, but she stopped short at the sound of the cell phone trilling in her pocket. "That's got to be Dahlia, wondering when I'm going to come to her rescue. Before I was so rudely interrupted by that visitor, I was busy packing. The aide is sick, so I'm going to fill in overnight. Maybe longer, depending on how soon our coordinator can find someone else to relieve her."

"Really? That's going above and beyond the call of duty." His lips curved in a strangely sensual smile. "Who's the client?"

"It's confidential," Claire began. Then she stopped short, remembering. "But he and his family are already involved with Oaktree. Since we share a professional interest, I guess there's no harm in letting you know. It's a man with Parkinson's disease. George Cropsey."

Chapter 34

*G*abriel stood in the doorway, watching as Claire disappeared back into the darkness. The feeble light from her flashlight carved a shaky trajectory up the road, then faded from sight. He heard the dogs bark, fall silent. Presumably her gentleman caller was gone, and she'd made it safely back inside.

How ironic, his worrying about her safety, when she'd already sealed her fate with her ill-timed visit. What had she seen? He had no way of knowing. He'd stashed the body in the trunk of the car barely ten minutes before she arrived, and she could well have been watching. And those cadaver drawings – she hadn't commented on them specifically, but she had to have gotten an eyeful, maybe even recognized the client. She'd seemed unusually edgy tonight. Said it was because of her creepy visitor, but for all Gabriel knew, she could be on to him.

In a way, it was for the best. He'd been waffling for far too long, but now it was time to act.

He strode to the kitchen, grabbed the large canvas and carried it back to the easel. The fluorescents bathed the surface in their unforgiving light. He'd told her the truth: the painting was a mess.

He had tried that Botticelli thing, roughing in three versions of Claire's figure, tripping the light fantastic through the woods near the lifeless body. But now he could see it was crap. The figures were grotesque, awkward, like a trio of ungainly scarecrows. The flesh tones were muddy, the textures slimy and scrofulous. What had ever possessed him to think he could become a decent painter?

As he stared glumly at the chaotic melange of colors on his palette, the glint of a stainless steel palette knife caught his eye. He grabbed the wooden handle, began scraping at the canvas. Gobs of paint came off on the blade. He grabbed a rag and wiped the knife clean, then attacked the figures again, more angrily this time. The knife left an overlapping pattern of angular swathes, slashing through the bodies as if a samurai warrior had taken a sword to them.

His breath coming in ragged gasps, he stepped back and studied the painting. Interesting, if you were into chaos and annihilation. An art therapist would probably have a field day interpreting the work. *Hmmm, this artist seems to have some issues around impulse control and anger management. Note the raw aggression of the slashing knife strokes. His ego boundaries are in acute danger of dissolution. Definitely a danger to self or others. I'd say he's in urgent need of crisis intervention. Therapy, medication, probably hospitalization.*

Bullshit! Gabriel hurled the palette knife at the picture window. It ricocheted off the glass, leaving a murky smear like a squashed bug on a windshield. My ego boundaries are just dandy, he thought. Or at least they will be, as soon as I resolve the Claire Lindstrom problem.

Dahlia's hug was so warm, so comforting, that Claire hated to pull away. But the meter was running on the taxi that idled in George's driveway, waiting to drive the aide to the station.

"I'm worried about you, Dahlia," Claire said. "Are you sure you don't want to go to the emergency room up here, rather than waiting till you get back to New York?"

"I'm positive. You know those ERs – they'd probably keep me sitting around for hours, and by that time I can be back in Brooklyn. I've been slugging down Pepto Bismol, so I should make it all right."

"I hope so. Just promise me you'll see a doctor first thing tomorrow."

"I promise." Dahlia glanced back at the house. "Are you sure you'll be okay with George? I've got a funny feeling about him – something's not right."

"How do you mean?"

"He seems even more depressed than usual. He perked up when he heard you were coming, though."

Claire felt a stab of apprehension. "The staffing changes have to be hard on him. I'd better get back inside. You said you gave him his last insulin injection before dinner, right?"

"Yes, and that should be it until morning. Don't forget to check his glucose before you give him the shot. If you prepare the dose and hand it to him, he self-administers."

"I know the drill." Claire squeezed Dahlia's arm. "I oriented you just two days ago, remember?"

The aide gave an embarrassed giggle, then winced. "Ouch, it hurts when I laugh. You're right, I'm sorry."

"Don't be. I'm glad you're so conscientious."

"By the way, where's Stephen? Why am I taking a taxi?"

He's busy breaking up with Maria. Or at least I hope so. Claire had a sudden impulse to share, managed to suppress it. "He had some personal business to take care of tonight."

Dahlia narrowed her eyes, scrutinized Claire. "Oh, I see. Well, I'd better go. As soon as I'm back home, I'll do a little ceremony for harmony and healing."

"That's a good idea, Dahlia. You deserve it."

"I didn't mean for me. I'll do it for everyone up here. You need it worse than I do."

Dahlia was right, Claire decided as she reentered George Cropsey's room. The man was definitely depressed; she saw it in the bleakness of his flat blue stare. As she approached the bed, his eyes veered sideways, away from hers. His gnarled hands scuttled crablike across the sheets. Just before they burrowed beneath the covers, she caught a glint of something. A cylinder –

"George, what's that you're holding?" She flew to his side, yanked back the sheets. He was clutching a syringe.

Her heart plummeted. "Give me that!" She grabbed his hand in both her own, forced his fingers apart. The vial rolled sideways, away from his grasp.

"You have no right!" He gasped out the words, tears running down his cheeks.

"I'm sorry, George. Maybe I overreacted, but what in God's name are you doing?"

She retrieved the syringe from the bedclothes, held it up to her eyes. The cylinder was full to the brim with colorless liquid. "Insulin, right? Dahlia told me you had your last injection before dinner. And this syringe has triple your usual dose."

He sank back into the pillows, looking terminally exhausted. His words came out in a wheeze. "I thought that would do the trick, if I took it soon enough after the last shot."

"So you wanted to kill yourself?"

"That was the idea, yes."

"I can't let it happen, George. Not on my watch." She glanced at the bedside table, where the bottle of insulin stood within easy reach. "Did Dahlia leave this here?"

"Yes, God bless her. Usually she puts it right back in the refrigerator, but the poor woman has been in so much pain, she must have forgotten." He paused, gasped for breath. "Please don't blame Dahlia. By the time you got here, she was practically beside herself. Pain can rob you of rational thought."

"I'm not out to blame anyone." *Except myself.* Claire should have gotten there sooner, but no, she was too busy touring an artist's studio. And when she made the switch with Dahlia, she should have noticed the insulin by the bed. She reached for the white plastic cap, clicked it carefully into place over the syringe. "I'll just go dispose of this."

George reached out a hand. "Don't go now. Since you've thwarted my efforts, we might as well talk."

"You're absolutely right." She stashed the syringe in the hip pocket of her jacket, then pulled a chair over to the bedside. Taking both George's hands in hers, she felt the tremor. "So tell me. Are things really that bad?"

"Isn't it obvious? I can see it in your eyes – all that pity. I can't stand being the object of pity. This endlessly prolonged dying process is an abomination against nature. Our society has taken it too far. We should be like the Eskimos, just put our elders on the nearest ice floe and float them out to sea."

He said that the first time we met. I should have taken the words more seriously. Claire attempted a smile. "That's a graphic way of putting it."

"Yes, unfortunately I still have my wits about me, at least most of the time. That makes this damn degeneration all the worse. If I had Alzheimer's, at least I'd be out of it before the end." George closed his eyes, sucked in a lungful of air. "Animals have a big advantage. They don't understand death, aren't cursed with all this precognition. I'm a big dog lover, had to have a couple of them put down. I remember my last one, a German shepherd named Caesar. He had hip dysplasia and a tumor on his spleen. All his systems were failing. The vet gave me time alone with him to say goodbye. He licked my face, and I asked him to forgive me. When the injection hit, I saw the light go out of his eyes, and that was it. He was dead in less than two minutes. That's how it should be with people." Tears spilled from his eyes and down his cheeks as he subsided into silence.

Claire felt her own eyes well with tears. She squeezed his hands tighter. What to say? He had a valid point. Death by insulin overdose wouldn't have been nearly so peaceful, but this was hardly the time for a lecture on the subject.

"So," he said suddenly, withdrawing his hands from hers and hunching forward. "You know anything about this Oaktree Associates? What do you think of the outfit?"

What a non sequitur. She'd wanted to hear what George had to say about Oaktree, but the thought had flown out the window in the wake of the crisis. Might as well take advantage. She tried for a neutral tone. "I don't know that much about them. What's your opinion?"

"I'm not sure. Paul seems to think they're okay."

"Have they ever sent anyone out here to meet you? That social worker, Gloria Wallender, maybe?"

"The lawyer came one time. Patrick something or other. Sleazy bastard."

That was odd, she reflected. Patrick denied ever having been here. And the other day, George had told her no one from Oaktree had ever paid him a visit. But then his memory might well be erratic because of the Parkinson's.

"We went over my Health Care Proxy and my Advance Directives," he continued. "I signed a DNR order – closest thing our society has to the Eskimos' ice floe. If I have the great good fortune to be totally out of it, I don't want anybody banging on my chest or shocking me back to life."

"You have my word that we'll honor your wishes in that respect," Claire said. "I've been over the DNR with our staff, and the paper is hanging on the refrigerator, right next to your plan of care."

He gave her a cockeyed grin. "So you won't try to abort takeoff, the way you did when you grabbed that syringe out of my hand?"

She grinned back. "George, your sense of humor is –"

The doorbell chimed, and she stopped mid-sentence. Who on earth? "George, are you expecting any visitors?"

"Not a soul."

"Then hang on a minute, and I'll go see who it is." She did a quick visual sweep of the room, detected no stray syringes or other weapons of potential self-destruction. "You promise to stay out of trouble till I get back?"

He nodded, and she headed out of the room and down the hall. At the front door, she flicked on the porch light and peered through the glass pane. Justin Greylock's pale blue eyes peered back at her.

She turned the latch, unlocked the deadbolt and swung the door open. "Justin? What on earth are you doing here?"

He smiled. "It feels as if we have some unfinished business together. I wasn't exactly cordial back at my house."

"That's understandable. I'm not big on unannounced visitors either. And I interrupted your painting."

"Even so, I could at least have offered you a drink. I decided I should come over and apologize in person. Besides, it's synchronicity that you're staying with an Oaktree client. I've been planning to meet George Cropsey, and I decided that since you're on duty here, tonight is the perfect night to do it."

Chapter 35

Claire opened the door wide. "Come on in, Justin. Strangely enough, George was just asking me what I thought about Oaktree."

His eyes narrowed as he stepped into the hall. "That's a coincidence. What did you tell him?"

She closed the door, relocked it behind them. "Nothing yet. He was just starting to tell me about his own experience with Oaktree when you rang the bell. Wait here while I see if he's up for company." She leaned closer, lowered her voice. "I shouldn't leave him alone. If this were a hospital, I'd have him on one-to-one suicide precautions right now. He tried to overdose on insulin."

"The poor guy, he must be desperate. Insulin is a lousy choice for suicide. Go ahead, get back to him. I'll wait."

Claire hurried down the hall to George's library-turned-sickroom, crossed quickly to his bedside. He was sound asleep, no doubt exhausted from the events of the past hour. Gently, she rested two fingers atop the carotid artery. His pulse was steady, his breathing slow and regular. *His vital signs are strong. Like it or not, he won't be sailing off on that ice floe anytime soon.*

She leaned down over the bed, her lips close to his ear. "George, we have company. A man from Oaktree Associates, the company we were just talking about. I'm going to bring him in to visit, so you won't have to be alone."

There was no response. She retraced her steps into the front hall. "Come on in," she told Justin. "He's sound asleep, so I can't introduce you right now, but let's bring in another chair. That way I can keep an eye on him."

"Great." Justin gestured toward the living room. "Looks like there are a couple in there. I'll grab one." He strode into the room, emerging with a dark wood chair. "Classy design. Arts and crafts style. Wonder if it's a Stickley?"

"I wouldn't know."

Justin had changed clothes. The jeans and sweatshirt were gone, replaced by a black cashmere sweater, black ultrasuede pants and black running shoes. He must have showered too; she was picking up a fresh shampoo scent along with an understated but masculine cologne. She felt a flutter of excitement at the thought that he'd gone to all this trouble for her, like a gentleman caller on a date. But although the unrelieved blackness matched his hair and brought out his lean, sculpted features, it reminded her unsettlingly of criminals in Hollywood caper movies. At least he's not wearing a ski mask, she thought wryly.

When they reached George's room, Justin set his chair down in a corner, then let out a low whistle. "Wow, some library! This guy must be a heavy intellectual."

"Yes, he's a retired English professor."

"And you said he has Parkinson's, right?"

"Yes. That and diabetes."

"Parkinson's is a lousy way to go. Slow and painful, but with enough remaining insight to be acutely aware of his own deterioration."

Claire sighed. "That's exactly what he was telling me before you got here."

"And did you manage to convince him it's worth soldiering on, no matter what?"

"Not really, no."

Justin padded toward the hospital bed, his footsteps soft and soundless. He studied the frail figure in the bed for a long moment, then walked quietly back to Claire. "Let's sit over in the corner and talk."

They drew their chairs close together, angled toward each other almost knee to knee. Surrounded by the walls of books, Claire found it natural to converse in whispers. This was a library, after all.

"So tell me the truth," Justin said, his blue eyes boring into hers. "Do you really feel you're performing an ethical service by prolonging this man's suffering?"

"That's a difficult question."

He leaned closer. "Didn't you say he tried to kill himself tonight?"

"It could have been just a gesture, a cry for attention. Or a momentary impulse."

"But you'll never know, because you interrupted him. In other words, you deprived him of his freedom to choose the time and manner of his death."

"I'm not sure he was thinking clearly. And as you said yourself, insulin is a lousy way to go. The person could experience all kinds of side effects. Seizures –"

"I know, and if the dosage isn't high enough, they could lapse into coma. A permanent vegetative state." He reached out, laid a hand atop hers.

She shuddered. For an account executive, he knew a great deal about insulin. She'd have to ask him about that later. For now, though, George Cropsey was her primary concern. "A coma is the last thing George would want," she said. "Above all else, he fears the loss of dignity. He told me he hates being the object of pity."

"What if there were a way to bring about his death quickly, humanely, so that he experiences virtually no pain?"

"You mean euthanasia? Strange, he talked about that too. He described taking his German shepherd to the vet, said how quickly and peacefully it was all over."

Justin smiled. "Odd, isn't it. When it comes to the end of life, we treat our animal companions with more kindness and compassion than we do our own kind."

"I'm not sure . . ." She lapsed into silence, suddenly uneasy about the direction of their conversation. Where was he going with this, and what would happen if she disagreed with him? The fluttery feeling in her stomach escalated into something more ominous.

Something told her to avoid getting confrontational. "It does seem ironic, doesn't it," she said. "All my training, all my natural inclinations point toward saving and prolonging human life, but you may be right. It may not always be for the best."

"Sounds like you're teetering right on the cusp. You could swing either way."

Not really. I'm a nurse, and I still choose life. Probably always will. All at once she thought of Rick Kozlowski. His burnout, his fascination with death. She'd found him unsettling, but now she realized Justin frightened her more. His façade was suave, dispassionate, but especially in his studio, she'd glimpsed a dark, mercurial energy.

He cupped her chin in his hand, tilted her face to his. "What's wrong? You haven't answered me."

She fought the impulse to pull away. "Sorry, I got distracted. For some reason, I was thinking about your paintings."

"Funny you should say that, Claire, because I have a confession to make. You know that painting I didn't want you to see?"

"The big one you took into the kitchen? Yes, what about it?"

His eyes widened, the pupils huge, like black holes in the dim room. "It featured three images of you. Three different poses, like the three graces in Botticelli's *Primavera*."

She shook her head, trying to break contact, but his fingers tightened on her jaw. "You were painting me?" she gasped. "Why on earth?"

"I realize we barely know each other, but you've become very special to me. I'm convinced that on some level, you and I are soul mates. Besides, you're very beautiful. I couldn't ask for a better model."

"But I've never modeled for you."

"I have a photographic memory. And in a way you've modeled without knowing it. Did you notice that scope on the tripod by the window?"

"No." Claire's heart began pounding harder.

"It has night vision capabilities, but I've watched you in daylight too, when you've been out walking the dogs. I've done some figure studies, but unfortunately, they weren't enough to go by, and the canvas is a mess. Just before coming here, I took a knife to it and scraped off a lot of the pigment. At this point, the painting looks hopeless. I'll probably destroy it."

Her gaze darted away from his, fled to his free hand. Strong, with elegant tapered fingers. She could easily picture it wielding a knife. "Give the painting some time," she said, trying to still the quaver in her voice. "It may be better than you think, and you can always rework it."

346

"Time is a luxury I don't have." He edged closer. "So you didn't see the telescope. What exactly did you see at my house?"

"Paintings, drawings. I don't know, Justin. I wasn't there long."

"I think you saw more than you let on."

"I have no idea what you mean."

"Don't lie to me, Claire. You saw the cadaver studies, the drawings on the floor."

"You mean those male figure studies? I barely glanced at them."

"Bullshit, I saw you studying them. That was Ray Rienzi, your missing client. You recognized him, I know you did." He let go her face, grasped her by both wrists. "Ray Rienzi was Oaktree's client too. He was next on the list, along with the gentleman in the bed over there, George Cropsey. By sheer good fortune - if I were religious, I'd call it divine intervention - I had a golden opportunity to take care of Ray ahead of schedule. I can show you if you don't believe me. His body's in the trunk of my car."

Claire's blood went cold. The stains in the dirt road, the way Ray had vanished virtually into thin air - it was all beginning to make horrible sense. *I'll never get out of here alive,* she thought. *He's going to kill me. He wouldn't be telling me this otherwise.*

She forced herself to meet his gaze. Keep him talking, buy some time. That was the only chance she had. "What did you do to Ray?" she asked.

"I hit him with my car last night, on a road near his house. An accident, pure and simple. At first I thought I'd hit a deer. I didn't realize who it was until I saw his ID bracelet. He died almost instantly. Like I said, divine providence. I brought him back to my studio to do some figure drawing before rigor mortis set in. I was about to take off and dispose of the body when you showed up. Did you see me loading him into the trunk, by any chance?"

Claire could scarcely breathe. "I told you, I didn't see anything," she stammered.

"So you say, but how can I be sure? It's too bad you forced my hand, but in a way it's for the best. Athena was right: my feelings for you were getting too intense. It was unprofessional, and it was jeopardizing my work."

His voice had turned carefully cool, and she shuddered. He was using the past tense, as if he'd already made his decision. *I'm as good as dead, unless I can buy some time. Keep him talking.*

"You mentioned a list," she said. "Who else is on it? Are they all Oaktree clients?"

"In a way. Even Lester Schatz, when you think about it, since he engaged Oaktree's services to take care of his mother. He wasn't on the list, strictly speaking, but as it turned out, his death served the agency's purposes."

"You killed Lester Schatz?"

"Yes, to save your life." He pressed her wrists harder. "You owe me, Claire. I just happened to be checking out your place with my night-vision scope. He was out to murder you. Said you were snooping around, asking too many questions. I'd have to agree with him there. You're too inquisitive for your own good. That's why I need to take drastic action. Much to my regret."

She dropped her eyes, tried frantically to frame a reply that didn't involve a question.

"You're dying to know more, aren't you?" He smiled thinly. "Go ahead, ask away. I won't bite your head off, I promise. I take pride in my work, and as a nurse, you of all people should appreciate it. I'm a nurse too, you know."

"No, I didn't know. I thought you were an account executive."

"That's just a convenient cover. Call me Gabriel, by the way. I prefer it to Justin."

"Gabriel, like the guardian angel?" She pitched her voice low, tried to conceal the quaver. "I like that. It suits you."

"Thanks, I think so too. That's why I chose it."

"I'm the one who should be thanking you, for saving me from Lester. Tell me, Gabriel, how did you kill him? Did you inject him with something?"

"Yes, potassium. Injected directly into the carotid artery, it stops the heart almost instantaneously. It's a quick, merciful death. Better than he deserved, actually, considering what he did to his mother."

Claire's own heart threatened to stop. "What do you mean?"

"He ordered her death, but she wasn't terminally ill or suffering. It was a needless death. Not one I'm particularly proud of."

She forced a breath. "But there are others you're proud of?"

"Oh, yes. The Alzheimer's victims, for example. In the advanced stages, they lose all remnants of personhood. It's sheer hell for the families. Parkinson's is no picnic, either. Take Mr. Cropsey here. You told me he tried to kill himself tonight, but you thwarted his wishes. I have the magic potion to grant him the deliverance he seeks, but first I need to know: have I succeeded in convincing you how wrong you were to prolong his suffering?"

Here it is, the clincher. Give the wrong answer, and you're dead. So is George.

Suddenly she remembered the insulin syringe in her pocket. Less lethal than potassium, at least in the short term, but it might be enough to subdue Justin, knock him out until she could get help. But how to reach it? He was still gripping her wrists. Somehow she would have to convince Justin that she bought into his madness, get him to trust her just long enough to drop his guard and let her out of his grasp.

She sighed, leaned closer. "You're right, Justin. I mean, Gabriel. George has suffered enough; he's told me that repeatedly, every time I've seen him. He's ready to let go of life, and I've been preventing him. Maybe I need to reexamine my priorities."

"A paradigm shift." His grasp relaxed slightly. "I made the transition; so can you. Let me show you how easy it is."

He stood, pulling her up with him, then let go one of her wrists and wrapped his arm around her waist. "It's usually even easier. Oaktree sends someone a few hours ahead of me to administer a sedative, so the client is nice and drowsy by the time I arrive."

Allyson Quigley! Claire almost blurted out the name, stopped short. "So it's a real team effort," she said carefully, trying to keep the irony out of her voice.

"You could say that, although we never meet as a team. Oaktree operates strictly on a need-to-know basis. I barely even know the woman who gives me the assignments."

Gloria Wallender, maybe? Again, Claire stifled the urge to ask. "That must be frustrating," she said.

"A little, although I understand the rationale behind it." He leaned closer, and she felt his breath, warm against her cheek. "The organization is growing incredibly quickly, since there's such a demand for their services. I have a hunch they might be into recruiting new staff. Qualified nurses, especially. They put you through rigorous screening, though. Make you take all sorts of personality profiles."

To seek out the coolest psychopaths, no doubt. "Are you thinking of me, by any chance?"

"Why not? True, eldercide requires an attitude adjustment, but it's a compassionate service in its way. I think you could make the transition."

"Eldercide, hmmm?" Claire felt a surge of hope. In the space of a few minutes, she'd gone from potential murder victim to potential job recruit. Would Gabriel get a finder's fee if she came on board? Something told her she'd better not ask. At any rate, her act seemed to be working.

"I don't know," she murmured. "It sounds intriguing, but I don't know if I'd actually be able to end someone's life, even if it's the humane thing to do."

"There's a surefire way to find out." One hand still grasping her wrist, the other arm around her waist as if in a slow, courtly dance, he guided her toward George Cropsey's bedside. "I'll give you the opportunity to do it, right here and now."

"Sorry, but I'll pass this time."

"Believe me, it's a feeling like no other, holding someone's life in the palm of your hand. The power is indescribable." His gaze hardened. "Besides, you have no choice. It's your life or his."

As they reached the bedside, she leaned over the metal side rails and looked down at George. To her dismay, his eyes were wide open, awash with tears and staring into hers.

"George!" she exclaimed. "How long have you been awake?"

"Long enough to get the gist. Most of my systems are failing, but my hearing's still pretty sharp." The tears spilled onto his cheeks. "If I understand correctly, this gentleman caller of yours has some kind of elixir at his disposal that will put me out of my misery quickly and with relatively little pain?"

Justin nodded. "How do you do, Mr. Cropsey? You can call me Gabriel."

"Ah, an angel of mercy. Just what the doctor ordered. Or didn't, but I wish he had." George's hands crept out from beneath the covers, lay limp and pallid atop the white sheet. "Time for show and tell. What did you bring me?"

Justin turned to Claire. "I meant what I said. If you want to live, you need to give the shot."

She nodded numbly.

"I have the syringe in my pocket, ready to go," Gabriel said. "Since it's your first time, I'll guide you, but one wrong move and you get the shot instead of him. It'll kill you in minutes, and there's no antidote. You got that, Claire?"

She nodded again.

"Do what he says, Claire." George's words came out in a wheeze. "Don't worry about me, I'll be all right."

"I know you will." Her eyes clouded with tears; she blinked them furiously away.

Justin reached in his pants pocket, extracted a syringe. He held it chest-high, removed the cap, then turned to Claire. "With the other clients, I used the carotid artery, but any site will work fairly quickly, especially since he's so frail. It's your choice, Claire. What will it be?"

From the corner of her eye, she saw George's hands fly up from the covers, clasp Justin's hands in his own. Holding on for dear life, he pulled himself to a sitting position, ducked his head and buried his teeth in Justin's hand. Justin screamed, yanked his hands away as the syringe plummeted onto the sheet.

Claire darted forward, grabbed the syringe. "It's all right, Gabriel. I've got it."

Did he even hear her? Hard to tell. He was glaring down at George, his hands around the old man's neck. "You little shit! How dare you double cross me like that?"

Claire groped in her jacket pocket, grabbed the syringe of insulin. *Seconds to spare.* She turned her back to the bed, uncapped the insulin. Thank God, the syringes were alike. She switched the cap to the vial of potassium, dropped it into her pocket, then turned back to the bedside. Gabriel was leaning over the side rails. His hands were on George's shoulders, shoving him down, down against the mattress.

She stepped quickly behind Gabriel, slammed the syringe into the soft tissue at the side of his neck, depressed the plunger. She watched the clear liquid drain into his neck. A second or two at most; then he whirled around to face her, clawing frantically at her hands. The syringe pulled free and tumbled to the floor.

His face was crimson. "You bitch! You've killed me!"

"No, it's not –" Claire stopped short. If he thought it was the potassium, so much the better. Maybe he would be too distraught to kill her or George. On the other hand, people reacted unpredictably to insulin, and she wasn't sure how much had gotten into his system. Maybe she really had killed him. Within minutes, she would know.

He lunged toward her. "I'll take you with me. We'll die together."

She twisted away, out of his grasp. "Not on my life we won't."

Chapter 36

Claire shrank back, felt Gabriel's fingertips graze her neck as she pulled away. She pivoted and ran full-tilt for the door.

George screamed. "Don't stop! He's after you!"

She careened down the hall toward the front door. Could she outrun Gabriel? She had to try. The insulin should slow him down, make him dizzy and disoriented, but it could be minutes before that happened. Meanwhile, he would have ample time to kill her.

She threw open the door, hurtled down the stone steps onto the walkway and dodged sideways onto the lawn. A massive clump of overgrown yews hugged the house. *Hide! It's your best shot!* She dashed toward the shrubs, threw herself into their midst. The branches scratched her face and hands as she hunkered down.

"Claire! No use hiding, I know you're out there!"

He stood on the bluestone porch, a black silhouette in the light that spilled from the doorway. Was he weaving slightly, or was her own terror swaying her perceptions?

She crouched in silence, taking shallow breaths she prayed he wouldn't hear. The evergreen boughs poked and jabbed her body, and her knees gave off pangs of protest, but she willed herself to remain immobile, a beast of prey panicked and paralyzed in the darkness.

"Come to me, Claire! I don't want to die alone. I want to take you with me." He gave a low, guttural moan, stumbled to the edge of the steps. He started down slowly, placing each foot with infinite care, feeling his way like a blind man. He was definitely wobbly now; it wasn't her imagination. At the bottom, he stood shaking, his feet planted far apart. "I don't feel right. It's not supposed to happen like this."

Far in the distance, an owl hooted. A dog howled in reply.

"Cerberus," Gabriel said. "The three-headed dog. He's waiting for me. Time to cross over the River Styx." He staggered onto the lawn, headed in her direction. She held her breath as he passed, taking short, tentative steps as if walking the edge of a precipice. He veered off the grass and waded into a bed of myrtle beneath a gigantic maple. "Need to rest a minute," he murmured. "Before I enter the river." His foot caught on some unseen obstacle – a maple root, she guessed. He pitched forward face down into the glossy ground cover.

I should go to him, Claire thought. Check his vitals, then run inside, get him something sweet. There's still time to save him. She remembered a canister set on the counter. George kept sugar there for exactly this kind of emergency.

Are you crazy, Claire? You want to save him, so he can rally and kill you? She stared in the direction of the fallen figure. Was there movement? The regular rise and fall of breathing? Beneath the maple, the blackness was practically impenetrable, and she couldn't be sure.

She waited what seemed an eternity, then rose from her crouch and crept out from among the yews. Still Gabriel didn't stir. Giving the maple a wide berth, she tiptoed across the grass to the bluestone steps, then up and into the house. She paused in the front hall. Her purse, her luggage were still there, beneath the antique table where she'd abandoned them when she came in what seemed a lifetime ago.

She grabbed her handbag, extracted her cell and punched in 911.

"There's a man here in hypoglycemic shock," she said when the operator came on. "Can you send the EMTs immediately? I need the police too. He's potentially dangerous."

"Is he diabetic?"

"Not to my knowledge."

"Then how –"

"Look, it's an emergency. I don't have time for a lot of questions. How fast can you send somebody?"

"It'll be a few minutes. Give me directions and I'll get right on it."

"Thanks." Claire complied, clicked off, then headed at a trot to George Cropsey's room.

The old man was hunched up in bed, his blue eyes alert and sparkling. "What the hell was that all about?" he asked when she reached his bedside.

"I don't have time to explain right now." She reached over and patted his hand. "I just wanted to make sure you're all right, and to thank you for being a hero. You probably saved both our lives, but you really caught me by surprise."

"I surprised myself too. Guess I'm just too ornery to let someone else have the final say over how and when I make my exit from this world."

"Good for you!" Her mind raced as she kissed his forehead. How long till the EMTs arrived? If Gabriel was truly heading into a diabetic coma or worse, even a few minutes might be too long. She needed to get some sugar into him. But if he came to . . .

Suddenly she flashed on the sterling silver wire in her jewelry case. She must have fifty feet of it, more than enough to bind his hands and feet. That way he couldn't attack her while she gave him the sugar. If she could even rouse him, that is. Or she could just let him lie there beneath the maple, maybe let him die . . .

No, that makes me as guilty as he is. Besides, I need him alive to help me learn the truth and bring down Oaktree Associates.

She dashed back to the front hall, popped open her tool box. The sterling wire lay coiled at the bottom, a gleaming halo. She grabbed the silver and a pair of wire cutters, headed for the door. No, wait, bring the sugar. No time for extra trips. She tore into the kitchen. The sugar was right where she remembered it. She grabbed the canister, a tablespoon. A carton of Tropicana for good measure. Then she headed back out into the darkness.

Gabriel was still sprawled motionless beneath the maple. Like Lester Schatz, she thought, but face down – and hopefully alive. Cautiously, she reached out and touched one wrist. She felt a pulse. Otherwise, no response. She grabbed the other wrist, brought his arms together behind his back. She could barely see. Too bad – she'd have to work by touch. She uncoiled the wire, began wrapping the wrists in a figure eight pattern. *The sign of infinity.* Pulled tight, knotted the wire, wrapped some more, knotted some more.

That should do it. Now for the feet. She clipped the wire at his wrists, taking care to bind and crop the loose ends securely. Then she crept down the length of his body, repeated the process at his ankles.

She stood to study her handiwork. With his black hair, his black clothes, Gabriel melted into the inky darkness; only the silver gleamed dully. Crouching again, she placed a hand on his shoulder, another on his hip, and pulled him toward her. He flopped onto his back, lay flaccid.

"Gabriel! It's Claire! Can you hear me?"

He moaned softly.

Good. He wasn't comatose, not yet. She leaned down over him. "I gave you insulin, not potassium. You're going to be all right, but you're in hypoglycemic shock."

His voice was faint. "Help me . . ."

She opened the canister, gouged out a tablespoon of sugar as he shook his head from side to side. "Hold still and open your mouth. I'm going to give you some sugar."

The shakes escalated to thrashing. "No, no, no . . ."

"Yes! Like it or not, I'm going to save you." With one hand, she grabbed his jaw, squeezed. His lips parted, and she poured in the sugar. "Swallow!"

He gulped convulsively, coughed.

"You need more. Open up!" She reached for more sugar, poured it in.

He swallowed, more purposefully this time, and she caught the dim gleam of his eyes as they flickered open. His shoulders flexed, then his arms. "What did you do to me? I'm paralyzed! I can't move!"

"I tied your hands and feet. It's 20-guage sterling silver, dead soft but very strong. You're not going anywhere, so you might as well relax. Help is on the way."

He struggled to sit upright, strained to pull his arms and legs apart. "Damn it, this wire is cutting into my skin! It hurts like a son of a bitch!"

"It won't hurt if you stop fighting it. It's jewelry wire; it's meant to lie against the skin. I use it for necklaces and bracelets; I wear it myself. How are you feeling, Gabriel? Do you know where you are and how you got here?"

He sank back, strained upright again, as if doing abdominal crunches at the gym. "I came here to kill George Cropsey. You too, but that was the hard part. If you'd seen it my way, I might have spared you, but you betrayed me."

"Let's not get into that now. At least you remember – that's a good sign. The insulin must not have done any damage."

"I'm not brain dead, if that's what you mean."

He was sitting now, knees bent, shoulders back, arms trussed behind his back. She leaned over, checked his wrists, his ankles. Was the metal holding firm? She'd tied the knots so quickly, almost sight unseen, and silver had an uncanny way of uncoiling and sliding on itself, seeking its former position. She prayed the knots would hold.

He turned to face her. "Claire, I don't understand. Why didn't you use the potassium instead? You could have killed me."

"I know, but I had a choice, and I made it instantaneously."

"What if there'd been no other choice? Would you have killed me then?"

"Maybe. I guess I'll never know."

The wail of sirens sounded in the distance, drew closer. Through the trees, she saw the flash of red and blue light bars. "That'll be the police," she said. "And the ambulance."

He sighed. "The night is young, and I'm dying of thirst. Can you get me something to drink before they get here?"

"It so happens I brought some orange juice to help wash down the sugar." She fumbled in the darkness for the carton, found it and unscrewed the cap. "Tropicana Grovestand, with pulp. I'm not sure how fresh it is. Let me check." She sniffed, took a swig. "Delicious."

She knelt beside him, held it to his lips, heard the glugging sound as he swallowed. "Say when," she murmured.

The sirens split the night, then stopped abruptly as the cop car and ambulance careened into the driveway. The carnival lights whirled crazily, red, white, blue and amber.

Gabriel jerked his head away. "When," he said.

Chapter 37

*P*aula folded the newspaper, added it to the stack on the coffee table in her office. "Careful, Claire. Don't get any pizza on this. It's my only copy."

Claire smiled. "Don't worry, I've got another one."

"Oh, so you've been saving them too? I thought you were sick of all the media coverage we've been getting since you brought down the Eldercide Killer."

"I am, but I've realized I might as well come to terms with it. It's not going away any time soon. And all the press coverage has been positive in a way. It's drawn attention to the incredible stress families face caring for their elders, and the importance of open, honest discussion about end-of-life decisions."

Maria grinned. "Come on, Claire, knock it off. You sound like you're giving another interview. You're practically a media superstar. And you photograph so well, it's not fair. The camera loves you. I'm insanely jealous."

"Don't be. It's a mixed blessing, believe me." Claire flashed on the memory of Gabriel, talking about his obsession with her allegedly Botticelli looks. She'd never seen his painting of her. Probably never would, now that he was locked up in the county jail, no doubt headed for life in prison. She wondered what would happen to all those canvases. He'd had genuine talent. And oddly enough, his own brand of compassion.

"Earth to Claire," Paula said as she reached for a slice of pepperoni and mushroom. "What are your plans for Thanksgiving? It's only a week away."

"I'll be with my neighbors, Angelo and Regina. I'll go over in the morning, spend the day in the kitchen with Angelo, make a traditional dinner with all the trimmings. They're the closest to family I have, and this will be her last Thanksgiving."

Stephen materialized in the doorway. "Can you wangle me an invitation? Angelo's a cool guy, and I make dynamite gravy."

Claire felt a rush of warmth, then a jolt as she noticed Maria watching her intently. "That's a possibility, Stephen. I'll check with Angelo and get back to you."

He lounged casually against the door frame. "So, ladies, what's happening? Are you having a party without me?"

"Just an impromptu treat," said Paula. "I realize it's been over a week, but I guess I'm still making amends to Claire for the way I kept blowing off all her suspicions. Besides, she needs the calories to keep up her energy for the extra caseload. We're down a nurse, after all."

Stephen crossed to the table, helped himself to a slice of the anchovy pizza. Good, Claire thought. Most people can't stand anchovies. One thing we have in common.

"What's up with Allyson Quigley, anyway?" He bit into the pizza, let the grease dribble down his fingers. "Have they carted her off to prison yet?"

"I have a feeling that won't happen any time soon," Claire said. "She made bail, and she's a star witness for the prosecution."

"And she's got a first-rate criminal lawyer," Paula said. "He'll probably manage to plead the charges down to practically nothing. She didn't actually kill anybody, after all."

"No," said Claire. "She just sedated them into submission, laid the groundwork so Gabriel could waltz in and kill them."

"At least he's behind bars." Stephen edged behind the table, plopped down on the sofa next to Claire. "Lucky for him. If I could get at that guy, I'd make him wish he'd never been born. When I think about what could have happened that night at George Cropsey's house –"

Claire leaned toward him, raised her finger to his lips. "Let's not think about it."

"I agree," Maria said. "Especially since I was out to dinner with Stephen that night, and he kept saying he felt guilty about not making the switch at Cropsey's. Stephen, I was going to break up with you anyway. I met this neat guy, and we were already dating –"

Stephen held out a hand in protest. "I know, Maria. You already told me. Several times, in fact. No need to rub it in."

"I know, but the thing is, I went out on that dinner under false pretenses, because I love going to nice places. If I'd refused, maybe Stephen would have been at George's house, and none of this would have happened."

"And the killer might still be at large," said Claire.

Maria frowned. "I should have tried harder to find another aide when Dahlia got sick. If I had, Claire wouldn't have been stuck there. But Claire, I was mad at you about Stephen, even though I was going to dump him. I thought it served you right to be stuck in that house. *Lo siento mucho.* I'm sorry."

"It worked out for the best," Claire said. "George was next on Gabriel's hit list, and if I hadn't been there, he would probably have succeeded in pulling off another killing. It was only because I told him I'd be there alone that he deviated from the prescribed plan. And I wouldn't have told him at all if Rick Kozlowski hadn't come calling and gotten me so unnerved that I paid that unscheduled visit to Gabriel's studio."

"I don't blame you for bailing on Rick," Stephen said. "He's a total creep."

Claire sighed. "Maybe, but I jumped to the wrong conclusions. I saw him last week at the Y. He told me the police grilled him for hours, but they found absolutely nothing that tied him to the killings or to Oaktree."

Maria brightened. "He's a nurse, isn't he? Maybe he'd want to come work for Compassionate Care."

Claire shuddered. "We'd have to be desperate."

"We *are* desperate," Paula said.

"Let's see what other nurses are out there," Claire replied. "Anyway, If Gabriel had waited and proceeded on schedule, if Allyson had managed to get in there and sedate George ahead of time, he'd probably be dead today."

"I'm glad he's still around," said Stephen. "I've taken a liking to that old guy. But wasn't he suicidal? He's probably bummed out because Gabriel didn't succeed in knocking him off."

"George seems to have turned a corner," Claire said. "He still gets depressed, but he's really proud of the role he played in uncovering Oaktree's eldercide operation."

"Not to mention the media coverage," said Paula. She ruffled through the stack of newspapers, extracted a section. "Look at this headline. 'Feisty Grandpa Brings Down Killer.' The photo is flattering, too."

"And that's just the Albany paper," said Maria. "It's made the national news too. I've been buying the New York City papers at the supermarket. I'm clipping all the articles. I'm checking Google every day too, and printing out the stories from the papers we can't get locally."

"Sounds like a full-time job," said Paula. "How are you managing that on top of your coordinating duties?"

"I'm coping." Maria grinned. "But we could use a second coordinator. I'm about ready to be a supervisor, don't you think?"

Paula smiled back. "The way the case load is growing, that's a distinct possibility. I could never have afforded this kind of media exposure, not in a million years. We've got more referrals than we can possibly handle. People who never considered live-in care before, who never knew Compassionate Care even existed."

Adding another coordinator? Claire wondered if Paula was getting too manicky – extravagance was a tell-tale sign. But she decided not to rain on her boss's parade. "We've got a waiting list for the first time ever," she said. "And I'm glad you agreed we can be more selective, and accept only those clients who can truly do better at home."

"No more Ray Rienzi's," said Stephen.

Maria lowered her eyes, made the sign of the cross at her chest. "That poor little man. I felt so terrible for him."

"And all the others," said Claire.

"So have they shut down Oaktree yet?" asked Stephen.

"No," Claire said. "I gather the D.A.'s office is building a case, but it'll probably be months before they go to trial. I have a hunch the higher-ups at Oaktree will try to weasel out of everything and blame the killings on a few aberrant underlings who were pursuing some weird, perverted agenda of their own."

"You may be right," Paula said. "I've made a few discrete inquiries myself. This is by no means a slam-dunk, open and shut case. They'll identify a few scapegoats, like Gabriel and Gloria Wallender –"

"I knew there was something weird about that woman," Claire said. "For a social worker, she was so cool and detached, at least on the phone. I never met her in person."

"I gather she was a legitimate social worker." Paula frowned. "She needed a fair amount of clinical savvy to psych out the families and determine which ones might be desperate enough to turn to euthanasia as a final solution for their unwanted relatives. She also helped coordinate the killings. Went by the code name Athena."

Maria's eyes widened. "Paula, this is so exciting! How on earth did you find out all these juicy details?"

Paula smiled cryptically. "I can't reveal my sources. Anyway, at this point it's mostly speculation. A lot will depend on plea bargaining, and who's willing to rat out whom in hopes of drawing a lesser sentence. I gather they've called in quite a few family members too."

"What about Herb Davidson?" Claire asked. "I heard him leave a phone message that day I visited Oaktree in New York City. I got the feeling they had some kind of business arrangement."

"Could be." Paula reached toward the pizza box, then withdrew her hand. "The coroner's name has come up. There's the suggestion he may have been negligent in not calling for autopsies in unexplained deaths, but the problem will be in establishing hard evidence. My source says Oaktree was pretty cagey about not leaving a paper trail. And they do offer some legitimate services. Undoubtedly those are the ones they'll have thorough documentation for."

Stephen rose, began pacing. "So Oaktree could come out of this smelling like a rose while the little guys take the fall for just following orders? That's typical bureaucratic BS. Reminds me of certain governments."

Claire had never heard him sounding so impassioned. "It makes me mad too, Stephen. To think this might not be over –" The phone rang, and she stopped short.

Maria jumped up. "Let's hope it's Dahlia. I've been waiting for her to get back to me about that new case we were discussing this morning." She crossed to Paula's desk, grabbed the receiver. Listened a moment, then grinned and gave a thumbs-up sign.

"Wait a minute, Dahlia, I'm going to put you on speaker phone. We're all here in Paula's office, and we want to hear how you're doing."

Maria pressed a button, and Dahlia's lilting voice filled the room. "The doctor cleared me to go back to work. It was an ulcer, but as long as I take my meds and avoid stress, he says I'll be fine."

Paula let out a guffaw. "Avoid stress? Are you kidding? In our business, stress is the name of the game. If you can't handle it, you shouldn't be in home health care."

"But there's a positive kind of stress," Claire said. "The kind that energizes you and gives life meaning. Without it, we might as well be dead."

"Right," said Dahlia. "It's sad that my clients are sick and that they might not have much time left, but it doesn't stress me out to care for them. I feel like I'm making their lives a little easier, more pleasant. I miss my work." She chuckled. "I even miss you folks."

Maria grinned. "We miss you too, Dahlia. How about if I have Stephen meet you at the ten o'clock train tomorrow?"

"Okay, I'll be there."

Stephen leaned toward the phone. "Hey, Dahlia! Don't forget your candles."

Afterword

*C*ompassionate Care, the home care agency in *Eldercide*, is inspired by my experiences as President of ElderSource, Inc., in the Hudson Valley of upstate New York. All the characters, organizations and events in this novel are the product of my imagination, however, as is the town of Kooperskill where the story unfolds. Any resemblance to ElderSource staff, clients, or families is purely coincidental. Mike D'Attilio is a real person, but he bears no resemblance to the fictional Dr. Michael D'Attilio. The character name was a gift from his wife Ann, who was high bidder on an auction item at the First Unitarian Universalist Society of Albany.

When I founded ElderSource in 1990, I had no idea of the challenges that lay ahead. Years of work on the geriatric unit of a psychiatric hospital had convinced me how much elders could benefit from the creative arts therapies and family therapy, and I wanted to offer these modalities in a home setting. But research convinced me that practical hands-on care was what our potential clients needed most. After an exhaustive application process that included hiring a Nursing Supervisor and submitting a Policy and Procedures Manual the size of a PhD thesis, we received our approval from the New York State Department of Health as a Licensed Home Care Services Agency.

Up against stiff competition from established agencies, we built our reputation and our case load with an ever increasing emphasis on live-in care. As a Registered Art Therapist with training in family therapy, I couldn't legally provide hands-on care, so I became trained and certified as a Personal Care Aide. A bad idea, other agency directors said – that way I might actually have to work as an aide. And so I did, on many occasions when other staff couldn't be found. I learned the business at the most basic level, helping clients cope with their declining bodily functions, comforting Alzheimer's patients through sleepless nights, waiting impatiently for relief staff to arrive. In the process, I developed enormous respect for the aides who make home care their life's work. I dedicate this book to them.

Compared to Compassionate Care, ElderSource had relatively smooth sailing. We had our share of staffing and medical crises, and some clients died during our watch, but all of natural causes. The only complaint serious enough to trigger an unannounced visit by a Department of Health inspector came about when a woman discovered an aide had briefly left her father alone to go pick up a pizza in town. But as the agency grew, so did my stress. Like Paula Rhodes, I agonized over meeting the payroll and packed on pounds while trying to cope by means of comfort food and antidepressants. Robb Smith, my husband, served as vice president and provided invaluable support as we weathered the ups and downs. Even so, I eventually came to realize that the agency could quite literally be the death of me. We transferred our staff and clients to another agency, and ElderSource closed its doors on Halloween of 1997.

Most of our clients were fortunate in that they had the resources to pay privately for round-the-clock live-in care, but that isn't true for the majority of today's rapidly aging population. Over eighty percent of home care services are provided by unpaid family members at enormous emotional and economic cost. Home care aides are in short supply; the work is difficult, with uncertain schedules and shamefully low pay. Medicare covers only a limited amount of home health care, and insurance coverage is woefully inadequate.

Thanks to modern medicine, our allotted life spans are growing steadily longer, but the quality of those additional years is often open to question. As our society ages, the ethical questions raised in *Eldercide* will grow ever more urgent. These issues deserve far more attention than I can give them here, but they are bound to resurface when I revisit Claire, Paula, and Compassionate Care in the next Kooperskill novel. In the meantime, please visit my website, www.julielomoe.com. Share your thoughts and feelings on these important subjects. I'd love to hear from you.

Printed in the United States
203063BV00002B/82-105/P